TO SARAH, HE WAS JUST A MAN

His body hardened even more when he remembered the way her heartbeat had sped up at his touch.

Her pulse was slow and steady now, the blood in her veins calling him to come and satiate his hunger. As he listened to the steady thrum of it, his own heart began to pound.

Roland slid one hand up her back, tunneling through soft, thick curls, and rested his fingers upon the satiny skin of her neck just over her pulse.

What would she taste like? Sweet like her smiles? Or spicy like her daring spirit?

Would drinking from her merely dull the pain? Or would it set him aflame?

His body was struggling to heal itself. The need for blood lacerated him.

Roland felt his fangs descend and lengthen.

Just one taste. Sarah is sleeping. She need never know.

DARKNESS DAWNS

Dianne Duvall

ZEBRA BOOKS
KENSINGTON PUBLISHING CORP.
http://www.kensingtonbooks.com

ZEBRA BOOKS are published by

Kensington Publishing Corp.
119 West 40th Street
New York, NY 10018

All Kensington titles, imprints, and distributed lines are available at special quantity discounts for bulk purchases for sales promotion, premiums, fund-raising, educational, or institutional use.

Special book excerpts or customized printings can also be created to fit specific needs. For details, write or phone the office of the Kensington Special Sales Manager: Attn. Special Sales Department. Kensington Publishing Corp., 119 West 40th Street, New York, NY 10018. Phone: 1-800-221-2647.

ISBN-13: 978-1-4201-1861-2
ISBN-10: 1-4201-1861-7

First Printing: February 2011
10 9 8 7 6 5 4 3 2 1

Printed in the United States of America

ACKNOWLEDGMENTS

My deepest appreciation goes to my editor, Megan Records, and everyone on the Kensington team. Heartfelt thanks go to my parents for their continued love and support. Most of all, I would like to thank my husband for always believing in me and encouraging me and for bringing so much love and happiness into my life.

Chapter 1

A strident screech pierced the predawn quiet.

The hair on the back of her neck rising, Sarah Bingham surveyed the meadow around her. The sky had gone from black to charcoal gray, a harbinger of sunrise that did little to alleviate the gloom. In the nine months North Carolina had been her home, she had heard some creepy animal calls, but that one had sounded downright human.

Couldn't have been. She lived way out in the boonies with no nearby neighbors.

Struggling to shake off her unease, she impaled the soil with a shovel, turned it over, then repeated the process that would ultimately culminate in a vegetable garden. The unseasonable heat she had hoped to avoid by starting early added a glimmer of moisture to her skin as she grappled with the drought-hardened ground.

Oh yeah. A few hours of this and she would definitely collapse into an exhausted slumber. *Screw you, insomnia!* The spring semester was over. Her students were gone. She was going to sleep tonight if it killed her.

Loud snarling, growling sounds abruptly split the air, accompanied by cracks and thumps and the snap of branches.

Starting violently, Sarah gripped the wooden handle of the

shovel and stared at the heavy undergrowth in front of her with wide, unblinking eyes.

The foliage began to thrash and sway. Her heart slammed against her ribs.

Oh crap! Weren't there bears in North Carolina?

Branches and leaves exploded outward as a massive dark form, moving so fast she couldn't see it clearly, charged toward her.

Too panicked to even scream, she dropped the wooden handle and raised her arms to protect her face, head, and neck.

A heavy weight crashed into her left side. Feet flying up, she hit the ground hard on her back two or three yards away. Dry soil and twigs abraded her hands as she threw them out to the sides. Something tore through her right shirtsleeve and cut her elbow. A painful throbbing invaded her ribs.

Rolling onto her stomach, Sarah jerked her head up and looked around wildly in time to see the trees that bisected this end of the meadow envelop . . . whatever had barreled into her.

Quiet settled upon the clearing.

Wincing, she pressed a hand to her aching side and scrambled to her feet.

The growls and thrashing resumed, even louder than before.

Adrenaline surging through her veins, shortening her breath, speeding her pulse, she grabbed the shovel with shaking hands, turned it upside down, and held it like a baseball bat.

She didn't know what that thing was, but if it came back, she was going to knock it six ways from Sunday.

"Where'd they go?" a voice called out breathlessly.

Sarah jumped and glanced at the trees that bordered the meadow on her right.

"That way! Straight ahead! Don't lose 'em!"

Two figures, mere shadows amid the dense, dark brush, moved as quickly as they could in the same direction as the . . . thing. Only visible for a brief moment before the trees swallowed them again, they didn't appear to have noticed her. The long-sleeved grecn shirt she wore over a black tank top and sweat pants must have made her blend into the dim scenery.

The growling ceased. So did the thumps and thrashing.

Sarah took a cautious step backward. Then another.

"Ah man!" the first voice blurted. "I think I'm gonna puke!"

"Don't be such a wuss."

What the hell was going on? Had those guys been chasing a bear?

It had to have been a bear, right?

"Aren't you gonna kill him?" the second voice asked.

"Let the sun finish him," sneered a new voice, deep and full of malice.

"What do you want us to do?" the second countered.

"Stay until it's over," the third instructed, his words softened by a British accent, "then bring me whatever is left of him."

Sarah continued to inch toward the wall of greenery that separated the meadow from her backyard, trying not to make any sound that might alert them to her presence.

Who were you supposed to call when you thought someone was torturing wild animals? 911? Animal Control?

"Is he gone?" the first voice asked uneasily.

"Yeah," the second responded.

"Are you sure?"

"Yeah-yeah. He's gone. He's gone."

"Dude! That was the most awesome thing I've ever seen in my life!"

"Didn't I tell ya?"

Wasn't torturing animals the first step toward becoming a serial killer?

"Hey, what are you doin'?" the first asked.

"Cuttin' his clothes off."

Sarah froze, ice filling her veins. *His clothes?*

"Dude, that's so gay."

"I'm not gay, asswipe. I wanna see what the sun's gonna do to him."

"Oh. Cool."

"Get his boots."

A man? That couldn't have been a man that had knocked her down. It had been huge, had growled, and had crossed the clearing *way* too fast to have been human.

Yet, it sounded as if their victim *was* a man, not an animal.

And, apparently, they weren't through with him.

Spinning around, she took three quick steps, intending to hurry home and call 911.

"Hey, Bobby," the second said, "you ever stabbed anyone before?"

She halted.

"No."

"Check this out."

Thud.

Grunt.

"Dude!"

Crap! Reversing direction, she crossed the clearing as quickly and quietly as she could. Her stinging hands tightened around the shovel handle. Sweat beaded on her skin. The bitter taste of fear invading her mouth, she entered the trees and crept forward.

This is crazy. This is crazy.

She was a music professor, not a police officer!

But it would take too long for the police to arrive. She lived so far from town. . . .

"You wanna try it?"

"Won't they be pissed if we cut him up?"

"Not as long as he's still breathin' when the sun hits him. And if he's not, who cares? How're they gonna know?"

The trees weren't as thick here as she had thought. After just a few steps, Sarah stood at the edge (with any luck, still concealed by their branches) and peered anxiously into the next field.

A whiff of rank body odor struck her.

There were three men. One, whose face was hidden from view, lay on the ground on his back, what she could see of him bare. His arms had been pulled away from his sides and appeared to be held down by something she couldn't glimpse through the tall grasses. Closer to her, his ankles had been lashed together with . . . rope? The weeds obscured them too much to tell. But they, too, were held down, judging by the way his thigh muscles continually flexed and strained.

A blond in faded jeans and a yellow T-shirt straddled the man's thighs, his back to Sarah. A second with brown hair stood beside him, mostly turned away, gaping down at the naked man.

Though she only caught a quick impression of their faces, Sarah guessed the assailants were around twenty years old.

The blond suddenly raised both hands above his head, his fingers curled around the grip of a pocketknife, then slammed them down.

Thud.

The naked man jerked and grunted with pain.

The brunet yelled, "Dude! Awesome!"

Sickened, terrified, trembling uncontrollably, Sarah stepped out of the trees, skulked forward, and swung the shovel.

The blond looked up at his accomplice. "You wanna—"

Thunk.

Yellow Shirt slumped sideways, hit the ground, and lay still.

The second man gaped at his friend in stupefaction, then spun toward Sarah . . . just as she swung again.

Thunk.

Right between the eyes.

"*Oww!*"

Uh-oh.

Staggering back a step, he swore profusely, blinked hard several times, then frowned.

Thunk.

That did it. His pale eyes rolled back in his head as he sank bonelessly to the ground.

When Sarah turned her attention to the naked man, her stomach lurched and she thought for a moment she might be sick.

He had indeed been restrained. Thick, rough rope stained with blood bound his ankles and had rubbed his skin raw. A T-shaped metal spike as thick as her thumb had been driven into the ground between them, immobilizing him and cutting deep grooves into his flesh. Identical spikes had been driven through the palm of each hand, pinning his arms to the ground.

It was as if they had wanted to crucify him but, lacking the necessary lumber, had staked him to the ground instead.

"Oh shit." The whisper escaped her involuntarily.

If the stakes weren't enough, two stab wounds marred his abdomen, courtesy of the blond. Deep gashes, weeping copious amounts of blood, scored the man's muscled arms, chest, and legs.

As she fought back nausea, Sarah directed her gaze to his face.

He was perhaps in his mid-thirties and handsome, despite the clenched jaw and lines of pain that bracketed his mouth and eyes. Short, jet black hair. Matching brows. Straight nose. Piercing, dark brown eyes that caught and held hers as she unlocked her stiff limbs and forced herself to move forward.

Gritting his teeth, Roland watched the woman kneel beside him and set the shovel down within easy reach.

He had heard someone approaching while the damned blond plunged his blade into him and had expected yet another of the vampires' minions to join them. Gathering what little energy was left in him, he had been preparing to make an unlikely attempt to telekinetically force the bastard to stab *himself* on the next go-round when the kid had suddenly stiffened, then keeled over, revealing a woman in a Bugs Bunny baseball cap.

She couldn't be more than five feet tall and wouldn't weigh a hundred pounds dripping wet. As she grabbed pieces of his discarded shirt and put pressure on his wounds, Roland could feel her violent trembling.

Who was she?

She had risked her life to save him. Why?

"Thank you," he managed to bite out past the increased pain she unintentionally caused him in her attempt to staunch the flow of blood.

She nodded, wide hazel eyes meeting his. "I—I have to call 911," she said, her voice soft and shaky. "Do you have a cell phone?"

"No." The vamps who had ambushed him—those who had survived, anyway—had nabbed it.

She looked at the unconscious men. "Maybe one of *them* has one. If they don't, I can run to my house, call, and be back in—"

"There isn't time," he interrupted, sensing the rapidly approaching dawn. "I suffer from a condition that causes extreme photosensitivity."

Her brow furrowed. "Is that like an allergy to bright light?"

"Yes. If I'm still here when the sun rises, the pain I'm experiencing now will multiply a hundredfold."

She glanced past him at the brightening horizon, her pretty face filling with dismay. "Please tell me you're joking."

"I'm not."

She met his gaze. "You're serious?"

"Very much so. Already weakened as I am, the sun will probably kill me."

"But I . . . I mean, you're . . . What should I do?"

"Free me."

"*How?* There are metal spikes in your hands!"

"Pull them up."

Her face blanched. "What?"

He couldn't blame her for hesitating. He didn't relish the idea himself but would really prefer it to roasting. "Please. I tried to do it myself and couldn't."

She looked at the hand closest to her with obvious dread.

"There's no other way."

Swallowing hard, she scooted over and placed a knee on the ground on either side of his hand.

Roland braced himself as she gripped the horizontal bar at the top of the spike, squeezing her fingers between it and his palm. Flames shot through his hand and up his arm at the slight jostling. He thought he hid it well until she apologized.

"I'm sorry. I'm sorry."

He gave his head a swift shake. Even that hurt. "Just pull."

Nodding gamely, looking a bit green about the gills, she pulled.

The stake didn't move.

Lips compressing, she tried again. The spike shifted, lifted perhaps an inch, then stopped.

She paused, tossing a panicked glance at the treetops that were beginning to acquire a golden glow. "It's in too deep!"

"Keep trying," he encouraged, imbuing the words with a calm he didn't feel. In peak condition, he could withstand brief contact with the less harsh light of dawn without sustaining any damage. However, with so many injuries currently sapping his strength and much of his life's blood soaking into the thirsty ground beneath him, even minor exposure would prove disastrous and, in all likelihood, fatal.

Drawing her feet up under her in a squat, she pulled on the spike again, this time aided by the muscles in her thighs.

Agony sliced through him like razor blades as it moved, slowly ascending. Roland helped as much as he could, biceps bunching as he pressed upward, trapping her fingers between the horizontal bar and his slick, ravaged skin.

At last, the spike released its hold on the earth and leapt free, nearly robbing the woman of her balance.

Withdrawing her hands, she stared at it with disbelieving

eyes. Still lodged in his palm, it was roughly a foot and a half long and covered with clumps of dirt and roots.

He motioned to his legs. "I'll remove the other one while you go to work on my ankles."

Nodding, she turned toward the blond and nervously searched the ground around him.

"It's by my hip," Roland told her, assuming she sought the knife.

Her gaze moved to Roland's hip, skipped to his groin, then back again. Pale face flushing, she retrieved the knife and hastily moved to his feet.

Did he not suffer so much, Roland would have smiled. Instead, he was just glad he still had something that could make her blush. For a moment there, when the kid had cut away Roland's clothes and crouched over him with the knife, he had feared the boy intended to geld him.

As the woman started sawing through the heavy rope at his ankles, Roland rolled his upper body toward the restrained arm until his hands touched. Though bone, muscle, and tendon had been damaged, he forced the fingers of his free hand to link with those of his other and began the excruciating task of pulling the second spike free.

"I saw a thing on the news once," the woman said, her voice taut with tension, "about these kids who had an illness like yours. And once a week they gathered at a park after it closed so they could socialize and play on the equipment in the dark."

Roland struggled to pay attention while he steadily forced the spike out of the ground. He hadn't felt this weak since . . . well, since before he had been transformed over nine centuries ago.

"In the car on the way there," she continued, "the children had to wear protective suits and helmets because even the headlights of passing cars would hurt them. Is your skin that sensitive?"

"Yes," he growled as the spike came loose.

Panting, he lay still for a moment, trying to shut out the pain. The knife she wielded slipped and sank into his flesh.

"I'm sorry," she said quickly.

He shook his head. It wasn't her fault. The rope was so tight he doubted even *he* could cut it off without giving himself a few nicks.

The pressure on his ankles loosened, then fell away. The woman dropped the knife and began to tug on the spike, raising it enough for him to slip his feet free.

Sitting up set the stab wounds in Roland's abdomen ablaze.

While he caught his breath, the woman moved to his side. Every few seconds she cast the horizon an apprehensive glance.

Seizing the bar lodged against one palm, he started to pull.

She grabbed his wrist. "Don't. If you remove it now, you'll drag dirt, bacteria, bugs, and who knows what else into the wound. And the spike might be curbing the flow of blood. Let the paramedics do it later."

Leaning forward, she pressed her face to his chest and slid her arms around him.

Roland was so shocked it took him a minute to realize she was trying to haul him to his feet.

She couldn't, of course. He weighed twice what she did. But he appreciated the effort.

His ankles (and most of the rest of him) screamed in protest as he dragged himself upright. As soon as he stood, the woman shifted to his side and carefully drew one of his arms across her narrow shoulders. The top of her cap barely reached his chin.

"Can you walk?"

He nodded wearily and let her steer him toward the trees.

The cool shade there provided welcome relief from the burning that already lashed his skin. Despite their hurry, his petite rescuer took great pains to protect him, holding back branches that would have otherwise brushed his wounds or jostled the spikes in his hands. She even warned him of sharp twigs and other hazards on the ground that might harm his barc feet.

When they reached the edge of the trees and he saw the bright, empty meadow ahead of them, Roland swore.

The woman bit her lower lip and cast him an apologetic look. “I live on the other side of those trees. Should we take the long way around and stay in the shade or can you make it across the clearing?”

Damn it. He needed to get to shelter before he fell flat on his face. “Cross the clearing.”

She didn’t hesitate or second-guess him. She merely propelled him forward, righting him when he stumbled and hastening him until they were practically jogging.

“Is it me or are you already turning pink?” she asked.

“It isn’t you.” A few more seconds and blisters would begin to form.

They made it to the trees, where she again warded off combatant branches. On the other side of the cluster of foliage, Roland saw a small frame house preceded by a deck and a densely shaded backyard.

He would be shielded from the sun all the way to the back door.

“Just a little farther,” she said breathlessly, the arm she had looped around his waist giving him a faint squeeze of encouragement he found oddly endearing.

Across the grass. Up the steps. A brief pause on the deck while she retrieved her keys from her shirt pocket and unlocked the door. Then the two of them squeezed inside a very narrow laundry room and secured the door behind them.

Both Roland and the woman at his side emitted simultaneous sighs of relief.

“What’s your name?” he heard himself ask.

“Sarah Bingham. Yours?”

“Roland Warbrook. Thank you for saving my life, Sarah.”

Chapter 2

Still tucked under his arm, Sarah ushered him into a small, spotless kitchen. "Who were those guys? Why did they do this to you?"

His sore feet soothed by the cold wood floor, Roland opted not to answer and instead took in the adjoining living room.

Of average size, it was divided into two areas. One half housed exercise equipment: an inclined sit-up bench, a treadmill, a spincycle, and a Total Gym. The other boasted a black futon with solid red and white throw pillows, a glass coffee table with a matching entertainment center, and tall black bookshelves full of DVDs, VHS tapes, and books. Black curtains covered the windows and blocked out the morning light. Several modern paintings that immediately appealed to him adorned the white walls. Strategically placed about the room in black wrought-iron stands, a dozen or so large houseplants formed splashes of color and lent the room a warm, cozy feel.

Sarah moved past him and ducked through a doorway into a miniscule bathroom. When she emerged, she carried a stack of towels in her arms.

All but one she tossed on the futon. The last—a large white one—she shook out as she approached him. Her gaze met his, then flickered away as a blush once more climbed her cheeks.

Stepping close to him, she wrapped the towel around his lower body and tucked the ends in at his waist, sarong-style.

"Thank you."

"Sure." Staring up at him with concern, she gently grasped his elbow. "Come sit down."

Roland let her lead him to the futon and sank down onto the surprisingly comfortable cushion. His head began to throb unmercifully.

"I'll call 911," she said, moving away, "then see what I can do to—"

Roland grabbed her wrist, hissing when his mutilated hand protested.

Her head snapped around. "What is it?"

"You can't."

Her forehead crinkled beneath the bill of her cap. "Can't what?"

"Call 911."

Her gaze turning wary, she twisted her arm to free her wrist and backed away. "Why? Are you wanted by the police?"

"No."

Hell. What was he supposed to say? It had been so long since he had spoken to any human who wasn't a cashier in a grocery store that he didn't have an explanation readily available.

He couldn't tell her the truth: that he was an immortal who had been led into an ambush by the vampire he had been hunting. She would think him insane.

Yet he had to tell her something.

What was that bullshit line Marcus fed his human friends?

"I'm with the CIA." That was it. "If you call 911, you'll blow four years of undercover work."

"CIA?" she parroted doubtfully.

He didn't blame her. It sounded ridiculous. How the hell did Marcus make that crap fly? "Yes."

"Why would calling 911 blow your cover?"

"The men who tried to kill me think I'm an illegal arms dealer wanted by the FBI. If—"

"How do I know you *aren't* an illegal arms dealer wanted by the FBI?"

Roland wanted to moan with frustration. Hunger and the need for blood twisted his insides into knots and the pain of his injuries constantly clawed at him, making it hard to think straight.

"If you're asking if I have ID that proves I'm CIA, carrying that sort of thing around when I'm undercover isn't exactly feasible."

She nibbled her full lower lip. "I suppose that's true."

"If it will ease your mind, I'll call my handler and he can confirm who I am." Hopefully Seth, the leader of the Immortal Guardians, would catch on fast and play along. Or maybe come up with something better. Roland just wasn't up to the task himself. "He's going to have to send someone in to extract me anyway." And would no doubt use this as an excuse to lecture him again about his refusal to have a Second.

Seconds (a rather outdated term, he supposed) were humans who protected immortals like himself during the day and generally came to their aid whenever they needed it. They and the rest of the human network Seth had fostered also helped hide the existence of immortals, vampires, and *gifted ones* from the general public by presenting facades of normalcy and providing a number of other services.

Seth required every Immortal Guardian to have a Second. Roland, however, steadfastly refused. It was the only issue over which he had ever butted heads with Seth, whom no one sane would ever want to piss off. The eldest amongst them, the immortal leader was so powerful he could walk in daylight without suffering any adverse effects at all. He possessed abilities the rest of them lacked that could make even Roland's hair stand on end. And had. On more than one occasion.

When it came to this, however, Roland absolutely would

not capitulate. Anything else Seth asked of him he would do. He owed the man a great deal and would not hesitate to die for him if need be. But welcome a Second into his home and give him his trust?

No way.

The dozen or more poor sods who had been sent to him over the years as his Second had all left . . . eagerly . . . of their own free will within twenty-four hours and damned near wet their pants in fear if they ran into Roland again later, so Seth had long ago stopped sending them.

The issue remained a contentious one, though.

Roland watched as Sarah crossed to the entertainment center and retrieved a black telephone. The cord trailing after her, she returned and set it beside him on the futon.

"No cell phone?" he asked curiously. It seemed as though everyone and their grandmother had one these days.

She smiled wryly. "No, I like my brain the way it is—tumor free—and plan to keep it that way, thank you."

"The phone companies claim they're safe."

She snorted. "And cigarette companies claimed cigarettes were safe. I think I'll listen to the neurologists who don't profit from the product sales and stick to landlines."

Fortunately, as an immortal, he didn't have to worry about that sort of thing.

When he would have picked up the phone's receiver, Sarah stopped him. "Use the speakerphone. I've seen too many news reports about criminals who posed as law enforcement officials to gain their victim's trust and would like to hear for myself that you are who you say you are."

That would make this a bit trickier.

Roland pressed the speakerphone button and dialed Seth's cell number.

As he watched, Sarah knelt on the floor beside him, pulled off her baseball cap, and ran a careless hand through her hair. A lovely dark chocolate brown that contrasted vividly with her alabaster skin, it fell in shining, subtle waves down to her waist.

"You have beautiful hair," he told her as she picked up one of the discarded towels and pressed it to the stab wounds in his abdomen.

A masculine throat cleared. "Roland?"

That could not possibly be a blush he felt climbing his cheeks at the sound of the immortal leader's deep, accented voice. He hadn't blushed since his days as a squire. "Yes."

"What—are you high? You just told me my hair is beautiful."

From the corner of his eye, Roland saw Sarah unsuccessfully attempt to stifle a smile. "I wasn't talking to you," he grumbled.

"Uh-huh. So, what's wrong?"

Sarah leaned forward to whisper, "How does he know something is wrong?"

Seth answered for him. "Because he only calls me when he's desperate. Who is that you have with you, Roland?"

"Sarah," she answered for him.

"That explains the caller ID."

"Who might you be?" she asked.

"Seth."

"And what is the nature of your relationship with Roland?"

There was just no way this was going to go well.

"I suppose you might call me his boss," Seth said slowly. "Why?"

"Something has come up," Roland interjected before Sarah could ask any more questions.

"Clearly," came his dry reply. "Are you injured?"

He glanced down at himself. "Yyyeah. A little bit."

Sarah's mouth fell open. "A little bit?" she repeated incredulously. "There are two-foot-long spikes sticking out of your hands!"

"Actually, they're more like a foot and a half."

"Roland, are you all right?" Seth asked, concern coloring his voice.

"Yes."

"No, he isn't," Sarah insisted. "He needs medical attention but he doesn't want me to call 911."

Seth, Roland thought, *if you can hear me, I told her I'm a CIA agent working undercover, posing as an illegal arms dealer, and can't call 911 because it would blow four years of undercover work.*

Several seconds of silence ticked by while he waited and hoped for a response.

That is so weak.

Both relieved and astounded that Seth could truly read his thoughts over long distance (the man was just too freakin' powerful), Roland responded rather belligerently, *Well, it works for Marcus.*

Marcus doesn't tell *mortals he's CIA. He leads them toward drawing the conclusion themselves.*

"Have you taken this woman into your confidence, Roland?" Seth spoke aloud.

"I have. She saved my life."

"Then you have the CIA's gratitude, ma'am. However, I must ask that you comply with his wishes. If you call for an ambulance, the police will get involved and four years of undercover work will go down the drain."

Disbelief washed across her pretty features. "Did you not hear me mention that they drove metal spikes through both of his hands?"

"Roland, explain."

He drew in a deep breath, wincing at the pain in his cracked ribs. "I was tracking a potential buyer"—*vamp*—"and was basically led into an ambush that included six of his colleagues." *There were seven vampires plus two human minions. I took out four of the vamps and seriously injured two others before they staked me to the ground and left the minions to guard me until the sun rose. Had Sarah not come along when she did and freed me, I'd be toast.*

"An ambush," Seth muttered thoughtfully.

"It was a very well-orchestrated attack." *Have you ever heard of vampires doing such?*

No. I've seen them travel in pairs, occasionally even threes, but—because of the madness that gradually afflicts them all—most prefer solitude.

"Something isn't right, Seth. I don't think this was an isolated incident." *The last vamp standing took a sample of my blood. It seemed to be the entire purpose of their attack. They knew who I was, that I was an immortal, before I ever confronted the bait vampire. How is that possible?*

Were it another immortal, I might think you had simply been careless. But I know how paranoid you are and how meticulously you guard your privacy. The fact that so many vampires are living together—let alone investigating, plotting, and planning attacks—is unheard of.

"I would join you and get to the bottom of this, but I can't," Seth said, his voice grim. "I have a situation here that requires my full attention."

Roland was not surprised. The leader of the Immortal Guardians frequently had his hands full. "No problem. I'll look into it myself."

"Um, hello?" Sarah called. "Are you people insane? You aren't going to be able to look into anything at all if you bleed to death on my futon."

How bad are your wounds?

I've stopped the bleeding, but they aren't healing. I could really use some blood.

Too bad you don't have a Second who could bring you some.

Roland ground his teeth. "What is David's number? I'll call him and see if he'll let me borrow Darnell for a few hours."

David was a fellow immortal, Darnell his Second. And, as luck would have it, they lived only an hour away.

"David can't help you. He and Darnell are here in Texas with me."

That gave him pause. Whereas Roland had lived centuries, David had lived millennia. The second-oldest immortal, David enjoyed powers that only Seth's exceeded.

Sending for David was tantamount to calling in the big guns.

"David is with you?"

"Yes."

Forcing his fingers to do his bidding, Roland picked up the receiver and brought it to his ear.

Sarah started to protest but quieted when he touched her shoulder in a silent bid for leniency.

"What kind of situation are we talking, Seth? Do you need my help?"

"No, David and I can handle it."

"Are you sure? I can put this on hold and be there in a few hours."

"I appreciate the offer, but I would prefer that you remain there and see what you can uncover."

"All right."

Sarah pursed her lips, raised one dark eyebrow, and looked pointedly at the phone.

Returning the receiver to its cradle, Roland switched back to speakerphone.

Sarah couldn't believe the man had just offered to fly to Texas to aid his boss, who clearly was also a good friend, when he sat before her covered in blood and ravaged by wounds that would make anyone with a weaker stomach than hers vomit.

That was loyalty. That was dedication.

Two qualities that seemed regrettably rare nowadays.

She studied Roland curiously. If he had opened the telephone conversation by saying, *Hey, Seth, do me a favor and tell this woman I really am a CIA agent,* she would have remained skeptical. But Seth had confirmed his status as an undercover agent—as well as the length of time he had been working this case—with no verbal hints from Roland, so she was inclined to believe him.

Besides, foolish though it may be, she *wanted* to believe him.

The fingers of one of his hands still rested on her shoulder, the spike carefully angled away from her face.

How could he stand it? How could he bear such horrific wounds so casually? So stoically? And what exactly did he plan to do about them if he didn't intend to call 911?

"Who else can I call?" Roland asked. His words carried a British accent.

"Marcus." Seth's accent wasn't as easy to identify.

Roland's forehead, speckled with blood, crinkled in a frown. "How is that going to help me? Marcus is in Houston."

"Not anymore. I transferred him to North Carolina last month. He's staying just outside of Greensboro."

"He is?"

The news seemed to please him.

Sarah peeled back the towel she held to his stomach, relieved to see that the stab wounds no longer bled. On the outside. Was he bleeding internally?

"Who is his Second?"

"What's a Second?" she whispered.

Roland lowered his voice. "It's like a partner whose sole duty is to watch your back throughout your investigation."

"Oh." Where had Roland's Second been this morning? It didn't look as though anyone had been watching *his* back. Other than her. And she had just stumbled onto the scene.

"Marcus doesn't have a Second," Seth said. "And before you say anything, he wasn't assigned one because Marcus is dangerous to be around right now. You simply *refused* one because you're antisocial."

Roland scowled. “I’m not antisocial. I just want to be lcft alonc.”

Sarah must have made some sound of amusement, because Roland met her gaze, then smiled sheepishly.

Her heart gave a little flutter.

Even with his face smeared with blood and dirt, he was attractive.

Then he frowned. “Wait. What makes you think Marcus is dangerous?”

“His behavior has grown erratic of late. I’m afraid any Second I place with him will quickly end up dead. Lisette is still in the area, though, and has a very competent Second. Would you prefer to call her?”

“No, just give me Marcus’s number.”

Sarah released her hold on the towel and picked up the pen and small tablet she kept on the coffee table. As Seth dictated the number, she wrote it down with Marcus’s name beside it.

Roland thanked Seth. “Don’t forget to call me if you need reinforcements.”

“Don’t worry about me. Just see what you can find out. And keep Sarah safe.”

Sarah’s stomach sank. Keep her safe?

Roland pressed the speakerphone button to hang up.

Her gaze met his.

The truth lay in his troubled, dark brown eyes.

“He thinks they’re going to come after me for helping you, doesn’t he?”

She thought she caught a flash of guilt before he looked away, down at his stomach, then at his hand.

When he spoke, his voice was hushed, weary. “Sarah, would you please clean these spikes up for me so I can remove them?”

Swallowing hard, she nodded and rose.

As Roland stood, the white towel loosened and started to fall. She hastily grabbed it and resecured the ends at his narrow waist.

"Thank you."

Again Sarah nodded and led him over to the kitchen sink.

He was so polite . . . in a gruff sort of way. It just made all of this seem that much more surreal.

Turning on the cold tap, she picked up the hand sprayer and began to carefully rinse the dirt, roots, and other crud off the long, pointed length of metal protruding from the back of his right hand.

It just couldn't be real. Any of it.

The violent struggle that had left this man staked to the ground in the field.

Her knocking two men unconscious with a shovel.

The frantic race for shelter.

His refusal of medical attention.

Finding out the sickos who had done this to him would now be after her.

It was all a bad dream, right? One of those really nasty nightmares in which you knew you were dreaming and needed to wake up, but couldn't?

Roland sucked in a breath through clenched teeth when the cool water made contact with his wound.

"Should I pour alcohol or witch hazel on it to disinfect it?" she asked, reluctant to hurt him more.

Adam's apple bobbing, he shook his head. "Soap and water will do."

Sarah obligingly poured dish liquid onto her hands and lathered up the spike.

Its surface wasn't smooth as she had thought. Rather, it abraded her skin like coarse-grained sandpaper, making it sting.

As soon as she finished rinsing the spike clean and turned off the water, Roland grabbed the horizontal bar wedged against his palm and tensed.

"Wait!" she practically shouted.

He looked at her, a muscle in his jaw twitching.

Stomach clenching, she stared up at him with pleading

eyes. "There's a clinic just fifteen miles away from here. I can—"

He started to pull. Lips drawing back from his teeth in a grimace, he emitted a long, bestial growl that made the hair on the back of her neck rise.

Sarah clapped her hands over her mouth to suppress a horrified cry.

When the spike slid free, crimson liquid began to pour from the large puncture wound left behind, dripping into the sink.

Unrolling several sections of paper towel, she folded them and wrapped them tightly around and around his hand.

"That's fine," he said hoarsely, holding the makeshift bandage in place with his thumb. "Now the other one."

Turning the cold water on again, she began to rinse the second spike. The first, still wet with Roland's blood, lay in the sink, where he had dropped it.

Her hands started to quake. The rest of her followed suit until her whole body trembled so violently Sarah thought she might shatter.

After shutting off the tap, she reeled off several more sections of paper towel and watched him remove the last spike.

The tendons on his neck stood out. Sweat beaded on his forehead. Yet Roland made no sound as the metal came free.

Sarah blinked back tears as she wrapped his hand.

He hadn't wanted to upset her. She didn't know how she knew it, but she did. He had seen how removing the first spike had shaken her and hadn't wanted to make it worse, so he had borne the pain silently.

Agony radiating from seemingly every cell in his body, Roland stared at Sarah's bent head. He could see her shaking, the rapid movement of her long lashes as she fought back tears.

She had been such a trouper about all of this. Strong. Fearless. Doing anything he asked of her no matter how difficult.

To see her suffering now with that glimmer of moisture on her pale cheeks tore at his fossilized heart.

Staring at her helplessly, he found himself at a loss as to how he might comfort her. He couldn't remember ever being confronted by a weeping woman. At least not one he knew or gave a damn about. Certainly not one who had helped him at such great risk to herself.

A sniffle escaped her as she finished wrapping his hand.

Unable to bear it, Roland reached out, tore off another paper towel, and, ignoring the sting of it, wiped as much of the blood and dirt from his chest as he could. After tossing the soiled paper towel into the sink, he hesitated briefly, then drew Sarah close, wrapped his arms around her, and awkwardly patted her back.

"Don't hurt your hands," she cautioned, her voice warbling slightly as she rested her face against his chest and slid her arms around his waist.

Unbelievable. Even as her tears dampened his skin, she looked out for him.

Him. A total stranger.

"I'm more concerned about you than my hands," he admitted.

"I'm okay," she said. "It's just been a very . . . nerve-racking morning."

Roland held her tighter. "And it isn't even 7 a.m."

She groaned. "That's just not right."

Closing his eyes, he rested his chin atop her hair and let his senses feast upon her. Her scent was a pleasant blend of woman, baby powder, and sunscreen. Her warm body, pressed to his, seemed fragile in comparison to his own bulk and strength.

Though thin, she was by no means built like the emaciated models and actresses other men inexplicably preferred. The breasts brushing his chest and interfering with his ability to moderate his pulse were enticingly full, her waist tiny, her hips nicely rounded, her thighs slender, but not sticklike in the worn sweatpants that hugged them.

Her small, almost childlike hands remained motionless on his back as if she feared moving them might hurt him.

Most likely it would. His back sported as many lacerations and bruises as the rest of him. She simply hadn't had time to notice them yet, what with the spikes.

Roland was glad she didn't know. If she did, she wouldn't be holding him like this, with such tenderness and trust. When was the last time a woman had done so?

Centuries surely. It felt . . . foreign to him.

Having been betrayed one time too many, Roland had long ago given up on relationships. When the strain of celibacy grew too much, he simply sought out prostitutes or women looking for one-night stands and allowed them to sate his needs.

Those women never held him like this, though. Only two women had embraced him so tenderly. And he didn't care to think of that right now.

In truth, he found it more and more difficult to think at all. Every inch of his body either ached, stung, throbbed, or burned. His head swam. His vision started to blur. His stomach churned.

Strangely, Sarah's presence, the comfort of her embrace, helped him distance himself from it all.

Gradually, her tremors subsided, as did her tears.

Sighing, she released him and eased a step away.

As Roland withdrew his large, hastily bandaged hands, he swayed and realized, to his dismay, that she had been anchoring him and helping him remain upright.

Several long strands of her hair clung to the stubble on his jaw. Reaching up, he gently disentangled them.

"I'm sorry," she said, wiping her cheeks. "I didn't mean to fall apart on you."

He shook his head, alarmed when the small movement

made the kitchen around him tilt and roll. "I'm the one who should apologize. I'm sorry you were dragged into all of this."

She nodded, her expression filled with anxiety.

Roland cupped her face in his hands, smoothing his thumbs across her soft, damp cheeks. "I won't let anyone hurt you, Sarah. I vow it."

Heart pounding, Sarah held his earnest gaze. His touch, his nearness, began to stir her in a wholly unexpected way. He stood before her, his gorgeous body riddled with severe wounds, and suddenly all she could think about was what it would feel like if he kissed her.

What is wrong *with me?*

Something dark flared in his eyes. One of his thumbs slid down her cheek to caress the corner of her mouth.

His head dipped. Her breath stopped. Anticipation rose.

Her lips a hair away from tasting his, Sarah heard a rustling sound followed by a soft thump. She glanced down, then swiftly up again as she realized the towel wrapped around his waist had fallen to the floor.

Emitting a sigh, Roland lowered his hands. "It's going to be one of those days," he said with a look of such pained chagrin that Sarah had to smile.

As he bent over to retrieve the towel, he listed to one side and would have fallen had he not reached for her. The moment his hand made rough contact with her shoulder, he cried out and yanked it back. His balance faltered.

Gasping, Sarah threw her arms around him and tried to steady him.

He staggered. She staggered with him.

Jeeze, he weighed a ton! Six foot one or two, maybe two hundred pounds of muscle. She would never be able to get him up off the floor if he fainted!

Finding it a lot harder to support him when he reeled away

from her, she drew his upper body toward her, took two steps back, and leaned all of her weight into him to prop him up.

Success! They were both still on their feet.

This time, when Roland's arms closed around her, he carefully avoided touching her with his hands. "Sarah," he rasped.

"Yes?"

He blinked hard and stared over her shoulder, his gaze unfocused. "If I pass out and you can't wake me up—"

Oh crap.

"—wait until an hour before sunset, then call Marcus."

"Shouldn't we call him now?"

"No, he won't . . ." Roland's dark eyes started to roll back in his head.

"No, no, no! Don't pass out on me! We have to get you to the futon!"

He blinked sluggishly when she shook him.

Hurriedly maneuvering them so her back was to the futon, she began shuffling toward it, dragging him with her.

He took one step, two, three, then his knees buckled and his weight sank down on her, pulling her toward the floor.

Swearing, unable to keep him upright, she twisted and shoved him away from her as hard as she could. The not-very-controlled fall that resulted landed him on his back on the futon with most of his legs hanging over the metal arm closest to her.

Whew!

That had been pure dumb luck.

"Roland?"

Rounding the futon, she leaned over him and patted one stubbled cheek. "Roland?"

Nothing.

He was definitely out for the count.

High above Houston, Texas, two figures stood on the roof of Williams Tower, the toes of their boots inches from the edge. Sixty-four stories high, the building loomed over the normally bustling Galleria area and was lauded as the tallest building in the country located outside of a city's urban core. Soon the sun would rise and sparkle off the countless windows of the steel and glass structure as though reflected in a gargantuan mirror. At its base, a large horseshoe-shaped multistory wall of water glowed amid the fading darkness.

Had the two imposing men currently positioned near the building's peak have instead stood on the street, they would have attracted unwanted attention despite the decreased activity predawn Sunday mornings generally heralded. One was six foot eight with a golden tan, wavy black hair that fell to his waist, and beautiful patrician features that inspired many a female double take. The other was an inch shorter with similar patrician features but had skin as dark as midnight and masses of pencil-thin dreadlocks that reached his hips. He, too, drew many admiring feminine gazes and caused hearts to flutter.

Both were clad all in black, wore leather urban dusters, and were fatigued from two long days and nights of searching.

Frowning, the taller of the two returned his cell phone to his pocket and mulled over all that Roland had told him.

"This is an interesting turn of events," his friend commented in a faint Egyptian accent.

"Yes." David possessed the preternaturally enhanced senses all immortals boasted and would have heard both sides of the conversation. Not just Seth's.

"Is this an isolated incident, or have you received other such calls?"

"So far it's isolated." But his gut told Seth it was only the beginning. "I don't like it. Usually when people band together to hunt and destroy us they are human, not vampire. *Never* vampire."

David nodded somberly. "Change is in the wind." He stared toward the west. "Do you think the attack on Roland is in any way related to *this?*"

This referred to the situation Seth had mentioned to Roland.

"No, this is something different."

There were roughly five and a half million people living in the Houston metropolitan area. A population that large, pervaded with crime, tended to draw a greater number of vampires. Currently, half a dozen immortals stationed around the city guarded the humans, hunting down the vamps who would make them their prey.

About a month ago, those immortals had begun to call Seth—one by one—and tell him there was a *funny feeling* in the air, puzzled because they could not pin down its origins.

Seth had been overseas at the time. Vampires were taking advantage of the violence and genocide afflicting Sudan and had dramatically increased their presence there. The immortals stationed in and around Darfur were having a tough time curbing the vamps' population and he had been lending them a hand.

As there had been no emergency, Seth had been reluctant to leave—even briefly—and had advised the Houston contingent to find out what they could and keep him posted.

They had found nothing. There had been no escalation in vampire activity. No escalation in human-on-human violence. Yet the feeling had remained. When Seth had asked them to describe it, they had all responded the same way: that it was as if the sound of fingernails scouring a chalkboard were being broadcast on a frequency too low or too high for them to hear, but nevertheless affected their bodies, leaving them feeling anxious. Every day the *volume* increased incrementally, as did their anxiety.

Both curious and concerned, he had ordered another Immortal Guardian to take his place in Sudan, then teleported to Houston to check it out. Seth possessed all of the gifts unique to immortals (who usually only had one or two) combined, as well as some the others lacked. But his were much stronger. As a result, upon his arrival he had heard what they had been unable to: a woman screaming in agony and, presumably, begging for help. She communicated telepathically on a frequency the other immortals could barely sense, none of those in the city being capable of telepathy.

She spoke a language he couldn't understand, which was odd. He pretty much knew them all, both current and ancient. None enabled him to garner her location, though he thought she could hear him, because her screams would dim down to whimpers whenever he attempted to communicate with her.

Knowing he would find her sooner with someone else who could hear her, he had summoned David.

"Is it me," David asked in his deep, mellifluous voice, "or did Roland sound rather taken with his rescuer?"

"It isn't you. I heard it, too."

"I hope she doesn't distract him too much."

Seth shook his head. "Roland is a professional."

David's lips quirked. "And antisocial, as you said. The poor woman probably can't wait to be rid of him."

If the mystery woman weren't screaming in his head, Seth would have laughed. He closed his eyes and tried yet again to hone in on her location as the already hot Texas breeze buffeted him.

"You were right," David murmured beside him. "It's coming from the west."

Seth opened his eyes and looked to his friend. "I'll go southwest. You go northwest and let us see if we cannot narrow it down."

David nodded. "She is weakening. Can you hear it?"

"Yes. I fear she will die if we do not find her soon."

"I'll search as long as I can, then let you know when I seek shelter." As one of the oldest and strongest immortals, David could withstand several hours of sunlight. Most could withstand only minutes.

"And I will continue searching throughout the day."

"You should rest."

"Not until I find her."

"Very well. I will rise as soon as I can."

"Thank you, my friend."

Ready to begin their search once more, the two stepped off the edge of the roof.

Chapter 3

Pressing two fingers to Roland's tanned throat, Sarah was relieved to feel a slow, steady pulse.

She straightened and stared down at him, filled with equal parts of awe over his beauty and the utter perfection of his body, and compassion for the agony his injuries must be inspiring. He looked extremely uncomfortable.

Moving to stand at the other end of the futon, she bent down, tucked her hands under his arms, and pulled until his head rested only a few inches from the metal arm on this side and only his calves hung over the other. A simple endeavor, one might think, yet it took her half an hour and, by the time she finished, she was sweating and out of breath.

All of those movies she had seen in which women her size dragged unconscious men his size across the floor, hoisted them up, and tossed them in the backseat of a car or across the back of a horse were very misleading. She exercised and lifted weights six days a week and had barely been able to move him two friggin' feet.

It hadn't helped that he weighed a lot more than the futon, which had insisted on moving with him every time she pulled. Her shins were going to be every shade of the rainbow tomorrow.

After carefully tucking a pillow beneath his head (his hair

was so soft), she went into the bathroom and retrieved all of the first aid supplies she could find.

There were quite a lot of them. When she had moved up here from Texas last summer, she had cut her hand badly on a broken glass while unpacking. (Thinking of how much the small, though deep, cut had hurt, she couldn't imagine what Roland must be experiencing.) She had been unable to get it to stop bleeding, and the box containing her first aid stuff had remained stubbornly elusive. Since she hadn't had health insurance at the time (she could barely afford it now), a trip to the emergency room would've proven too costly, so she had wrapped a washcloth around her hand, held it in place with a tight layer of duct tape, driven fifteen miles to the nearest Walmart, and bought enough gauze, nonstick pads, first aid tape, butterfly closures, and antibiotic ointment to take care of the cut and any other gashes the moving boxes' contents might inflict during the next few months.

Fortunately for Roland, there had been very few.

Dumping the gauze and other paraphernalia on the coffee table, she went back for washcloths and two bottles of witch hazel, swung by the kitchen to grab a couple of bowls, then added them to the pile.

Sarah seated herself beside Roland on the futon, her hip touching his. Her gaze fell to his groin and lingered wickedly. The towel remained where it had fallen on the kitchen floor, leaving him bare.

He was very impressive. She felt guilty for noticing, considering the condition he was in, but . . . how could she not?

Forcing her gaze away, she poured witch hazel into a bowl, saturated a washcloth, wrung it out, then carefully began to bathe away the blood and dirt that coated Roland's skin.

His face had escaped much of the devastation to which the rest of him had been subjected. On the left side of his high forehead was a pink mark that would be a large bruise tomorrow. Another darkened the opposite cheekbone, disappearing into the coarse stubble. His full lower lip was split. Other than that, his face was flawless. No swelling marred his lowered eyelids or the skin his crescent-shaped lashes shadowed. His straight nose, neither too long nor too short, was unbroken.

He really was handsome. Not a soft, pretty-boy, male model handsome, but an overtly masculine, smoothly angular, *I'm hot, but can kick ass* handsome.

His hands made her want to cry. Again. And she was not one to cry easily. If she weren't so exhausted, she would have held it together much better earlier. But two nights of little or no sleep had taken their toll. (Damned students, stressing her out. Thank goodness the spring semester had finally ended.)

His fingers were long and tapered, his nails neatly trimmed . . . and a hole the width of a nickel went all the way through each palm. It was despicable, the atrocities some people could commit without a qualm.

Sarah rinsed the first hand well with witch hazel (she had chosen witch hazel over alcohol to clean his wounds because it would hurt less), applied thick sterile nonstick pads to both sides, then wound gauze around and around it, topping it off with first aid tape. The other hand received the same treatment.

She opted not to use antibiotic ointment because she thought she had read somewhere that it wasn't supposed to be applied to the insides of puncture wounds. She did spread the ointment over the numerous lacerations on his arms, torso, hips, and thighs, though. Some of those were shallow. Some were so deep she had to use the butterfly closures to hold the sides together.

Witch hazel. Antibiotic ointment. Butterfly closures if necessary. Gauze. First aid tape. She really didn't know what else to do.

None of his wounds were still bleeding, which was good.

But weird.

Her hand had bled for hours, stopping only while she had kept pressure on it. When she had later removed the duct tape and towel to replace them with bandages, it had started to bleed all over again and had done so off and on for a couple of days.

Yet Roland didn't appear to be bleeding anywhere. Not even his hands.

How was that possible?

Was it part of his illness? Did whatever caused his photosensitivity also make his blood clot faster? The news segment about the photosensitive children hadn't mentioned anything about that.

Even the stab wounds in his eight-pack abs no longer bled. It was a little unsettling.

Okay, majorly unsettling. It just didn't seem natural. If his chest weren't rising and falling with each breath, she would think he was dead.

Sarah rinsed out the bowl and filled it with more witch hazel. Amid a great deal of unladylike grunting, she managed to roll Roland onto his side away from her so she could inspect his back.

It, too, sported long, deep gashes and what appeared to be more stab wounds, all of which were encrusted with blood, dirt, grass, and weeds. And, like those in front, these wounds no longer bled.

Sarah went to work, cleaning and doctoring them, starting at his wide, strong shoulders. His back was broad, muscular, naturally tanned like the rest of him. A long slash began where his neck met his right shoulder and sliced down toward his left armpit. It took the rest of her butterfly closures to secure it. Another looked as though the weapon that had carved it had glanced off his ribs down on his left side. A third slit his narrow waist on the right.

It all seemed a little off.

Didn't most criminals sport guns now? Even petty criminals?

She would think that whatever enemies Roland had acquired posing as an illegal arms dealer would have *shot* him, not attacked him with knives.

Sarah mulled that one over for several minutes while she ministered to him.

Maybe they hadn't wanted to attract attention? Sound did tend to carry out here, echoing through the countryside.

But there wasn't much gun crime in this area. At least not compared to Houston, where she had been born and raised. She would think if someone heard a gunshot way out here, they would attribute it to hunters, target practice, a truck backfiring, or someone shooting off fireworks.

Plus, there were always silencers.

Sarah blushed as she bathed the dirt and blood from Roland's lower body. He had the sexiest butt she had ever seen. While every guy she had dated in the past had *had* no butt, Roland's was firm and muscular. And his legs . . .

Like the rest of him, they were well-muscled and honed to perfection (that perfection broken by a cut where one of his attackers had tried to hamstring him).

It felt decidedly intimate, touching him like this while he slept. She tended to be a little shy around men and had never taken sex as lightly as her peers. (Most of the women and girls she had known had treated sex like a recreational sport and were insanely unconcerned about disease.) Consequently, she had only had two lovers thus far, both of whom had been long-term relationships.

Her first lover had been reed-thin. The second had been similarly thin when they had begun dating and a good fifty pounds overweight by the time their three-year relationship had fizzled out. Neither man, as far as she knew, had ever so much as touched a weight, let alone lifted one.

Roland, on the other hand, was built like an Olympic athlete and, for just a moment (okay, maybe two or three . . . or four), made her wish he was uninjured and she was easy.

Shaking her head, Sarah decided she had drooled over the poor guy long enough and set the damp cloth and bowl of witch hazel on the coffee table. The black material of the futon where he had lain was smeared with as much dirt, blood, and plant materials as his back had been. She had no idea how she was going to clean it later and, for now, did not want any of that sneaking back into his wounds.

Rising, she strode to the narrow linen closet next to the bathroom and withdrew two white sheets. The first, she shook out, folded in half, and spread across every inch of the futon's seat that Roland didn't cover. Then she eased him onto his back and covered him with the second.

Her work done, she stood, staring down at him for several minutes.

He seemed at once a stranger and not a stranger to her. Strong yet vulnerable.

Sarah bit her lower lip.

The rise and fall of his chest was barely discernible.

He had told her to wait until an hour before sunset to call Marcus. Though she wanted to do otherwise, she decided to respect his wishes.

For now.

In the basement of a large, isolated farmhouse, a pair of russet eyes opened. Bastien perused the darkness briefly to ensure no one had encroached upon his sanctuary.

When he had confirmed that all was safe and secure, a malevolent smile rife with triumph stretched across his handsome features.

Revenge was so sweet.

At last, his enemy was dead.

The Immortal Guardian who currently went by the name of Roland Warbrook had killed four of Bastien's men when they had ambushed him the previous night, but Roland had paid for that with his life.

Paid for that and so much more.

Bastien closed his eyes, savoring his victory. How the bastard must have suffered as the sun rose and baked him like an oven.

He wouldn't have burst into flames the way vampires did in movies. No, he would have blistered, then charred like meat left too long on a grill. His body, already damaged, would have been unable to heal itself. Deprived of blood, thanks to the large sample Bastien himself had extracted, the parasitic virus that infected them all would have turned on its host, devouring him from the inside out until there was nothing left upon which it might feast.

It was an agonizing death.

And one Roland had richly deserved. He and all of those like him.

Rising, Bastien donned the black clothing that allowed him to blend in with the night and topped it off with a long black coat. Once he had armed himself with his usual weaponry, he unbolted the door and left his chamber.

The ground beneath his farmhouse was riddled with catacombs painstakingly created by himself and his followers. It was a place where they could all rest without fear. Safe from sunlight. Safe from humans. Safe from Immortal Guardians who thought them too stupid to devise such.

He let a smirk curl his lips.

Would the immortals still sneer at them when the vampires began to pick them all off, one by one? Or would they realize they were outnumbered and beg for mercy, as so many vampires had in the past?

Bastien stepped out into a winding tunnel that, like a maze, branched off into numerous dead ends. He had dug and paved this wing himself and he alone knew the way to and from his chamber. Anyone else who tried to find it would inevitably end up lost and answer to him when he heard their pitiful cries for help and hunted them down.

Upon reaching the central hall, which was an expansion of the original basement, he scaled the stairs that led into the house itself. Though the house was dark, all windows carefully covered, the sun had not yet set. His brethren would sleep awhile longer. As the oldest vampire in their midst, he tended to rise before them.

His human servants, however, were up and about.

Tanner, the highest-ranking human, awaited him at the top of the steps. Roughly six feet tall with short blond hair and glasses, he looked, dressed, and sounded more like an accountant than the devoted employee of a vampire.

"They're in your study."

Bastien nodded, anticipation thrumming through him. With two wounded vampires he had needed to get belowground, he had ordered Derek and Bobby to remain behind and collect whatever was left of Roland after the sun had risen. They would be here now to deliver it.

Several men lounging on the living room sofas scrambled to their feet as he walked past. Bastien acknowledged the humans with a short nod and continued on, thinking with some amusement of ways he might display Roland's remains.

That amusement died as soon as he entered the study.

Something was wrong. Something Derek and Bobby apparently thought would spark his dangerous temper. He could smell their fear, see the tension in their stiff postures, their nervousness in the bobbing knees they couldn't keep still as they shifted in the chairs positioned in front of his desk.

"You have something for me."

They leapt to their feet and spun around at his words, faces paling. These two would do just about anything for him in hopes of earning a taste of the vampire's gifts. It was why he had chosen them to complete this task.

"Where is it?" he demanded.

The twenty-somethings exchanged a terrified look. Bobby had a large bruise in the center of his forehead.

Derek, the one with the bolder nature, girded his loins and spoke. "He, uh . . . he escaped."

A haze of fury instantly filled Bastien's vision, painting the world around him red. In a heartbeat, both men were lifted and slammed to the surface of the desk. His hands tightened around their throats, restricting their airways and pinning them in place.

"He was completely immobilized and at your mercy when we left," Bastien snarled at the quivering lumps. "What did you do?"

"It wasn't us!" Derek cried hoarsely as Bobby whimpered and wet himself. "We were watchin' over him like you told us to and were attacked!"

"By whom? He had no way of contacting his fellow Guardians."

"I don't know." He gagged and coughed until Bastien loosened his hold minutely. "I didn't see who it was. Bobby said it was some crazy bitch with a shovel. She knocked us both out and helped the Guardian get away."

"A woman?" he growled furiously. "A mortal woman armed with nothing but a gardening tool bested you?"

"W-we didn't hear her coming," he blurted. "She was . . . she was crazy quiet."

One of the immortals' Seconds, perhaps?

If so, why hadn't she been better armed?

Bastien lifted the men and slammed them back down again hard enough to crack the heavy wooden surface of the antique desk. "Damn you! We had him! You say you want to be one of us, but when I give you a task—one *simple* task—you *fuck it up!*"

Incensed, his wound from the previous night still paining him, he roared his fury so loudly he woke the slumbering vampires below.

Fangs exploded from his gums.

Derek and Bobby began to scream.

Uncaring, Bastien bent and sank his teeth into Derek's throat.

Hunger clawed at Roland with razor-sharp talons as he slowly came awake. The need for blood was strong. His wounds had not healed as he slept, as they would have if he had had a few units on hand. He should have taken a minute to feed on the punk who had stabbed him.

But then Sarah would have been afraid of him.

Sarah.

Eyes flying open, Roland saw her in the kitchen. She was closing the oven door and reaching over to return a pot holder to its hook on the wall.

Her bloodstained clothing had been replaced with pale blue, low-riding jeans and an olive green T-shirt that hugged her shapely figure, emphasizing a small waist, full breasts, nicely rounded hips, and a tempting ass. Her hair was still damp from a shower and spilled in thick waves down her back.

He frowned. Was one of her elbows scraped? Had that happened when she'd saved him?

She glanced at him over her shoulder, looked away, then did a double take. Face brightening, she spun around. "You're awake."

"Yes."

Brow furrowing, she crossed to his side. "How are you feeling?"

"About the same." May as well be honest whenever he could. "How long have I been out?"

"Almost four hours."

It wasn't until then that he realized the blood and dirt that had coated him had been washed away. He now sported numerous neat white bandages and was covered with a sheet.

"Did you do all this?"

"Yes."

He tested the bandage wrapped around his left hand. "Nice field dressing. Are you a doctor?"

She offered him a wry smile. "Not the medical kind. I have a doctoral degree in music theory and teach over at UNC Chapel Hill."

Beautiful *and* smart. A marvelous combination. "Well, you did an excellent job. Thank you."

Her kindness continued to astound him. Even a Second wouldn't have cleaned him up and made him more comfortable. He would have just bitched and moaned over his sleep being disrupted and given him blood.

Roland's imagination temporarily soared with images of her touching his bare body while he had slept.

If only he could have remained conscious.

Sarah worried her lower lip and clasped her hands in front of her, suddenly appearing uncertain.

He frowned. "What is it?"

"I've been trying to figure out a tactful way to ask you something. . . ."

Oh shit. Had his fangs descended while he was unconscious? A hasty feel with his tongue reassured him that they were receded, as they should be. But if she had seen his fangs earlier, it would explain why she seemed so uneasy.

"Forget tact," he told her, wondering how he would respond if she asked him if he were a vampire. "Just ask."

Nodding, she drew in a deep breath, then blurted out, "Are you HIV positive?"

His eyebrows flew up. Not what he had been expecting. "No."

"Are you sure? Because a lot of people who have it don't know they have it."

"I'm 100 percent sure. No HIV. No hepatitis. Nothing. I'm clean."

The tension left her as she gave him a relieved smile. "Thank goodness."

Considering how much contact she had had with his blood, he could understand her concern, especially if she had any open wounds of her own.

Again he frowned. "Were you injured, Sarah?"

Wrinkling her nose, she held up her hands to show him scratched and abraded palms. It also allowed him to see her scraped elbow. "I forgot all about it until after I finished cleaning you up. And when I saw it . . . I admit I got a little worried."

Roland slowly sat up, clenching his teeth when the movement made it feel as if he were being stabbed anew in the stomach.

"What are you doing?" she asked as he swiveled and lowered his feet to the floor, ensuring the sheet continued to cover him to the waist.

Once the pain had subsided enough for him to unlock his jaw, he motioned to the empty space beside him. "Sit with me for a moment." It was more a question than an order.

A sweet shyness entered her features as she obligingly sat next to him.

Roland took her hands in his and turned them palms up so he could study the angry red marks. "What happened?"

"Something knocked me down in the meadow before I found you," she answered. "It was so big and moved so fast I thought it was a bear, but . . ." She tilted her head to one side, drawing his gaze to hers. "Was it you? And the others?"

It must have been. He didn't recall seeing her or bumping into her. But, when fighting three vampires (he had already dispatched four at that point) and traveling at preternatural speeds, the details of one's surroundings could sometimes blur.

"I don't know. I was focused on my opponents and saw little else."

Spying what was left of her first aid supplies on the coffee table, he released her hands, picked up a half-empty bottle of witch hazel, and snagged a clean cloth.

"Did I miss a wound?" she asked, her eyes roving his exposed skin.

Roland gave his chest and arms a cursory inspection. "Not as far as I can tell." Thanks to her ministrations, he would heal more swiftly when he fed.

The lid came free easily. Dampening the cloth, he returned the witch hazel to the coffee table.

"Then what are you . . . ?"

Her words faltered as he reclaimed one of her dainty hands and gently cleansed her palm.

"Oh. Oh, no. No, no, Roland, you don't have to do that."

"Yes, I do," he responded, quiet but determined.

This woman had knocked out two men bent on torturing him to death, unstaked him, helped him up, dragged him a hundred yards uphill, welcomed him into her home, given him shelter for the day, and cleaned and bandaged his wounds.

He *wanted* to do this for her.

Sarah's heart turned over as she watched him painstakingly tend her abrasions. Her hand looked so small cradled in his.

She really had forgotten about the scratches until she had washed his blood off her hands. The water had stung and, when she had seen the raw, red marks, they had immediately begun to throb and burn.

Dropping the cloth to his lap, Roland located the tube of antibiotic ointment and struggled to remove the cap. A muscle leapt along his jaw.

It must be killing him to move his fingers like that. She thought it fairly miraculous that he could move them at all. A hole that size must have broken bones and damaged nerves and tendons, too.

She reached for the tube with her free hand. "Let me . . ."

He sent her a warning glare.

Sarah swiftly withdrew. "Okay."

At last succeeding, he squeezed a generous dollop of clear goo onto his index finger and applied it to her palm with a featherlight touch that made her pulse race.

As if he heard her heartbeat pick up, he raised his dark brown eyes, meeting hers.

She wanted to look away but couldn't.

What was it about this man that affected her so?

His fingers resumed their slow strokes. "Am I hurting you?" he asked, his voice as smooth as melted chocolate and just as appealing.

Unable to find her own, Sarah shook her head.

The ache in her palm receded beneath his touch, replaced by a warm tingling.

Roland gently covered the scratches with a nonstick pad and wrapped some of the remaining gauze around her hand, just as she had done for him.

Her other hand received the same careful treatment. When he was finished, Roland held both of her hands in his.

"We match," she teased.

His dark eyes lightened with amusement as he drew her attention to the fact that the whole of one of her hands barely filled his palm. "Not quite."

She smiled.

"Sarah, there is something I must ask you."

Sobering at his earnest expression, she leaned forward. "What?"

He shifted infinitesimally closer, his eyes boring into hers. "Is that pizza I smell? Because I am *famished.*"

The corners of his lips twitched.

Sarah laughed. "Yes, it's pizza." She glanced at the clock on the DVD player. "And it should be about ready."

Roland smiled up at her as she rose, his raven hair falling forward across his bruised forehead and lending him a boyish charm.

"I was hoping you would wake up," she said as she headed for the kitchen, "and tried to think of something you could eat that wouldn't require hurting your hands with the use of utensils. I figured you would balk at my spoon feeding you."

"You were right. I would. Pizza is perfect. Thank you."

Grabbing a pot holder, she hoped he wouldn't change his mind when he saw it. Heat blasted her as she opened the oven door, removed the pizza, and set it on the stovetop. For some reason, most of her fellow Americans seemed to think any food that didn't contain chemicals that had been banned in every other industrialized nation or that didn't increase their risk of cancer, Alzheimer's, and other debilitating illnesses must taste like crap and turned their noses up without èven trying it.

If Roland was like that, too bad for him. He was going to go hungry.

She sighed and closed the oven door. Who was she kidding? No, he wouldn't. She'd just fix him something else and be pissed about it.

"Would you like tea or water with it? The tea is decaf."

"Tea, please."

She smiled. Roland had said "please" and "thank you" more times in the hours she had known him than Tom, her ex-boyfriend, had in the entire last year they were together.

Carrying two glasses and a pitcher of iced tea over to the coffee table, she set them down, then went back for plates and napkins and finally the pizza.

Roland stared down at it as she sliced it. "That pizza is organic."

Here we go. "Look, I know it doesn't contain artificial crap, genetically modified organisms, irradiated vegetables, recombinant artificial bovine growth hormone, pesticides, or other harmful chemicals, but if you'll just give it a chance—"

"I don't have to give it a chance," he interrupted. "I eat this all the time. It's delicious."

As Sarah gaped at him in astonishment, he grabbed a goat cheese– and vegetable-laden slice and practically swallowed it whole.

Ho-ly crap! This man might very well be perfect! He was handsome, kind, brave as hell, loyal to his friends, fought bad guys for a living, *and* ate natural?

If he didn't ask her out when the danger was over, she was

damn well going to find a way to overcome her shyness long enough to ask him!

A second piece of pizza disappeared as quickly as the first.

"You know, I have another one of these in the freezer," she said, trying not to laugh. "Would you like me to heat it up, too?"

"Yes, please," he said as eagerly as a boy who had just been offered a piece of double-decker chocolate fudge cake.

Sarah gladly popped another pizza into the oven, then seated herself beside Roland again and, having eaten nothing since dinner the previous evening, dove into pizza heaven herself.

Roland, she soon learned, was even a sweetheart when he ate.

"Here, take this one," he said as she finished her first piece. "It's the cheesiest."

He ate the pieces with crust that was a little too brown himself and saved the best pieces for her. Whenever the level of tea in her glass dipped, he refilled it. And he was fun to talk to. Now that they'd discovered they had something in common beyond the fact that both their lives had been in danger a few hours earlier, they chatted like old friends.

"Have you tried the baked waffle fries?" she asked him.

"Not only have I tried them, I am addicted to them."

"What about soy ice cream?"

"There are three flavors in my freezer right now."

"Tofurky?"

"Poor tofurky. It's gotten such a bad rap."

They both laughed.

Sarah even liked that about him. The deep rumble rolled up from his chest and seemed to catch him off-guard as if he didn't laugh very often and was surprised to be doing so now.

It wasn't long before both pizzas were gone, the pitcher of tea was empty, and the two of them were slumped against the back of the futon, shoulders touching, sleepy and sated.

* * *

Roland watched Sarah hide a yawn behind a small, bandaged hand. She looked as exhausted as he felt and, with a full belly, was probably as close to conking out as he was.

This all seemed so surreal . . . almost like a dream induced by eating a heavy meal right before bedtime. He hadn't hurt this much physically since he had been transformed; yet he had actually enjoyed the past hour, laughing and talking with a beautiful woman, sharing a meal and a warm camaraderie with her as if they weren't an immortal and a mortal.

As if he weren't 937 years old to her, perhaps, twenty-eight or thirty.

As if he were still capable of trust. Of friendship. Or more.

In his mortal life, before he had been transformed, he had treasured moments like this. Sharing a trencher with his wife at the high table in the great hall. Offering her the choicest morsels. Winning her smiles and tinkling laughter.

But, if that treacherous bitch had accomplished nothing else, she had taught him that things weren't always what they seemed.

"I think I'll call Marcus now, if that's all right with you."

"Sure."

Sarah dug through the napkins and assorted litter that had collected on the coffee table until she found the tablet with Marcus's number on it.

"Here you are." She handed him the tablet and the phone.

"Thank you."

Her smile broadened, then turned into another yawn. "Sorry. I didn't sleep last night."

Roland frowned. "Why?" Had the vampires who had lured him out there been terrorizing her before he arrived?

She grimaced. "The spring semester just ended and one of my spoiled Fundamentals students went whining to the department chair, claiming he got a D because I didn't like him. I've only been teaching there for two semesters, so I wasn't sure how the chair would react."

"Did you get in trouble?"

"No. The student hadn't turned in half of his assignments and had failed most of the exams. The whole department knew he was full of crap and leapt to my defense. It just really ticked me off."

"I would imagine so."

"That's actually why I was in the meadow this morning. I figured several hours spent turning over the soil for a veggie garden would tire me out enough to rid me of my insomnia and let me sleep tonight."

He winced. "Sorry I spoiled the plan."

She smiled. "No apologies necessary."

Assuming Sarah wanted to listen in as she had before (*he* would, but then the other immortals claimed he was paranoid), Roland pressed the speakerphone button and dialed Marcus's number.

On the fourth ring, an irritable voice hoarse with sleep answered. "*What?*"

"Marcus, it's Roland."

"Roland?" He sounded understandably surprised. It had been a decade or so since the two had last touched base. "Hey, man. How's it going?"

"Actually—"

"Wait. You only call me when you're desperate. What happened?"

Roland looked askance at Sarah.

She smiled and whispered, "I'm beginning to see a pattern."

"Who the hell was that?" Marcus demanded, shocked no doubt that Roland would have anyone, particularly a woman, with him during daylight hours.

"An innocent who came to my rescue."

"*You* needed rescuing?"

"Yes, I'll explain it all later. Right now I need a favor."

"Name it."

"I need you to bring me some *medical* supplies," he said

meaningfully, then asked Sarah for her address and relayed it to Marcus.

"How badly are you injured?"

As Roland opened his mouth to respond, Sarah blurted out, "Badly."

He raised his eyebrows.

She shrugged. "I'm sorry. I know that was rude, but I was afraid you were going to downplay it again."

"How much blood have you lost, Roland?" Marcus pressed.

"A lot," he admitted.

Sarah beamed her approval and patted his arm, making him smile.

"Can you hold out until evening?"

"Yes."

She frowned.

"Okay. I'll bring you everything you need tonight."

"Great."

Leaning forward, Sarah whispered, "Don't forget clothes."

"Right," he said, distracted by her nearness. "I'm also going to need some clothes."

There was a long silence.

"Clothes?" Marcus repeated.

"Yes."

"Should I ask?"

"No."

"Okay then," he said, clearly amused. "Medical supplies and clothing. I'll be there as soon as I can."

Roland pressed the speakerphone button and returned the phone to the coffee table.

Sarah was watching him with a slight smile, her hazel eyes twinkling with merriment.

"I'm not antisocial," he said. He really was, but it suddenly seemed important that she believe otherwise.

Her smile widened. "You just want to be left alone?"

"Not always," he countered with a smile of his own. "Not today."

"You're just saying that because I baked you pizza," she teased.

"In part," he teased back and she laughed. "I don't suppose you have any clothing that might fit me, do you? Marcus will never let me hear the end of it if I'm wearing nothing but a sheet when he arrives."

"No. Yes. Well . . . nnno. I thought maybe the long-sleeved shirt I had on when I found you might fit you, but you're a lot bigger than my ex."

"Ex-husband?"

"Ex-boyfriend. And everything else I have is my size."

Nodding absently, he couldn't resist asking, "Is there a current boyfriend I should worry about coming home and finding me naked on your futon?" *Subtle.*

"No. What about you? Is your wife or girlfriend going to give you grief when she finds out you spent the day with me?"

"No wife or girlfriend," he responded automatically, surprised she would ask.

Was she interested in him?

If so, why? He was a mess and she could very well have gotten killed trying to help him.

"I had a friend in Houston who was with HPD, and he said women always seemed to react badly when he told them he was a policeman. I guess the whole relationship thing must be even harder for you since so much of what you do has to be kept hush-hush."

You have no idea. "It does tend to complicate things."

She stifled another yawn.

"Would you like to go lie down?" he asked. "I'm fine now that you've patched me up."

"You are *not* fine," she protested with a disbelieving laugh. "You're in pain. You're miserable. And there's no way I'm going to leave you alone. Until your friend comes by tonight, I'm afraid you're stuck with me."

He smiled. "Quite a pleasant fate, I admit."

She smiled back and started gathering their napkins onto the pizza tray. “Why don’t I clear some of this mess away? Then we can watch a movie or find something on TV to help pass the time.”

“Sounds good.” Heart light despite the many aches bombarding him, he watched her carry the tray to the kitchen.

Chapter 4

Roland awoke as the sun was setting, his body wracked with pain. It took several minutes of intense concentration before he was able to distance himself from it enough to open his eyes and take in his surroundings.

The television was on, tuned to a news channel, the volume low.

He was lying on his back on the futon, his left leg bent at the knee and resting against the cushioned back. His right leg was stretched out with his foot hanging off the end. What utterly astonished him and nearly made him forget the pain, however, was Sarah, who was sprawled atop him, peacefully ensconced in slumber.

Her cheek was pillowed by his chest. Emitting a pleasant citrus scent, her hair again clung to his stubbled jaw and fell across his shoulder in curly disarray. One of her small hands loosely clutched his shoulder. The other was tucked into his side. Her full breasts warmed his stomach. Her hips rested against his groin, arousing him despite his discomfort.

Damn, but it felt good.

Giving in to temptation, he wrapped his arms around her and buried his face in her silky hair.

She stirred, her hand tightening on his shoulder as she snuggled closer, then fell still.

He hadn't slept with a woman in the literal sense in over nine centuries, refusing to let down his guard enough to experience such intimacy as this. Not even with Mary, who had feigned such devotion. He had obeyed the proprieties when he had courted Mary and, fearing her reaction when she found out what he was, had never left himself so vulnerable.

But Sarah didn't know what he was and he had no intention of telling her. He didn't want to see the same loathing in her eyes that had darkened Beatrice's or the fear that had widened Mary's.

To Sarah, he was just a man.

His body hardened even more when he remembered the way her heartbeat had sped up at his touch.

Her pulse was slow and steady now, the blood in her veins calling him to come and satiate his hunger. As he listened to the steady thrum of it, his own heart began to pound.

Roland slid one hand up her back, tunneling through soft, thick curls, and rested his fingers upon the satiny skin of her neck just over her pulse.

What would she taste like? Sweet like her smiles? Or spicy like her daring spirit?

Would drinking from her merely dull the pain? Or would it set him aflame?

His body was struggling to heal itself. The need for blood lacerated him.

Roland felt his fangs descend and lengthen.

Just one taste. Sarah is sleeping. She need never know.

He could ease her up his chest, lower his lips to the delicate skin of her throat. . . .

Groaning, Roland drew his tongue across her pulse . . . then froze.

Rearing back, he stared down at her in dismay.

When had he moved her?

One second he had been wondering what she would taste like and the next his lips had been on her flesh. Was he that close to losing control?

He forced his fangs to retract.

"Sarah." He shook her gently.

She didn't rouse.

Something like panic struck him. Had he already drunk from her? Was he so far gone that he had drained her and not even been aware of it?

Brushing the hair back from her face and neck, he searched for but found no bite marks. His wounds weren't healing either, so he couldn't have fed yet.

"Sarah," he said louder.

"Hmmm."

"*Sarah,*" he practically shouted.

Her eyes flew open, rising to meet his. "What?"

Roland almost laughed, he was so relieved. She was just a sound sleeper.

She blinked three times, then gave him a sleepy smile. "Oh. Hi."

He smiled back. "Hello."

Wait for it. . . .

Her eyes widened as Morpheus released his hold and she became aware of her position. "Oh! I fell asleep!"

"We both did."

"But I fell asleep on you."

"And normally I wouldn't complain, but you're putting pressure on my cracked ribs."

A blush climbed her cheeks. "I am so sorry!"

Sarah sought a place to put her hands that wouldn't harm Roland as she endeavored to rise. When her shifting and squirming made her aware of the heavy erection that was pressing into her stomach, she stilled. Her eyes flew up to meet his.

"Yyyeah. Sorry about that," he said sheepishly. "I can't help it. You're a beautiful woman and my body is reacting accordingly."

His wasn't the only one. Her mouth went dry at the feel of him. Heat pooled low in her belly.

His smile fell away.

Sarah swallowed hard as she held his gaze, then . . .

Her breath caught.

His eyes were glowing—actually *glowing*—with a strange amber incandescence.

Hurtling herself up and off him, she scooted backward until the cold metal arm of the futon hit her butt.

A veil descended over his features as he sat up. "What is it?"

Her heart trip-hammering with alarm, Sarah virtually leapt off the futon to place more distance between them. "Your eyes."

He glanced down and readjusted the sheet that covered him to the waist. "What about them?"

"They're—"

He looked up.

His eyes were brown again. Deep, dark brown. Guarded. "Yes?"

Had it been a trick of the light?

Don't second-guess yourself. You know what you saw.

"They were glowing," she finished and waited for him to deny it.

"Ah," he said as if she had mentioned it might rain tomorrow. "I apologize. With everything that has happened, I didn't think to warn you about that."

"Warn me about what?" she queried nervously.

What would make someone's eyes do that? It was like something out of a science fiction movie.

"The affliction that causes my photosensitivity also affects my eyes. I'm told that when the light strikes them at a certain angle, they appear to glow or shimmer strangely."

"Oh." Her heartbeat began to slow. "Yes, they do."

"Forgive me, Sarah. I didn't mean to frighten you."

"You didn't," she lied, feeling awful now. *Jeeze.* It wasn't *his* fault. And she had made such a big deal about it, leaping away from him as if he were a friggin' cobra. "It just . . . caught me off-guard, that's all," she finished lamely.

When he swung his feet around and planted them on the floor, she sat beside him and tentatively asked, "Do you mind my asking what your affliction is?"

He shook his head. "Porphyria."

Porphyria, she repeated silently. She couldn't remember if that was what those kids on the news had had or not. "Is it fatal?"

"It would have been this morning had you not found me before the sun did."

The thought of it made her feel sick. "So as long as you avoid the sun and other bright lights . . ."

"The illness won't kill me."

Good. "Does it cause blindness?"

"No, my eyes are a bit sensitive to bright light but, other than that, function normally if you can overlook the occasional luminescence."

Reaching out, she rested a hand on his arm. "I'm sorry. I shouldn't have reacted the way I did. And I'm sorry I fell asleep on you, too."

"Don't worry about the former. It is perfectly understandable. And as for the latter . . ." He leaned toward her and proffered a wicked grin. "The latter was my pleasure."

Sarah laughed. "I wouldn't have thought someone with injuries as severe as yours would be capable of *reacting* to that pleasure."

He grimaced. "I wouldn't have thought it possible either, but there you have it."

It was the closest he had come to a verbal admission of the agony he must be suffering.

His strength was simply extraordinary. If she were in his position, she would be bawling her eyes out and begging for painkillers. As would most people, male or female.

The crunch of gravel outside heralded the arrival of a vehicle as it pulled into her driveway. The engine fell silent.

Rising, Roland wrapped the sheet around his waist and crossed to one of the two windows that looked out onto the front yard.

Sarah grabbed the remote and shut off the television. She heard a car door open and close as Roland brushed the curtains aside and peered through the blinds.

"It's Marcus."

She stood, wondering if she should go to the door or wait for Roland to give the okay.

The tension that had stiffened his spine at the sound of the car did not lessen as he continued to stare through the window.

Did he worry that his friend may have been followed?

Boots made hollow thumps on the wooden porch. A knock sounded.

Roland left the window and went to the front door.

Sarah followed and stood a couple of steps behind him as he unlocked and swung it open.

Night had fallen. The moon was almost new. In the country, that meant it was pitch black outside, the darkness broken only by the tiny sporadic flashes of fireflies.

Though the porch light was off, enough light spilled forth from the house to illuminate their visitor.

He was tall, perhaps an inch shorter than Roland, so that would put him at about six foot one. His hair was dark as midnight and fell halfway down his back. Clad in black jeans, a black T-shirt, a black leather jacket, and biker boots, his body was slender but ripped. His jaw was shadowed by several days' growth of beard and his eyes . . .

Though he looked to be about the same age as she was—thirty—his brown eyes seemed much older.

"Marcus." Roland held out a bandaged hand.

Marcus entered and set down the duffle bag and briefcase he carried. "Roland." Bypassing the hand, he clasped

Roland's forearm and pulled him into a hug. "It's good to see you."

Roland winced and gingerly clapped him on the back, then retreated.

Marcus met Sarah's curious gaze and raised his eyebrows.

Moving to stand beside Roland, she held out a hand. "Sarah Bingham."

His large, callused fingers clasped hers. "Marcus Grayden. A pleasure to meet you." His words were endowed with the same British accent that flavored Roland's.

"Nice to meet you, too."

Stepping back, he propped his hands on his hips and looked Roland up and down. "I have to admit . . . if you didn't look like hell, I'd be laughing. What happened to your clothes?"

Grunting, Roland urged Marcus back toward the door. "I'll fill you in in a minute. First I need you to have a look outside. Around the house and in the meadow behind it."

"All right." Walking out onto the porch, he paused and tilted his head as though listening for something. Then he seemed to sniff the air, almost like a lion seeking the scent of prey. "Do I know what I'm looking for?"

"Yes, more than one."

His face brightened. "More than one?"

"And possibly a couple of wannabes."

"Interesting." Descending the steps, he vanished into the darkness.

Roland closed the door.

"Don't you think he would have better luck if he used a flashlight?" Sarah asked, puzzled. There were no streetlights or any other form of ambient light, so the man may as well have been walking around blindfolded.

"He'll ask if he needs one."

If he *needs* one? How could he not?

"Is Marcus your brother?"

"No, why do you ask?"

She shrugged. "You both share the same hair and eye coloring. You're almost the same height. You're both handsome, have the same build—"

"You think he's handsome?" he interrupted.

"Sure. Not as handsome as you are. I mean, even covered with blood and truly scary wounds, you—" She broke off. What was she doing?

Clearing her throat, she mumbled, "I just thought you might be related."

Boots again sounded on the porch.

Marcus must have conceded defeat and decided he needed a flashlight.

"It's Marcus," she heard him call.

Roland opened the door. "Anything?"

"All clear," Marcus responded as he strode inside.

At first, Sarah thought he was joking. There was no way he could have checked her backyard and the meadow beyond already. Even with good lighting and running at top speed he would have only had time to reach the site of her future veggie garden.

His next words, however, belied that and stunned her speechless.

Scowling at Roland, he asked, "Is all the blood on the ground near that spike yours?"

"Yes," was Roland's clipped response.

Swearing, Marcus bent and grabbed the handles of his duffle bag, his eyes snagging Sarah's. "Where's your bathroom?"

She pointed to it. "You saw the meadow where they staked him to the ground?"

"They staked you to the ground?" he roared, turning on Roland.

"Yes. I don't suppose you found a couple of corpses lying about, did you?"

"No."

Sarah looked at Roland. "So the guys I hit with the shovel didn't die?"

"Apparently not." He didn't seem pleased.

She swallowed. "You think they're going to come back."

He nodded. "And since you're the only person nearby, they'll draw the obvious conclusion that you were the one who helped me."

That's what she had feared. "What should I do?"

He hesitated, as though waging some internal debate. "Pack a bag. You can stay with me until this is all sorted out."

Marcus's mouth fell open. "*What?*"

Roland frowned belligerently. "She'll be safe with me."

"You *never* let anyone stay with you. *I* don't stay with you. I don't even know where you live and I've known you freakin' forever!"

"Well, I'm sure as hell not going to let her stay with you. You're dangerous to be around."

"According to whom?"

"Seth."

"Well, Seth doesn't know everything."

Roland raised one eyebrow.

"All right. All right. Sometimes Seth does seem to know everything. It's incredibly annoying. But I would never purposefully endanger an innocent."

"The key word being 'purposefully.'"

Sarah raised a hand. "Is anyone here interested in where *I* might wish to stay?"

Both men turned to her with guilty expressions.

"I'm sorry, Sarah," Roland said wearily. "I didn't mean to make you feel you have no say in the matter. I'm only concerned with your safety."

"I appreciate that."

Marcus stared at Roland as if his friend had just sprouted a pair of horns. "You're *apologizing?* Seriously, what happened to you? Have you been taken over by a pod person?"

Roland's face darkened with promised retribution.

Sarah touched his arm to calm him and glared at Marcus. "Marcus, don't poke the bear. In case you haven't noticed, Roland is in a lot of pain and doesn't need the added aggravation of you taunting him. Are you here to help him or what?"

Remorse rippled across his features. "I'm sorry. Hurry up and decide this so I can patch him up."

Roland's hand brushed the small of her back. "Would you rather stay with family until—"

"No," she answered immediately, unable to repress a shudder. As far as she was concerned, she had no family. "No, I want to stay with you."

He nodded. "Pack whatever you'll need for the next few days. Hopefully, we'll be able to resolve this swiftly."

Roland watched Sarah until she entered the bedroom and left their sight, then allowed his shoulders to slump and some of the pain he was feeling to show in his face.

Marcus's lighthearted facade evaporated. "Hope I didn't irritate you too much. I was trying to keep her attention focused on me so she wouldn't notice your eyes." Slipping an arm around Roland, he practically carried him to the bathroom.

Roland sat on the side of the bathtub as Marcus closed the door. "Are they glowing again?"

"Yes."

"She's already seen them. Please tell me you brought sustenance."

Marcus unzipped the duffle bag and withdrew a small cooler. Inside were half a dozen bags of much-needed blood.

With great relief, Roland allowed his fangs to descend and plunged them into the first bag, draining it swiftly. His body was so depleted it took a second, then a third before his wounds began to heal. His hunger ebbed, as did some of the pain.

Marcus waited patiently, exchanging each empty bag for

a full one until Roland was glutted. Putting the cooler away, he handed Roland the clothes he had brought. "Now tell me what happened."

Roland did so in tones too low for Sarah to overhear, pulling on a pair of black cargo pants and a long-sleeved black T-shirt that would hide the fact that some of the cuts Sarah had tended would soon be gone.

"I've never heard of such a large group hunting together," Marcus commented as Roland sat on the tub again to pull on socks and boots.

"Nor have I and I was definitely their prey. This was no random incident."

"Why would they take your blood?"

"I don't know. There have been vamps over the centuries who thought they could avoid the madness that afflicts their brethren by subsisting entirely on the blood of one of us."

"But if that had been their goal, they would have taken *you,* not a sample."

Roland shook his head. "I don't know their goal. I just know Sarah saved my life and is now caught in the middle, so we need to dispatch these assholes as quickly as possible."

"She thinks your eyes and photosensitivity are the result of porphyria?"

"Yes."

The wood floor outside the bathroom door creaked. "It's awfully quiet in there," Sarah called worriedly. "Is everything okay?"

"Yes," Marcus replied loudly.

"Roland?"

He smiled. "I'm all right, Sarah. We'll be out in a minute. Marcus is just giving me a few stitches."

"Okay. Feel free to yell if it hurts too much."

"Marcus would mock me if I did."

"Not if I hit him with my trusty shovel."

Both men laughed.

"Beautiful, brave, and possessed of violent tendencies. I like her," Marcus declared.

Beyond the door, Sarah laughed.

"Speaking of beautiful, brave, and violent women," Roland broached hesitantly, "I was surprised to learn you were in North Carolina. I didn't think anything could drag you away from Texas."

All levity fled as Marcus's face turned to stone. "There's nothing there for me now."

"What happened?" Roland asked, fearing he knew the answer.

Marcus's dark eyes filled with grief. "It's over. Bethany is gone."

A deep sorrow invaded Roland. He had only met Bethany Bennett once, curious to see the woman who had held Marcus's heart for eight hundred years.

She had been all that his friend had described. Small. Smart. Strong, both physically and emotionally. Brave. Beautiful. Possessed of a great wit and a tendency to tease. (All words and phrases he might use to describe Sarah, now that he thought of it.) Roland had liked her. And didn't know what Marcus was going to do now that she was gone.

"When?" he asked softly.

Marcus's throat worked. "Seven years ago."

Roland closed his eyes. "I'm such a bastard. I didn't know." And he should have. Marcus had told him the year he would have to say goodbye to her, but the time had slipped past unnoticed.

"I knew all along how it would end. How it *had* to end. There was nothing you could have done."

"I could have been there for you." The way Marcus had been there for him when Mary had betrayed him.

Marcus snorted. "And done what? Watched me fall apart?"

Roland studied him closely. "*Did* you fall apart?"

Avoiding his gaze, Marcus closed the cooler and returned it to the duffle bag.

"Marcus?"

"What?" he snapped, jerking the zipper shut. "Do you want me to admit I took it badly? Fine. I took it badly. So badly that Seth now thinks I'm fucking suicidal."

Alarms sounded. "Are you?"

"No, Roland. I'm just . . ." Sighing, Marcus raked a hand through his hair. "Tired. And numb. You of all people know how wearying this existence can be when there's nothing to look forward to and no one to share it with."

"I do." And he had hoped Marcus, a hundred years younger and the first immortal he had personally trained, would never come to experience such weariness himself.

Roland was out of his element here. For the second time today, he found himself faced with someone who needed comfort and he was still uncertain how to render it. "You don't want a hug, do you?" he asked uneasily.

Marcus's look seemed to question his sanity. "Hell, no."

Roland nearly wilted with relief. "Good."

Shaking his head, Marcus produced a half smile. "I should have said yes and dredged up a few tears just to watch you squirm."

"I'm surprised you didn't," Roland returned sardonically.

Upon leaving the bathroom, they found Sarah back in the den, setting a large tote bag down on the futon.

She glanced over her shoulder, then turned to face them. "Wow. You look . . ." Her gaze made a slow excursion down Roland's body and back up again, speeding his pulse. "You look great."

The admiration in those hazel depths made his body harden.

"Are you feeling better?" she continued. "Was Marcus able to help?"

"Yes to both questions."

Brow furrowed with concern, she closed the distance between them. "You *are* going to see a doctor now, right?"

"No, I need to get you to safety first."

"Surely the CIA has emergency medical facilities available for their operatives. Wouldn't I be safe there?"

Marcus passed them on his way to the front door. "You told her you're CIA?"

"Yes."

Sarah turned to Marcus. "It wasn't his fault. I know it's supposed to be kept secret, but if he hadn't told me I would have called 911 and blown his cover."

As soon as she looked away, Marcus rolled his eyes and mouthed, *Lame.*

Ignoring him, Roland asked Sarah if her bag was packed.

"Almost. I need a few things from the bathroom, then I'm good to go."

Roland moved aside so she could slip past him, then crossed over to Marcus.

"You aren't supposed to *tell* them you're CIA," he said, his voice muted, as he set the duffle bag down and picked up the briefcase. "You're supposed to let them infer it."

Roland sent him a warning scowl. "I haven't had to explain myself to a mortal in centuries. Cut me some slack."

Balancing the briefcase on the back of the futon, Marcus flipped the latches up and opened it.

Roland smiled when he saw its contents. "You thought of everything, I see."

"I figured if you had lost your clothes, you'd probably lost your weapons, too."

"You were right. I did." He was distributing sais, daggers, and throwing stars to various pockets, boots, and belt loops when Sarah returned and dumped a toothbrush, hairbrush, comb, hair ties, and several small bottles and jars into her tote.

Eyeing his weapons, she crossed her arms beneath full breasts. "Okay, would someone please explain to me why a man posing as an illegal arms dealer doesn't carry a gun?"

"Amateur," Marcus mumbled beneath his breath before continuing more clearly. "The knives are part of the persona we created to reinforce the belief of the criminals he deals with that he is a member of a particularly violent eastern European crime family. He also usually carries a couple of .45 semiautomatics but lost them in the fight."

"Why didn't you bring him replacements?"

"A miscommunication."

Since they rarely fought more than one vampire at a time and wanted to avoid drawing attention to their battles, immortals tended to avoid using guns. Vampires did as well, knowing even in their madness that more than one careless vamp had experienced an excruciating death in a sunlit cell after being taken into custody by law enforcement officials.

Pursing her lips in a way Roland found adorable, Sarah left them, disappeared into the bedroom, and returned carrying a Glock 9mm and a spare clip.

"Here," she said, holding them out to him. "You can use mine."

Roland raised his eyebrows.

She shrugged. "I used to live in Houston. Crime is pretty bad there and, when a woman in my apartment complex was raped by a burglar, I decided that any man who broke into my place was going to have to be carried out."

Damn. He really liked her.

Sarah watched him palm the weapon and give it a quick inspection. She kept it in good condition. Clean. Well-oiled. No rust or dust in any of the grooves or crevices. He seemed satisfied.

"There's a bullet in the chamber and fifteen in the clip," she told him.

"You any good with it?" Marcus asked.

"Very good," Sarah answered matter-of-factly. "There's no point in owning a gun if you aren't prepared to use it."

Roland handed it back to her.

"Don't you need it?" she asked, taking it.

"I want you to hold on to it. If my assailants catch up with us before we reach my home, aim for the major arteries." Using his index and middle fingers, he pointed out the key arteries on his own body in his neck, arms, abdomen, and inner thighs. "Here, here, here, and here. Got it?"

"Yes." Every man she had ever chatted with at the shooting range, including cops, had told her to aim for the chest. Then, after seeing what a good shot she was, amended that to the head and chest. Yet, Roland was telling her to aim for major arteries?

That was odd.

"Don't hesitate," he stressed earnestly. "If you even *think* one of them is moving toward you, start shooting."

"Will do," she promised.

Marcus cleared his throat. "And don't shoot *us*."

She frowned up at him. "I just told you I'm good. I never miss my target."

"And I'm asking you not to target us," he countered, eyebrows raised. "Please?"

She looked at Roland and caught him exchanging a somber glance with Marcus.

Feeling as if she were missing something, she addressed Marcus. "Fine. If it will make you feel better, I promise I won't shoot you."

He nodded. "Good. I'm going to hold you to that."

If she didn't know better, she would have thought he truly believed she might turn her gun on them later.

Roland grabbed her tote bag. "Let's get going."

Marcus collected the duffle bag and briefcase and headed outside.

Sarah stuffed the spare clip into her back pocket and gripped the 9mm tightly with her right hand, nervous all of a sudden.

His expression softening, Roland touched her left arm. "Don't worry. I won't let anyone harm you."

She forced a smile.

Sliding his hand down until their palms met, he linked his long fingers through hers and gave her hand a light squeeze.

Butterflies erupted in her stomach as she followed him onto the porch.

How could something as innocent as holding hands sometimes feel so intimate, she wondered as he locked and closed the door behind them.

Darkness enfolded them, so complete Sarah couldn't see an inch in front of her face.

When Roland started down the front steps, she remained where she was.

"What's wrong?" he asked, tugged to a halt.

"I can't see."

The porch light flickered, then came on.

Blinking at the sudden brightness, she looked up at the glowing bulb, back at the closed door, then at Roland, who waited on the steps.

He shrugged. "Must be faulty wiring. I turned it on as we were leaving. Come on. We need to hurry."

Descending the steps, Sarah followed him across the uneven front lawn, then glanced back at the light.

The house *was* old. The wiring, too. Perhaps she shouldn't have exchanged the dim yellow bulb that had originally been in the archaic fixture with a hundred-watt one. There had just been too many nights when she had tripped on the uneven ground between the gravel driveway and the front steps because the lower wattage bulb only lit the porch.

The brilliant white light of *this* bulb spilled down the stairs onto the grass and extended all the way to Marcus's shiny black Prius, which was parked close behind her sixteen-year-old grungy white piece of crap Geo Prism.

Marcus handed Roland the briefcase, unlocked the passenger door, and started around the front of the car.

Roland released Sarah's hand and reached for the passenger door handle, then paused.

Marcus stopped short.

Both men tilted their heads to one side, like an animal that hears a noise pitched too high for human cars. As one, they dropped the bags they carried and spun around to face the trees on the opposite side of the house.

Ice skittered down Sarah's spine as they raised their faces to the sky, drew in deep breaths, and held them.

Man, these guys could be creepy.

Roland's chin dipped. "They're here."

Chapter 5

Such menace glittered in Roland's dark gaze that Sarah found herself taking an involuntary step backward.

As if the movement drew his notice, he took her arm and urged her to stand behind him. Marcus moved to Roland's side, the two forming a solid barrier that protected her front while the car protected her back.

"I count eight," Marcus murmured, his stance alert.

"As do I."

Eight men? How could they count eight men, she thought wildly, when she couldn't hear anything but frogs and that weird bug she had never encountered before moving to North Carolina that sounded sort of like a cicada, but not really?

Ch-ch-ch . . . ch-ch-ch . . . ch-ch-ch.

"I thought you said you took out four of them," Marcus said as Sarah strained to hear whatever it was they heard.

"I did." "Took out" as in killed? "And severely wounded two others."

"Then who the hell are we facing?"

Roland shook his head. "I don't know who he is or what he wants, but he appears to have raised quite an army."

"The one who staked you to the ground?"

"Yes."

"Unbelievable."

Sarah concurred. This was *all* unbelievable. Shouldn't these guys be nervous or tense or sweating or something? Maybe jumping in the car so they could get the hell out of there? Especially when one considered how the previous night's confrontation had ended.

Instead, they seemed relaxed, their bodies loose, their deep voices casually ominous.

Unlike them, she was a bit of a wreck. Her palms were sweating. Every muscle was tense. And her fingers were clutching the Glock in a death grip.

The foliage on the opposite side of the large front yard parted in several places. Dark figures emerged from the shadows, growing more distinct as they stepped into the dim outer reaches of the porch light. Men. Six, no seven. All young, in their late teens and early twenties.

Marcus and Roland stood with their arms at their sides, feet shoulder's width apart.

Peering between her two massive protectors, Sarah anxiously took stock of those they were up against.

There were three, around twenty years old, who were decked out in goth gear. Black T-shirts with skull faces emblazoned on them in dramatic patterns. Ragged black jeans. Big black boots. Lots of chains and spikes and studs and body piercings. They were all around five-ten and sported the same hairstyle: two-inch shocks that stood up like porcupine quills. The only difference was the coloring. One had cherry-red hair. One had royal blue hair. And one was bleach blond.

The next in line looked to be a boy no older than sixteen or seventeen. Standing five foot eight, he had brassy orange hair, was liberally covered with freckles, and had a feral look about him that screamed *serial killer in the making.*

On the other side of him stood a pair of identical twins who nearly matched Roland and Marcus in height. Unlike their comrades, who were all thin and lanky, these two had broad shoulders and thick muscles clearly defined by tight gray T-shirts and faded jeans. With long, straight, flaxen hair, they would've looked perfectly at home dressed as medieval Vikings.

The guy on the other side of them had shoulder-length greasy brown hair and looked like he had just stepped off the pages of an ad for an '80s grunge band, plaid shirt and all. He, too, stood around five foot ten or eleven.

As Sarah completed her visual inventory, an eighth figure materialized from the darkness and moved to stand in front of the others, who fanned out in a loose horseshoe around him.

She swallowed.

This man was almost as scary as Roland when Roland was at his most intimidating.

He was tall, an inch or two above six feet, with shoulder-length black hair. His taut, muscled body was clad in black jeans and a black T-shirt, his broad shoulders encased in a long black coat. His face was clean-shaven, his jaw strong.

He would be quite handsome if he didn't give her a major case of the creepin' willies.

"So," he spoke, his attention focused on Roland, "it's true then. You can't imagine my disappointment when I arose, expecting to be handed your remains in a coffee can and was instead informed that you had been rescued."

Sarah recognized his voice as that of the Brit who had told the kid stabbing Roland to let the sun finish him off.

Beside Roland, Marcus snorted. "This is the prick you mentioned earlier?"

"He's the one."

The feral ginger turned to the leader. "You still want him dead?"

"Yes."

"And the other one?"

"Take him alive."

"Look," Marcus said, amiably apologetic, "I know I'm prettier than he is. And I'm flattered. Really. But I feel like I should tell you . . . I'm really not into guys."

Clearly they were all homophobes.

An explosion of violence erupted in the front yard.

As Sarah looked on, immobilized by shock, the grunge kid, Vikings, and ginger attacked Marcus while the leader and the three goths went for Roland. Fear, more intense than any she had ever experienced, cemented her feet to the ground and made her heart slam against her ribs.

It wasn't right.

It wasn't normal.

Roland whipped out a couple of sais—long steel daggers with sharpened prongs that extended on either side of the main blade—while Marcus drew short swords. Together they expertly engaged their opponents, who were armed with everything from big bowie knives to machetes to short swords of their own. Fending off three and four at a time, Roland and Marcus forced them back and kept them distanced from Sarah. It was like watching Neo and his friends in *The Matrix* fight, only these men all wielded deadly blades and moved so swiftly they became a blur.

This isn't possible, her panicked brain whispered.

No one moved that fast. World record–breaking Olympic athletes didn't move that fast!

And, of them all, Roland and Marcus were the fastest.

Blood sprayed in an arc, light from the porch sparkling off the crimson droplets as the blue-haired goth stumbled back, his throat sliced open. He didn't even have time to raise a hand to it before Roland buried one of his sais in the kid's chest, spun, and parried a blow the leader aimed at his back with a short sword.

Roland's eyes were glowing again. And his weren't the only one's. Marcus's. The leader's. The Vikings'. *Everyone's* eyes glowed green or blue or amber.

Everyone's but hers.

And their teeth . . .

The blue-haired goth sank to his knees, emitting horrible gagging and gasping noises, mouth open to expose what could only be described as *fangs.*

Her heart skipping a beat, Sarah looked at the leader, whose lips were drawn back in a snarl of rage, revealing more fangs.

Oh shit.

The Vikings—fangs.

The ginger kid—fangs.

These guys weren't . . .

They weren't . . . *vampires* . . . were they?

Vampires don't exist.

Then why did the ginger kid just sink his fangs into Marcus's arm?

Marcus rewarded him by cutting his femoral artery, damned near severing the kid's leg in the process.

Were Roland and Marcus vampire hunters?

"The woman is his weakness!" the leader growled suddenly.

Instantly, the goth with the bleach-blond hair dropped back, slunk to one side, and edged his way around Roland. His glowing cerulean eyes fastened on Sarah. There were several cuts and slits in his clothing, which glistened damply. The material parted as he moved toward her, revealing pale, blood-coated flesh torn open where Roland had scored hits with his arsenal of blades.

His mouth twisting in an evil smile, the boy stalked her slowly, fangs gleaming. Sarah took a step backward, then belatedly remembered the weapon in her hand.

Raising the Glock, she flicked the safety off and fired once. The bullet entered dead center between the goth's eyes and exited the back of his head, accompanied by a disgusting amount of flesh.

His head snapped back. "Ahh!" Then he glared at her. "Bitch, that hurt!"

Crap. Aim for the arteries.

As he started toward her, Sarah fired three more times in quick succession. Blood spurted from his neck, abdomen, and thigh.

His face contorting in fury, he lunged toward her.

Wind stirred her hair as a blur of motion swept past her and hit the goth. Metal glinted in the dim light. The goth fell to the ground. Above him, Roland paused, panting, bleeding from several wounds on his torso and arms.

His eerie eyes met hers. "Are you all right?"

She nodded, too frightened to speak.

The leader's short sword swung while Roland was distracted and sliced into his neck. Blood splattered Sarah's face and front.

"No!" she screamed as Roland reeled backward, scarlet liquid pouring down his chest.

Turning the Glock on the leader, she fired repeatedly, eyes filling with tears. His body jerked with each impact.

Sarah paused, blinking to clear her vision.

She had hit him once in the head and five times in the chest and he was still standing. A throwing star embedded itself in his collarbone, drawing the leader's attention to Marcus.

Sarah turned to Roland.

Holding one hand to his neck, he staggered and nearly fell. His shirt and pants were already saturated. His face was utterly colorless.

"Roland."

It was her fault. He had been protecting her. If she hadn't distracted him, he would've seen the blow coming and avoided it.

She started toward him.

The last goth kid hissed and sprang at her.

Roland moved in a blur, intercepting her attacker. There was a loud crack. The cherry-haired goth screamed as a jagged bone protruded from his forearm.

Roland twisted the other arm up behind the kid's back. His face contorted in agony, the goth held himself motionless.

Roland raised his head and met her gaze.

Every ounce of blood in her body sank to Sarah's feet.

His eyes glowed even brighter than they had before. His face was lined with pain.

And now Roland sported a set of fangs as sharp and deadly as the others'.

Terror engulfed her. Her limbs began to shake.

"Look away, Sarah," he growled, his handsome features harsh.

She shook her head, nearly tripping over the briefcase and tote as she stumbled back until Marcus's car stopped her.

"Look away!"

She couldn't.

Roland swore fiercely, then bent and sank his teeth into the goth's neck.

He was one of them. Roland was one of them! He was a vampire!

Sarah looked around wildly.

The Vikings were down. So was the grunge guy and the ginger kid, whose body, she saw with horror, was beginning to shrivel up like a mummy's.

Marcus was fighting the leader. Her front lawn was awash with blood. A dozen more men with glowing eyes were exiting the trees across the yard.

She glanced back.

Roland was drinking the goth kid's blood, his luminous gaze watching her every move.

Sliding along the car, away from Roland and his prey, Sarah fought down hysteria. Her breath came in short, panicked gasps, while a voice in her head shouted, *Go! Run! Get the hell out of there!*

When she reached the front bumper, her foot kicked something that made a tinkling noise. Barely visible in the shadow she cast lay Marcus's keys.

Sarah bent, grabbed them, and bolted for the driver's door. Scrambling inside, she slammed the door shut, locked it, locked the passenger door, set the gun on the seat beside her, and shoved the key into the ignition.

She couldn't reach the pedals.

Groping around the base of the seat, she found the adjustment lever, pulled it, and scooted the seat up as far as it would go.

Through the passenger window, she saw Roland drop the goth's limp body to the ground.

Sarah turned the key. The engine roared to life.

His eyes met hers for one drawn-out moment, full of rage and something else, before he turned and met the onslaught of the new vampires.

Putting the car in reverse, she stomped on the accelerator and turned to look behind her just as the back bumper slammed into a vampire who had circled around and been heading for Roland's back.

She hadn't even seen him coming.

His body rolled up, hit the back windshield, and slid off to the side as she turned the wheel, backed into the two-lane blacktop road in front of the house, and hit the brakes.

Putting the car into drive, she flipped on the headlights and floored it.

Tires squealed. The smell of burning rubber filled the air as the car rapidly accelerated.

Trees whipped by, dark, unfocused giants. Fireflies blinked and sparkled as she passed. The only sounds that met her ears were the humming of the engine, those weird North Carolina bugs, and her rasping, gasping breaths.

In the rearview mirror, her tiny house, its porch light, and the macabre battle taking place in front of it shrank, then disappeared from view as the road curved, rose, and dipped.

Sarah's whole body was trembling. Her thoughts were scattered. Her actions driven solely by the need to get away. Fast. Too fast to navigate the bends and curves of the road safely, but she couldn't bring herself to slow down. She turned on the high beams, hoping it would compensate for the lack of streetlights and let her see any deer that may have ambled onto the road in time to avoid hitting them.

Vampires, she thought hysterically.

Vampires were real.

And Roland was one of them.

The hood of the car abruptly buckled when a man seemingly dropped out of the sky and landed on it in a crouch.

Sarah screamed as the front of the car nose-dived into the pavement. The air bag exploded into her face, slamming her head back into the headrest. The rear end of the car kept moving forward, tires squealing as the car spun around and came to a jarring halt facing the trees on the side of the road.

Not wearing a seat belt, Sarah was hurled like a rag doll into the driver's side door. Glass shattered, showered her, cut her as pain shot through her head and the left side of her face and body.

The engine sputtered, then faltered into silence.

Dazed, she grabbed the armrest to lever herself upright. Shards of glass sliced into her forearm and through the gauze bandages on her palm. Wincing, she yanked her hand back and sluggishly straightened in her seat.

The air bag wilted as it deflated, allowing her to peer blearily through the front windshield.

The dark figure crouched on the hood slowly rose to his full height.

It was the lead vampire in the long black coat.

Sarah whimpered when he met her gaze and smiled menacingly, fangs glinting in the ambient light of the high beams.

Terrified, she searched for the Glock but couldn't find it. It wasn't *on* the seat, *under* the seat, or on the floorboard.

The vampire stepped off the car and landed gracefully on the pavement.

Seeing nothing else she could use as a weapon, Sarah gritted her teeth, picked up a triangular piece of glass, and curled her fingers around the wide end.

Aim for the major arteries.

Blood welled and saturated white gauze as the sharp edges cut through the bandages and sliced her skin like a knife. The odor of burned rubber spoiled the late spring breeze that ruffled her hair.

Strolling to the driver's side door, the vampire stopped within striking distance.

Sarah tensed, biding her time.

Something large slammed into the vampire, knocking him back at least fifteen yards.

The glass shard cut deep as Sarah jerked in surprise.

Leaning forward, she saw . . . Roland, picking himself up and turning to swing his sais at the other vampire.

Was he protecting her? Or was he saving her for himself so he could—what—bite her? Suck her blood? Kill her?

Screw that!

Turning the key, she mentally urged the engine to start. *Come on.*

It coughed a few times but did no more.

Come on!

She tried again and again. But it wouldn't start.

Damn it! Her hands slick with blood, she fumbled with the door's lock, unable to grip it. Close to screaming with frustration, she wiped her fingers on her shirt, then finally succeeded.

Throwing the door open, Sarah lurched out and raced for the trees illuminated by the headlights. They were denser than those around her house, the underbrush thicker. Weeds that reminded her of ferns brushed her thighs as she surged forward.

The light faded, penetrating the shadows only so far, and Sarah soon found herself stumbling blindly through complete darkness.

Unable to see where she was going, fearing she would run headlong into a tree and knock herself unconscious, she slowed to a brisk walk, hands outstretched before her.

Branches slapped her in the face, neck, chest, and hands, embedding the glass particles more deeply and tugging at her bandages. Her many cuts stung. Her head throbbed. Moisture welled in her eyes.

If she could just get away . . .

Far, far away.

She could no longer hear the grunts and thumps and sounds of the fight. Only the thrashing of the foliage as she plowed ahead, the *ch-ch-ch* sound of those freaky bugs, the croaking of frogs, and her own frantic heartbeat pounding in her ears.

Sarah didn't know how far she had gone or how long she had been fleeing when her foot unexpectedly met empty air.

Flailing her arms for balance, she lost the battle and tumbled forward as the ground dropped off in front of her. Her hands and knees hit the dirt hard but didn't stop the momentum that sent her rolling and jouncing down a hill.

The trunks of saplings felt like baseball bats striking her as she went, the thin branches of bushes and weeds like whips. Pain burst through the back of her head just before she skidded to an agonized halt.

Moaning, Sarah rolled onto her back. Flashing lights that had nothing to do with fireflies winked at the edges of her vision. Dizziness assailed her, making her feel as if she were lying on the deck of a ship being tossed about by a violent storm. If she could see her surroundings, no doubt they would be spinning nauseatingly.

Shifting to her side, she braced her aching hands on the cool grass and cautiously sat up.

The throbbing in her head intensified, as did that in her newly bruised ribs. But she couldn't just sit there. She had to keep moving.

Unable to suppress a groan, Sarah managed to gain her feet with the help of the tree that had ultimately ended her descent.

With the hill behind her, she headed forward, arms extended.

There didn't seem to be any more trees or shrubs. Just tall weeds or grasses that stroked her knees.

North Carolina was full of rolling meadows and hay fields. She must have wandered into either one or the other.

A branch snapped behind her, somewhere up the hill.

Panic returning with a vengeance, she took off running. Though she had left the shadows of the trees, her surroundings were no brighter, so she couldn't see a thing.

Blindly racing forward at top speed was nearly as terrifying as knowing that a vampire was pursuing her. Sarah had not experienced this kind of darkness until she had moved to North Carolina. (The sky of a sprawling metropolis like Houston was never completely dark unless a hurricane like Ike took out the power.)

Tripping over some unseen object, she went down hard on her hands, elbows, and knees. Got up. Raced forward, breath coming in gasps that spawned sharp, stabbing pains in the right side of her chest. Fell hard. Got up. Raced forward, tears now streaming down her face. Tripped. Stumbled. Kept going. Tripped. Fell hard.

She almost couldn't get up this time. Pain and fatigue clawed at her. If only she could see where she was going. . . .

Holding her right side, where one of the saplings had struck her ribs, she took off at a jog, too damned tired to go any faster, and slammed face-first into a tree.

Rebounding off it, she staggered back a step. Strong hands abruptly gripped her upper arms as amber eyes blazed down at her.

It wasn't a tree.

Screaming, she fought with all of the measly strength she had left.

"Sarah!" a familiar voice called as the hands gently shook her.

She sagged weakly. "Roland?"

"Yes."

The dizziness returned.

"P-please don't kill me," she murmured, then sank into oblivion.

Roland caught Sarah as she fainted. Slipping one arm around her back and the other beneath her knees, he lifted her up and settled her against his chest. Her head lolled and came to rest on his shoulder.

Fiery pain shot through the arm his new nemesis had broken. Because Roland had lost so much blood again, the limb had only healed superficially.

It didn't matter. Pain he was familiar with. Fear he wasn't.

And it had definitely been fear that had gripped him when he had seen the lead vampire take off and chase Sarah after she had driven away.

Bastien, he had heard one of the flunky reinforcements call him.

Giving in to impulse, Roland buried his face in Sarah's tangled, leaf-strewn hair. The pleasant citrus scent was now suppressed by that of the forest mulch she had collected in her flight.

His preternaturally enhanced senses reassured him that her heartbeat, though rapid from sprinting and panic, was strong.

The intense relief he felt was disquieting.

Roland raised his head. She looked like hell. Unlike Sarah, he could see clearly in full darkness and his first glimpse of her had been a shock.

The left half of her face was smeared with blood that oozed from a gash near her hairline. Her clothing was torn in half a dozen places and coated with so much dirt, leaves, and grass that even if he hadn't seen the path she had cleared on her way down the hill, he would have known she had taken a bad fall.

The bandages he had carefully wrapped around her hands were gone. Her fingers and palms bled from numerous cuts, some of which still had pieces of glass lodged in them. So did her left forearm. Her right forearm and elbow were scraped. Both arms, her chin, and her collarbone sported pink patches that would no doubt morph into ugly bruises over the next few days.

She must have been in agony. Yet she hadn't given up.

When he had reached the bottom of the hill, Roland had been astounded to see her running blindly across the meadow.

Running. Not walking.

He frowned down at her.

Had she been running from *him* or from Bastien?

Just as he had hoped, she had wasted no time in leaving after he had tackled the bastard, breaking several of the vamp's ribs, so she couldn't have known who the victor would be.

Not that he would call himself the victor. He hadn't defeated Bastien. Bastien had decided a strategic retreat was in order when it had become clear he wouldn't win.

Worried about Sarah, Roland had elected not to pursue him.

If Sarah had known Roland was the one trailing her, would she have stopped or continued to run? He had seen the horror suffuse her face when she had realized what he was. It was the same he had seen consume Mary when he had mistakenly taken her into his confidence.

He barely knew Sarah, so it shouldn't have hurt.

But it had.

"Arghhhhhhhhh!"

Roland stiffened when that male roar rent the air.

A warning? A charge sounded?

"What the hell happened to my car?"

Marcus.

Relaxing, Roland shook his head and started back to face his friend's wrath, jostling his precious burden as little as possible.

He snorted, a sound rife with self-mockery.

Precious burden? Sarah didn't mean anything to him. Never *would* mean anything to him. Never *could.*

It didn't matter that she was one of the most intriguing women he had met in centuries. Nor that she had been all that is kind to him, laughed with him, teased him, slept curled up against him on her futon. So soft and sweet.

Now that she knew what he was, she would despise him.

And, knowing that, only a fool would allow himself to care for her.

Sighing deeply, the self-proclaimed fool trudged up the hill and forged through the trees.

Marcus paced back and forth beside his car in long, angry strides that would've been more impressive if they weren't hampered by a pronounced limp. When the lead vampire had taken off after Sarah, Roland had quickly finished off his foes and followed, leaving Marcus behind to battle the half dozen who were left of the new arrivals. Not that he had minded. He could handle it and had, though not before a Marilyn Manson look-alike (why did so many new vamps find it necessary to submerge themselves in goth facades?) had shattered his right kneecap.

That particular vamp had then unwillingly supplied the blood that had healed his leg enough for Marcus to continue and eliminate all comers.

After which he had raced here and found this.

Freakin' vamp would pay!

Swearing fluently, he stepped into the open driver's door and, despite his wounds, effortlessly pushed the vehicle off the road. He wasn't sure what was wrong with it beyond the obvious damage done to the body (it looked like someone had dropped a wrecking ball on it), but it wouldn't start.

Slamming the door shut, he resumed his pacing.

He was full of rage and pain and adrenaline and hadn't felt this alive in years.

Seven years to be exact.

And Marcus liked it.

A lot.

Which was why Seth was worried about him.

Seth must have intuited it. Marcus didn't know how, because Seth had not hunted with him or witnessed the change firsthand. Yet Seth had accused him of taking unnecessary risks and being self-destructive before banishing him to small-town North Carolina, where vampires were generally fewer in number.

Marcus smiled grimly.

Ah, but Seth's plan had backfired.

Tonight had been great. Tonight he had been presented with a challenge that could very well have defeated him. Tonight he felt alive.

The foliage on the other side of the car parted and Roland emerged, carrying a bloody and battered Sarah.

Marcus halted, thinking her dead until he picked up her racing pulse. "Is she okay?"

"She will be." Roland glanced at the white Geo Prism parked several yards behind the Prius.

Marcus shrugged. "I thought we might need it to catch up with her if the vamp didn't get her first."

"Sorry about your car," Roland muttered, heading for the Prism.

Marcus followed and opened the passenger door for him. "Don't worry about it. I already called Reordon. He and his cleaning crew will take care of it."

Roland said nothing, just eased inside the cramped vehicle.

Marcus watched his friend curiously. Roland wasn't behaving in his usual irascible, distance-himself-from-everything-and-everyone manner. In fact, he didn't seem to want to distance himself from Sarah at all, curtly refusing Marcus's offer to take her until Roland was settled, instead tightening his hold on her and keeping her with him.

Roland's touch was downright possessive as he cradled Sarah on his lap and arranged her just so, ensuring she would be comfortable. Under Marcus's bemused gaze, he then gently cupped a hand protectively over her head and motioned for Marcus to close the door.

Marcus closed it, fascinated, and circled the rear of the car.

Who the hell was this woman and how had she managed to snare Roland's interest so quickly?

Because she had definitely snared it.

Squeezing his long frame behind the wheel, he closed the door and turned the key. The engine sputtered to reluctant life. "Where to?"

"My place," Roland said, not looking up as he carefully began to pick pieces of glass out of Sarah's hair and drop them to the floorboard.

Marcus pulled onto the road and followed Roland's directions. "Did the vamp do that to her?"

"In part. He jumped onto the hood of your car and brought it to a crashing halt."

Marcus frowned. Judging by the way the tires had squealed and smoked as Sarah had sped away from the house, she had been going damned fast. "How did he catch her?"

From the corner of his eye, he saw Roland shake his head. "I don't know. I've never seen a vampire move so swiftly. Fortunately, I got there before he could lay a hand on her and she ran away while we fought."

"Did you kill the fucker?"

"No, Bastien chose to retreat."

And Roland hadn't gone after him? Very telling. "His name is Bastien?"

"That's what one of his men called him. By the time I found Sarah, she had tumbled down a wooded hill and was racing across a field."

Glancing away from the road momentarily, Marcus saw Roland tenderly smooth his big hand over her hair after the last particle of glass was tossed away. "Was she running from Bastien? Or from you?"

Roland's lips tightened. "Both, I think."

"What did she say when you caught up with her?"

Roland's eyes were grim when they met his. "She begged me not to kill her."

Silently, Marcus swore and returned his attention to the road.

That did not bode well.

Twenty minutes later, Roland gently deposited Sarah on the dark brown sofa in his living room and placed a pillow beneath her head. That she was still unconscious worried him.

As he knelt beside her, he noticed the blood that coated his hands and forearms and turned to Marcus. "Get me a towel, will you?"

Marcus disappeared into the kitchen, then returned to the entrance and tossed Roland a towel. "What are you doing?"

Roland began wiping the blood from his hands. "She has a nasty head wound and some bad bruises and scrapes. I'm going to heal her."

"Oh, no, you're not. Not until you feed. You've lost a lot of blood and have much more severe wounds of your own. You know what will happen if you heal her without feeding first."

"I'm not going to put my needs before hers, Marcus. She saved my life."

"And you saved hers, so the two of you are even."

"Hers would not have been in danger if she hadn't found and helped me."

"Oh, please. Do you really think that after babysitting you and watching the sun roast your hairy ass, Ren and Stimpy would have walked past her with a smile and a wave and continued on their merry way? She's a lovely woman living alone in the middle of nowhere with no one nearby to hear her screams. They were stabbing you because they wanted to know what it felt like. What makes you think they wouldn't have raped and tortured her just to see what *that* felt like? If you ask me, she's damned lucky she *did* find and help you. So you can stop playing the martyr and feed."

Ignoring him, Roland tossed the towel aside and settled his palm on the ribs he had seen Sarah clutching as she ran. Just as he had suspected, three of them were cracked.

His hand heated as he focused his flagging energy. His own ribs began to ache as hers healed beneath his touch.

Releasing her, he shifted uncomfortably.

"Here."

A bag of blood appeared a few inches in front of his face. Roland's gaze followed the arm offering it to its owner.

Marcus now stood behind the sofa. "I brought it to you in case you were simply too tired or lazy to get it yourself."

Roland brushed it aside impatiently. "Get that out of here."

"Stop being stubborn," Marcus demanded. "You need it and she's unconscious."

"But she could wake at any moment."

Actually, she already had.

Chapter 6

Sarah had been flirting with consciousness ever since Roland had settled her on what felt like a very comfortable sofa.

Roland was a vampire. Marcus was, too. And she was now alone with them and terrified of what they meant to do to her. She needed to escape but had no hope of outrunning them. So she had enacted the only plan she could think of with her head pounding and sharp pains darting through her chest every time she drew in a breath: feign sleep, eavesdrop, gather information, then sneak away at the first opportunity.

The hardest part so far had been keeping her heartbeat steady and slow despite her fear and not flinching when Roland had touched her sore ribs.

Well, no. The absolute hardest part had been not freaking out when Marcus had told Roland to feed, assuming she would be the main course.

The more she listened, though, the more uncertainty crowded her. Roland didn't sound like the soulless predator she had seen suck the blood of that goth kid in her front yard. He sounded like the nice guy she had spent the day with. The one who had let her sleep on him without copping a feel, disinclined to complain about her weight resting on his many wounds.

He sounded protective of her.

"And Seth thinks *I'm* unreasonable," Marcus muttered. "She knows what we are."

"And she's already seen me feed once, Marcus. I don't want her to see me do it again. She'll be scared enough when she wakes."

"Not necessarily."

"Clearly you didn't see her face when she dove for the car and screeched away."

Inwardly, she winced. Jeeze, that sounded cowardly.

"I was preoccupied, if you'll recall," Marcus responded dryly. "Besides, she was only afraid because she thought you were a vampire like the others. Once you explain that you're not, that you're an immortal, she'll come around."

He wasn't a vampire? What was an immortal?

"The way Mary did?" Roland asked dryly.

Who was Mary?

Marcus snorted. "Mary was a twit, infected by the superstitions of her time and easily influenced by others."

"She was not a twit. She was well-educated."

"She was a bluestocking, a student of the classics with her head in the clouds. Despite her love of books, she knew little more of the world than her female peers and, as I said, was easily influenced by others. Perhaps if she had been capable of thinking for herself, she wouldn't have betrayed you the way she did."

Roland grunted.

"None of that matters, anyway, because Mary and Sarah are two different people. Mary would never have hit a man in the head with a shovel to save you. Sarah did."

Well, that made her feel better.

"Plus, I happened to see a number of paranormal romance novels on her bookshelves when we were at her place, so she may not freak out at all."

"What do you know about romance novels?" Roland asked skeptically.

"Bethany liked them. I recognized several she had read."

"Well, liking the fiction doesn't mean Sarah will like the reality."

The pain in her head increased minutely when Roland carefully prodded the left side of her forehead, then brushed her hair back.

"I don't really care whether she likes it or not as long as she accepts it and doesn't rat us out."

"I'm not worried about that."

"Really? You, the king of paranoia, aren't worried she'll blab our secret?"

"If she did, who would believe her? She'd be locked away in a looney bin faster than she could say *Nosferatu.*"

"Not if she led the police here."

"I'd make sure she couldn't. She didn't see the way here. A blindfold or a sedative will prevent her from seeing the way back. Or, better yet, I could have Seth pop in and transport her."

Sarah sensed movement above her face before Roland's hand withdrew.

"What are you doing?" He sounded surprised.

"Stopping you from doing something stupid."

"Let go of my arm, Marcus."

Fear surged to the surface again at that ominous warning.

"Feed first, then heal her."

What did that mean—*heal her?* Heal her as in render first aid? Why was it so imperative that he *feed* first?

She recalled the soothing heat that had suffused her chest when he had touched her ribs moments ago. The sharp pains had vanished, as had the ache. She was once more able to take deep breaths.

What had Roland done to her?

"When she wakes, I don't want the first thing she sees to be me holding a bag of blood to my lips," Roland bit out.

Oh crap. He is *a vampire.*

"Then hurry up and feed before she wakes."

"She's already close. Her breathing is changing."

She swore silently.

"Then leave the room and feed."

"And have her wake up alone? No."

A charged silence followed.

"Oh, man," Marcus breathed. "You like her."

Against her will, Sarah's eyes flew open and sought Roland's reaction.

He was kneeling beside her, his hair mussed and damp with perspiration around his face. The terrible wound in his neck was sealed and no longer bled. A long cut followed his jawline from his right earlobe to his chin where one of his opponents must have tried to slit his throat again and miscalculated, laying open the flesh so deeply that she feared she would see bone if she rinsed away the blood.

His shirt was saturated with the red liquid, his clothing torn in numerous places. He was also holding his left arm close to his body in a way that made her wonder if it weren't broken.

Battered and looking no better, Marcus stood behind the sofa. In one hand, he held a bag of blood similar to those used in hospitals.

Neither man paid her any attention as they stared at each other.

Marcus looked concerned. Roland looked bitter.

"You do, don't you?" Marcus pressed. "You like her."

A muscle in Roland's cheek jumped. "Don't you think that would be rather foolish, considering?"

"Considering what—that she's smart, pretty, and good with a gun?"

"No," Roland said, his voice laden with sarcasm. "Considering she would have used her gun on *us* if you hadn't made her promise not to. As soon as she wakes up, she's going to run screaming for the door."

Okay, she knew he was a vampire or whatever, but felt guilty anyway because running and screaming *had* been her first impulse and he looked as if he knew that and his feelings were hurt.

Marcus stroked his chin thoughtfully. "I think you're wrong."

"Why, because you know her so well?"

"No, because you're so distraught over her injuries and her potential fear of you that you've missed something pertinent I have not."

His gaze still on Marcus, Roland brushed his fingers through her hair in what seemed an unconscious gesture of affection. "And what might that be?"

Marcus smiled smugly. "She's been awake ever since you laid her on the sofa and has *not* run for the door."

Roland's head snapped down. His brown eyes widening when they met hers, he snatched his hand back as though afraid he would be reprimanded for daring to touch her.

Minutes passed.

The silence stretched.

Sarah cleared her throat. "Um, hi?"

He frowned. "Why aren't you screaming?"

Why indeed? "Because my head is killing me?"

It wasn't a lie exactly. Her head *was* killing her. Yet the truth was that the longer he went without baring his fangs and diving for her throat, the more calm usurped fear's place.

Maybe she had a concussion.

"May I take a look at it?" he asked hesitantly.

She nodded, then groaned at the agony the small movement spawned.

His fingers went to her forehead.

"I don't think it's that one," she whispered, afraid talking louder might make her skull explode. "I think it's the one in back."

His frown deepened. "Forgive me. I didn't know there was another." Very carefully, he eased his hand between her head and the pillow it rested upon, tunneling through her hair.

She flinched and, for a moment, thought she was going to vomit, the throbbing got so bad.

"I'm sorry," he murmured. "It'll get better in just a second."

"Roland," Marcus warned.

"You're going to feel a momentary warmth," Roland continued, ignoring his friend.

What was he . . . ?

Sarah blinked. His hand was getting hotter. And, as it did, the pain lessened. It almost felt as though he were holding a heating pad to the wound.

She looked at Marcus, who was scowling his displeasure, then at Roland again.

Was he paler than he had been a moment ago?

He slipped his hand around and covered the cut on her forehead where it had slammed into the driver's side window.

Again that odd warmth heated her head where he touched her.

He closed his eyes. His jaw clenched.

The pain receded.

Sarah opened her mouth to thank him and ask him what he had done but ended up sucking in a startled breath instead. As she watched, an abrasion formed on the left side of his forehead high up near his hairline. It darkened, widened, swelled. A deep cut opened his flesh. Blood spilled down his cheek.

Swearing, Marcus reached down and yanked Roland's hand away from Sarah's face.

Roland opened his eyes. "What?" His voice was hoarse. "What happened?"

"You *know* what happened," Marcus snapped, releasing him.

Roland raised a hand and gingerly probed his new wound. His fingers were wet with blood when he lowered them. "Oh." He glanced at Sarah, then hastily wiped his hand on his shirt as though he hoped to conceal what had just taken place.

Sarah touched her own forehead and confirmed it.

No cut. No swelling. Her wound was gone.

Now Roland sported one just like it.

The large knot on the back of her head was gone, too. If she were gutsy enough to stroke the back of Roland's head, would she find a large lump there as well?

"Are you feeling better?" he asked, voice tight with suppressed pain.

"Much better." Her head was fine. Her ribs were fine. What had he done?

"Please, don't be afraid, Sarah."

"I'm not." Her answer had been automatic and took even her by surprise.

It was true. She wasn't afraid anymore.

"If you'll excuse me for a moment." Rising, Roland staggered and would have fallen into the glass coffee table had Marcus not leapt over the sofa in the blink of an eye and caught him.

Sarah sat up, heart pounding. "Roland?"

Careful not to touch his friend's broken arm, Marcus drew the other across his shoulders and began dragging Roland toward the dining room. "I told you to feed first," he groused in furious undertones.

Now she thought she understood why. At least in part.

Sarah stood. "Is he going to be okay?"

Marcus nodded and waved her back. "Yes, just . . . stay there, Sarah. We'll be back in a moment."

He wouldn't *feed* in front of her.

"Is there anything I can do?" she asked uncertainly.

"Don't leave," Roland whispered as they entered the small dining room and passed through it into what she assumed was the kitchen, out of her line of sight.

"Sit here," she heard Marcus command.

The refrigerator door opened and shut.

Sarah looked around the living room, comfortably if sparsely decorated with very attractive modern furniture.

This was her chance to sneak away. Roland and Marcus had both been weakened by their wounds. Roland was even worse off after *healing* her, which apparently entailed transferring her wounds to his own body. Marcus was distracted, tending him. They probably wouldn't notice she was gone for several minutes.

Sarah raised a hand to her forehead, drawing her fingers across the healthy flesh that now lay beneath the drying blood.

Don't leave. Roland's words had been not a warning, but a request, almost pleading.

She looked toward the kitchen.

Drawing a deep breath, hoping she would not come to regret her decision, Sarah sat down on the sofa to wait.

Roland couldn't believe it. She hadn't left.

He had emptied several bags of blood as quickly as possible, ears straining to hear the creak of a floorboard or the sound of the front door opening and closing or a window shattering. Anything that would indicate either a stealthy or frantic attempt at escape. He had taken a moment to rinse the blood from his face, strode through the dining area into the entrance of the living room, and . . .

She hadn't left. Sarah was still there, sitting on the sofa, studying her hands.

He watched her for a moment, both relieved and puzzled.

Why wasn't she freaking out? Did she merely feign calm in order to gain his trust so she could leave, then return later with a band of humans to kill him?

Sarah glanced over and noticed him standing there. "Are you feeling better?"

"Yes, thank you."

"You look a *lot* better." Unease flickered across her expressive face. "Is it because you . . . because you fed?"

"Yes." No point in denying it. He felt awkward as hell admitting it, though.

"Oh."

Oh? That's it? "You still aren't screaming."

"Is that the usual reaction you get when people realize you're, um . . ."

"Different? Yes, generally."

Marcus stepped up beside him. "We also get shrieks, curses, pants wetting, bowels releasing"—Sarah grimaced—"religious recitations. . . ."

Her eyebrows rose. "Religious recitations?"

"You know—Get thee back, you, ah . . ." He nudged Roland. "What was it that priest called us?"

Roland rolled his eyes. "Which one?" They had had run-ins with quite a few.

"The one in London."

"What century?"

"Eighteenth."

Sarah's mouth fell open.

"The one with hair like Albert Einstein?"

"Yes."

"Spawns of Satan."

"Right." Adopting a raspy, elderly man's voice, Marcus shook his fist at Sarah and intoned dramatically, "Get thee back, ye spawns of Satan. Return thee to the bowels of hell where ye belong!" Lowering his fist, he proceeded in a normal voice. "Then he hurled numerous biblical verses at our heads as we walked away. And this after we saved his arse from a fairly nasty vampire he had mistaken for a poor parishioner." He shrugged. "But screaming is by far the most common reaction, from both men and women."

She looked a bit flabbergasted. "Uh-huh."

Marcus clapped his hands together. "Well, Sarah is conscious and calm." He turned to Roland. "You no longer appear to be at death's door. I could really use a shower. So, if the two of you are good, I'm going to go have a wash and lie down so my leg can heal more swiftly."

Roland nodded, glad he would have some time alone with Sarah, though he didn't know what to say to her. "Use the guest room. Down the hallway, second door on the right. It has a private bath."

"You have a guest room?"

"Seth stays here occasionally."

Marcus scowled.

"What? It's not like I invite him. He just does it to annoy me because he knows I don't like having other people in my home."

Marcus looked pointedly at Sarah.

"I don't mean you," Roland hastily assured her. "I wouldn't have invited you if I didn't want you here."

"What, did *my* invitation get lost in the mail?" his friend demanded acerbically.

Roland's reluctance to trust had always rankled Marcus. "You're here, aren't you?"

"Yeah, because you needed a ride."

Roland wondered briefly how much it would frighten Sarah if he were to throttle Marcus in front of her. "Weren't you going to take a shower or something?" He gave him a shove in the right direction.

"All right. I'm going."

"Call Lisette before you do and let her know what's going on. Killing me seems to be the vamps' primary goal, but they also appear to be interested in capturing an immortal, since he told them to take you alive."

Marcus smiled wickedly. "The fact that they had to avoid striking a killing blow made my job much easier."

"Lucky you."

Chuckling, Marcus strode down the hallway, entered the guest bedroom, said, "Hey, this is nice," and closed the door.

Roland turned back to Sarah and found her staring at him somberly. Futilely, he searched his brain for something to say that might put her at ease and—what—make her *like* him?

Dream on.

"I'm still not screaming," she pointed out softly.

He felt a smile tug at his lips. "I noticed."

She looked down at the hands resting upon her knees, palms up. "I might scream once I start picking the glass out of these cuts, though. Do you by any chance have a pair of tweezers I can borrow?"

He ducked back into the kitchen and snagged the tweezers from his first aid drawer. Adding a bowl of water and a clean towel, he rejoined Sarah in the living room.

The coffee table was glass set in a heavy wood frame with a sturdy base more than capable of supporting his weight. Roland seated himself on it directly in front of her and parked his big feet on either side of hers, knees comfortably splayed. Setting the water and towel down beside him, he leaned forward, braced his elbows on his knees, and, arming himself with the tweezers, held his left hand out to her.

Sarah eyed the tweezers with dread but trustingly placed her right hand in his.

Damned if that didn't make him feel all warm and fuzzy inside.

Roland studied her palm and the underside of her fingers. There were numerous small pieces of glass embedded in her tender skin. The base of her thumb and the bend of every finger closest to their tips boasted deep cuts that looked as if they had been carved by a knife. While the other punctures, scrapes, and cuts had ceased bleeding, these five were still oozing.

He cast her a questioning look.

"When that guy landed on the car and wrecked it, I lost track of the Glock. The only other weapon I could come up with was a chunk of glass."

"Quick thinking," he praised. She was a fighter, kept a clear head, and didn't give up easily. He liked that.

Positioning the tweezers over one of the bloody shards, he warned, "This is going to hurt."

"I know. Let's just get it over with."

Roland plucked out the first piece of glass.

She winced as he removed another and another and another.

He hated to hurt her, but it had to be done.

"I feel like such a wuss," she admitted as he worked, "squirming over a little thing like this when you had metal spikes driven through your hands."

He shrugged. "I'm accustomed to such. You aren't."

"Are you serious? That sort of thing happens to you often?"

"Actually, no. I usually only come up against one or two opponents at a time. But even then, broken bones, deep lacerations, and gunshot wounds can result." He double-checked her palm, made sure he had removed every sliver, then moved on to her fingers.

She jumped. "Ow! Sorry. That just slipped out."

He shook his head. "I know how much glass can hurt."

He had been chucked through many a window, glass door, and mirror over the centuries.

When Roland heard her heartbeat accelerate a little later, he wondered at its cause.

"So," she broached hesitantly, "are you a vampire?"

Ah. "No, the men who attacked us were vampires."

A moment of silence passed.

"But you have teeth like them. And their eyes glowed like yours. And I saw you drink that kid's blood."

She also knew he had been imbibing in the kitchen, thanks to Marcus's lack of subtlety.

"It's a little complicated."

"I'm an intelligent woman."

He smiled. "I know you are. I'm just trying to think of the best way to explain it."

She cocked her head curiously. "Surely you've done it before."

"Yes," he acknowledged, "but it's been a long time."

"How long?"

He thought of Mary. "Almost four centuries."

A quick glimpse showed him wide hazel eyes.

"How old *are* you? Ow."

"Sorry. Nine hundred and thirty-seven."

"You're 937 years old?"

"Yes."

"You have fangs, drink blood, and have lived almost a thousand years, but you're *not* a vampire."

"Correct."

"Explain, please."

"Give me a moment first. I think I've got all the glass out of this one."

Setting the tweezers aside, Roland sandwiched her hand between both of his and closed his eyes.

Heat built in his hands, then entered hers, seeking and healing her wounds. Pain, like needles, pricked his right palm and fingers before swiftly receding.

Opening his eyes, he relaxed his hold and bent his head to examine her hand.

Sarah did, too, leaning forward until her forehead nearly touched his, her curious expression morphing into one of fascination when she saw her cuts were wholly healed. "That's amazing."

Shifting so that he held her hand over the bowl of water, Roland rinsed it with the cool, clean liquid. Dirt and blood were washed away, revealing healthy flesh bereft of either wounds or scars. He dabbed her skin dry with the towel and set it aside, then trailed his fingers over her palm in languid strokes. Soft circles that widened gradually. Down the length of one finger. Up the next. Dipping in between.

He told himself he was just checking to be certain all was healed, but he really just wanted to touch her.

Her heart began to race, the sound easily detected by his immortal ears.

He raised his eyes and met hers. "Am I hurting you?"

"No," she answered, her voice a little breathless.

Not pain. "Am I scaring you?" he asked, still stroking.

"No."

Not fear. "Your pulse is racing."

"It is?" She licked her lips.

His eyes followed the motion, the sight of that small pink tongue moistening her full lower lip speeding his own pulse until it nearly matched hers. "My senses are heightened. I can hear it."

Her eyes widened. "You can't read my thoughts, can you?"

"No."

"Thank goodness," she whispered and his interest spiked.

"Why? What would they tell me if I could?" Something naughty, he hoped.

"Nothing." Yet she blushed as she said it.

Gently extracting her hand from his, she pressed it to his muscled chest above his heart.

Roland sucked in a sharp breath.

"You have a heartbeat."

He nodded, caught off-guard by her tender touch. "I'm not dead. Or undead, as I believe much of the vampire lore claims."

She slid her hand up his chest, over his collarbone, and splayed her fingers on his neck.

The strength of the desire that small caress inspired shocked him.

"Your pulse is racing, too," she said softly.

And it certainly wasn't because he was afraid of her.

Although there was a hidden part of him that *did* fear her.

The feelings she raised in him were too intense. Too alarming. He wanted to watch over her, protect her, keep her safe. He wanted her to accept him for who and what he was.

He wanted her to like him.

It was insane. He had known her for too brief a time to be this drawn to her. This vulnerable.

He couldn't afford such weakness.

She cupped his jaw in her tiny hand, flooding him with more of that foreign tenderness. Her thumb slid across his chin to the other side.

It was all he could do not to turn his head and bury his lips in her palm.

"Your wounds have healed." Her gaze flickered from his neck, where Bastien had cut his throat the first time, to his jawline, where Bastien had tried again and missed, to his forehead, where her wound had opened on his body when he healed her. All three were either gone or had been reduced to scars that would fade while he slept.

"Many of them have, yes." A few, like his broken arm and a couple of deep stab wounds, were better but would require more blood and rest to mend completely.

"But you're not a vampire."

"No, Marcus and I and others of our ilk prefer to be called immortals. Our human assistants call us Immortal Guardians."

She lowered her hand and leaned back against the sofa cushions. "Whom do you guard?"

"Humanity."

"From vampires?"

"Yes."

Roland picked up her left hand and readied the tweezers, reluctant to begin anew and cause her more pain.

"I'm not really understanding how you differ from the vampires other than that they're assholes and you're not."

He laughed. "Some of my colleagues might disagree with you on that one."

"Then they must not know you well," she protested, and warmth engulfed him once more.

Forcing himself to focus on the glass that sparkled like diamonds amid the blood and torn flesh of her palm, he removed a long sliver. There was a lot more of it lodged in this hand. Unlike the right, the glass was also embedded in her forearm all the way up to her elbow.

"Vampirism," he explained, "and the characteristics associated with it are the result of a very rare parasitic virus."

* * *

"A virus," Sarah repeated, flinching as Roland withdrew a particularly deep shard.

"Yes."

"What precisely are those characteristics?" A lust for blood? A penchant for biting?

He tilted her hand a little to catch the light. "Neither vampires nor immortals are dead. You've felt my heartbeat. You know I breathe."

And his heartbeat had quickened beneath her touch.

"We all have heightened senses."

Sarah remembered the way Roland and Marcus had seemed to hear the vampires' approach long before she had. "Is that how you knew they were coming?"

He nodded, brow furrowed in concentration as he worked on her wounds. "We heard them coming when they were still a couple of miles away and knew how many there were by their individual scents."

It boggled the mind.

"Wow," she joked weakly. "Life must have really sucked for you before deodorant was invented."

He chuckled. "Advances in personal hygiene have indeed made things more pleasant for us, though this latest generation seems to be regressing."

"Tell me about it. I have students who roll out of bed and come to class without even brushing their teeth. Ow!"

"Sorry."

Sarah pondered his keen sense of smell and cringed at the aromas *she* must be emitting. "Maybe I should be the one apologizing."

He glanced up at her. "Why?"

"I'm all sweaty and covered with blood and dirt and who knows what else I picked up rolling down that hill. I wouldn't imagine I'm generating the most pleasant of fragrances."

"The scent of blood is as enticing to me as chocolate is to you."

Her face scrunched up involuntarily. "It is?" That was kind of gross.

He smiled wryly. "Yes. Beyond that, you smell like the forest, your citrus shampoo, baby powder deodorant, and your own unique scent." She saw him inhale subtly. "And even sweaty, your scent is very appealing."

Her heart skipped. He said it as if it turned him on. "Really?"

His eyes darkened, then gained a hint of that unearthly glow. "Your pulse is racing again."

Boldly, she reached out and touched his neck. "So is yours."

From the corner of her eye, she saw his fingers tighten around the tweezers.

"What are some of the other characteristics?" she asked, withdrawing.

"Our vision is far sharper than yours."

"Can you see in the dark?"

"As clearly as a cat."

No wonder Marcus hadn't needed a flashlight to inspect the field. "So what makes your eyes glow?"

"We still don't understand some of the physiological changes that take place in our bodies, and why our eyes glow is one of them. All we know is that it occasionally happens when we feel pain and almost always happens when we experience extreme emotions, such as anger."

Or arousal? she wanted to ask but couldn't bring herself to do so. When she had touched him, stroked the pulse in his strong, tanned neck, his eyes had begun to glow.

Had he felt desire for her? Been as affected by the light caress as she had?

"We're stronger than humans," he went on, cataloging his differences, "a great deal stronger, and can move very fast."

So fast he had blurred. It was cool and creepy at the same time. "What else?"

"We heal swiftly, as you've seen. And we're sensitive to sunlight."

"Is that everything?"

"No, those are only the traits we have in common with the vampires. The virus affects those of us who call ourselves immortals differently. We all start out mortal like you, then become infected through the bite of a vampire."

"Only a vampire? Not an immortal?"

"Immortals very rarely transform humans."

"Oh. So you were turned by a vampire."

His lips tightened. "Yes."

"I assume by your expression that it was against your will."

"Yes. I was fortunate. My body is one of the few capable of mutating the virus, reshaping it, and altering its effects." He paused while he chased down a piece of glass that seemed intent on making a home for itself in her thumb.

Sarah gritted her teeth and clenched her right hand into a fist. Jeeze, it hurt.

If plucking tiny pieces of broken glass out of her hands hurt this much, what kind of hell must Roland have suffered yanking those spikes out of his palms?

Her tense muscles relaxed slightly when he succeeded in capturing the rogue sliver.

He met her gaze. "Do you need to take a break?"

"No." In a way, knowing how stoically he had endured his wounds made getting through this easier for her.

"The virus has negative consequences in vampires that it does not have in us. Vampires subsist entirely on blood. They become addicted to it like some do to cocaine or crystal meth. Immortals, on the other hand, lack this flaw and don't ingest blood nightly."

"Hence the pizza."

He smiled. "Except when injured, those of us who are older need only feed once or twice a week and, otherwise, have a diet similar to your own. Lots of vegetables and fruits. Very little meat. Organic chicken, turkey, or other fowl.

None of the heavier meats, processed, or artificial foods that contain known carcinogens or other harmful chemicals. The same things that cause cancer, heart disease, and genetic mutations in humans increase our need for blood because of the damage they spawn in our bodies that the virus must heal, so we simply avoid them."

"Makes sense. So your diet is different from theirs. What else?"

"Vampires don't live as long as we do. The virus causes a slow descent into madness in them. It's why we hunt them. Their madness and addiction lead them to kill their victims by draining them completely."

"Human victims?"

"Yes. When the vampires are young, the deaths are swift because the vampire's only desire is to satisfy his or her hunger. But after a few years, as portions of the brain deteriorate, madness infects them and they begin to toy with their prey as a cat would with a mouse, terrifying and torturing them. Either way, we cannot allow such slaying of innocents."

"Do *you* drink from humans?" The idea of him sucking on some other woman's neck was disturbing.

Which was not to say she wanted him to suck on *her* neck. Although . . .

Wait. What was she saying?

"Until the last century and the advent of blood banks, we had little choice. But we never killed those we fed upon and were always careful not to weaken them too much." He paused and seemed to think a moment. "Actually that's not true. As much as I wish to avoid frightening you, I want to be honest. We were always careful not to kill or weaken the *innocents* we fed upon. Pedophiles, rapists, and murders, however, were often not treated as kindly."

In other words, they were killed.

Well, she didn't have a problem with that. Sarah had always had a rather biblical sense of justice. "But . . . how does that work? I mean, don't they . . . didn't they tell people about you?"

"No. When our fangs descend, the glands that formed above them during our transformation release a chemical much like GHB under the pressure of a bite, so those we feed upon are left with no memory of it."

That was pretty slick. "And you don't drink from humans anymore?"

"Only when we're desperate. We own a chain of blood banks, to which our Seconds and their families routinely donate, and receive our sustenance in the form of bagged blood now."

"Is there no cure for the virus?"

"No cure."

Something in his voice suggested he would've taken it if there were.

"What about antivirals? They've been making strides with antivirals lately."

He shook his head. "We've tried them. They have no effect on us at all, in part because this virus behaves like no other on the planet. And testing antivirals is dangerous. Some of our scientists believe that if one did prove successful and kill the virus, we would die along with it because the virus essentially replaces our immune system."

"That's a hell of a catch-22," Sarah said. "Remove the virus and you'll be left with no immune system."

"Yes."

"How long do vampires live, then?"

"They rarely live a century. Either we kill them, they grow careless in their madness and accidentally destroy themselves, or they kill each other in blind rages and territorial battles."

A century of madness and killing. That was messed up.

"And immortals? How long do immortals live?"

"We don't age, so . . . indefinitely as long as no one

decapitates us, burns us until we're reduced to ash, or stakes us out for the sun."

The image of him staked to the ground in the meadow flashed through her mind and shook her anew. "You really could have died this morning."

"Yes." He met her gaze intently. "And I must thank you again for saving my life, Sarah."

She nodded. "I'm just glad I was there to help."

Chapter 7

Roland finished removing the glass from Sarah's palm and moved on to her wrist and forearm.

"Why does the virus affect you differently?" she asked curiously.

"Until recently we could only speculate. Like other immortals, I was different as a human, before my transformation, but didn't know why. Back in the day, as they say, we were called *gifted ones:* men and women who were born with special talents we hid more often than not in order to avoid being accused of witchcraft and drowned or burned or stoned to death."

He was both pleased with and wary of how well she was taking all of this. His explanation seemed to fascinate rather than horrify her.

It also appeared to be distracting her from the pain he was causing her.

"It became apparent early on that I had been born with the ability to heal with my hands."

"That isn't a result of the virus?"

He shook his head. "One of my earliest memories is of finding a bird with a broken wing in the bailey not far from the steps of the keep. I felt sorry for it and picked it up, cupping my hands around it to hold it still. The next thing I knew, the wing was mended and the bird was flying away. Several men and women who had seen it crossed themselves. I didn't understand why."

His mother, having witnessed the miracle, had rushed to his side. "My mother stared at me with such fear in her eyes."

You have been blessed, sweetling, with a wondrous gift. But others will not see it so, she had told him in the seclusion of her solar. *They will think you cursed. They will fear you and seek to harm you. You must* never *again use it when the eyes of others are upon you. Only heal in secret.*

"Your mother was afraid of you?" Sarah asked, brow furrowed.

"No, she was afraid *for* me. With good reason. Many a *gifted one* was slain because of his or her differences."

The eleventh century in which he had been born had lacked the legions of lawyers and hate-crime legislation that kept most men's sadistic natures in check today. Anyone viewed as different had been hated, distrusted, or feared outright and had been made to suffer for it. (One of the downsides of living so long was seeing firsthand how little progress mankind made in certain areas.)

He repositioned her arm so he could better see her elbow. The glass pieces here were deeper as a result of her tumble down the hill and other falls.

"Thank you, Roland."

He looked up at the softly spoken words. She was staring at him with what might almost be mistaken for fondness in her hazel eyes.

"Thank you for healing my ribs and my head."

He held his breath when she raised her free hand and drew her fingers lightly across his forehead where it had bled.

"Why did you do it? Why did you heal me without feeding first when you knew it would hurt you?"

Why did her every touch affect him so? He was so distracted, he could think of no other answer but the truth. "I could not bear to see you suffer."

"But you could've fed and rebuilt your strength in just a few minutes."

"A few minutes were too many."

When she lowered her hand, her palm fitted itself to his kneecap, then slid to one side as her fingers tucked themselves into the crease of his pants along the bend.

Roland's vision honed in on that small, pale hand resting on his knee. Fire licked its way up his thigh to his groin as she exerted enough pressure to urge his leg against hers.

It seemed to be a gesture of affection. One he didn't know how to respond to or how to interpret. Damn his antisocial ass.

Had he isolated himself from the world so much that he couldn't decipher the meaning of a woman touching his knee?

His body reacted as though it were a sexual overture. He wanted desperately to kiss her. To taste those full, pink lips. Press her back against the sofa. Lean his hard body into hers. There was just something about Sarah that constantly set him aflame.

But he seriously doubted she had meant it as such. The way she pressed his knee against hers felt almost like a hug.

If he were seated next to her, would she have embraced him?

"Thank you," she said again.

An adequate response eluding him, he nodded and went back to digging for glass.

"Did healing my hand just now hurt you?" she queried.

"The wounds didn't open on me," he assured her. "That only happens when I've been weakened physically first and haven't fed or if I try to heal mortal wounds."

"But did it *hurt* you?"

He didn't want to answer that. She was softhearted and—

"Roland?"

Persistent.

He sighed. "Only for a moment. But it was worth it."

Her frown told him how much she disliked that. "Can all immortals heal with their hands?"

"No, whatever gifts we were born with—healing, precognition, telepathy, telekinesis—remain with us after the transformation. The older the immortal, the greater and more varied the gifts."

"What can Marcus do?"

Roland grimaced, thinking of it. "Marcus's gift is rather unsettling. He can see spirits."

"Spirits as in ghosts?"

"Yes. And when I say he sees them, I mean he really *sees* them. It isn't like those charlatans on television who claim your dead Aunt Esther is talking to them and says to tell you not to worry about the money."

Sarah laughed.

"Marcus is the real deal. He sees dead people and it is neither cool nor comfortable."

She bit her lip. "I'm sorry. I wasn't laughing at Marcus's gift. I was laughing at your description of the fakers."

He raised his head long enough to smile at her. "I know, Sarah."

She smiled back.

"I should warn you, he's a bit sensitive about it." Extremely sensitive. "When Marcus was a boy, his stepfather thought he was mad and beat him nearly every day until Marcus was old enough to run away and squire for the Earl of Fosterly. He was careful after that never to reveal his ability, even when he met other *gifted ones*. It wasn't until after he was transformed that he finally mentioned it, and then, reluctantly."

"I can see why. Do you have any gifts in addition to the healing?"

"I have minor telekinetic abilities, but they're weak enough that they aid me little in battle."

"Telekinetic? That's wild."

Concentrating, Roland made one of the pillows beside her rise into the air without warning. Sarah jumped and stared at it with wide eyes. It hovered there for a heartbeat, then flew forward and gently bounced off her face.

Laughing, she caught it with her free hand and met his gaze.

"I couldn't resist," he confessed with a grin.

"Uh-huh." She set the pillow aside. "Your telekinetic abilities don't seem so weak to me."

He shrugged. "It requires time to focus that I often lack when fighting vampires." Roland set the tweezers aside. "I think that's it." He started to cover her palm with his free hand.

Sarah grabbed his wrist. "Don't."

He raised his brows. "Don't what?"

"Heal me. I don't want to hurt you."

Roland stared at her. He had just spent a good half hour or more hurting her and she was worried about the few seconds of discomfort healing her cuts would cause him? If it weren't for him, she wouldn't *have* any cuts.

He waved away her concern. "I told you. The pain is fleeting."

Her chin jutted forward. "Fleeting or not, I won't let you do it."

She wouldn't *let* him? *She,* a five-foot-one-inch, ninety-five-pound mortal female, wouldn't let *him,* a six-foot-two-inch immortal sporting two hundred pounds of muscle—

Oh, screw it. He had never been the bully type. If she didn't want him to heal her, he wouldn't force it. *Damn it.*

Roland let his gaze wander over her charmingly stubborn expression, then focused on those lush, pink lips.

Although . . . perhaps he wouldn't have to force her. Perhaps there was another way.

She had been wreaking havoc on his thoughts and senses with her innocently provocative touches ever since he had met her. If he were to take a page from her book . . .

Without giving himself a chance to think about it or to point out that he was probably only using this as an excuse, he leaned forward and pressed his lips to hers.

Her breath caught at the tentative touch, but she didn't pull away. Her lips parted in surprise.

Hell. This was a mistake.

She tasted as good as she looked. As good as she smelled. She was intoxicating, like a fine wine that went straight to Roland's head. One sip wasn't enough. He needed more and took advantage of her parted lips to deepen the kiss.

When Roland's tongue stroked her lower lip and delved inside to duel with her own, flames whipped through Sarah, searing her from her head to her toes. Her heart began to pound. Her whole body flushed.

Releasing his wrist, she cupped his face. The coarse stubble on his jaw abraded her palm as he tilted his head to heighten the contact, teasing, exploring, tantalizing.

The man kissed as though he had spent centuries learning everything there was to know about it. She had never been so turned on so quickly in her life!

When Roland leaned farther toward her, she met him halfway, scooting to the sofa's edge, wanting to feel him against her.

He continued to devour her lips even as he began to stroke her fingers.

Sarah at first attributed the warmth that suffused her hand, then her forearm, to the burning desire Roland's kiss was kindling. She felt his hand slide up her arm, curling around her elbow in a gentle caress, and delighted in his touch, wanting more . . . until awareness of what he was doing finally penetrated her hazy thoughts.

He was healing her!

Tearing her mouth from the heat of his, she looked down at the arm he was still fondling. Sure enough, the cuts had all healed.

Sarah glared at him, feeling absurdly hurt as she struggled to catch her breath. It had been a ploy? "You tricked me."

Roland returned her stare blankly, his eyes all aglow.

That made her feel a little better. He had said they only did that when he was experiencing strong emotions.

Or sometimes pain. Maybe it wasn't desire. Maybe it was a result of the pain healing her cuts had caused him.

"You tricked me!" she repeated, clinging tenaciously to her anger. "You knew I didn't want you to heal me, so you kissed me to distract me, then healed me anyway."

"I did?" He glanced down at her arm and slid his fingers across her newly mended skin, making it tingle.

"Don't even bother trying to deny it."

"I'm not denying it. I'm surprised it worked." Then, in more of a mutter, he added, "Never in my life have I had such a hard time concentrating. I can't believe I even remembered to heal you."

Her anger evaporated.

He stilled . . . as though realizing he had said too much.

Satisfaction sifted through her. He had been as swept away by the kiss as she had.

His beautiful, iridescent eyes met hers.

A slow smile curled her lips. "Caught in your own web?"

"Very much so."

She liked that he didn't deny it. And her ego liked that he was attracted to her.

Unfortunately, he showed no such elation.

"You have that look about you again," she told him.

"What look?"

"The same one you had earlier, like you're waiting for me to scream or freak out or something."

"Probably because I am."

It was a little heartbreaking to see that spark of vulnerability fused with resignation in his eyes.

Sarah captured one of his hands in hers. "If I didn't scream earlier, why would I scream now?"

He studied their clasped hands and said simply, "It's what most women do when they realize they've just been kissed by a monster."

"A monster?" she repeated derisively. "What kind of crackpots have you been dating?"

His lips twitched as he met her gaze. "I would not be so quick to judge. Did you or did you not run from me in fear earlier?"

Busted. He *would* have to remember that. "I wasn't running from you. I was running from the vampires."

Knowing better, Roland raised one eyebrow.

"Okay, I was running from all of you. But I thought you were like *them.* Give me a break. I didn't even know you weren't human until . . . what . . . an hour ago? I'm still trying to catch up and think I've done fairly well under the circumstances."

"Remarkably well," he agreed. "I suppose that's why I keep waiting for the axe to fall. It's so contrary to what I've dealt with in the past."

"That really sucks."

"Yes, it does."

She looked down at their hands, turning his palms up. "Are you okay?"

Roland stared at her, perplexed. "Okay?"

"You healed my hand and arm. I'm sure it must have hurt."

"I'm fine." His perpetual arousal in her presence pained him more than healing her minor cuts and scratches had.

"Good. No more tricks then?"

"Not as long as you allow me to heal you whenever I deem it necessary."

She raised her head, eyes narrowed in mock anger. "You left out stubbornness when you were listing the characteristics of an immortal."

He grinned, feeling unusually light at heart. "I was stubborn as a human."

"I can believe that."

"Perhaps because it is a trait you're personally familiar with?" he teased.

"I plead the Fifth." She brushed her hair back from her forehead, making a face when she felt the blood and dirt that matted the tangled strands. "I know you very sweetly assured me that I don't stink, but I would love to wash all of this off me."

"Of course." Rising, he unsuccessfully tried to banish an image of her standing naked beneath a steaming spray of water.

That one was going to linger.

He eased around her knees, then pulled her up to stand beside him.

She winced.

"What is it?" He did a quick visual inspection of her body and found no obvious injuries. There could be bruises, though.

Her face went blank. "Nothing."

"You winced."

"No, I didn't."

"I was looking right at you."

"Maybe it wasn't a wince. Maybe I was trying not to sneeze. There was a lot of pollen in that field, you know."

"No more than there was in the meadow behind your house and you didn't sneeze once all day."

She tapped her chin with one finger. "Dust?"

"Try again. I'm what you humans call a neat freak. My home is immaculate."

She looked around, taking in the modern living room and what could be seen of the dining room. "You're right. It is. And beautifully decorated."

"Thank you. You aren't going to tell me why you winced, are you?"

She gave him a bright smile he found impossible not to return. "No. Now, how about that shower?"

He shook his head, vowing to discover whatever bruises, aches, or pains troubled her later. "As you wish."

Perhaps when she was resting. She was a pretty sound sleeper. He wouldn't be doing anything to her that she hadn't done to him if he were to sneak in, examine her while she slumbered, and rid her of any lingering bruises and scrapes.

Women were funny, though. And she was again looking at him as she would a normal man. The last thing he wanted to do was jeopardize that and once more become a monster in her eyes.

Turning her hand in his, he laced his fingers through hers and led her out of the living room, down the hallway, and into the master bedroom. All the while, he waited for an objection or a casual withdrawing that didn't come.

How sad was it that he had been without human contact for so long that simply holding a woman's hand set his heart to racing?

Well, not holding *any* woman's hand. Holding *Sarah's* hand set his heart to racing.

He flicked on the overhead light.

Sarah stopped short.

Unwilling to relinquish the warm contact, he stood at her side and entertained himself by stroking the back of her hand with his thumb while she perused the large bedroom.

"This is beautiful, Roland." Sarah took in the forest-green walls, the beautiful hardwood floors, the postmodern paintings, and the ebony-stained armoire, four-poster king-size bed, and matching bedside tables.

"You like it?" he asked tentatively.

"I love it. Green is my favorite color."

His face lit with a gorgeous smile that made the butterflies return to her belly. "Mine, too. The shower is right through here."

Her hand still in his, she followed him to an open door on the far wall. Roland leaned in, flicked on the light, then stepped aside so she could join him in the doorway.

"Oh, wow," she breathed as she peered inside. "This is totally my dream bathroom." Wanting to hold his hand a little longer, she drew him in after her as she moved to the center of the room and turned in a slow circle.

"Believe it or not, the house had no bathroom when I bought it. There was only what the locals called a johnny house out back."

"How long have you had this place?" she asked, unable to imagine it.

"A century or so. There were originally five bedrooms. I kept two, made one a library, one a home gym, and converted the fifth into a small bath for the guest room and this larger master bath."

"You did all this yourself?" she asked incredulously.

"There wasn't much else for me to do during the long days."

"I am beyond impressed."

All earth tones, it was like something out of an interior design magazine. Lovely stone tiles in complementary shades. A shower large enough to hold half a dozen people. A whirlpool bathtub so long Roland could stretch out completely in it (with room left over for her to join him, not that she should be thinking that). Rich mahogany cabinetry. Brushed nickel hardware. Plants galore and candles in wall sconces and scattered around the tub.

She stared at Roland, unable to turn her mind away from images of him soaking in a warm bubble bath with candlelight glinting off his damp, golden skin.

"You do realize you're going to have to pry me out of here with a crowbar, right?"

He laughed. "Take as long as you want. Shower. Soak in a nice hot bath." He opened the cabinet beneath the sink to show her several bottles containing bubble bath in varying scents.

Oh jeeze. He does take bubble baths.

Now she would never get those drool-inspiring images out of her head.

"I think I saw your tote in the backseat when we arrived," he went on. "I'll go look and, if Marcus brought it, will leave it outside the door for you. Otherwise, you're welcome to borrow some of my clothes. Take anything you need from the closet."

"Thank you."

He gave her hand a squeeze, then released it and crossed to the door. "Call me if you need anything."

Like his large hands smoothing over her slick, soapy body?

"Will do."

With one last smile, Roland exited and closed the bathroom door behind him.

In the blood-soaked front yard of Sarah's small frame house, a silhouette emerged from the trees. A light breeze toyed with the hem of his long black coat as he strode forward, limping heavily. The sweet scent of late spring blossoms was tainted by the pungent odors of blood, sweat, and decaying corpses.

Bastien stared at the remains of the men he had led into battle. *His* battle.

The vampiric virus was hard at work. In a frantic bid to live despite the cessation of flowing blood, it would feast upon the dead flesh of its host until there was nothing left. Not even bones. Minutes hence, the only evidence of the violence that had taken place here would be the crimson-stained grass and ragged pieces of clothing that no longer housed bodies.

Rage boiled up within him, muting the pain of his many wounds. He had thought to find survivors here, unable to believe all nineteen of his men could have been annihilated.

Last night, when they had made their first attempt to kill Roland, four had been destroyed, but three of their seven had survived. Had the mortal woman not intervened, his enemy would now be dead and he and the rest of his men would be celebrating their victory.

He growled deep in his throat, a rough, bestial sound.

He had returned tonight to finish Roland off. To seek his vengeance. Confident that it would at last be done.

Finding two Immortal Guardians instead of one had surprised him but had not overly concerned him. With another dozen vampires—flushed from feeding—on the way, they had outnumbered the immortals ten to one.

The woman had posed no threat. She was a human and, based on her panicked flight, not Roland's Second as he had previously supposed. They should have had no difficulty destroying his enemy and taking the other captive.

Yet Bastien alone remained. His men were dead, disintegrating beneath his baleful gaze. And his enemy had again escaped his clutches.

Swearing foully, he strode purposefully into the darkness.

This wasn't over. He would seek new victims to alleviate his pain, then devise another plan.

One way or another, Roland Warbrook would die.

After retrieving Sarah's tote for her, Roland had grabbed a change of clothes (shoes, socks, boxer shorts, T-shirt, and slacks—all black) and slipped into the guest bedroom. Marcus must have been injured worse than he had let on, because he had not roused the whole time Roland was showering and changing. Sleep that deep among immortals was a clear indication that significant healing was taking place.

Now, as Roland stood in the kitchen, peering into the refrigerator, he became aware of Sarah's presence in the entrance.

"Hi," she said softly.

Roland looked over at her and stared, arrested by her beauty. "Hi."

Her slender figure was encased in low-riding jeans and a

comfortably formfitting gray T-shirt that made his body react in ways that would soon have his eyes glowing if he wasn't careful. Surrounded by thick curls that were still damp at the ends, her lovely face was clean and makeup free. Her ears, where they peeked through the heavy strands, were pink from the heat of the hair dryer.

That made him smile.

Her tiny feet were bare.

"Would you be interested in a salad?" he asked, surprised he sounded so casual.

"If I can have a taste of whatever is producing that wonderful aroma afterward, yes."

Pulling organic lettuce, carrots, spinach, tomatoes, and sliced almonds from the refrigerator, he set them on the counter beside the sink. "It's eggplant Parmesan."

Her hazel eyes—more green than brown tonight—widened. "Eggplant Parmesan?" She moved toward him as though he held in his hands the key to a great treasure. "You made eggplant Parmesan while I was in the shower? Seriously, don't tease me. It's one of my all-time favorite meals, so if you tell me you made it and you didn't, I may have to hurt you."

He smiled. "If by making it, you mean removing it from the fridge and popping it in the oven, then yes, I made it while you were in the shower."

"Ooh, goody goody goody goody." She danced over to his side, outwardly as happy as a child on Christmas morning. "I didn't even realize I was hungry until I smelled it and now I'm *ravenous*." She took two carrots from the bag. "Perhaps now might be a good time to warn you that I may be small, but I can put away a *lot* of food."

He laughed. "Nothing wrong with a healthy appetite."

She used his environmentally friendly dishwashing soap to clean the carrots, rinsed them, then looked at him expectantly. "Where is your carrot peeler?"

"In the drawer to your left. What are you doing?"

Opening the drawer, she retrieved the peeler. "Helping you make the salad."

He frowned. "You don't have to do that, Sarah. You're my guest." Guests weren't supposed to prepare their own meals, were they?

She shrugged. "I know. But I want to."

Since he enjoyed her company, he didn't press it. And was soon glad he hadn't. Shoulder to shoulder, they prepared the vegetables. Sarah peeled the carrots while he washed the lettuce and spinach.

He felt a moment's uneasiness when she pulled out his butcher knife. Roland and humans with sharp knives generally did not mix well. More often than not, one or the other ended up bloody. But he said nothing and was careful to hide the sudden tension he felt.

Or so he thought.

Glancing at him from the corner of her eye as she sliced the carrots with the speed and dexterity of a professional chef, she said, "If you don't stop looking at me like you expect me to plunge this between your shoulder blades, you're going to forfeit your portion of the eggplant Parmesan."

He shook his head, feeling another smile tug at his lips. "You really *aren't* afraid of me, are you?"

Pausing, she lowered the knife, turned toward him, and leaned one hip against the counter. "I *was* . . . when I saw you bite that goth kid. And when I was running through the meadow, mostly because I was in a full-blown panic and didn't know whether it was you or the vampire chasing me."

"When you saw it was me, you fainted," he pointed out. That bothered him far more than it should, as did her begging him not to kill her just before she lost consciousness.

"Yeah, I've never done that before," she said with some amazement. "But I knew *you* knew that I had seen what you are and assumed you would be angry. And, in my defense, I had just slammed my head into both a car window and a tree."

True. "And now?"

"No," she said simply. "I'm not afraid of you."

Though he was beaming inside, he nodded solemnly. "Then you may continue wielding the knife."

She tossed a carrot slice at him.

Both grinning, they finished preparing the salads.

Sarah carried them to the table, setting one on the end and the other in front of the chair catty-corner to it. Roland followed with plates loaded with eggplant Parmesan.

"Is tea all right?" he asked. "I'm afraid we don't consume wine or other alcoholic beverages."

"I don't, either. Tea is great," she answered.

While he took a large pitcher from the refrigerator and pulled two glasses down from an upper cabinet, she gathered the utensils.

"Isn't Marcus going to join us?"

"He's still resting." At least he had been when Roland had finished showering. "He'll eat later, once his knee is better."

Holding her chair for her, Roland seated Sarah, then himself. He was glad she had arranged their plates close together instead of putting them at opposite ends of the table. This was more pleasant. Cozier.

"You never told me why immortals were different from everyone else as humans," she said as she started on her salad.

He even liked the way she ate. She hadn't been kidding when she said she could put away a lot of food. She had an amusingly healthy appetite, but impeccable table manners.

"We didn't know ourselves until the last few decades when DNA and gene mapping were tackled by scientists and members of the medical community."

"That must have been tough, being different without knowing why."

"Actually, the why of it remains a mystery. It is only the *how* that we have finally come to understand."

Her salad soon a thing of the past, she slipped her first

forkful of the eggplant Parmesan between her lips, closed her eyes, chewed, and hummed in ecstasy. “Man, this is good. I love eggplant Parmesan but don’t know how to cook it.”

Roland’s gaze fell to her lips, the gentle motions of her throat as she swallowed. “Perhaps you would like to join me the next time I prepare it.”

“I’d love to,” she answered without hesitation, seemingly unaware of how her easy acceptance of his rare invitation affected him.

“So what did you find out? How are you different from the rest of us?”

It took him a moment to recover. “Apparently, every human being has forty-six DNA memo groups that provide the blueprints for their existence. Our scientists have discovered that those of us who were *gifted ones* have seven thousand.”

Chapter 8

Sarah stared at Roland as he forked a piece of eggplant into his mouth and chewed. "Seven thousand?"

He nodded and took a drink of tea.

"And the rest of us only have forty-six."

"Yes."

"All of us."

"Yes."

"You have seven *thousand.*"

He ate another piece of eggplant.

"How is that possible?"

"We don't know."

Her mind raced as she savored the delicious meal. There didn't seem to be that many explanations.

"I feel a little weird asking this," she said hesitantly, "but is it possible you guys are aliens?"

"As in extraterrestrials?"

"Yes."

"Some have suggested as much, that perhaps we are the descendants of aliens who either crashed or came to Earth, seeking a new home."

Wow. "You sound like you don't believe that's the case."

He shrugged. "It just seems like we'd know if such were true. Wouldn't the aliens have wanted their children and future generations to know why they're different, what planet their ancestors came from? Wouldn't they have told them and passed the story down from generation to generation?"

"*I* would have."

"Other immortals hypothesize that there have always been two species of humans living on Earth. Those who believe in evolution ask why humans would *not* evolve into separate species. Animals certainly have."

"And creationists?"

"Creationists point out that, in the Bible, when Cain slew Abel and was banished, he went to live in the land of Nod and was marked by God so those he met there would not kill him as punishment for murdering his brother. There was no information given regarding the inhabitants of Nod. Until then, the only humans mentioned were Adam and Eve and their children. But clearly there were others on the planet. Some speculate that those were the *gifted ones.*"

Sarah had only read the Bible from cover to cover once and tried to remember Cain's fate. "You're right. There *were* other people. I had forgotten that."

"Who we are is anybody's guess," he went on. "Alien race? Separate species? Either would explain why our gifts have lessened over the centuries, why younger immortals have fewer gifts than older ones. The bloodline has been diluted over the millennia as a result of procreating with humans, the gifts weakened. Some, we know, have been lost altogether."

"What about the older immortals? Who is the eldest amongst you?"

"That would be Seth."

"Doesn't he know why you're different?"

He hesitated. His gaze slid toward the guest room, making her wonder if perhaps he was debating telling her something he didn't want Marcus to hear. "He refuses to speculate."

"I sense a *but* in there."

He smiled faintly. "But he knows. He confessed as much to me when I was . . . at a particularly low point in my existence and questioned him on the subject. I think he didn't want to add to my disappointment."

She couldn't help but wonder what that low point was. "What did he say?"

"That revealing the truth inevitably leads to a great deal of bloodshed, so he has resolved to keep his counsel."

She frowned. That not only sucked, it raised more questions.

"I don't imagine he will change his mind after so many millennia, so I doubt we'll ever learn the truth."

Sarah rested her hand on his muscular forearm. "I'm sorry, Roland. I hope he *does* change his mind. I can tell it troubles you."

He covered her hand with his own. "Thank you." His thumb caressed her knuckles, speeding her pulse.

When she dampened her lips, his gaze dropped to follow the delicate swipe of her tongue. His grip on her hand tightened.

He leaned forward.

She held her breath.

"I take it I missed dinner?" A voice spoke from the dining room's entrance.

Sarah and Roland sprang apart.

Marcus, clean but clad in his dirty clothes, raised one ebony eyebrow.

Roland cleared his throat. "I thought you were sleeping."

Marcus nodded to their empty plates. "Got any more of that?"

"In the oven. Still warm."

"Thanks."

Marcus headed into the kitchen.

From his position at the table, Roland could see him opening and closing cabinets and drawers in search of plates, flatware, and a glass.

Her back to the kitchen, Sarah turned her gaze to the tabletop near him.

Roland glanced down to see if he had spilled something and saw nothing amiss. "What is it?"

Surprising him, she took the hand that had just been stroking her own and studied the mottled dark pink scars that marred it. There were two: one where the spike had entered and another where it had exited.

As she drew the fingers of her free hand gently across his skin, a sensual tingle raced up his arm. He could not seem to get enough of her touch, no matter how casual or innocent.

"I can't believe how quickly you heal."

"All immortals do after the transformation. But I was like this before, when I was human. It's part of the gifts I was born with."

From the corner of his eye, he saw Marcus open the refrigerator door, extract a bag of blood from the meat compartment, and close it again. The bag rattled faintly when he lifted it to his lips and sank his fangs into it.

Roland sent Marcus a scowl, not wanting him to feed in front of Sarah. (Vampirism was easier to accept when the more unpleasant aspects of it weren't tossed in one's face at every turn.)

Marcus shrugged.

Sarah gripped Roland's hand more firmly. Though her eyes were wide when they met his, indicating she had guessed what Marcus was doing, she didn't turn around to look.

"Is he drinking blood?" she whispered.

"Yes."

"Out of a bag?"

"Yes." Her expression lent him no hint of her thoughts.

"How do you feel about that?"

Even Marcus contemplated her curiously now, awaiting her response.

"I don't know. Does blood taste as gross as I think it does?"

He fought a smile. "Do you remember what I told you about its scent?"

She nodded. "You said it smelled as good to you as chocolate does to me."

"The same holds true for the taste. Immortals and vampires find it very appealing."

"Hmm."

Marcus tossed the empty bag into the trash. After filling his plate, he carried it, the utensils, and his glass into the dining room and sat across from Sarah.

"You don't think we're damned for drinking blood?" he asked dryly.

They had heard whispers and shouts of such from humans all of their existences.

She appeared to ponder it for a moment. "There are a lot of commandments regarding diet in the Bible. Not drinking blood is just one of them. So if you two are damned for drinking blood, then anyone who eats rabbit, pork, meat with blood in it, shellfish, things that swarm, and birds of prey or scavenger birds is damned, too. And those are just the restrictions I can remember off the top of my head."

It was a surprisingly logical and pragmatic approach to take.

Marcus raised his eyebrows. "Do you eat any of those foods?"

She wrinkled her nose. "No. If you ask me, that crap just isn't healthy, which is probably why it was banned in the first place. Pigs eat their own feces and tend to carry more diseases and parasites. Rabbits eat their own feces, too, so—yuck. Shellfish are the vacuum cleaners of the ocean and can accumulate high levels of toxins. No thanks. Scavenger birds eat roadkill. Again, yuck. And I've personally never seen the appeal of eating things like chocolate-covered ants or roaches."

Roland laughed. "Neither have I. What about meat with blood in it?"

"As far as I know I don't. I don't eat red meat, so no rare bloody steaks. And any fowl I prepare is organic and either boiled or baked until the meat is so tender it falls off the bone. I assume any blood there might be in it would be cooked away."

"Well, technically speaking, we don't *drink* the blood," Roland said. "Our goal is to get it into our circulatory system, not our digestive tract. So our fangs behave like IV needles, drawing the blood in and carrying it directly to our veins."

Sarah pursed her lips. "But you do swallow some."

Marcus nodded. "There's always a drop or two of overflow."

"And you like the taste of it?"

"Yes," they answered.

Again she wrinkled her nose. "Weird."

Both men laughed.

As Marcus went back to eating, Roland wondered how long it would take Sarah to realize she was still holding his hand. (He hoped a long time.) "What did Lisette say when you talked to her?"

"That all vampires appear to have fled Raleigh. She hasn't so much as caught a glimpse of one in the last two nights."

"That's because they were all too busy attacking me," Roland said. "Or rather us."

Marcus nodded, chewed, swallowed. "She said she would be more than happy to come join the fun if we need her."

Roland considered it. If the attacks continued to escalate, they could use the backup. However, killing him was not the vampires' sole motive. They wanted to get their hands on an immortal for undoubtedly unsavory purposes, and he would never forgive himself if the French Immortal Guardian were captured.

"Let's hold off on that, shall we? I don't want to risk her falling into the vampires' clutches."

"I agree."

* * *

As the men discussed the other woman in fond, protective tones, Sarah became aware of a semi-seething emotion infiltrating her that she eventually identified as jealousy.

"Who is Lisette?"

Roland answered, "She's the Immortal Guardian stationed in Raleigh."

"Do you know her well?" *Jeeze, don't beat around the bush.*

"No, we've only run into each other a few times over the centuries."

Marcus grinned. "He's antisocial." While Roland shot him a glare, Marcus filled his fork again and started to raise it to his mouth. Pausing with it halfway there, he turned to Roland, looking puzzled. "Do you have a dog?"

Roland released a long-suffering sigh. "No."

Lowering his fork, Marcus looked into the kitchen.

Sarah turned to follow his gaze and saw nothing. Was he staring at the door on the opposite side?

"What the hell *is* that?" Marcus went on. "It sounds like a wolf or coyote howling, but not really."

Sarah didn't realize she was still holding his hand until Roland gently withdrew it, pushed back his chair, and rose. "It's Nietzsche, my cat. He howls like a dog whenever he's about to pick a fight with something."

Marcus frowned. "Nietzsche? Didn't you have a cat named Nietzsche, like, forty years ago?"

Roland shrugged. "I like the name." As he walked past Sarah, he briefly rested his hand on her shoulder. "I'll be back in a minute."

Her pulse gave a little leap. "Okay."

Lips tilting up in that handsome smile of his, he strode through the kitchen and opened the door. Beyond she saw a room the size of her bedroom that seemed to be a mud room/laundry room and boasted two doors.

Roland headed through it without turning the lights on, bypassed the door that she assumed led to a garage, unlocked and opened the back door, slipped outside, then closed it behind him.

Silence fell in his absence.

Sarah turned around and found Marcus staring at her thoughtfully.

She gave him a tentative smile.

As though it was a sign he had been waiting for, he set his utensils down, leaned forward, and braced his forearms on the table. “It appears a window of opportunity has opened before me, Sarah, and I’ve decided I’m going to take it.”

“Um, okay.”

“While Roland is busy cursing his cat and trying to talk it out of rumbling with an apparently rotund raccoon, he’ll be too distracted to listen to our conversation.”

“You aren’t going to ask me out, are you?”

He smiled. “No, I can see that Roland has already snared your interest, just as you have snared his. Anyone with eyes can see the affection growing between you.”

“We’ve only known each other for a day,” Sarah protested weakly. He was right, though . . . at least on her end of it. Roland definitely made her heart go pitter-patter and she liked him more with every minute she spent in his company.

Marcus shrugged. “It happens that way sometimes. And since it appears to be happening that way for the two of you, I thought you should know a couple of things.”

“Okay.” She really didn’t know what else to say.

“The first is that Roland has serious trust issues.”

She smiled. “I already knew that one.” It didn’t take a genius to recognize Roland’s lack of faith in others.

“The fact that he has welcomed you into his home speaks volumes.”

“Not really. I didn’t exactly give him a choice.”

“Believe me. He had a choice. He could have easily pawned you off on me or Lisette or sent you to one of the safe houses our human colleagues maintain if he didn’t want you here.”

Hmm. That was thought-provoking.

"I razz Roland about his inherent distrust," Marcus continued earnestly, "but the truth is it has tragic origins. I won't go into details. Suffice it to say he has been royally fucked over not once, not twice, but three times by people he loved and trusted above all others. And each betrayal nearly cost him his life."

Had *Mary the twit* been one of those who had betrayed him? Sarah wondered.

"I wasn't there for the first two, but I had a front-row seat for the third." He shook his head, regret crowding his features. "Which is why, after eight centuries of friendship, I try not to let it bother me that a part of him still secretly expects me to turn on him and stab him in the back."

Roland didn't trust Marcus after *eight centuries* of friendship?

Maybe his trust issues went deeper than she had thought.

"Anyway, I said all that to say this, my second point: You seem like a very nice woman. You're smart and attractive and are handling all of this exceedingly well."

She had fled into the forest, thinking them monsters. *That* was handling this well? "What exactly are you trying to say, Marcus?"

"Simply this. I don't know if you're planning to leave at the earliest opportunity or linger to help us sort this out. Whether you're going to keep things casual between you and Roland or will try to break past his barriers and pursue a relationship with him."

Sarah stared at him in disbelief. "Are you asking me what my intentions are?"

He snorted. "Roland would be mortified were I to do anything so horrific. No, I merely thought it pertinent to mention that I consider myself to be an easygoing guy. However—and I cannot stress this enough—should you unwisely choose to betray Roland, I will not hesitate to kill you."

There was nothing easygoing in his expression when he

said it. Sarah didn't doubt for a minute he would carry through on his threat.

"I have no intention of betraying him."

He smiled and picked up his fork. "We're good then." Once more the genial fellow, he tucked into the remainder of his meal.

"You know," she said slowly, "I realize you're only looking out for him, but if you've given that warning to every woman he's had dinner with, you've probably made him miss out on a lot of second dates."

He shook his head. "You're the first woman he's shown this much interest in in centuries."

"I am?"

"Yes, and he would be equally mortified to know I'd told you *that,* so . . ."

"Mum's the word."

"Thank you."

A faint yowling met her ears.

Sarah rehashed Marcus's words. "Was one of the people who betrayed him Mary?"

"Yes." He drank several swallows of tea.

She would have questioned him further had he not placed a finger to his lips and looked pointedly at the back door.

Sarah swiveled in her seat, waiting.

A low howling that really did sound like a wolf filtered in, accompanied by the rumble of Roland's voice.

The door swung inward and Roland entered, carrying a gray tabby that looked like it wasn't yet full grown. The fur on its striped and speckled back was bristling as it licked its lips repeatedly. One last howl escaped it before Roland closed the door, locked it, and set his burden gently on the floor.

"Was it a raccoon?" Sarah asked and smiled when he rolled his eyes.

"The biggest damned raccoon I've ever seen. I'm fairly certain it was rabid, but did that deter him? No."

The cocky little cat trotted into the kitchen ahead of him,

then stopped short when he saw her and Marcus, nearly tripping Roland.

"Damn it, Nietzsche."

Laughing, Sarah made kissy noises to draw him nearer. Nietzsche regarded her uncertainly and slunk closer to Roland.

"He isn't used to strangers," Roland said apologetically. "He'll warm up to you once his belly is full and his insatiable curiosity kicks in." Reaching up, he pulled a combination food and water dish down off the top of the refrigerator.

Sarah gathered her dirty dishes, stacked Roland's on top of them, and carried them to the sink as Roland filled one bowl with water and the other with canned food that smelled very strongly of what could only be liver. After peeling off the label, he rinsed the can out and dropped it in a recycle bin hidden inside one of the lower cabinets.

Marcus followed and added his dishes to the pile in the sink. "I didn't ask earlier. Is it okay if I stay the night, or do you want me to hit the road?"

Roland bent to put the dish on the floor. "Stay. We'll give you a ride home tomorrow night."

We.

"Thanks, man."

Sarah smiled when Nietzsche began to hungrily devour his stinky meal.

Roland patted his striped head, then straightened and looked at Marcus. "How's the knee?"

"Hurts like hell. I think I'm going to call it a night."

Sarah and Roland bade him goodnight, then turned their attention to the dirty dishes.

"I'll take care of this," Roland said right about the time she realized he didn't have a dishwasher and would be doing them by hand. "Why don't you go relax in the living room? It's been a long, difficult day."

"Long day" was an understatement. It felt like insomnia

had shoved her out of bed and driven her to go out and start digging a veggie garden weeks ago, not this morning.

And difficult?

Yes, parts of it had been scary as hell. Several parts, in fact. But she had really enjoyed the quieter times she had spent with Roland today . . . when it had been just the two of them, chatting and getting to know each other without the immortal revelations and vampires-trying-to-kill-you stuff interfering.

She wouldn't mind recapturing some of that and maybe learning more about him.

"That's okay. I'd rather be in here with you."

She smiled when he looked at her with *Why the hell would you want to be with me?* stamped across his forehead and reached for a green and yellow sponge.

The man truly didn't know his own appeal.

Normally, doing the dishes was one of the most tedious tasks Sarah performed each day. (Her little house didn't have a dishwasher because there simply wasn't room.) But, standing side by side with Roland, her shoulder touching his arm, their fingers brushing each time he handed her a soapy dish to rinse and place in the drainer, she had to admit it could be fun.

Roland was quiet at first, almost shy, making her wonder just how isolated a life he had led. Seth and Marcus had both nagged him about being reclusive. Was she really the only guest he had willingly brought here? Did he have no friends with whom he could kick back and relax?

Sarah suspected the answer was no and didn't think there had been a great deal of happiness in his long life. Whenever she made him laugh, it emerged as that sort of rusty chuckle as though he had almost forgotten how to do it.

"Thank you for letting me stay with you, Roland."

"You're welcome." He met her gaze from the corner of his eye and sent her a faint smile. "Much more welcome than Marcus."

She grinned.

Electricity skittered up her arm when he placed a couple of sudsy forks in her hand, his fingers stroking her palm as they withdrew.

"You seemed rather . . . emphatic in your refusal to stay with your family," he mentioned cautiously.

"Yeah, I kinda got shafted in the family department."

"How so?"

Sarah grimaced. "When my mother was eighteen, she had the not-very-original idea to get pregnant on purpose in order to trap her boyfriend into marrying her. Her boyfriend told her to kiss his ass, walked away without a backward glance, and nine months later my brother Jason was born. When she was twenty, she decided to try again with man number two, who hung in there for a few miserable months, then left before I was born. After that—though there were no more children, thank goodness—it was one man after another after another. Some were nice to me and Jason. Some were indifferent. Some were physically or verbally abusive. It didn't exactly endear her to me."

Roland's face darkened. "I know this is a personal question, but did any of them . . . ?"

"Abuse me sexually?"

He nodded.

"No." Sarah accepted another fork from him. "Although there was one she started bringing home when I was thirteen . . ." She shuddered, remembering. "He had a way of looking at me that made my skin crawl. Mom dumped him fairly quickly."

"Good."

"She didn't dump him because she was afraid he might hurt me. She dumped him because she was jealous. She accused me of intentionally trying to steal him away from her."

Roland paused in his washing and stared down at her in apparent disbelief.

Sarah shrugged. "My mother is one of those women who

refuses to grow up. When Jason and I were in high school, she wore my clothes, tried to act like a teenager, embarrassed the hell out of Jason if he brought a girl home, and hit on all of my dates. Not that there were many. I avoided dating completely once I realized she was going to try to seduce every boy who showed an interest in me."

He grunted. "I've met a few of those over the centuries."

"And as if that weren't bad enough," Sarah continued, "the woman couldn't hold down a job for more than a year at a stretch. We were always short on money. And once Jason and I started working as teenagers, she decided *mooching* off of us was a lot easier than supporting us. She basically made our lives miserable. I couldn't get out fast enough and moved away to college as soon as I graduated high school."

"I don't blame you. What about your brother?"

She sighed. "My brother became an alcoholic and beats his wife, who refuses to leave him. I cut ties with all of them a long time ago."

Silently, he handed her a glass.

She gave him a guarded look. "Aren't you going to tell me I'm a horrible person for turning my back on them?"

"No, I don't buy into that *you have to love them because you're related to them* tripe. Life is short. At least for you humans. Too short to waste on people who treat you badly and do nothing but make you miserable."

The tension in her eased. "There don't seem to be very many people out there who agree with that."

"More than you might think." He handed her another glass, his shoulder rubbing hers. Or rather his arm. She was about a foot shorter than him. "Besides, I know how much families can suck."

She eyed him curiously. "Lousy parents?"

"Lousy brother," he corrected, passing her the last glass, and grimly met her inquiring gaze. "My brother is the one who arranged for me to be captured by the vampire who transformed me."

Shock ripped through Sarah as she stared up at him. She had assumed Roland had been the random victim of some vampire lost to madness and bloodlust, not gift-wrapped and handed over to one by a family member.

"How could he do that to you?" she whispered, appalled.

"Very easily, as it turned out. I trusted him implicitly."

What a terrible betrayal. Marcus had told her Roland had been royally screwed over three times. This had to have been one of them.

"Did you ever find out why he did it?"

"I was the heir. He was the younger son. When my father died, I inherited the title, the lands, and all the wealth. I had everything Edward wanted."

"But that's how it *was* back then. I mean, it couldn't have come as any surprise to him. And there were other ways he could have gained lands and money."

"None so expedient as getting rid of me, however. I wasn't the first heir to become the victim of a younger brother's envy." He shook his head. "He was good, I'll give him that. Not once did he reveal his resentment in any way. He wasn't distant or angry or bitter. He was a good friend to me. My closest friend. I trusted him more than any other and would probably have slain any man who questioned his honor."

Wiping her wet hand on her jeans, Sarah touched his arm. "Some people are superlative actors, never showing those around them their true thoughts."

"Edward could've won an Oscar. Even after I was captured, I thought him innocent. He was there when it happened. We were on our way to court when the vampire's human minions attacked. I knew Edward couldn't fight worth a damn, so I sent him fleeing into the forest while I cut down as many as I could. I was so glad he got away safely."

Though he spoke softly, there was a wealth of anger and hurt in his words. His brother's deceit had profoundly scarred him.

"It wasn't until I escaped that I learned the truth."

Sarah frowned. "If he wanted you dead, why did he have the vampire transform you?"

"He didn't. He assumed the vampire would kill me and leave my corpse for the wolves. And the vampire would have, I'm sure, had I not been one of the *gifted ones.*"

"I don't understand. Did that make the vampire change his mind?"

"No." Roland handed her the last fork to rinse. "There are two ways humans and *gifted ones* can be transformed. The first, and most merciful, is for the vampire to drain them almost to the point of death, then infuse them with his blood until they are replenished. In this way, the virus invades the body in such numbers that the change is swift."

When Sarah finished rinsing the fork and placed it in the drainer with the rest of the dinner dishes, the two of them took turns washing the soap off their hands and drying them on a clean hand towel.

"What's the other way?"

"To feed from the human repeatedly. When a vampire or immortal drinks from a human, the human is exposed to the virus in trace amounts. Unless the human's immune system has already been compromised—by HIV, for example—a single bite isn't a problem. The immune system can fight it off in small quantities, but it takes a hit while doing so. Now, because this virus is so different, the body can't produce memory B cells for it the way it can for the flu or the measles and—"

"What are memory B cells?"

"Memory B cells enable the immune system to easily recognize and swiftly defeat a virus the next time one is exposed to it. So if the human is bitten and the vampiric virus attacks again, without those memory B cells, the immune system doesn't remember it, must start from scratch to fight it off again, and is weakened more. With repeated feedings, eventually the immune system is crippled enough that the virus destroys it completely and takes its place."

"Does it . . . does the change hurt?"

"The first method isn't that bad. I've heard it's a bit like having the flu and is over in two or three days' time. The second method, however, makes the human very ill. Dangerously high fevers. Delirium. Severe muscle and stomach cramps. Vomiting. Convulsions. The pain becomes so unbearable it makes one pray for death and, depending on how often the vampire drinks from you, can last anywhere from a few weeks to months."

The expression on his face when he mentioned praying for death was so haunted. Sarah feared he was speaking from experience, not merely reciting symptoms he had observed in others. "Is that how it happened to you?"

Turning to face her, he leaned one hip against the counter. "Yes. After my capture, I was taken to an isolated castle that looked as if it had leapt from the pages of a gothic novel and was manacled to a wall in the dungeon. There were six others there, both men and women. Every night the vampire came down and fed from us. A different victim for each day of the week. We were his own personal blood bank, given just enough food and stagnant water to keep us alive."

She couldn't bear to think of him that way. Chained to a wall, suffering such torturous pain. "Did the others turn?"

"We all did in time. Because of the conditions in which we were kept, the madness that usually seeps into vampires slowly struck my cell mates almost immediately. When it did, the vampire killed them and replaced them with new victims. But I was a *gifted one.* My body didn't react the same way theirs did. I didn't become vampire. I became immortal, though I admit there were days I wished I *could* seek refuge in madness."

"How long did it take?" she asked. How long had he suffered?

"Six months, give or take a week. Had he fed from me daily, it would have happened sooner. But my immune system had a week to recover between feedings and, because of my gifts, I healed swifter and more fully than the others."

Six months.

"The rest continued to weaken after their transformation. They couldn't seem to stomach food and had no blood to nourish them. I could still eat and naively thought that meant I could yet be saved. My senses sharpened. My body cramped, needing blood, but the other symptoms faded away. My strength returned, increasing until I was able to yank the chains that bound me straight out of the wall."

"Did you kill the vampire?"

Slowly, he nodded. "I killed the vampire *and* his minions, set free those victims who were salvageable, put the others out of their misery, then razed the castle and went home, where I was ultimately forced to face the truth of my brother's perfidy."

Sarah didn't know how he had survived it.

Well, she knew how he had survived it physically. The more advanced DNA he couldn't explain. But how had he survived it mentally? Emotionally? He must have been clinging by a thread.

And then to find out his brother had engineered it all . . .

Curling her hand around his strong biceps, Sarah rose onto her toes and kissed his freshly shaven cheek.

Chapter 9

Roland's pulse increased as warmth unfurled in his chest like a cat awakening from a nap. Sarah returned her heels to the floor and gazed up at him with tenderness softening her hazel eyes.

"Why did you do that?" he asked, reaching up to touch the tingling skin her lips had brushed.

She smiled. "I wanted to. And you looked like you might need it."

Had he? The old anger had risen up to choke him as it always did when he thought of Edward. Yet it had dissolved the instant she kissed him, her delectable scent sweeping over him, intoxicating him.

He *had* needed it. Needed that and so much more. He needed her. He needed . . .

Slowly lowering his head, Roland claimed her lips in an excruciatingly gentle exploration.

Her breath caught. Eyelids drifting closed, she parted her lips and invited him within.

Roland eagerly complied, his tongue gliding in to stroke and tease hers. His body tightened as lust hit him hard. Touching her sides just beneath her arms, he drew her nearer. She was so small. So delicate. He could feel the faint ridges of her ribs beneath his fingers as his thumbs brushed the sides of her full breasts.

Sarah thought her heart might burst from her chest as Roland's lips seduced hers, first gently, then hungrily, speeding her pulse. Fire danced through her as his thumbs stroked the sides of her breasts, straying ever closer to the sensitive peaks. Again she rose onto her toes so he wouldn't have to bend down so far. Smoothing her hands up his chest and around his neck, she leaned into him and buried her fingers in his hair, clutching a silky fistful.

He wrapped his arms around her and pressed her to him, a low growl rumbling in his throat. Sarah winced when one of his hands slid up her back and put fleeting pressure on the large bruise a tree had spawned. At least, she assumed there was a bruise. She had forgotten to look earlier, but it hurt badly enough.

His other hand followed the same path, triggering the same sharp pain.

A niggling thought pricked her.

Dragging her lips from his, she turned her head aside and tried to clear her muddled thoughts.

Roland merely kissed a path along her jaw and down her neck, making her knees go weak.

"Wait," she protested feebly.

His body hard and throbbing with need, Roland drew his tongue across the pulse that beat rapidly just beneath the soft skin at the base of Sarah's neck. "You smell so good," he whispered hoarsely.

"That isn't me. It's your expensive bath products."

He shook his head. "It's you." He drew in a long, deep breath and held it a moment. It was stronger now and mingled with the even more enticing scent of her budding arousal. "You could set me down blindfolded in the middle of a packed football stadium and I could find you by your scent alone. No perfume on the planet can compare."

She tasted good, too, he discovered, brushing his lips over

her soft skin. And there was so much more of her he wanted to taste. To feel. To stroke. Explore.

Resenting the T-shirt that kept him from touching bare flesh, he caressed her back and sought her succulent lips once more.

"Wait," she said again, pressing against his chest. "Where are your hands?"

A groan of frustrated desire welled up inside him, but he didn't let it escape. Swearing silently, Roland forced himself to take a step back, held his hands out to his sides where she could see them, and wished fervently that she had waited a little longer to come to her senses. They were both breathing hard as she stared up at him with lips red and swollen from his kisses. Her lovely breasts rose and fell rapidly beneath the cotton of her T-shirt, making him clench his hands into fists to avoid reaching for her.

He supposed he should apologize. He had taken an innocent gesture of affection and turned it into something else entirely. Not what she had expected, he was sure.

"Were you healing me again?" she demanded breathlessly.

He blinked at the odd question. "What?"

"Your hands were on my back. Were you trying to heal me on the sly again?"

He frowned. "What's wrong with your back?"

Her fingertips still touched his chest, holding him at bay. She waved the other hand dismissively. "Just answer the question. The last time you kissed me, you only did it to distract me while you healed me."

She didn't really believe that, did she?

The suspicion and hurt reflected in her eyes suggested she did.

Well, hell.

"Distracting you while I healed you was only an excuse. I've wanted to kiss you ever since I woke up with your beautiful body stretched atop mine and your enchanting scent making my head swim." He paused. "No. No, that's not true. I've wanted to kiss you ever since you held me in your kitchen after helping me remove the spikes. That was a bit earlier."

Her hands falling limply to her sides, she swallowed visibly. "Really?"

He nodded slowly, then took a step closer as a spark of heat returned to her eyes.

When she backed into the counter, he braced his hands on either side of her, trapping her in between. "You don't know how much I regret passing out this morning. Missing the feel of your hands bathing my naked flesh." Leaning down until his lips nearly touched the sensitive skin beneath her ear, he drew in a slow, deep breath. "I love your scent." He let his lips follow a path down her neck to the hollow where it met her shoulder, still close but not touching, breath warming her skin. "Your every touch inflames me, leaves me hard and aching, unable to hide my reaction to you." Raising his head, he stared down at her. "Can you truly not know how much I want you?"

Reaching up, she rested her palm against his cheek. Roland covered her small hand with his and held it there, savoring her touch.

"Your eyes are glowing again," she whispered.

"They'll always glow when I want you." He hesitated. "Does it . . . frighten you?" *Disgust you?*

Smiling, she shook her head. "I think it's beautiful." Her hand moved beneath his and he released it, expecting her to withdraw. Instead she curled her fingers around his neck and drew him toward her. Leaning forward, she brushed her lips against the base of his throat, tasting him with her tongue.

Roland did groan then, pulse leaping, and rested his hands on her hips, gripping the material of her jeans tightly.

She placed her other hand on his chest and slid it down, burning a path across his stomach, making the muscles there quiver until she was cupping the heavy erection that strained against the front of his slacks.

Igniting at her bold caress, he stared down at her and saw the glow from his own eyes reflected in hers.

"I want you, too," she murmured.

Roland swooped down and captured her lips, devouring her even as the hunger devoured him from the inside out. Finding her breast with one large hand, he stroked a hardened nipple through the thin T-shirt and lace that covered it.

She tore her lips from his with a gasp and began to stroke him through his slacks. "What are you doing to me?"

He licked and kissed a fevered path down her throat. "If you have to ask, I'm not doing it right."

She responded with a sound that was part laugh, part moan. "If you weren't doing it right, I wouldn't be this tempted."

Continuing to stroke and squeeze him, she drove him nearly mad with lust.

Giving her nipple a pinch, he poised his mouth above her other breast. "How tempted are you?"

"*Extremely* tempted."

Roland fastened his mouth onto her breast, dampening the material of her T-shirt, finding the hardened peak and teasing it with his teeth.

She groaned, inflaming him further. When she abandoned his erection, he nearly protested. Then both of her small hands reached around, grabbed his ass, and pulled him flush against her as she rose onto her toes.

"I'm not like this," she gasped.

Leaning his body into hers, he slid his free hand down the outside of her thigh, tucked his hand beneath her knee, and drew her leg up over his hip. "I like you like this," he murmured around her breast. He could feel her heart beating wildly in her chest.

He rocked against her, urged on by those hands on his ass and her leg over his hip.

"You don't—" She moaned, arched into him. "Y-you don't understand. I don't"—another gasp—"I don't have sex with men I've just met."

He slid the hand at her knee up her thigh, down over her lovely ass and farther until he was stroking her hot, moist center through the damp material of her jeans. "By sex I assume you mean intercourse?"

"Yesss."

He raised his head and met her hungry eyes. "No problem. I can give you orgasms without it."

Sarah stared into those glowing eyes, then grabbed a fistful of his hair and dragged his mouth to hers. His fingers continued to stroke her through her jeans as his body thrust against hers, increasing the pressure, raising the pleasure, making her wild with need.

She began an almost frantic foray with her hands, gliding them over his back, his arms, his chest, feeling the hard, heavy muscle ripple beneath her palms. His lips left hers, sweeping down her neck, briefly closing over the pulse that raced just beneath the skin before returning to her breast. Her head fell back.

The hand teasing her other breast slid around her back and crushed her to him.

Pain burst through her in a shattering wave. Sarah stiffened and thought she may have cried out.

His head jerked up, his eyes seeking hers.

Blackness swam at the edges of her vision.

She didn't know what he saw in her face, but his hands left her in a rush.

Concern flooding his features, he eased her thigh off his hip and lowered her foot to the floor. "Sarah?"

She shook her head, unable to speak, unable to breathe it hurt so badly. Tears welled in her eyes.

"Where does it hurt?"

She shook her head again.

Gently cupping her face in one large palm, he held her gaze as the amber glow in his began to fade to brown. "Breathe," he commanded softly.

She did, each breath choppy and torturous, realizing only

then that she was clutching fistfuls of his T-shirt. Jeeze, it hurt. Every time she inhaled, it felt as though someone were pounding her back with a sledgehammer.

His thumbs brushed aside a few tears that escaped as she gradually began to recover. "If you can't tell me," he enjoined quietly, "show me. Is it your upper or lower back?"

Had the pain not begun to mellow from agony to hurts-like-hell, she probably would have told him, knowing he could end it. But she remained silent, breath coming a little easier now.

Perhaps her expression revealed that it was no longer that she *couldn't* tell him, but *wouldn't,* because she could actually see the frustration well up within him and spill over his handsome features.

"Don't be stubborn. I'm at full strength. It won't harm me."

"Yes, it will." Uncurling her hands, she let them fall to her sides and did her best to appear normal.

Roland's jaw clenched as he released her and took a step back. "Don't make me regret being honest with you, Sarah."

Clearly he wasn't buying it. "You said it hurts you when you heal, that you absorb both the wound and the pain."

"It is fleeting!" he practically shouted. "Do you have any idea how much pain I have suffered over the centuries?"

"Yes, and I don't want to be the source of any more," she insisted.

He started to respond, then clamped his lips shut. Silence filled the kitchen as he visibly wrestled with his temper. "Is that the *true* reason you don't want me to heal you? Or is there another?"

She frowned. What other reason could there be?

Before she could ask, he turned and strode, fuming, from the room.

Nietzsche, seated beside his now-empty bowl, gave her a condemning look, then began to groom himself.

She was still standing there, unconsciously staring at the cat, when Marcus poked his head in a few minutes later.

He took one look at her face and sighed. "That's what I thought." He entered the kitchen, his upper body bare, one hand holding a sheet wrapped around his waist. Pink scars that only hours ago had been open cuts marred the muscles of his chest, abdomen, and arms. "Here's the thing," he said. "When you reject Roland's gift, you're rejecting him."

How did he know . . . ?

Dread filled her. "How much did you hear?"

He smiled. "Enough. Sorry about that. Couldn't help it."

Heat flooded her face. She had forgotten about their hyper-acute hearing. "I'm not rejecting his gift," she said, trying not to think about the heavy breathing and moaning he must have heard.

"That probably isn't how he sees it." Coming closer, he leaned against the cabinets beside her. "Look, we immortals tend to be a little . . . sensitive about our gifts. Every one of us has been feared, ostracized, or even abused because of them in the past. And not just by strangers. If you let Roland touch you to bring you pleasure"—her flush deepened—"but don't let him touch you to heal you with his gift, what else is he supposed to think but that that part of him repels you?"

She threw her hands up. "That I don't want to hurt him!" Why was that so hard for them to understand?

He snorted. "Sarah, the vampire who transformed Roland didn't just feed on him, he tortured him. For months." Roland had left out that part of the story. "In comparison, healing whatever wounds you have would hurt him about as much as removing a splinter. And the pain would be just as fleeting since he's at full strength and your wounds aren't life-threatening."

She eyed him uncertainly, thinking he must be exaggerating the part about it being so painless, but . . .

Did Roland really think that part of him repelled her?

"Besides," Marcus added, "healing you will bring him peace. I could feel his concern for you all the way from the guest room and I'm not even an empath."

She thought about it a moment longer, her back still screaming at her.

When you reject Roland's gift, you're rejecting him.

Nodding slowly, she touched Marcus's arm in a brief gesture of thanks, then left the kitchen.

Steaming water flowed into the whirlpool tub with a dim roar as Roland stood in the bathroom, a packet of herbs forgotten in one hand. Since Sarah had refused to let him heal her, he had intended to run a bath for her that would soothe her aches and bruises. But that may not be necessary now.

Bending, he turned off the tap, tossed the herbs onto the counter, and crossed to the doorway.

Sarah stood in the center of the bedroom, looking uncertain, apologetic, and pained. "I'm sorry. I didn't mean . . . I don't want you to think I . . ." She looked away, brow furrowing, then met his gaze once more. "Would you please heal my back, Roland?"

"Of course," he said, heart pounding as he strode toward her, not stopping until they nearly touched.

She had to tilt her head way back to look up at him. "I wasn't rejecting you," she said earnestly. "I just didn't want to cause you pain."

"Knowing you're suffering pains me more than healing your wounds would."

She nodded, swallowing. "Would you help me remove my shirt?"

He stayed her hands when she reached for the hem. "Let me close the door." He didn't want Marcus to catch a glimpse of her on his way back to the guest room.

When the door was closed and ensured their privacy, he rejoined her and reached for the hem of her T-shirt.

Raising her arms, she winced and bit her lip, holding her breath until he had dragged the shirt over her head and she could lower them again.

Ignoring her bountiful breasts, barely covered in black lace, Roland tossed the shirt aside and examined the pale bruises forming on her chest that she had failed to mention.

"These don't hurt that much," she said, following his gaze. "In the front, my arms caught the brunt of it and you healed them when you healed my cuts."

Remaining silent, he circled behind her so he could view the damage there, then swore foully. A bruise the width of his fist, already livid against her pale, pale skin, crossed her back from lower shoulder blade to shoulder blade. Narrower strips of bruises crisscrossed it. Still others polka-dotted the flesh in between, giving the illusion that she had been beaten, whipped, and stoned all at once.

His gaze dipped down to her bottom and beyond. "Is this all of it?" he asked grimly.

There was the slightest hesitation. "No, I pretty much hurt all over. Except for my hands."

Reaching around her, he unbuttoned, then unzipped, her jeans.

He heard her heart begin to pound a rapid rhythm as he tucked his thumbs in the sides and drew them down her legs. Her hand came to rest on his shoulder as she stepped out of them and kicked them aside.

Roland knelt there for a moment, fighting down the arousal that had never left him. Her body was all that he had known it would be. Slender. Toned. Muscles causing gentle ripples. Her hips were full, not boyishly skinny like so many actresses' hips were, and—with her breasts—formed a perfect hourglass. Her bottom was round and firm and, beneath her black bikini panties, probably just as bruised as the rest of her. Had it not been, he might have leaned forward and sunk his teeth in for a love bite.

Roland shook himself and shifted his focus to healing her. Wrapping his hands around one delicate ankle, he summoned the energy within him and felt heat blossom in his palms, then suffuse her skin, mending tissue and withdrawing pain. Up her calf and shin he slowly trailed them, over her knee to her thigh. The higher they climbed, the faster her heart beat.

Stopping just short of the panties, still damp from their love play, he began again at the other ankle. Her skin was velvety smooth, tempting him to linger, feeding the need that still rode him.

When both legs were healed, the pain and blotchy bruising erased, he fingered the top edge of her panties, then peeked at the bottom beneath. She was bruised there, too. Sarah offered no protest as he stood and slipped his hands beneath the scrap of fabric to cup her succulent flesh. He saw her throat work as she swallowed, her eyelids fluttering closed.

Energy sizzled, passed from him into her, imbued her with warmth, then returned to him carrying her pain. Marcus hadn't lied. Roland barely felt it, an ache he easily dismissed until he worked his way up her back to the place where it looked as if she had been hit with a baseball bat. The skin there wasn't merely bruised. It was puffy and swollen.

Even the lightest touch made her jump and clench the hands at her sides into fists.

"I'm sorry," he murmured. "I have to touch it to heal you."

She nodded.

It hurt more to heal this one. He was surprised she had been able to hide it from him and wished she would have let him attend to it earlier and spare her that. As the swelling decreased, the tension in her shoulders eased, pouring out of her like water. After another minute or two, the marks above it were gone as well and the perfection of her narrow back was restored.

Sarah sighed with relief as the last of her discomfort vanished. She thought that was the end of it, that Roland was finished. But just as she started to turn around, he moved closer, pressing his front to her back. His fingers slipped between her arms and her sides. Those large hands flowed over the twitching skin of her stomach and settled low over one hipbone.

A now familiar tingling heat filtered into her as he absorbed the bruise forming there. He nuzzled her ear with his lips as his hands caressed their way up to the ribs on her left side. Once the soreness she had forgotten there was healed, he slid his hands up the sides of her breasts to her chest and shoulders, then very slowly down over her upper arms, which sported quite a few faint bruises, particularly on the left side where her body had slammed into the car door as the Prius had careened to a halt.

By the time the last bruise, cut, or ache was healed, there was very little of her that had gone untouched. It was almost as if Roland were not only healing her, but learning her—every curve, dip, and valley—much as a sculptor would a subject he wished to commit to memory so that he might reproduce it later with clay or stone. It wasn't sexual (though heat that had nothing to do with his *gift* lingered long after his hands had moved on). But tender. So tender.

And intense.

When he finished, he surprised her by wrapping his arms around her shoulders, just above her breasts, and resting his cheek atop her hair. Peace filtered through her, as though they had stood like this many times, basking in each other's nearness.

Reaching up, she lightly grasped the arms crossed over her chest. "Thank you, Roland."

He nodded, a contented sigh ruffling her bangs. "Sleep with me tonight," he murmured, so softly she nearly missed it.

With his supernatural hearing, he probably had no difficulty hearing the increase in her pulse rate.

Leaning to one side, she looked up at him over her shoulder.

His eyes found hers, reading the question in them. "Just sleep," he promised. "I want to be near you."

And she knew that it was not for the purpose of protection, but because he felt the same pull she did.

"Okay."

He pressed a light kiss to her temple, then stepped back and dragged his T-shirt over his head.

Sarah swallowed and decided she would forgo the nightgown she had brought with her and sleep in her underwear so she could feel that warm, hard, muscled flesh pressed against her with as little material between them as possible.

They took turns in the bathroom, Sarah first. As she climbed into the bed, she marveled at the soft white sheets and just how big the mattress was. It was comfortable, too, she discovered as she snuggled down against the pillows, wondering why the thought of sharing it with Roland didn't make her nervous.

Roland emerged from the bathroom, leaving the light on and the door cracked. "The dark curtains prevent sunlight from getting in, so it's pretty much pitch black in here with the light off. If you rise before me, I don't want you to trip and hurt yourself."

"Thank you."

He doffed his slacks and tossed them onto a chair. Clad only in black boxers, he crossed to the door, muscled thighs rippling with every movement, and flipped the overhead light off.

Sarah was glad the bathroom light was still on so she could watch him approach.

"I always sleep in the buff. Is that all right?"

She nodded and watched, breath held, as the boxers hit the floor. He was so beautiful.

The mattress dipped as he slid beneath the covers. Turning toward her, he propped himself on one elbow and studied her intently. Then, leaning down, he brushed her lips with a light kiss. "Goodnight, Sarah."

"Goodnight."

It felt like the most natural thing in the world when he

urged her to roll onto her side, facing away from him, and spooned up behind her. His chest was warm and solid at her back. His hips and thighs cradled hers. Even as the erection trapped against her bottom sped her pulse, exhaustion swept over her and seemed to seep into her very bones.

One of Roland's heavy arms circled her waist and held her tight against him as he buried his face in her hair.

Wrapped comfortably in his embrace, Sarah drifted into sleep.

Seth and David's search took them well outside the city of Houston. Venturing farther and farther west, they passed through grazing and farmlands and one small town after another until they thought they had finally found what they sought.

Seth stood in the shadows of numerous tall pine and oak trees. It wasn't even June and the hard clay soil beneath his boots was already cracked with drought. Pine cones, pine nettles, decayed leaves, and an abundance of acorns carpeted the bare ground where grass and weeds should have been growing, but couldn't. Though the hot, humid breeze carried with it many annoying mosquitoes, none buzzed around his tall, still frame.

Ten yards from the trees' edge stood a chain-link fence with razor wire strung across the top. A single two-lane road led in and out of a gated entrance guarded by men in camouflage carrying assault rifles. Beyond lay an open field the size of a football stadium, a mostly empty parking lot, and a large three-story structure that was curiously devoid of windows, save those that bordered the front entrance.

There were plenty of surveillance cameras anchored to the building's roof and more heavily armed men in camouflage on the grounds.

David emerged from the darkness behind Seth without a

single rustle of leaves or snapping of twig. "This is it," he said softly. "I'm certain of it. The woman is being kept in there."

Seth nodded. Her cries were so loud here he had to partially block them out to keep them from distracting him.

"I circled the building," his friend continued. "The fence has no weak points. Not that a fence could stop us. Guards walk the perimeter on all sides. As far as I could see, there are no blind spots in the video surveillance."

We are here, Seth told the woman soothingly. *We will be with you soon, little one, and will take you far away from here.*

The screaming stopped, the silence that followed almost painful in its absence.

Had she understood him? Could she sense that they were near?

Just a little longer, then you will be free.

She spoke an unintelligible sentence or two. Then her words dissolved into whimpers of pain.

David cocked his head to one side. "Does the fact that it's guarded either by the military or by mercenaries concern you at all?"

"A little," Seth answered honestly. "Not because we cannot breech it, but because I cannot puzzle it all out. What is this place? It's not a prison or a military base, yet soldiers guard it. Why is she kept here? Whoever she is, they have been torturing her for months. Why would they do that?"

"Who are *they?*" David posed rhetorically.

"Exactly. What information could she possibly have that would make this acceptable and why the hell would she continue to withhold it?"

"You don't think she's a vampire, do you? Or an immortal who was taken without our knowledge? Because if the government ever finds out we're real, we're going to have some serious problems on our hands."

"If she were vampire or immortal, I would understand what she is saying."

"I can't decipher her speech either and I know almost as many languages as you do. Hers doesn't sound at all familiar."

"Well, we'll know the answers soon enough."

David nodded slowly. "This is going to get ugly."

"Most likely," Seth agreed. "Be careful not to let any of the bullets pass through you and hit our mystery lady."

"Of course."

"Shall we?"

While the guards continued their slow stroll about the building, oblivious to the encroaching menace in the shadows, Seth's and David's silhouettes blurred, then shifted, becoming something altogether different.

Sarah jerked awake, heart pounding as it often did when something yanked her out of a sound sleep.

What had done it?

Rolling onto her back, she turned her head.

Roland was sprawled on his stomach, arms tucked beneath his pillow, sound asleep. He looked so sweet, so boyishly handsome, she had to smile.

Until a *thunk* came from the front of the house.

Roland didn't stir as she slipped out of bed and hurriedly donned her T-shirt and jeans.

It was probably just Marcus up and about or Nietzsche getting into something he shouldn't, but she wasn't going to take any chances. She would check just in case.

Opening the bedroom door, she crept down the hallway.

A quick peek showed her an empty living room. Sarah continued through it and into the dining room, then the kitchen, keeping an eye out for Nietzsche.

Another *thunk* sounded, louder this time. It was the sound of a car door closing.

The sun had been up for at least an hour, so it wasn't vampires.

Sarah told herself not to panic. It could always be UPS or FedEx or the postman making a delivery.

Two more *thunks* sounded.

Or not. Postal delivery men and women did not arrive in groups of four.

"Pop the trunk," a man called out.

Gravel crunched as another car pulled up out front.

Oh, crap.

Grabbing the butcher knife from the dish drainer, Sarah ran for the bedroom. She could hear multiple male voices now as four more car doors opened and closed.

Roland's enemy worked with humans (if you could call those two flunkies she had hit with her shovel humans). He must have sent more here to kill Roland while daylight weakened him.

"Roland!" she hissed in a loud whisper, hurrying into the room and around the foot of the bed. "Roland, wake up!" Grabbing his shoulder, she shook him hard.

Oh, no! She'd forgotten about Marcus!

She glanced toward the bedroom door, then squeaked when Roland turned onto his back, grabbed her by the throat, flipped her over him, and slammed her down on the bed so fast her head swam.

His hand tightened, robbing her of air. His face, above hers, was twisted in a snarl, fangs extended, eyes glowing brightly.

"It's me," she croaked, struggling to breathe.

He blinked. The snarl vanished. "Sarah?" His grip loosened abruptly. "I'm sorry. Did I hurt you?" His fingers stroked her abused throat. "I should have told you that I sleep much more deeply when I'm healing from an injury and don't react well to being startled awake."

Before she could answer, his gaze strayed to the knife she clutched, then returned to hers filled with betrayal.

Okay, he had woken up with her standing over him with a knife in her hand. It looked damning, true. But the fact that he thought her capable of killing him really pissed her off. Especially after what had passed between them last night.

Sarah placed her empty hand in the center of his chest and shoved. "I didn't come in here to kill you, damn it!" she whispered with a snarl of her own. "I came in here to warn you!"

Rolling out of bed, he rose smoothly to his feet.

Far less graceful, Sarah scooted off the bed beneath his watchful gaze. "I'm pretty sure your enemy has found you. A noise woke me. I went to check it out and heard two cars pull up out front. At least eight men got out, by the sounds of it."

"How did they know where to find me?" he asked, the implication being she had told them.

"Ooh, I am *so* going to kick your ass for that later. I don't *know* how they knew. I don't even know where *here* is. I was unconscious when you brought me here. Remember?"

Roland had forgotten that. Grabbing the slacks and T-shirt he had discarded last night, he tugged them on and crossed to the armoire. Uncertain what to think, he yanked the doors open and began plucking weapons from the substantial display within.

Sarah joined him, stiff with indignation. The part of him that felt remorse for accusing her vied with that which silently suggested she could have seen his address on a piece of mail and called someone while he slept.

"They're human," she snapped, tossing the knife inside and grabbing a Sig Sauer P226 X-Five Tactical 9mm and two twenty-round clips. "Use guns."

Lips clamped tight with fury, she turned and stomped toward the door.

He grabbed a Glock 10mm. "Where are you going?"

"To warn Marcus."

"The hell you are."

The front door could burst open at any moment. He wasn't about to let Sarah put herself in those men's sights.

Catching up with her before she could take another step, he curled a hand around her upper arm.

Jerked to a halt, she turned on him and growled, "Don't touch me."

Oh yeah. She definitely had a temper and he had clumsily ignited it.

But now wasn't the time.

Roland yanked her toward him. "Look, this isn't the first time I've awoken to find the woman I care about standing over me with a knife in her hand. I drew a faulty conclusion. I was wrong. Be pissed at me later. Right now you need to get your ass in the bathroom, put your back to the wall either in the tub or behind the toilet, and shoot anyone who comes through the door who isn't me or Marcus."

He pushed her none too gently in that direction as Marcus hurried into the room, hair tousled with sleep, completely naked. "What's going on?"

Sarah stopped and gaped.

Roland grimaced and threw up a hand. "Put some fucking clothes on before I go blind."

Marcus rolled his eyes. "My clothes are a torn, bloody mess. I was hoping I could borrow some of yours."

Grumbling, Roland crossed to the closet, displeased to notice Sarah still staring. "Sarah, get in the bathroom."

He almost smiled when the abrupt command yanked her attention back to him.

"I'm not your dog to do your bidding," she snapped.

Well, hell.

Marcus raised one eyebrow. "Trouble in paradise?"

A pair of jeans and a sweatshirt hit him in the face. "Shut up."

While Marcus bent to pull on the jeans, Roland returned to stand in front of the petite, seething beauty he was so smitten with, effectively blocking her view.

"I'm trying to protect you, Sarah."

Some of the anger left her face, allowing him to see the

fear beneath. "I know you are, but I'm not going to cower in the bathroom and let you two take on all of them yourselves when I can help. I told you, I'm very good with a gun."

"How many are we talking?" Marcus asked as he zipped his pants.

"At least eight," Roland told him.

Sarah took a step closer, her body nearly touching his, and tilted her head back to look up at him. "Let me help you, Roland. Please."

He couldn't bear it. He had to touch her.

Slipping his free arm around her waist, he drew her up against him, dipped his head, and took her lips in a long, thorough kiss that resurrected memories of the previous night.

Her face was flushed, her pupils dilated, when he released her.

"Stay low," he instructed. "And remember that bullets go through walls. You don't have to be exposed for them to shoot you."

"Or vice versa," Marcus added, dragging the sweatshirt over his head and raking a hand through his hair. "Oh shit. Do you smell that?"

Roland had caught the pungent scent a half second before Marcus had spoken. Fury swept through him. "Yes."

Sarah inhaled deeply. "What is it? I can't smell it."

"Gasoline," they both answered grimly.

Roland urged Sarah over to the wall beside the door frame. "Remember what I said. Stay low. Shoot as many as you can. If they set the place on fire, go out the window and hide in the forest."

"What about you? It's morning. The sun's up."

"We're both back to full strength. We can tolerate brief exposure to sunlight."

Marcus stuffed his pockets with knives, throwing stars, and ammunition, grabbed a shotgun, and left the room.

Roland returned to the armoire, stuck several daggers into

his back pockets, added several clips for the Glock, then headed for the doorway.

Sarah watched his approach with wide eyes full of trepidation.

As he drew even with her, he paused, kissed her again, then pressed his forehead to hers. "Don't get hurt."

"Be safe."

Roland could hear the men speaking in low murmurs as they doused the exterior of his home with gasoline. They must think immortals lapsed into the same near comatose state vampires did when the sun rose.

"Don't light it yet, man," one said. "Remember? We're supposed to go in and get the Guardian's whore out first."

"What for?"

"Hell if I know. But no way am I fuckin' up the way Derek and Bobby did."

Leaving Sarah, Roland strode down the hallway and entered the living room. His eyes met Marcus's. This was sounding more and more like a personal vendetta.

He had assumed that, like the rest of his kind, Bastien simply despised all Immortal Guardians and had thought to bag himself one. But this vamp had tried to kill him two nights in a row, tenaciously tracked him to his home so he could send his human minions to finish the job, and now he wanted Sarah because he thought she was Roland's woman?

"What are you doin'?" another asked.

"Pickin' the locks."

"I thought we were just gonna break the door down."

"Nuh-uh. These guys are supposed to be dead to the world, but I don't want to take any chances. We're goin' in quiet."

Roland held up his left hand, fingers extended, touched the tip of his middle finger to his thumb, indicating eight, and pointed to the door. Then, pointing to the east side of the house, he held up two fingers.

Marcus nodded and held up two, pointing to the west side.

Melting back into the shadows, they waited.

Chapter 10

Sarah's heart was racing, her hands clammy, as she listened to the front door creak open. Two men cried out simultaneously. Victims of knives or throwing stars?

Gunfire erupted, so loud she jumped a foot. (She always wore protective earmuffs at the firing range.) Squatting with both hands wrapped tightly about the Sig Sauer's grip, she peeked around the doorjamb.

What she could see of the living room was utter chaos.

No wonder Roland and Marcus had looked more angry than concerned that they might be killed. The two of them moved so swiftly that, in the split second it took the humans to aim their weapons, the immortals could leap across the room, leaving them firing either at empty space or their own men.

A tall, thin man stepped into view and stayed there. Sarah raised the 9mm, sighted down the barrel . . . but hesitated to pull the trigger. Roland and Marcus kept swooping past in a blur and she was terrified of accidentally hitting one of them.

Her target glanced up, saw her, and yelled, "She's in the back!" over the nearly constant gunfire. He took a step forward and went rigid, the hilt of one of Roland's daggers protruding from his throat.

Another man dove into the hallway and ran toward her.

Sarah fired three shots and he collapsed on the floor. Two more followed. The one in front raised a .45.

Sarah ducked back and sank lower as he fired. Wood splintered from the door frame above her head.

Scooting backward, she aimed at the wall between her and the hallway and fired several shots in the men's direction. One cried out and created a series of thuds as he went down. The other burst into the bedroom, firing as he came.

Had she been standing, he would have hit her.

Instead, Sarah took him out with a bullet to the head.

"*Sarah!*" Roland bellowed from the living room.

"I'm fine!" she shouted back, unable to look away from the dead man's blank stare.

There were tiny pauses in the shooting as the men ran out of ammunition and replaced their mags. These were, more often than not, punctuated by screams of pain as Roland and Marcus took advantage of the lull and the men's divided attention and struck.

Even though bullets from the other room would sporadically burst through the wall above her with a spray of Sheetrock, Sarah began to think they might just make it through this intact.

Then the acrid scent of smoke teased her nostrils, spurring an even greater influx of fear.

The house was on fire.

Roland swore as two more bullets ripped through his shoulder and arm. Humans had been a lot easier to defeat before semiautomatic and automatic weapons had been invented.

When the bastards had registered that the two Immortal Guardians they had come to kill were not only awake but also as strong and fast and powerful as they were at night, the minions had decided their best bet at making it out of this alive was to back themselves against the front wall and spray the room with bullets.

It was a very effective strategy. Even with his preternatural speed, Roland couldn't get near them without being hit. He only hoped Sarah was staying low in the bedroom.

As Roland yanked the gun from one man's hand, turned it back on him, and fired multiple times, he saw another duck out the front door.

The sun had risen over an hour ago. The last thing Roland should do with blood loss weakening him and his body struggling to heal the eight or nine bullet wounds he now sported was expose himself to direct sunlight. But he had no choice.

In the blink of an eye, he was outside, squinting against the bright light and gritting his teeth as his skin instantly began to redden and burn. The man he had followed gaped at him as flames leapt up from the lighter he had dropped and rapidly spread around the gasoline-soaked side of the house.

"But it's daylight," the man blurted stupidly as Roland closed in on him.

"Surprise, asshole."

The idiot's cry for help ended when Roland snapped his neck.

Darting back inside, Roland slammed the door shut. The abrupt shift from light to the darkness provided by heavy curtains covering the windows left the humans panicked and discombobulated. Unfortunately, it didn't last long. Flames snuck in windows shattered by stray bullets and latched onto curtains. The thick material quickly ignited, allowing daylight in and escorting the fire inside. By the time only two humans remained, most of the living room was engulfed, so he and Marcus couldn't take time to feed and replenish their strength.

Smoke formed a dense cloud near the ceiling as the last human fell. Both Roland and Marcus had been shot roughly a dozen times. Though none of the bullets had severed arteries, at least as far as Roland could tell, some had damaged major organs and were taking their toll.

Marcus was having a difficult time breathing, thanks to several chest wounds. Every cough the smoke spawned was agonizing for both men as they staggered down the hallway to the bedroom.

"Sarah," Roland called so she wouldn't shoot them as they stepped over two dead men and approached the doorway.

"I'm here."

He nearly tripped over a third as they entered the otherwise deserted bedroom.

Emerging from the bathroom with a damp towel held over her mouth and nose, Sarah stopped short. Her eyes widened as she beheld the holes in his blood-soaked clothing and the sunburn that painted his skin a mottled maroon.

"We have to go," he rasped. "Now."

Her heart in her throat, Sarah watched Roland cross to a window and open it, weaving on his feet. He looked terrible. As did Marcus, who leaned against the wall, wheezing and coughing up blood. Hurrying to Marcus's side, she handed him one of the damp cloths she held.

Nodding his thanks—she wasn't sure he was capable of speech—he held it over his mouth and nose.

"Sarah."

She turned to see Roland punching out the screen. At his urging, she swiftly joined him.

He waved away the cloth she offered and took her hand, helping her through the window. Once she was out, he grabbed his cell phone off the bedside table and thrust it at her. "Get to the trees."

"What about you?"

"We'll be right behind you."

"I'm not leaving without you."

He swore.

The flames had followed the gasoline trail around the house and were creeping closer and closer to the window.

"The fire is spreading," he choked out and gave her a shove that nearly sent her sprawling. "We're immortal. You aren't. Now go."

Unwilling to abandon him, she backed away a few feet and waited anxiously as he ducked inside and disappeared from view. At least a full minute passed before he returned, helping Marcus through the window.

Sarah glanced up at the smoldering roof. The eaves were narrow, providing not nearly enough shade to protect them as Roland exited the window with a grunt of pain.

Marcus's skin immediately pinkened. Roland's, already abused, began to blister.

Hoisting Marcus's arm over his shoulder, Roland started for the trees, half-dragging half-carrying his friend, every step a struggle.

Sarah ignored his scowl and hurried to his side. Pulling Marcus's other arm across her shoulders, she lent her own strength and herded them as quickly as possible to the shelter of the forest.

Pebbles and twigs poked and scratched her bare feet, but she ignored them, focusing only on the tree line ahead. Cool shade enveloped them and she was relieved to see the canopy above was dense enough to protect the men from most of the sun's damaging rays.

A few yards in, Roland and Marcus both sank to their knees, dragging her down with them.

"Sorry," Marcus gasped out and released her.

Sarah scooted around to kneel in front of Roland. "What can I do?"

He shook his head, breathing heavily through his mouth, and collapsed onto his back.

Marcus fell back beside him.

Panic rising, Sarah stared at them both helplessly.

She moved closer to Roland. "Do you . . . do you need

blood?" Not knowing how else to help him, she held her wrist above his parted lips.

One of Roland's hands came up. His long, bloody fingers gently clasped hers. But, instead of biting her wrist, he carried her hand to his lips for a kiss. "Not enough."

She frowned. "I don't have enough to help you?"

He gave her hand a squeeze and closed his eyes.

A lump in his shirt (which she hadn't noticed in the rush to get him to safety) moved, making her start. A plaintive meow sounded and tears spilled over her lashes. When he had gone back for Marcus, he must have unearthed Nietzsche and stuffed him down his shirt.

Roland's breathing slowed.

Marcus's was scarcely detectable.

Were they dying? Trembling, Sarah bit her lip and looked around. Didn't she even have enough blood to tide him over until . . .

Roland's cell phone lay where she had dropped it.

An idea forming, she lunged for it. There was only one phone number stored in it. Eyes glued to Roland's chest, Sarah swiftly dialed it and prayed it was the one she needed.

Flames stretched toward the clear Texas sky like golden fingers as the sun peeked over the horizon. Smoke billowed upward, cloaking the fading stars in charcoal clouds as cries shattered the dawn.

Sirens blared. Men in camouflage ran around in panicked disarray, dodging fire trucks and a few civilians who had made it safely outside. Firefighters raced about in their tan and yellow gear, dousing the roaring conflagration that used to be a three-story building with massive streams of water from numerous hoses.

Two figures materialized amid the chaos, their clothing and long black leather coats covered with blood and full of holes carved by bullets that couldn't kill them. Even as they strode toward the trees, small misshapen bits of metal emerged from their bodies and dropped to the ground, the wounds left behind sealing themselves within seconds.

Looped over David's shoulder was a duffle bag filled with laptop computers, exterior hard drives, CDs, DVDs, and junk drives packed with information they would comb through later.

Cradled in Seth's arms was the woman they had come for, her naked, malnourished body wrapped in a bloody lab coat, so light he doubted she weighed more than eighty pounds.

The darkness of the forest embraced them. Seth carefully adjusted his unconscious burden so her head would be pillowed by his shoulder.

A moan escaped her chapped, cracked lips between ragged breaths.

His mouth tightened in fury.

"We should have killed them all," David growled beside him.

"Those we left alive had no knowledge of this."

A trebly version of Disturbed's "Down with the Sickness" split the air.

Seth halted. It was his cell phone. Turning partially away from David, he said, "Back right pocket. See who it is."

David retrieved the phone. When he saw who the caller was, he frowned and met Seth's gaze. "It's Roland."

Sarah stared at Roland, willing him to keep breathing while she held the cell phone to her ear and counted the rings.

One. Two. Three. Four.

Please answer!

"Hello?" a lightly accented bass baritone voice said finally.

"Seth?" she practically sobbed in relief.

"Yes. Who is this?"

"It's Sarah. Sarah Bingham. Roland needs your help. I think he's dying."

A giant of a man suddenly appeared before her out of thin air.

Sarah shrieked and dropped the phone.

"What happened?" he asked.

Gaping up at him, she couldn't find her voice . . . which, in the end, wasn't necessary. As soon as he turned his head, he saw Marcus and Roland laid out on the ground and swore fluently.

He was quite an imposing figure. Standing over six and a half feet tall, he had broad shoulders and a slender, yet muscular, athletic build. His face was utterly flawless. Not too rugged. Not too pretty. Strong jaw. Patrician nose. No wrinkles or sagging skin or anything else she would think the oldest Immortal Guardian would sport.

Even more astonishing, his dark clothing was wet with blood and riddled with twice as many bullet holes as Roland's.

What the hell?

As he knelt between Marcus and Roland, who looked frighteningly close to death, his dark coat pooled around him and his long black hair fell forward to brush the ground.

"You are Seth, right?" she asked when she could speak again.

"Yes." Peering through the trees at the flames swallowing Roland's house, he said, "As succinctly as possible, tell me what happened."

"The vampire who staked Roland to the ground led another attack on us last night, then sent roughly a dozen men—humans—to finish the job today. I saw Roland follow one outside. The man set the house on fire. I assume Roland killed him. The others are all dead inside."

"Are you injured?"

"No."

He rested one of his large hands on Marcus's chest, then held the other out to her. "Take my hand, Sarah."

Roland seemed to trust this man, so Sarah decided she would, too.

Scrambling forward on her knees, she took his hand.

"Now, touch Roland."

She had no idea if this was a healing ritual or what, but obediently rested her hand on Roland's chest.

Seth's dark, enigmatic gaze caught and held hers. "You may find this a little disorienting."

Find *what* disorienting?

A feeling of weightlessness similar to that which one experiences in an elevator swept over her. Gripping Roland's T-shirt tightly, she abruptly found herself in complete darkness.

Lights flickered on and Sarah stared in astonishment at the spacious living room that had inexplicably replaced the trees.

Plush cream carpet provided a kinder bed for Roland and Marcus than the hard ground previously had. The scent of vanilla replaced that of smoke.

Seth released her hand and pulled a cell phone from his back pocket. As he dialed a number and held it to his ear, Sarah stared down at Roland.

His face was so blistered and bloody, he was nearly unrecognizable.

Taking one of his hands in hers, she gently stroked his sweat-dampened hair. The lump in his shirt moved and wriggled its way up to the neckline. A second later, Nietzsche's tousled head poked out beneath Roland's chin.

"Hi there," Sarah whispered, still fighting tears. "You okay, Nietzsche?"

The little cat looked around, wormed the rest of its body out of the T-shirt, then darted away to hide under a nearby chair.

Sarah lowered her gaze to Roland. The rise and fall of his chest was barely detectable, the time between breaths so long she feared each one may have been his last.

"Chris?" Seth spoke suddenly. "Seth. I have need of your cleaning skills. . . . Roland's house is on fire with approximately eleven humans inside, one outside, all dead. He lives in an isolated area, so I don't know how long it will take someone to notice the smoke and call the fire department. They could already be on their way."

He rattled off the address. "I doubt it. Knowing Roland, it will be impossible for anyone to trace the house to him. But go ahead, just to be on the safe side. . . . Thank you."

As he returned the phone to his pocket, Seth studied Sarah intently. "Roland told you what he is?"

"Yes, I know he's an immortal."

"And you have no problem with that?"

"No, I'm glad he is. Otherwise he would be dead right now."

Nodding thoughtfully, he leaned forward and placed his hand on Roland's chest.

Sarah thought at first he was feeling for a heartbeat.

Then his hand began to glow. Heat radiated from it.

Beneath her astonished gaze, the blisters on Roland's face, neck, arms, and hands shrank, then vanished. Pink skin returned to a natural golden tan. The angry bullet wounds in one of his arms and those visible through the ragged tears in his clothing sealed themselves, smoothed out, and faded to nothingness. A few in his torso spat out mangled lumps of metal she dimly recognized as bullets, then did the same.

By the time the glow faded and Seth removed his hand, Roland looked whole and healthy again, if a trifle pale.

Sarah watched Seth turn and place his hand on Marcus. "Roland told me immortals who are healers can't heal severe wounds without it draining their strength and the wounds opening on their own bodies." Even when they were in top form. And Seth appeared to have been shot more than the two men he was healing combined. Yet no wounds had opened on him.

"*They* can't," Seth said. "I can."

His hand began to glow again. Bullets emerged from Marcus's body as his burns faded.

She frowned. Was Seth stronger because he was older? Or was he different? "Are you not an immortal, then?"

He smiled, so handsome he would have taken her breath away if Roland hadn't already turned her head. "I'm about as immortal as they come."

Hmm. Sarah couldn't decide whether that answered her question or not.

The ethereal glow faded, leaving Marcus as whole as Roland.

"Does blood make you squeamish?" Seth asked, sitting back on his heels.

Sarah looked down at Roland's blood-soaked form, then at the stains on her own clothing. Smiling wryly, she said, "If it did, I'd pretty much be screwed, wouldn't I?"

He laughed.

She nodded to Roland, still holding his hand and stroking his hair. "Is he going to be okay?"

"Yes, but he needs blood."

"I offered him mine, but he wouldn't take it."

His eyebrows rose. "You did?"

She nodded. "He said it wasn't enough."

"More likely he was afraid that, in his condition, he might lose himself and take too much. There should be a goodly supply of it in the refrigerator. Would you mind getting some while I make them"—he motioned toward Roland and Marcus—"more comfortable?"

"Just point me in the right direction."

He did. "The kitchen is right through there."

Sarah stood and hurried to the kitchen, surprised to discover her legs were trembling. The room was dark when she entered. Sliding her hand along the wall, she found the light switch and turned it on.

Wow. She didn't know whose place this was, but it was friggin' huge! Most of the two-bedroom frame house she was renting could easily fit inside this kitchen.

Crossing to the very expensive-looking stainless steel

refrigerator, she opened the door on the right. It was nearly empty, spotlessly clean. Maybe *all* Immortal Guardians were neat freaks.

It was sort of weird to think of them doing housework. Killing vampires by night, then coming home to clean the fridge, mop the floor, or scour the bathroom by day.

Ignoring the club soda, organic fruit juices, and natural salad dressings, Sarah bent and pulled open what looked like a modified meat compartment drawer. Bags of blood were neatly stacked inside. There were more in the vegetable bin.

Seth hadn't specified how much she should bring, so Sarah took it all. Loading up, she filled her arms, shivering at the cold, elbowed the drawers shut, then let the refrigerator door close itself. The plastic bags weren't that easy to handle in bulk. They kept shifting and sliding and trying to slip out of her grasp.

Juggling them as best she could, she hurried back into the spacious living room.

Marcus and Roland were now conscious and seated, side by side, on one of the three sofas the room boasted. Seth was comfortably sprawled in an armchair across from them. The same one Nietzsche hid beneath.

Roland's eyes widened when he saw her.

"This is all there is," Sarah said, dumping her load on the coffee table. Seth leaned forward and deftly caught one as it slid off the side toward the floor. "Is that enough?"

"*More* than enough," Marcus said, grabbing a bag and biting into it.

"Oh. Did I bring too much?"

Roland leaned forward and picked up a bag. "Had Seth not done the work for us, it would take all of this and more to heal our wounds and replenish our strength. But, since he did, we need only enough to replace the blood we've lost."

Sarah nodded and tucked her hands behind her back. They were starting to shake and she was beginning to get that swollen-throated weepy feeling now that the danger was over and reaction was setting in.

She was so glad Roland was going to be all right. So relieved she wanted to crawl into his lap and wrap her arms around his neck.

Instead, she locked her hands together and did her best to look like she wasn't about to embarrass herself by falling apart.

Roland seemed hesitant to feed in front of her.

Hoping to reassure him, she pasted a smile on her face. "I won't freak out. I promise. You drinking blood is no more repellent to me than someone else eating one of those greasy triple beef hamburgers I see advertised on television."

Roland wasn't sure he believed that as he brought the bag to his lips. Watching her carefully, he bit down and drew hard with his fangs. No grimace. No shudder.

One would think she had just handed him a juice box.

Nietzsche chose that moment to creep out of his hiding place and rub against Seth's black fatigue–covered calf. His striped and speckled gray fur and white paws were sticky with Roland's blood and stood out in darkened spikes.

"Well, what have we here?" Seth picked the cat up, examined him briefly, then settled him in his lap. "Hello, Nietzsche. I didn't know you were still around."

Uh-oh.

The gaze Seth turned on Roland was inscrutable. "You do realize that cats aren't actually *supposed* to live nine lives?"

From the corner of his eye, Roland saw Marcus frown.

"Wait a minute," he said after draining the first bag. "That isn't the *original* Nietzsche, is it? That would make him—what—forty years old?"

"Forty-three," Seth clarified.

Roland opted to remain silent and glanced up to catch Sarah's reaction as their words sank in.

Her eyes widened. "An immortal cat?" she blurted incredulously. "There are *immortal cats?*"

"*One* immortal cat," Seth corrected as he stroked Nietzsche's messy fur.

Nietzsche closed his eyes in ecstasy and began to purr and work his little paws.

Seth's disapproval didn't have to be verbalized. Even Sarah seemed to sense it and edged closer to Roland.

Well, what's done is done.

"It was an accident," Roland began, setting his empty bag aside. "I came upon a vampire who was draining a woman dry. When I attacked and started kicking his ass, she freaked out and pepper sprayed me."

"Why?" Sarah demanded. "You were trying to help her."

"She wasn't lucid. She thought he was giving her a hickey, not killing her," he explained. "Before my vision cleared, the vamp got in a lucky shot and cut my carotid artery. It healed, but—by the time I dispatched the vamp, took care of the woman, and got home—I had lost so much blood that I passed out before I could feed. I awoke sometime later to the feel of Nietzsche's sandpapery tongue licking my neck." He shrugged. "I don't know how much he consumed, but he hasn't aged a day since."

Marcus studied the cat curiously. "Has it made him more violent? Is that why he attacked the raccoon?"

"No, Nietzsche has always been very territorial. The little nutcase."

Seth sighed. "Let's keep this between us, shall we? I have my hands full watching over all of you Guardians. I don't need immortal pets to be thrown into the mix, as well."

Roland and Marcus murmured their agreement, then each drained another bag.

Sarah perched on the sofa arm nearest Roland.

Seth waited until they were finished to speak. "Tell me what you know of the one who tried to kill you."

"Not much more than the last time I talked to you," Roland said, raking a hand through his hair in frustration. "His name is Bastien. He's British. And he has raised a small army of both vampires and human minions."

Seth's brow furrowed.

"He attacked us again last night, shortly after Marcus arrived, as we were leaving Sarah's home. There were seven vamps with him. A dozen more joined them after the fight began."

"All of whom deferred to Bastien and looked to him as their leader," Marcus threw in.

Roland nodded. "The plan was to kill me and take Marcus alive." He gave a quick rundown of the fight and of Bastien leaving to pursue Sarah, eventually ceding the fight and fleeing.

"You didn't follow him?" There was no censure in the question.

"No, I was worried about Sarah and wanted to make sure she was all right."

Seth stared at him a long moment, then looked to Sarah. "Were you hurt?"

"No," she said at the same time Roland said, "Yes."

A flush covered her cheeks as she shifted restlessly beneath their collective scrutiny.

Roland was about to reach out, take her hand, and draw her down to sit closer to him when she jumped up and bent to collect the full bags of blood that remained on the coffee table.

"If you're finished, I'd better go put these up. I'm sure they're supposed to stay refrigerated."

Watching her hurry toward the kitchen, he had to fight the need to follow.

"The humans who attacked us today were also Bastien's," Marcus added.

Seth rubbed Nietzsche's chin. "How did they find you?"

Guilt pricked Roland as he recalled accusing Sarah of helping them. "Bastien must have circled around, lingered downwind, and followed us."

Marcus shook his head. "If he followed us, he did it on foot. I would've seen and heard a car or motorcycle even with the headlights off."

"And considering his injuries," Roland said, "he would've had to have been damned determined. This feels like a personal vendetta to me."

"Personal vendetta or not, this needs to be taken care of," Seth decreed. "The more vampires he creates and humans he brings into the fold, the greater the risk of exposure. Too many humans have cell phones that take pictures now. With an army of vamps that size all feeding in one area, it's only a matter of time before someone catches something on video."

"We're working on it." It was a lame response, but the best he could do at the moment. "Where are we, by the way? Whose house is this?"

"David's. He said to tell you that you're welcome to stay as long as you need to."

"That's very generous of him. Thank him for me, will you?"

"Sure."

Roland exchanged a look with Marcus.

Marcus returned his attention to Seth. "All right. Since *he* won't ask, I will. Is the blood all over your clothes ours or yours?"

Seth glanced down, as though only then noticing his condition. "Mine."

That was it, nothing more.

His exasperation showing, Marcus sighed. "Are those bullet holes?" he pressed, motioning to the numerous small tears in his clothing.

"Yes."

Marcus turned to Roland. "You know, I didn't register until this very moment just how alike the two of you are."

Both Seth and Roland frowned. Seth, because he apparently

wasn't pleased with the comparison, and Roland because, for once, it bothered him that he was the thorn in everyone's side.

Was he really that big a pain in the ass?

"Yes," Seth answered the unspoken question, then grinned when Roland reached up and stroked one eyebrow with his middle finger.

"Look," Marcus said, "I only asked because there must be at least two or three dozen of them. Are you all right?"

"I'm fine, Marcus. When Sarah called, I was just wrapping something up and didn't have time to change."

"Do you need blood?"

He shook his head. "My wounds have healed."

Roland stared at him. "What exactly is going on in Texas? Could it be related to whatever is happening here?"

"No," Seth said decisively. "We aren't—" He broke off. Tilting his head to one side, he looked away as though listening to something. Pulling out his cell phone, he dialed a number and held it to his ear. "What's wrong?"

Roland glanced at Marcus, wondering to whom Seth was speaking.

"Where is she now?" Seth asked the unseen speaker.

Marcus raised one eyebrow.

"I'll be right there."

Nietzsche mewed a protest as Seth set him on the carpet and rose, tucking his phone back in his pocket.

"I have to go."

Marcus stood. "Wait. Does David have a computer?"

"A laptop, but he took it with him."

"Then can you drop me at my place? I want to do a little cybersleuthing and see what I can come up with."

In answer, Seth reached out and touched Marcus's shoulder. "Keep me posted," he told Roland.

Then the two vanished.

Chapter 11

All was quiet when Seth appeared in his Houston home.

Well, not entirely quiet.

The sound of rapid, jagged breaths drew him upstairs to one of the many guest bedrooms he kept for visiting immortals and their Seconds.

Darnell, David's Second, stood in the hallway out of sight of the bedroom, brow furrowed. David stood in the doorway, hands raised in a gesture of peace. That, coupled with his height, muscled body, and blood-soaked clothing, however, apparently did little to reassure the object of his attention.

Seth brushed by both men and entered the room, pausing a step inside. No doubt he was equally intimidating, though, for once, he did not intend to be.

Across the room, the young woman they had rescued cowered on the floor, squeezed into a corner between a dresser and the wall.

"What happened?" he asked David, his eyes on the woman.

"She awoke shortly after I began to heal her and panicked," David murmured. "With those wounds, she shouldn't move. But I couldn't bring myself to restrain her. I didn't want to frighten her." He shrugged helplessly. "I've tried talking to her, but she doesn't respond. Mine is not the voice she is accustomed to hearing in her head."

Seth nodded and took a step toward her.

The woman flinched and pressed her body tighter into the corner, knees practically touching her chin. Her red hair had been carelessly cropped and hung in short, lank strands about a pallid face. Dark hollows painted the skin beneath wide, fear-filled green eyes and sharp cheekbones. She was small and frail, so thin as to be skeletal. Clearly she had been starved. But her torture had not ended there.

Dozens, if not hundreds, of cuts, burns, and puncture wounds covered her arms and legs. The two smallest fingers on her right hand had been cut off at the first knuckle, the wounds still raw and unbandaged. Though he couldn't see her feet now—they were hidden beneath the hem of the robe David had wrapped around her—he knew that two of her toes were missing as well.

The worst of her wounds lay in her torso. When Seth and Marcus had burst into the room in which she had been confined, she had been naked, manacled to a table, her chest laid open as two men in surgeons' scrubs shocked her exposed heart with small metal paddles. Had he not heard her screaming in his head, Seth might have thought she had died during open heart surgery and that they were trying to resuscitate her. But she hadn't been dead. And because they hadn't sedated her, she had felt everything they were doing to her.

"Did you heal her chest?" he asked quietly.

"Not completely. I was almost finished when she awakened."

Cautiously, Seth took another step toward her, bending so he wouldn't tower over her quite so much. "Easy," he crooned when she gave another start. "Easy. We aren't going to hurt you. We want to help you."

Do you remember me? he asked her telepathically. Perhaps his voice sounded different when he spoke aloud than it did when he spoke to her in her mind. Or perhaps her captors had deafened her. There was no way of knowing yet how deeply some of her injuries went.

Her gaze flew to his, clung.

You called for help and I answered you.

Tears welled in her tragic eyes and spilled down sunken cheeks.

My name is Seth. He took another step. Then another.

She looked at David anxiously, then back at Seth.

David won't hurt you. He was trying to heal you when you woke up and became afraid.

Seth sank to his haunches so their faces would be on more of an even level, then eased ever closer, extending his right hand, palm up.

You are safe now. Those men will not find you here. Won't you let us help you?

Her gaze dropped to his bloody clothing and hand and a question arose amid the fear in her expression.

He smiled. *They did not want to let you go. But we heard you calling out to us and refused to leave without you. Both of us were injured, but we have recovered.*

He was close to her now. Almost close enough to touch.

Please. I can feel your pain. Let us ease it. Let us heal you as we did ourselves.

Hesitantly, she reached out and placed her left hand in his.

Seth smiled. Covering it, he slowly slid his other hand up her arm to her elbow. As he did, the cuts, burns, and bruises he touched healed and disappeared.

Her breath caught.

You see? We wish only to help you.

Taking her right hand, careful not to put any pressure on her damaged fingers, he drew her to her feet.

Her ordeal had left her severely weakened. Seth steadied her when she would have staggered and fallen, and sent her another smile. When he looked down to make sure he didn't tread on her bare feet with his big boots, he froze.

"David, did you heal her foot?" he asked neutrally.

"No, I started with her chest and got no further. Why?"

He met his friend's concerned gaze. "Her missing toes have grown back."

"What?" David took a step forward so he could better see her feet. "How is that possible? She's human."

Both men looked to the woman for an answer.

The fear returned to her face tenfold.

Chiding herself for being such a coward, Sarah left the kitchen and entered the living room only to find it empty save for Roland, who stood beside the newly stained sofa.

"Where is everybody?"

"Gone," he said simply, circling the coffee table and slowly approaching her. "Seth had some emergency that required his attention and Marcus was eager to get home."

"I didn't even hear them leave."

His lips quirked wryly. "They didn't use the door."

"Oh." Seth had done that teleportation thing again.

Freaky.

Sarah wrung her hands in front of her in a vain attempt to stop their trembling.

Pausing several feet away, Roland studied her, his crimson-streaked brow furrowed. "Are you all right?"

She nodded, lowering her gaze when her vision wavered with tears. A lump lodged itself in her throat as the trembling spread from her hands to the rest of her body.

"Sarah?" he asked, voice soft with concern.

Shaking her head—she was *so* not all right—she strode forward until her forehead met his chest.

His arms came around her, strong and reassuring.

Sarah slid her own around his waist and burrowed closer, tears streaming down her cheeks.

"Shh," he whispered. "It's all right." His large hands slid up and down her back in long, soothing strokes. "Everything is going to be all right."

She nodded, embarrassed by her tears, yet helpless to stem their flow.

He rested his chin atop her head and held her tight. "I'm so sorry about all of this, Sarah."

Shaking her head, she spoke between sniffles. "It isn't your fault some jerk wants to kill you."

He laughed and tightened his hold on her. "Yes, but I didn't have to drag you into it."

"You didn't drag me. I pretty much plowed my way in."

"And, though it's selfish of me to admit it, I'm very glad you did."

Her tears abated beneath his tender, calming influence. Raising her head, Sarah took a step back, a little disappointed when his arms fell away.

"I'm sorry I keep crying." She swiped at her damp cheeks. "You must think I'm a total basket case." Her body was still racked with shivers, yet he was as relaxed as though they had just spent a pleasant day sightseeing.

He raised a hand, brushing the hair at her temple back with gentle fingers. "If you knew what I truly thought of you, you would never stop blushing."

She stared up at him. "I wouldn't?"

He slowly wagged his head from side to side. "You were magnificent today. Confronted with a dozen men armed with semi- and automatic weapons, you didn't panic. You wielded your 9mm with cool precision and faced down three of them on your own, then saved my ass. Again. *And* Marcus's."

His view of what had happened sounded a lot better than her own. "I was terrified," she countered. Not cool under fire. Not magnificent. *Terrified.* "I thought you were going to die. When I saw you with all those wounds and the sun scorching your skin . . . I thought you were going to die, Roland." And damned if more tears didn't well up and spill over her lashes just at the thought of it.

He stared at them as though mesmerized. "Blood loss will not kill me. It may hurt like hell, but it won't kill me. I can slow my pulse and metabolic rate so that I can survive as long as it takes for another blood source to come along. But the sun . . . The sun will roast me, Sarah, when I'm that injured and I don't know that I would have made it to the forest if you hadn't hauled us there, then called in the cavalry. Are those tears for me?"

She almost didn't catch the question tacked onto the end with no pause. "Yes," she admitted. "I've gotten a little attached to you."

His brown eyes turned amber, began to glow. "I've grown attached to you, too." He stroked a finger along her jawline.

She didn't know what to say to that. "I can't seem to stop shaking."

Taking her hand, he gave it a squeeze. "I can remedy that." He turned and strode through the living room.

Sarah let him pull her along after him into a hallway with several closed doors.

"It's been a couple of decades or so since Marcus came to visit me," he said, opening a door on the right. The room inside appeared to be a library. "But he stayed here when he did and I seem to recall him mentioning . . ." He opened the door across from it and Sarah peered past him into a stairwell that led down into darkness. "A basement," he finished with a smile. "Excellent."

She didn't know how a damp, chilly basement was going to help her, but tromped down the stairs behind him anyway. Perhaps, after the incident with the sun, he found the idea of being underground soothing. She probably would if she were in his position.

The wooden steps were cool beneath her bare feet.

At the bottom lay a wide carpeted hallway that led to the left and to the right. Roland went right and opened the first door they encountered.

When he flicked on the overhead light, she saw it was a lovely bedroom. Not cold or damp at all. "It'll do," he announced dismissively.

She glanced up at him. "I liked yours better, too."

He gave her another of those heart-stopping smiles over his shoulder and drew her forward through the room and into a bathroom nearly as large as the bedroom.

Jeeze. Immortals really had a thing for luxurious bathrooms.

As she glanced around at her opulent surroundings, Roland took her by the shoulder and steered her away from the sinks. "Don't look in the mirror."

Which, naturally, made her gaze fly straight to one of the two mirrors mounted above the double sinks. When she saw her reflection, her eyes widened. There was blood smeared all over the middle and left side of her face from forehead to chin. She looked like friggin' Carrie on prom night.

Roland's reflection in the mirror grimaced. "Sorry about that. It came off my shirt when I held you."

"That's okay." She refrained from mentioning that seeing her pale, wide-eyed face liberally coated with ruby liquid gave her the creeps.

Crossing to the shower, Roland opened the glass door and leaned in. The faucet squeaked a little as he turned on the hot water. Almost instantly, steam began to spill forth. He turned on the cold tap, adjusted the temperature to suit him, then straightened and turned to face her.

"Now," he said, prowling toward her, "let's get those clothes off."

Her pulse skittered wildly. "What?"

"The best thing we can do to stop the shaking is get you into a nice hot shower. You'll feel much better once you're warm and the remnants of the day are washed away."

Sarah had no idea what he had just said. She couldn't concentrate when he was staring at her with those incandescent eyes. Especially since he was pulling his ragged T-shirt over his head while he spoke. Beneath lay bloodstained muscles that rippled and flexed as he tossed the material aside. There were no signs of any wounds. Only pure perfection.

"What am I supposed to be doing again?" she asked absently.

"Taking your clothes off and enjoying a steamy shower."

"And your plans are?"

He smiled and reached for the hem of her shirt. "To enjoy it with you."

Sarah let him pull her shirt over her head, her tongue inconveniently tied.

"Seth wouldn't have brought us here if he didn't think it was safe," he went on. "But until I double-check the security myself, I'm not letting you out of my sight."

She nodded. That worked for her.

"Don't worry." His face softened, though his eyes still glowed. "I'll respect your *No Sex with Strangers* rule and keep my pants on. *You,* however"—a teasing glint entered his eyes—"should feel free to take off as much as you want."

Even covered with blood, he tempted her.

She had told him she didn't have sex with men she had just met, men she didn't really know, but . . . when Sarah took into account what she *did* know about Roland, were the things she didn't really that important? So she didn't know his favorite color or his favorite ice cream flavor. No, wait. Actually she did know those. His favorite color was green and he liked banana nut soy cream, one of her own personal favorites. She didn't know his favorite movie or what kind of music he preferred, what his favorite television show was.

But she knew he was honorable, that he had spent every night for nearly a thousand years defending and protecting humans like herself from those who preyed upon them, suffering untold injuries in the process, then turning around and doing it all over again the next night. She knew he placed her safety above his own and wouldn't hesitate to risk his life in order to save hers. She knew he had willingly drawn her pain and injuries into himself to ease her discomfort and would do so again.

He had been nothing but kind to her since the moment they had met. He was patient with crazy kitties. He was very loyal to his friends and clearly felt affection for them, though he hid it behind a gruff facade when in their presence.

She knew his troubled past, some of it anyway, and suspected he was as leery of surrendering himself to another as she was. Yet he was capable of such tenderness, such passion, as she had learned firsthand last night. Just thinking about it made her body clench.

That little practical voice that usually stayed her when tempted instead taunted her by pointing out that, since he was immortal, she didn't have to worry about STDs. And this was a safe time in her cycle, which meant no pregnancy fears either.

What the hell was she waiting for?

Sarah smiled and unbuttoned the waist of her jeans.

She knew she felt as comfortable with Roland as she would with an old friend. And more drawn to him than she had ever been to another.

His gaze dropped to her hands.

She knew he wouldn't touch her if she didn't want him to, even with an erection already straining against the front of his slacks.

He watched every movement avidly as she slid the zipper down, then peeled the jeans down her legs and stepped out of them.

And she knew she *wanted* him to touch her. Needed it. Almost desperately.

"Roland," she said, reaching around behind her and unhooking her bra.

"Hmm?" His hands curled into fists at his sides as the black lace fell away.

"You aren't a stranger."

* * *

Roland stared at her, pulse racing. He wasn't a stranger? "Are you saying . . . ?"

"I'm saying take your pants off. The sooner we wash this blood off, the sooner you can do to me all of those things I can see you're thinking about doing."

Oh shit.

His pants were on the floor before she drew her next breath.

Sarah jumped at his super-quick movement, then laughed.

He grinned, shrugging sheepishly, then felt compelled to caution her. "This could be a reaction to the violence and having come so close to getting killed, Sarah." He had experienced such a reaction himself a time or two before he had been transformed—that need for a physical reaffirmation of life after coming so close to death.

"I know. I don't think it is. But if I'm wrong, I don't care. I just want your hands on me. Everywhere. As soon as possible."

"I can do that," he murmured, stepping closer.

She raised her face to his for a kiss, eyes twinkling. "I know you *can.* But do you *want* to?"

Placing his hands on her hips, he brushed his lips against hers. "You already know the answer to that."

Roland teased her with his tongue, grazing her lower lip, then gliding within. Withdrawing. Sliding within. Withdrawing. She tasted so good.

Moaning, she rose onto her toes, wrapped her arms around his neck, and leaned her nearly bare body into his. Her soft, full breasts came to rest against his chest. His cock, no longer restrained by his pants, was trapped against her flat belly.

It was torture. Wonderful, exquisite torture. Because he wanted to bury himself inside her and couldn't. Not yet.

Hooking his thumbs in the waistband of her black panties, he tore himself away from her lips long enough to slide the small scrap of material down her body to the floor. She made a light sound of protest at his retreat, then rested a hand on his shoulder as she liberated one foot and used the other to kick the panties away.

When he looked up, his face was nearly on a level with the triangle of dark curls he had touched through her jeans the night before. He wanted to lean forward, kiss her there. Lick her. Stroke her. He glanced up, saw her staring down at him, seeming to read every thought as it occurred to him.

"Maybe we can forgo the shower," she whispered. Shifting the hand on his shoulder, she moved it up to tunnel through his hair, grip a fistful, and give it a light tug.

Excitement shot through him.

Oh yeah. This was going to be good. This was going to be so fucking good.

But as he rose, preparing to pounce and please her in a hundred different ways, he caught a glimpse of himself in the mirror behind her. Unlike Sarah, who only had blood on her face, hands, and a little bit of her chest, he was covered in the crimson liquid. He had been shot a dozen times or more, had bled copiously, and had been spattered with the blood of his opponents as well. There was scarcely an inch of skin left clean. It even dampened his hair.

He couldn't come to her like this.

She glanced over her shoulder, caught his reflection in the mirror, and turned back, eyes questioning.

"I'm sorry," he said. "I wasn't thinking."

"I wasn't either." She looked at the steaming shower, then back at him, lips quirking. "Wanna race?"

He grinned. "I'll wash you if you'll wash me."

"Deal."

Laughing, they stepped into the shower and closed the door. Steam swirled around them, brushing their skin with spectral fingers. Sarah closed her eyes, ducked under the water, scrubbed her face, then gave the spray her back.

Roland's breath caught as she tilted her head back, ran her hands through her hair, elbows pointed at the ceiling. Water sluiced down her body, over her shoulders and full breasts, skipping off the hardened pink tips. Her long hair darkened to black, straightening as it molded itself to her slick form in a shiny curtain. One thin section slid down her chest, hugged her breast, and continued down to tease her belly button.

When Roland raised his gaze once more it was to find she had opened her eyes and was watching him. "You're so beautiful," he told her.

She smiled. Her lashes were dark and spiked with moisture. "So are you."

"I've never showered with a woman before," he admitted.

"Really? What do you think so far?"

He felt a slow smile stretch his lips. "I like it."

Grinning, she moved aside so he could take her place.

Roland stepped beneath the spray. Reluctantly ceding his ability to stare at her, he turned away and began rinsing his hair, face, and chest. The water turned red as it sluiced down his front, collecting more blood from his arms, abdomen, and legs. By the time it circled the drain, it looked like cranberry juice.

When his front was as clean as it would get without soap, he turned his back to the spray.

Sarah had taken a cloth from the recessed shelf and was lathering it up, her gaze firmly fixed on his ass. When he faced her, she hastily raised her eyes to meet his.

He grinned. "Caught you."

Laughing, she blushed. "What's good for the goose?"

"Is great for the gander." He grabbed a second cloth, randomly chose a shower gel from the selection provided, and started lathering it. "Turn around."

She gave him her back, so delicate beneath his large hands as he slid the thin soapy cloth across it. Shoulder to shoulder. Down to her narrow waist. Over the smooth round globes of her bottom. Following the curves of her lightly muscled thighs. He knew these curves. Every gentle flare, subtle dip, and hollow down to her tiny feet. He had learned them well last night. Memorized them. Dreamt of them.

He could hear her heartbeat pick up, her breath shorten, as he drew the cloth down the back of her thigh to her ankle, around and up the front to the bend at her hip, then down the outside, around and up the inside until his soapy knuckles grazed the curls at her center. A pause. Then down the back of the other thigh, up the front, down the outside, and slowly up the inside to end with another brush of his knuckles.

"Turn around," he said again, his voice raspy with the desire that made him so hard he thought he might burst if he didn't have her soon.

She swung around to face him, face flushed with need.

As he rose and reached toward her, she stayed his hand.

"My turn."

When he opened his mouth to protest, she made a twirling motion with her index finger.

Roland gave her his back.

Molded to her small hand, the soapy cloth touched his shoulder, then smoothed across his back in firm, but languid strokes, drifting lower, down to his waist.

The water from the showerhead pounded his front, pouring over his ultrasensitive shaft, adding to the pleasure of her every touch.

When both of her hands settled over his ass and squeezed, he moaned and dropped his head back. Her hands left him.

Her front pressed against his back. When he felt her reach around him, Roland glanced down and saw her dangle the cloth under the spray until the pink suds were whisked away.

She stepped back. He heard her add more soap to the cloth, lather it. Then it was brushing the back of his thigh, slipping down to his ankle, around, up the front, down the outside just as he had done to her and up the inside until her knuckles brushed his balls with just the lightest touch.

He hissed in a breath as pleasure darted through him.

Down the back of his other thigh, up the front, down the outside, and up, up, up the inside, anticipation as sharp as a knife. But she stopped without touching him this time. The cloth withdrew. He let his breath out in a faint sigh of disappointment, then sucked it in again when her small hand, slick with soap and free of the cloth, slid between his legs, cupped his sac, and fondled him, squeezing gently. His cock jumped. The need to be inside her was so strong he shook with it.

"Sarah," he moaned.

Her hand left him. "Turn around."

Sarah was practically panting with need when Roland spun around and faced her. His chest rose and fell as swiftly as hers. His eyes glowed brightly. His swollen erection strained toward her.

"Hurry," was all she could say.

He tossed his cloth aside and instead palmed her breasts with soapy hands. Dipping his head, he captured her lips in a feverish kiss. When his thumbs and fingers found the hardened peaks and strummed them, pinched them, circled them, a throaty sound of need unlike any she had heard herself make before escaped her.

Dropping her own cloth, she followed his example and drew her sudsy hands across his powerful chest.

One of his hands slipped down her stomach to the damp curls at the juncture of her thighs. Her knees nearly buckled when he stroked her clit with his thumb and, finding her entrance, dipped a finger inside.

Moaning, she trailed a hand down to his erection, curled her fingers around him (he was too large for her to enclose completely), and stroked him from base to tip.

He groaned, urging her on with his hips when she stroked him again and again. "Fuck this," he muttered. "We're clean enough."

Sarah sputtered, then laughed as he drew her back with him under the steamy spray.

They aided the water in swiftly sweeping the suds from

their bodies. Her hands teased him. His hands teased her. He shut off the water, then lifted her.

"Wrap your legs around my waist," he growled.

Sarah did so eagerly, trapping his long, hardened length between their bodies.

They didn't pause to dry off. He merely carried her into the bedroom and tumbled them smoothly onto the bed.

"No more preliminaries," she begged as he settled his weight atop her, his hips between her thighs, his upper body propped on his hands. "I want you inside me."

He groaned and reached between them, positioning his erection at her entrance, rubbing the smooth head against her. "Next time you'll let me taste you first," he vowed, then plunged inside her.

Sarah threw her head back as he filled her. "Yesss."

He withdrew almost to the crown, then plunged again.

"More," she purred.

A very masculine chuckle rumbled forth as he obliged her.

Sarah stared up at him raptly as he continued to thrust, grinding against her, driving her pleasure ever upward. Short, dark hair fell over his forehead in wet spikes that dripped cool water onto her every time he thrust. His luminous amber eyes were brighter than she had ever seen them. His fangs had lengthened and peeked out from between soft lips. Heavy muscles bunched beneath smooth skin beaded with moisture.

Sliding her hands down his back, she gripped his muscled ass and urged him on, arching against him as the pressure built and built and built. He felt so good inside her. So hard. Touching all the right places.

She screamed his name as she came, heard her own emerge from his lips on a groan as he followed her over the edge.

Their breath emerged in gasps as the pleasure gradually spiraled downward and a lazy contentment enfolded them. Drawing one of her legs up over his hip, Roland rolled them onto their sides, bodies still joined, and cuddled her close.

By the time she regained enough of her breath to speak, the fatigue brought on by too many days with too little rest and too much adrenaline caught up with her and she drifted into a deep sleep, surrounded by his warmth and soothed by soft caresses.

Chapter 12

"You said earlier that I wasn't the only woman you've cared about that you had found standing over you with a knife," Sarah broached softly. She had awoken some time ago to the wondrous feeling of Roland's hands and mouth exploring every inch of her.

It had been slow and sweet this second time, each of them leisurely learning where and how the other liked to be touched, what evoked the most pleasure, until they were once again swept away.

Roland sighed. He was lying on his back with her curled up against him.

"Who was she?"

His hand covered hers on his chest and toyed with her fingers. "There were two," he confided grimly. "The first was my wife."

Her heart clenched. While the thought of him with another woman was unpalatable, the knowledge that that woman had deceived him both infuriated and baffled her.

Why would any woman in her right mind want to hurt Roland?

Sarah propped her chin on his chest so she could look up at him, but he avoided her gaze, instead focusing on her hair as he combed his fingers through it.

“Once I escaped the vampire, all I could think about was getting home to Beatrice. Though ours was an arranged marriage, I loved her and thought she loved me. We had known each other since I was sent to foster with her father when we were children and shared a close friendship. Our marriage was a happy one and gave me two beautiful children before I was captured and transformed.”

If his children had looked anything like him, they had been gorgeous.

His lips formed a bitter smile. “They were all so surprised to see me when I strode into the great hall after making my escape. I had been gone for months. Everyone believed I was dead, killed with the rest of my party that day. Those seated around the trestle tables went absolutely silent. At the high table, Beatrice whispered my name and fainted. I thought my brother would, too, so pale did he turn. I didn’t know yet, you see, that he had betrayed me.”

He twined a lock of her hair around one finger. “Edward embraced me, told me how he had searched and searched for me. My wife, once she roused, ran to me, covered my face with kisses and tears of joy. I was such a fool I damn near wept, too.”

Sarah stroked his chest, wishing she could ease his pain, regretting stirring up such bad memories.

“She took me upstairs, bathed me, fed me, made love to me oh so tenderly”—that was hard to hear—“and tucked me into bed. I awoke an hour later to the feel of her plunging a dagger into my chest.”

Shock pierced Sarah. His wife had *stabbed* him?

Roland met her gaze, his brown eyes full of self-mockery. “She didn’t know what I had become—that I could live through such a wound—and, thinking I was dying, told me all.

“When my brother had returned home shortly after we married, she had fallen in love with him.”

Inside, Sarah cringed.

"Edward loved her as well and the two of them secretly cuckolded me from then on. The son and daughter I adored, she swore, were my brother's offspring, not my own."

"Oh, Roland."

"And it was she who had heard rumors of the vampire and talked my brother into arranging for me to be taken and killed so Edward could have both the title and Beatrice. By returning, apparently hale and hearty, I had ruined everything."

"So she *stabbed* you?" Sarah asked incredulously.

"That didn't work out quite the way she thought it would."

"I should hope not!" Sitting up, unable to contain the outrage she felt on his behalf, she settled back on her heels, facing him. "I can't believe she did that to you! That she would even *cheat* on you, let alone try to kill you! Your brother was clearly an asshole. And even if he wasn't, why the hell would she want *him* when she could have *you?* Was she friggin' crazy?"

His eyebrows flew up.

"What did you do?"

His gaze turned watchful. "I killed them."

"Oh." That took some of the wind out of her sails. "Well. Good then."

"You don't think me a monster for doing so?"

"No, I'm a firm believer in an eye for an eye. They tried to kill you . . . twice . . . and would have succeeded if you weren't different. If you had let them live, they probably would've tried a third time. As far as I'm concerned, it was self-defense."

He rested a hand on her thigh. "To be honest, it was an accident. I was newly turned and unused to my increased strength and hungers. The craving for blood is strong in the beginning and I was losing a lot from the hole in my chest. In my rage and pain, I drained her dry before I even realized what I was doing."

That must have made him feel even worse. "And your brother?"

"When he came to collect my body after she supposedly finished me off, I hit him too hard and fractured his skull. Badly. Because the wound in my chest had not had sufficient time to mend itself completely, healing him would have left me weak and at his mercy, so . . . I did nothing. I let him die."

There was guilt there, despite all that his brother had purposely done to him.

Lying down again, Sarah slid over and stretched out on top of him like a blanket. "I'm sorry, Roland."

His arms came around her and held her tightly. "It was a long time ago."

"But I can tell it still hurts."

"Yes," he reluctantly acknowledged.

"Maybe she lied about the children." That had probably hurt more than anything else.

"She did. I'm sure of it."

She looked up at him. "How?"

He smiled. "I told you I was born with special gifts."

"Yes."

"Those gifts were passed down to me from my mother, who had similar gifts. My father had none. When my mother died, he remarried and my stepmother bore him Edward and three girls, none of whom were *gifted ones.*" His smile softened. "My son was born a healer, my daughter with telekinetic abilities. Edward could not possibly have fathered them."

Clearly he had loved his children. Sarah could almost picture them. A smaller version of Roland, marching around in imitation of the proud papa his pretty sister had wrapped around her tiny finger. She smiled. "What were their names?"

"Thomas and Emma."

"What happened after . . . ? Did you stay?"

"Yes. I didn't know where else to go, so I buried Beatrice and Edward in secret and let everyone believe they had run away together. It was very difficult. I was still adjusting to the changes and feared what others would think. I explained my photosensitivity away as an exotic illness I had contracted when my captors *shipped me off to the Holy Land.*"

She pursed her lips. "Did it work?"

"Some accepted it. Others did not and feared me. Superstition had a stranglehold on many back then."

"So I've heard."

"I frightened myself at times. After what happened with Beatrice, I worried I might inadvertently hurt the children and was almost afraid to be around them. Then Seth arrived and helped me understand everything better."

"How did he know who and what you were? That you needed help?"

"I don't know. He's so much older than I am, his powers unimaginable. He always seems to sense when *gifted ones* have been transformed and makes his way to them to help them, teach them, and eventually train them in ways to protect themselves and hunt vampires. If he can't do it himself, he assigns another immortal to train them."

She frowned. "Why didn't he come to you when the vampire first took you? Why didn't he free you? You were down there for months."

"*Gifted ones* are harder for him to pin down than immortals and I didn't transform completely until right before I escaped. He had sensed I was turning and begun to search for me. But, you have to understand, there were fewer of us back then. So if he passed through an area with a vampire problem, he had to pause long enough to take care of it before moving on."

"Oh." Wrapping her arms around him, she hugged him tighter. "I just hate the idea of you suffering the way you did."

Roland pressed a kiss to the soft hair atop her head and rolled them to their sides. He felt . . . strange. Lighter, perhaps. As if sharing with Sarah the pain and anger that had pressed down upon him for so long had finally liberated him from it.

Was this *contentment* he felt, seeping into his very marrow as he twined his legs through hers? It had been so long, he barely recognized it.

With a wondrous sense of peace, he realized he could finally think of his children without their memory being overshadowed by Edward and Beatrice's betrayal.

"I presided over my home for a decade and was able to watch my children grow to adulthood before people began to notice I wasn't aging." He smiled. "Emma became a beautiful young woman, sweet-natured and generous. Thomas was nearly as tall as I am and so handsome the girls all fought over him. Both of them were incredibly bright. I could not have been more proud. Thomas was an immensely powerful knight and earned his spurs a year younger than I did," he boasted. "He had such honor within him, was so like my father."

"No," Sarah correctly softly. "He was so like *you.*"

Tipping his chin down, he found her smiling up at him.

She drew a finger along his jawline in a light caress that made his skin tingle. "Handsome, smart, and honorable? It sounds like he was a carbon copy of his father."

Roland's throat thickened and he was shocked to feel moisture well in his eyes. Abashed, he buried his face in her hair.

"Did you tell them what you were?" she asked, stroking his back.

He had to swallow hard before he could speak. "No, I stayed as long as I dared. Long enough to see Emma happily married to an earl who adored her and to ensure Thomas was ready to assume the title. Then I said my goodbyes, left, and had one of my immortal colleagues send them word of my supposed death."

Sarah pressed a kiss to his neck. "Did you ever see them again?"

"From a distance. I watched over both of them until they

died, then watched over my grandchildren until they died, and their children as well."

"Immortality must be difficult at times."

"It can be. I'm not the only Guardian who has isolated himself from others. Forming attachments with humans and having to watch them grow old and die generation after generation can become unbearable as the centuries accumulate."

It would be no different with Sarah. When she was stooped with age, her hair a snowy-white complement to the wrinkles mapping her sweet face, he would be the same as he was now, unchanged by the decades that had passed.

The thought was an unwelcome one he hastily pushed aside, unwilling to let reality intrude just yet and rob him of the happiness she inspired.

"I hate to ask this," she said, "but you said *two* women tried to kill you. Who was the other?"

"My betrothed."

She muttered something into his chest he couldn't make out. "Was her name Mary?"

He frowned. "Yes. What do you know of her?"

"Only what you and Marcus said about her while he was trying to talk you out of healing me."

Oh. "Well, it's a much shorter story. I met her in the seventeenth century, lost my head over her, asked her to marry me, and when she said yes, told her what I was. She freaked out, but I managed to calm her down, or so I thought. She said she needed time to think. I gave it to her. The next afternoon, she stormed into my home with half a dozen humans bearing knives, stakes, and torches and tried to kill me."

Even that memory lacked its usual bite with Sarah's soft form snuggled up against him. Marcus was right. Mary *had* been a twit. She had seemed to accept him by the time he had finished talking. So she had probably told her sister, then been swayed by *her* reaction.

Sarah's small hands came up to cup his cheeks, drawing his gaze to hers. "Roland?"

"Yes?" She was so adorable, with her mussed hair and kiss-swollen lips.

"I promise I will *never* betray you or try to kill you."

Another piece of the shield he had erected around his heart fell away.

He touched his lips to hers. "I believe you." It was true. He did. "And I have to tell you . . . that scares the hell out of me."

"I know. If I were in your shoes, it would scare me, too. But I would never intentionally harm you." The somber promise in her eyes, more brown than green today, morphed into amusement. "Notice I said 'intentionally.' Occasionally, I have what I call clumsy days when I just can't seem to do anything right, which tends to result in bruises, cuts, or burns. So if you hang around me long enough, you might unwittingly become a victim and acquire a few yourself."

If you hang around me long enough.

Was it a backhanded invitation?

Could she be implying she wouldn't be averse to spending more time with him when this was all over? That she might be interested in pursuing a relationship with him?

Is that what *he* wanted?

Hell, yes!

Rolling her to her back, Roland took her lips in a deep, devouring kiss and whispered, "I'll risk it."

The bleating of his cell phone woke Roland from a sound sleep. Cursing himself for leaving it upstairs, he carefully extricated himself from Sarah's tangled limbs—damn, he didn't want to leave her—then raced up to the living room in a blur of motion.

"What?" he growled, answering on the second ring.

"You must be Roland," a cheerful male voice said.

"Who the hell is this and how did you get my number?"

The man laughed. "Oh yeah. You're definitely Roland. This

is Chris Reordon. I'm this region's Cleaner. Seth gave me your number."

Reordon. Roland had heard of him. He was rumored to be one of the best, though Roland had never felt the need to call upon his services.

Concealing the existence of both the vampiric virus and the *gifted ones* from the rest of society was a full-time job that required constant vigilance and connections in various law enforcement and government agencies that immortals had difficulty cultivating due to their aversion to sunlight and the time they spent hunting vampires and reducing the threat they posed. The computer age and advent of video cameras, cell phones that took pictures, and the Internet made it all even more complicated.

Fortunately, Seth had long ago begun ferreting out trustworthy humans to build a support network that helped immortals with everything from investing their capital and multiplying their wealth to supplying weapons, providing new identities every few decades, studying the disease that transformed them, researching a cure, performing daytime surveillance when necessary, and running interference with humans who became too curious for their own good. The network had been in place and steadily expanding for centuries now.

Many of the humans employed by the network were descendants of previous members who had passed the torch to their sons or daughters. Absolute loyalty was imperative. Rules and guidelines were strictly implemented. Those who strayed and broke faith with the network—and there had been very few—were swiftly tracked down and punished by the network's human enforcers with no immortal interference.

The role of Cleaners was fairly self-explanatory: They cleaned up the messes immortals sometimes left behind.

"How did it go?" Roland asked, tamping down his irritation at being ranked on by a human he didn't even know.

"Just fine," the man responded in more businesslike tones.

"I'm sorry to say your house is a total loss. We managed to get there before anyone else did. Society's apathy really works in our favor sometimes. Most of the people who saw the smoke must have assumed someone else had already called 911 and not bothered to call it themselves, because we had plenty of time to stage it before the fire department arrived."

"Stage it as what?"

"A drug deal gone bad at a meth lab. You did a hell of a job covering your tracks, by the way. Even I couldn't find anything to link you to that house. Or the car in the garage, which was also destroyed."

"And the Geo Prism?"

"We got it out of there before the authorities arrived."

"Who exactly did the authorities think you were?"

"DEA, arrived too late to rescue an agent whose cover was blown and who subsequently died in the fire."

How did everyone else pass themselves off as federal agents so easily when Roland couldn't make it fly worth a crap?

"Do you want us to bring you a replacement car? We can have it there by sunset."

"What happened to the Prism?"

"Nothing. I just assumed it was stolen."

"It wasn't."

"Really? You should have put that hunk of junk out of its misery a long time ago."

"It isn't mine. It belongs to a woman who was caught in the crossfire." Sarah no doubt would have already replaced it if she could have. "She's here with me and, I'm sure, would appreciate getting it back."

"A human woman?" Chris asked, his voice deadly serious.

Roland stiffened. Having never called upon Cleaners, he wasn't sure how they dealt with humans who had been exposed to the truth. "Yes."

"I'll be there within an hour to pick her up."

"The hell you will."

"You know the rules, Roland. Any human who—"

"Fuck the rules."

"Her knowledge puts us all at risk," Chris reminded him. "At the very least I need to sit her down, have her sign a confidentiality agreement, and impress upon her what will happen if she ever violates it."

The threat was obvious.

Anger welled within Roland as he listened. After all Sarah had been through since finding him in that field, there was no way he was going to let Chris intimidate and frighten her.

"I said fuck the rules and fuck you," Roland snarled. "You stay the hell away from her."

"Your ass isn't the only one on the line here," Chris said, his own irritation beginning to show. "Do you have any idea how many laws my team and I broke today cleaning up your shit? This is standard procedure, put in place to protect us *all.* If she wigs out and decides to tell—"

"She isn't going to wig out, and my ass isn't on the line. I know that because she *saved* it. Now if you have any interest in keeping *yours* intact, you'll damned well steer clear of her!"

A long silence ensued.

Roland sighed and pinched the bridge of his nose, exhaustion beating at him. He really shouldn't alienate this man after the help he had rendered them earlier.

"Look, Reordon. I don't mean to bust your balls. It's been a long two days. I'm tired. I'm irritable. And I wouldn't even be here if it weren't for Sarah. She saved my life—twice—and has been through hell. I'm not going to repay her by letting you strong-arm her and threaten her. She has enough on her plate now that she's become as much of a target as I am."

"A target," Chris repeated, the antagonism in his voice melting away. "Why don't you clue me in to what's going on? I know you usually work solo, but if you've got humans attacking you by the dozen, I can probably be of some assistance. Were those at your house minions or independents?"

"Minions." Though disclosing information to a perfect

stranger made him uneasy, Roland filled Chris in on what had been happening.

"What's the name of the vamp?"

"I only have a first name. Bastien."

"Country of origin?"

"England."

"Physical description?"

Roland gave him one.

"Vamps don't have our resources, so they usually leave a money trail. If this one is lucid enough to organize and control an army, he can't be too old. He also must live in the area. I've already got a guy tracing the license plate and VIN numbers on the SUVs the minions drove to your place. We took them before the fire department arrived and replaced them with a couple of crap cars. We'll check them for prints and other forensic evidence, then let me see what I can come up with and I'll get back to you."

"Thanks, man."

"No problem. Call me if anything else comes up."

"I will."

"Do you want me to send out a team to guard you and Sarah while you sleep?"

"No thanks." He couldn't extend his already shaky trust to anyone else.

At least, not yet.

"Okay. Let me know if you change your mind."

"I will."

After hanging up, Roland put Chris's number on speed dial.

"Roland?"

He turned, warmth invading him as Sarah shuffled into the room.

Her long hair was tousled from their lovemaking and framed her face in tangled waves. Her eyelids were heavy, her lips still swollen from his kisses.

Only his black T-shirt, which he silently admitted had never looked so good, covered her nudity. The sleeves that were short on him covered her elbows. The hem fell a third of the way down her pale, faintly muscled thighs.

Seeing her in the too-big plain cotton shirt stirred him more swiftly than the sexiest lingerie would. He was filled with such tenderness and affection. Such possessiveness.

Mine.

He wanted to shout it to the world, place his mark on her so everyone would know she was his.

Hell.

If he wasn't careful, he was going to find himself falling in love with her.

And that way lay heartache and disaster.

It never ended well when an immortal fell in love with a human.

Only *gifted ones* could be successfully transformed. Those rare individuals with the extra DNA memo groups that bestowed upon them special abilities and enabled their bodies to mutate the virus so they would become immortal rather than vampire. So many *gifted ones* had been killed before they could procreate in centuries past by fools egged on by superstition, fear, or envy, that their descendants today were very few. The chances of an immortal finding and falling in love with one were astronomically low. Roland could number on one hand the times such had happened during his long existence (word tended to get around when it did) and those love affairs had ended badly when the *gifted ones* chose not to be transformed.

The fact that an individual *could* safely be transformed didn't necessarily mean he or she would *want* to be transformed.

But even that hope had been denied him here. Sarah had none of the special gifts that would have indicated she was different. She lacked the black hair and dark brown eyes characteristic of all those who possessed the bloodline that would prevent her from turning vampire. A relationship with her could only end one of two ways.

At best, he would have fifty or sixty years with her before she died in his arms of old age. His ability to heal may extend that a decade or so if he were lucky.

At worst, they would have . . . maybe twenty years of happiness before the signs of her aging could no longer be staved off. And those signs would gradually increase. The first time someone mistook her for his mother rather than his wife or lover would devastate her. She would feel self-conscious about the changes taking place in her body (while his remained youthful) and insist they only make love in the dark under the covers, where she thought she could hide from his preternatural vision.

As various parts of her continued to wrinkle and sag, she would begin to question his love for her. His attempts to reassure her by pointing out that if he were human and aging alongside her, he would feel no different—his devotion unfaltering—would fall on deaf ears. Each night, when he left to hunt, she would suspect he was seeing a younger woman on the side. She would grow increasingly bitter. He would become weary of her distrust and constant accusations, her lack of faith in him.

It was always the same.

He had been naive when he had courted Mary. Communication between immortals had been very limited at the time and further hampered by his self-imposed isolation. He had foolishly believed that as long as he loved her, the inevitable changes in Mary's appearance wouldn't matter.

It wasn't until the birth of the Internet that allowed immortals all over the world to meet and communicate with each other via chat rooms and message boards that he had understood the truth of it.

But as Sarah approached him, a sleepy smile lighting her face, there was a part of him that wished, just this once, it would turn out differently.

"When I woke up, you were gone."

Walking into his embrace, she wrapped her arms around

him and leaned her head against his chest. Her small hands were cold on his back, her toes icy where they brushed his.

He didn't mind. Feeling inexorably heartsore, Roland rested his cheek atop her hair and let her presence soothe him.

"Is everything okay?" she asked, rubbing his back.

"Yes, it was just Seth's Cleaner, calling to let me know everything had been taken care of. The police won't be questioning us about the fire or the dead men."

"Good."

He couldn't help but derive a certain masculine satisfaction from the fact that his scent was all over her. Beneath that was her own unique fragrance, tantalizing him as it always did.

She squeezed him tighter momentarily. "I'm sorry you lost your house, Roland."

He shook his head slightly. "The only things irreplaceable in it were you, Marcus, and Nietzsche, and you all made it out safely."

He felt her smile against his chest. "You're so sweet."

Roland choked back a laugh. *Sweet* was an adjective he didn't think anyone had used to describe him since he was in swaddling clothes.

"You know what?" she asked mischievously.

"What?" he responded, still smiling.

Raising up onto her toes, she tilted her head back and whispered in his ear, "You're wearing my favorite outfit."

He laughed and glanced down. "I'm completely naked."

She grinned. "And you wear it so well."

His spirits buoyed, he lowered his head.

Sarah hummed her approval as his lips brushed hers.

When she had awoken and found herself alone, she had felt a moment's panic. Then, from a distance, the faint murmur of his voice had reached her ears. The bed had felt so cold and empty. She hadn't been able to go back to sleep without his big, warm body spooned up behind her.

After listening to the indistinct rumble of his voice for

several minutes and hearing no responses, she had assumed he was talking on the phone, donned his T-shirt, gone in search of him, and found him standing gloriously naked in the living room.

For a moment, he had looked so sad. She had wanted only to hold him, comfort him, bring a smile to his face.

But now, with his sleek tongue slipping past her lips and speeding her pulse, all she could think of was how it had felt to have him inside her, moving in long, deep, hard strokes that had made her want to scream and had sped her toward one fantastic orgasm after another.

Withdrawing her arms from around his waist, she slid her hands up his muscled chest, over his shoulders, and tunneled her fingers through his short, silky hair.

He groaned as she raked her nails across his scalp and hungrily returned his kiss. Bending his knees so she wouldn't have to stand on her toes, he grasped her nape with one hand and locked her to him while he slid the other down over her hip and thigh.

She shivered when that hand dipped beneath the hem of the shirt she wore and slowly began to climb again, drawing the soft cotton along with it. Cool air rushed over her rapidly heating flesh as he cupped her bottom and squeezed, dragging her tighter against him. The long, hard length of his erection prodded her stomach as he insinuated a strong thigh between her legs and pressed against her sensitive core.

Sarah moaned, breath catching. She was already wet, dampening his skin as she rocked against him.

His hunger rising, Roland released her tempting ass and slid his hand up her slender back. His body began to tremble with the need to be inside her.

Abandoning her lips, he whipped the shirt over her head and bared her beautiful body. He stroked her breasts, pinching the hardened peaks. She jerked against him.

Smiling, he lowered his head and took one pink bud into his mouth, swirled his tongue around it, took it between his teeth, and bit, though he was careful not to break the skin. He glanced up when she moaned again. Her face was flushed with passion, her hips urgent as they rocked against him. She was so wet for him. He wanted to taste her. Now.

Dropping to his knees, he parted her legs and feasted upon her center. The dark triangle of curls was damp with need, her scent going straight to his head like a glass of champagne.

She cried out as his tongue sought her clit, rasped across it. His cock hardened even more as she clenched her hands in his hair and held him to her. Again and again he teased the nub of her desire, circling it, flicking it, sucking it as he slipped one finger inside her, then a second, stroking in rhythm with his mouth until she was panting and begging for release.

A first orgasm crashed over her, drawing his name from her lips as her body spasmed around his fingers. And still he did not cease, building upon it, extending it. Not until the last cry was wrung from her lips and her knees buckled did he withdraw.

Roland caught her easily and lifted her even as he stood, urging her legs around his waist. He was shaking with need, her taste lingering on his tongue. The kisses and love bites she delivered to his neck only enflamed him more.

Turning, he took two steps and pressed her up against the wall. Her ankles locked behind his back as she eagerly sought his mouth.

"Be careful," he warned softly. "My fangs are very sharp."

She nodded wordlessly, then shocked the hell out of him by stroking one with her tongue. A shudder of pleasure worked its way through him at this evidence of her acceptance of him.

Supporting her weight with one arm, he reached up with the other to palm one of her breasts. He lowered his mouth to the other and again worshipped it with teeth and tongue.

He couldn't wait much longer.

As if hearing his thoughts, Sarah reached down between them and took his cock in her hand. Roland groaned as she stroked him, squeezed him, drew her thumb in circles around the moist, sensitive crown.

"I want you inside me," she murmured, her breath warm on his ear.

Raising his head, he met her heated gaze and told her hoarsely, "Take me there."

Eyes fastened to his, she guided him to her moist entrance and drew him in.

He groaned. She was so warm and tight.

Sarah sucked in a breath as Roland sank to the hilt, loving the heavy feel of him.

His eyes glowed fiercely as he began to move, the amber bright against his tanned skin and dark eyebrows. His fangs were extended. Fangs he was careful to keep from cutting or puncturing her while he took her nipple between his teeth and stroked it with his tongue, sending shards of pleasure slicing through her.

"Roland," she moaned, burying her hands in his hair and holding him to her. "You feel so good."

His hands tightened. His thrusts increased. Quicker. Harder.

"Yes," she groaned, urging him against her with her legs, head falling back against the wall.

He trailed his lips up her breast, over her collarbone to her neck, found the pulse beating frantically just beneath the surface.

Was he going to bite her?

It wasn't fear that raced through her at the thought, but excitement.

He stroked his tongue across the skin. A gentle grazing of his teeth followed as he drew his free hand down her stomach, delving into the thatch of curls to tease her clit.

It was too much. Sarah splintered apart in his arms, crying out as a second climax even stronger than the first careened through her.

Roland joined her with a groan, her body milking his as wave after wave of pleasure buffeted her.

When the last ripples had faded, he leaned his forehead against the wall beside her, his damp cheek pressed to hers. Their breath came in gasps as he wrapped both arms around her and held her tightly.

"That was . . . incredible," she said between breaths, sliding her arms around his neck and holding him close, though her sated body wanted to sink into a boneless heap at his feet.

He raised his head, drawing back just enough to look down at her.

She smiled and cupped his face with one hand. "Those eyes," she murmured, entranced by their glow.

He nuzzled her palm, pressing a kiss to its center.

"You're so beautiful," she told him and couldn't care less that the word was more often used to describe women. He *was* beautiful. And despite his apparent misgivings, she liked seeing him like this. Eyes as bright as the moon. So consumed by passion that he couldn't hide his true nature from her.

His brow furrowed. "I almost bit you."

"I know." She touched a finger to his tempting (and talented) mouth. He had the softest lips she had ever kissed.

"I'm sorry."

Remembering his previous experience with women, she gave him a quick kiss. "It's okay, Roland. You didn't scare me." She felt heat climb into her cheeks. "To be honest"—she leaned forward to whisper in his ear—"it turned me on."

"It did?"

She leaned back again so she could see him.

His face was lit with the most adorable, boyish smile she had seen on him thus far, making her doubly glad she had told him.

"Really."

He gave her a quick, buoyant kiss that made her smile.

When he drew back, she was sorry to see his fangs had retracted.

Easing her feet to the floor, he held her steady until her rubbery legs would support her. "The desire to bite you was almost overpowering," he admitted, "but I have to resist it. As addictive as I find your scent, I'm afraid your blood would be even more so and make me want to keep coming back for more." He brushed her hair back from her face and gently cupped her cheek. "I can't risk infecting you, Sarah. I *won't* risk it. I care too much about you."

She covered his hand with hers and held it there, feeling surprisingly disappointed, yet touched that he cared so much for her he would deny himself to keep her safe.

Sending him a mischievous look from beneath her lashes, she murmured, "I guess you'll just have to keep tasting me in other ways and places."

Grinning, he shook his head. "You're an amazing woman."

Adopting an exaggeratedly somber look, she nodded. "I know."

Roland laughed and scooped her up into his arms. "Let's go try out that whirlpool tub."

Chapter 13

All was quiet when Bastien awoke. Glancing at the clock, he saw it was late afternoon. The other vampires would still be asleep, rousing only when the sun set. He supposed it was his age that allowed him to wake as early as he did. Perhaps the longer one was infected, the weaker the side effects became, requiring less rest and allowing brief exposure to sunlight.

His thoughts turned to Roland and the woman as he dressed, then began negotiating the underground maze.

Sarah Bingham.

After this morning's failed attempt had cost him twelve more men—all human—Bastien had set Tanner to seeking out information on her, wanting to know what her role in all of this was.

Apparently Sarah was neither a member of the network nor Roland's Second. She was a thirty-year-old music theory professor, who—as far as he knew—had never laid eyes on Roland until Bastien and his men had staked him out for the sunrise practically in her backyard.

She was a complication he had not anticipated, but one that may work to his advantage. Killing Roland was his top priority. He would accomplish that feat using any means necessary.

Crossing the basement's main room, he climbed the stairs.

The farmhouse's living room was empty. There were only four humans in his employ now. He could hear three of them trolling for snacks in the kitchen.

Bastien entered the study as the fourth, Tanner, pulled a stack of papers from the humming printer.

"Is that tonight's list?"

Tanner jumped, then turned to regard him with a worrisome amount of relief. "You're awake. Finally."

That couldn't be good.

"What's wrong?"

Tanner rolled his eyes and set the papers on the neat desktop. "It's Keegan. He's been calling every five minutes, wanting to meet with you."

"Did he say what the problem was?"

"No, he just kept cursing me out for not waking you up. Then cursed me out some more for not telling him where you live so he could do it himself."

"Thank you for that." Bastien was still unsure he had done the right thing by trusting the biochemist and didn't want to leave himself and the others vulnerable.

"Sure thing. Maybe you should call before he has a stroke." Lowering his voice, he muttered, "Or before I strangle him."

Bastien smiled. "I'll wait and go see him when it's dark."

"You want backup?"

"No, I can handle him."

Tanner laughed. "I'm sure you can."

The phone rang.

Tanner glanced at the caller ID, lifted the receiver, then slammed it down again. "How's the hunt going?"

"More slowly than I anticipated."

"Anything I can do?"

"Just what you're already doing."

Nodding, Tanner rounded the desk and held out the papers. "Here's tonight's assignments."

Each page had a name and address at the top and Mapquest directions below it.

"There seems to be an endless supply, doesn't there?"

Tanner's lips tightened. "Yes, there is."

Dr. Montrose Keegan fell into the *arrogant little prick* category. Bastien did not like him. However, that dislike was not intense enough to deter him from accepting an opportunity very few vampires had been given.

Montrose's twenty-three-year-old brother, Casey, had succumbed to the virus four years earlier. (Drunken college students were easy prey for vampires, which was why so many of Bastien's men had been under twenty-five years of age when they were transformed.) As commonly happened, the vampire who turned him had almost immediately abandoned him.

Bastien had found Casey and Montrose shortly thereafter and had taken the young vampire under his wing, offering him shelter and instruction as long as Montrose helped him search for a cure and Casey agreed to keep their lair's location a secret, even from his brother.

The arrangement had worked well so far. Unfortunately, Montrose forgot on occasion just who wielded the power in this game, and needed to be reminded.

Bastien silently let himself into the single man's house and followed the curses and frustrated thumps and thuds to the basement lab.

His back to Bastien, Montrose stood beside a cluttered desk with a phone receiver held to his ear. Swearing foully, he slammed the receiver down.

Bastien let his fangs descend their full length, made sure his irritation was enough to make his eyes glow, then put on a burst of preternatural speed so he seemed to appear out of nowhere directly in front of the good doctor.

Montrose was so startled, his feet left the floor. "Bastien! Where . . . H-H-How did you get in?"

Bastien curled his lip, flashing a bit of fang. "Tanner Long is both my employee and my friend. Would you care to explain why you verbally abused and tried to berate him into disturbing my rest?"

Sweat beading on his forehead, the average-size, prematurely balding man took a nervous step backward. "I-It was an emergency."

Bastien towered over him, scowling menacingly. "An emergency would be finding the teaspoonful of Casey's remains left behind after an immortal's attack."

Montrose paled.

"Casey is even now awakening from the rest you sought to deny me, so there *is* no emergency. Did you finish the suit?"

"N-no. It'll be ready tomorrow."

"Why is it not ready tonight?"

After stuttering several unsuccessful beginnings, Montrose said, "I just—I need to know where you got that blood sample you brought me. Not Casey's. The other one."

Bastien frowned. "You know where I got it."

"From your enemy? The Immortal Guardian?"

"Yes."

"Where can I find him?"

"In a few days, there won't be anything left for you to find."

Montrose shook his head wildly. "You can't kill him. He isn't human."

Bastien laughed. "Neither is your brother."

"But he was once," Montrose said earnestly.

Frowning, Bastien studied the man carefully. There was an almost fanatical gleam in his eyes, put there by something he must have found in Roland's blood.

"What are you saying, Keegan?"

Montrose crossed to one of the tables laden with computers, centrifuges, and assorted medical paraphernalia Bastien knew little about and picked up a labeled glass vial with blood in it. "I'm saying Casey may be a vampire now, but he started out human. *This* man"—he held up the vial—"didn't. This man was never human."

Bastien stared at him.

What the hell?

Though Sarah knew it irked him, Roland didn't go out to hunt that night. They bathed Nietzsche, shared what for others would've been dinner, but for them was brunch, did the dishes, let Nietzsche out, brought the cat back in again when he picked a fight with an opossum, then retired to the living room.

While Sarah caught up on world events through various satellite news channels, Roland paced restlessly. Back and forth. Around and around. Until she couldn't take it anymore and turned off the television.

"Roland."

"Yes?" he replied absently.

"Why are you still here?"

"What do you mean?"

"Shouldn't you be out hunting?"

He frowned. "I'm not leaving you here alone, unprotected."

"I'm not in danger here."

"As you were in no danger at my home?"

"You said yourself they must have followed us after the big paranormal rumble. Well, there's no way they could have followed us here. Seth zapped us here or flashed us or teleported us. Whatever you want to call it. There's nothing to lead them here."

He resumed his pacing. "Except me, if they see me out hunting and follow me home."

"Yeah, like that's going to happen. You're expecting it now and will know it if they even *try* to tail you."

"You have more faith in me than I do."

"I have *complete* faith in you," she told him honestly.

He stopped and turned to stare at her, his expression stunned. "How can you? I've failed you twice."

Now it was her turn to frown. "What? When?"

"When you were harmed running from that bastard Bastien—and me, I might add." He had never said as much, but she knew her initial fear of him when she had seen him sprout fangs and drink the goth kid's blood had hurt him. "And again when you were nearly shot and burned alive while in my home and under my protection."

"I'm here, am I not?" she retorted, coming to her feet. "Safe and secure and still in one piece."

"I'm not leaving you."

"What about Bastien? He almost killed you twice. Don't you want to find him?"

Hell, yes! his expression shouted even as he shook his head. "Your safety is more important to me."

"Then call Chris Reordon and have him send some guys over to protect me while you go take care of business."

"I'm not going to entrust your safety to a group of humans I don't know from Adam."

"So . . . what? Bastien goes free?"

His shoulders tensed. "Marcus is searching for him, as is Lisette."

Sarah crossed the room and stood toe to toe with him. "You know that isn't good enough." Reaching up, she stroked his clenched jaw. "You want to be out there with them, hunting this guy down and taking him out yourself."

Leaning down, he pressed his forehead to hers and sighed. "I don't see any way around this. I can't let anything happen to you, Sarah."

Her heart swelled at the emotion in his deep voice.

He didn't say it as though he felt obligated to keep her safe. He said it as though he couldn't bear the idea of her getting hurt.

Pressing a quick kiss to his lips, Sarah took his hand,

turned, and began leading him toward the hallway. Through the door to the basement and down the spiral staircase they went, Roland asking no questions.

When they reached the subterranean floor, she turned left instead of toward the bedroom they shared on the right.

"Where are we going?"

Sarah said nothing until they reached the training room, where she flicked on the light. "I want you to teach me how to kick vampire ass."

"What?"

"Knowing I can defend myself against a vampire attack will help put your mind at ease. Mine, too. So . . ." She motioned to the weapons and assorted equipment that filled the high school gym–size room. "Teach me."

He propped his hands on his hips. "No, you are not going to hunt vampires."

"I don't want to hunt vampires. Though your chauvinistic, autocratic, I'm-the-man-so-you'll-do-as-I-say attitude may prod me into it."

"I didn't mean—"

"I know. You're just worried about me and want to protect me. But you can't be with me every minute—"

When he opened his mouth to interrupt, she hastily covered his lips with her fingers. "Let me finish. You can't be with me every minute of every day for the rest of my life. Sooner or later I will be in a position where a vampire—not necessarily Bastien—could catch me alone. Don't you want me to be able to fight him off?"

Roland removed her fingers, kissed them, then linked them with his own. "Yes."

"Excellent. I should be in pretty good shape." She exercised six days a week, cardio and weights. "So show me what I need to know to kill something that moves faster than I can follow."

* * *

Three nights later, Roland called a halt to their latest training session. Panting heavily, Sarah took the towel he offered and mopped her damp face as she collapsed onto one of the padded benches the room boasted.

Roland tried but couldn't seem to wipe the grin off his face. It had been there for at least an hour now and his cheeks were starting to ache from it. He had not enjoyed himself this much in centuries.

Sarah was a natural. Already in near peak physical condition, she had listened to his instructions, earnestly mimicked them as proficiently as she was able, then—as he drilled her and tested her and put her through her paces—had rapidly begun to carry them out like a pro.

It helped that she had taken a couple of martial arts classes while she was in college. She was swift on her feet, graceful of motion, and such a joy to be around. Her quirky sense of humor reared its head at the most unexpected moments. She would be deadly serious one minute, concentrating on the lesson, then say something the next that would have him folding over with laughter.

"I am so screwed," she said, dabbing at her neck.

That managed to dim his smile a little. "Why do you say that?" He crossed over and seated himself beside her so their shoulders brushed.

She was dressed like a professional vampire hunter. Black cargo pants that resembled military fatigues with lots of loops and pockets for weapons and ammo rode low on her hips and fit her legs loosely. A black tank top clung to her narrow waist and full breasts in damp patches. New black boots fit her small feet snugly and, he feared, rubbed blisters as she broke them in.

The tote bag carrying her clothing had been destroyed in the fire, so she had had to make do with what she could find here at what she called "David's Estate."

Since he never knew when an immortal or one of the network's humans might drop by, David had made it a habit to keep a supply of men's and women's clothing on hand for any in need. Immortals' clothing tended to end up torn and blood-spattered after a confrontation with a vamp. Bloodstains were more difficult to discern on black material, often appearing as simply indeterminate wet splotches, so everything in David's take-what-you-need wardrobe was black and suitable for combat. Everything except the underwear that was still in new, sealed packages. It was bright white.

Sarah looked great in black. Her pale skin seemed almost to glow in comparison where it wasn't flushed from her exertions.

"I totally suck at this," she complained.

He looked at her in surprise. "No, you don't. I was just thinking that you seem to have a natural talent for it."

She eyed him dubiously.

Roland tucked a damp curl behind her ear. "I've trained many immortals who didn't learn as fast as you do."

"I didn't know you trained other immortals. I thought you preferred solitude."

"Seth doesn't always give me a choice in the matter. Sometimes he just pops in, drops some poor sod off, says 'train him,' then leaves before I can offer any protest."

She smiled wryly. "And now you're stuck training me."

He drew the backs of his fingers down her warm, damp cheek. "Training you is a pleasure. I told you, you're a natural. I have not enjoyed myself so much in a very long time." He sent her a wicked grin. "At least not fully clothed."

She laughed.

"Why are you so convinced you did poorly?"

"When you attacked me and tested me, you were holding yourself back."

"I want you to learn the moves and grow comfortable with them before I come at you in earnest with preternatural speed and strength."

"But you *will* come at me in earnest, right? Soon?"

"Yes, if you promise to let me heal the bruises or other injuries that will result."

"Ro-land."

"Sarah, please," he said somberly, taking one of her hands in his. "I'm not simply mouthing platitudes when I say I can't bear to see you hurt. I care about you. It's going to be very . . . difficult for me to train you in earnest, knowing I risk hurting you when my every instinct is screaming at me to protect you. I won't be able to do it unless you assure me I can heal you if anything happens."

He couldn't read her expression as she gazed up at him, nibbling her lower lip.

"Okay, you can heal me."

The tension that had been slowly gathering in his shoulders vanished. "Thank you."

Raising her free hand, she drew the soft pads of her fingers across his forehead, down his temple, over his cheekbone, and along his jaw in a tender caress that sped his pulse.

"Do you know how easy it would be for me to fall in love with you?" she whispered.

Roland closed his eyes. How could he feel elated and as if his heart were breaking at the same time? "That would be very unwise," he told her softly.

"Because you don't feel the same?"

Opening his eyes, he brought the hand he held to his lips for a fervent kiss and shook his head. "No, sweetling. I fear you may have stolen my heart in the first twenty-four hours we were together."

"Shouldn't that be a good thing? If we both feel the same way . . ."

"If I were human, it would be wonderful. We could fall in love with light hearts, marry, have children, grandchildren, grow old together, live happily ever after, and die. But I'm not human, Sarah. I'm immortal. My body will never age. I will remain exactly as I am now while you grow old. And, in time, you would become bitter and doubt my feelings for you."

She stared down at their clasped hands. "Maybe I wouldn't."

He smiled sadly. "If so, you would be the first. There have been other immortals who have loved humans."

Pulling his hand onto her lap, she toyed with his fingers. "Even if I didn't, I would still grow old and die."

He remained quiet, letting her ponder it.

"I would probably come to feel like a chain around your neck. A strong young—at least physically—man tied to a dying old woman."

"You see how it would be," he murmured, full of regret. "And I couldn't give you children."

"Did the transformation leave you sterile?"

"That's what we all believed since even those who wished to reproduce with their human lovers were unable to. However, our scientists have come to understand—"

"You have scientists?"

"Both human and immortal, learning everything they can about the virus. How it works. Researching a cure and, barring that, some way to force the virus to mutate in vampires the way it has in us so that we can end their madness and bloodlust."

"Have you had any luck with that?"

"None so far."

"What about the fertility problem?"

"We aren't sterile, but we may as well be. With our males, the virus dramatically decreases the lifespan of our sperm." He paused uncertainly. "Are you sure you want to hear this?"

"Yes, I want to know everything."

So be it. "Normally sperm can live inside a woman's body for up to five days. Ours, however, die pretty much as soon as we ejaculate. Because of the strange symbiotic relationship we have with the virus, it dies with the sperm before the woman can become infected, which is why I haven't been using condoms."

"What about immortal women? Can they get pregnant?"

"No, the virus present in the eggs their bodies produce attacks and kills the sperm of human males."

"And if she sleeps with an immortal?"

"We believe that, if circumstances are optimal, pregnancy could result." He sighed, reluctant to continue. But she had asked and she should know it all. "In truth, we're uncertain how the virus would affect a fetus. Or a baby if it were carried to term and delivered. Would the child of two immortals age or remain forever trapped in the form of an infant? Immortal females are always conscious of the time they ovulate and, when they do, refrain from engaging in intercourse with immortal males for fear of the consequences."

Her brow furrowed. "So, no children."

"No children."

How he wished he *could* give her children, watch her body swell with his babe, have a tiny replica of Sarah skipping through their home.

Sarah raised her chin and met his gaze. "If the trade-off is having you, Roland, I wouldn't need children to be happy."

His heart skipped a beat. "What are you saying?"

"What if you transformed me?"

Stunned, Roland almost forgot to breathe. "You would let me?"

She opened her mouth to speak, paused, then sighed. "I don't know. All of this is happening so quickly. I want to say yes. But considering what's at stake, I think I should take more time to think about it."

"Just knowing you would consider it means the world to me."

"Then you would do it, if I asked? You would transform me?"

Pleasure and pain again warred within him. "No."

Her lips parted in surprise. "Why?"

"I told you how the virus works. If you aren't a *gifted one,* your body won't mutate the virus and you will turn vampire instead of immortal." He fingered a satiny strand of brown hair that had escaped from her ponytail. "Every one of us has black hair and dark brown eyes."

Understanding dimmed her hazel gaze. "You think I would turn vampire, that I don't have the right DNA."

"Do you possess any special gifts you haven't mentioned?" he asked, not really holding out any hope. "Telepathy? Telekinesis? The ability to shape shift? Teleport? See the future? Know an object's history by touch? Heal with your hands? See the dead?"

She shook her head with the first gift mentioned and continued wagging it back and forth as he named a few others. "Nothing. No special gifts."

"Then I won't transform you and risk your turning vampire."

Sarah stared up at Roland, so depressed now she didn't really know what to say. No matter what path they took, they were screwed. They could either go their separate ways, maintain a human/immortal relationship he seemed to think would be doomed, or transform her, which would probably turn her into a bloodlusting lunatic vampire.

"This really blows."

"I know," he agreed fatalistically.

"Isn't there a blood test or something that would let us know for sure whether I have the right DNA?"

"Yes. If you decide you want to be transformed, I can take you to one of our labs and have a sample tested to be sure."

But she could tell he didn't think there was a chance in hell she would turn immortal.

Hmm. Alone without Roland. Bitter with Roland. Or murderously crazy.

Sarah wasn't too thrilled with the choices.

"Anybody home?" a voice called out upstairs.

Roland's eyes immediately flashed bright amber as fangs burst from his gums.

He was gone in a blink, moving so quickly he seemed to vanish.

Sarah took off after him, running from the room, down the hall, and up the winding staircase.

"Don't-kill-me-it's-Marcus!" was shouted, the words emerging one on top of another.

Indistinct masculine voices followed, growing more clear as she reached the ground floor and headed for the living room.

"David gave me the code to get through the security gate and a key," Marcus was saying. Roland must have asked how he had gotten in without tripping the alarm.

"When?"

"When I moved to North Carolina. Every immortal in the state has one."

"I don't."

"That's because you're antisocial," Marcus replied as though explaining it to a child.

Sarah pursed her lips. She was beginning to think the other immortals used that particular label just to aggravate him.

"If you had accepted his invitation," Marcus went on, "he would have given you one, too. Hello, Sarah."

"Hi, Marcus," she greeted as she joined them, noticing a third man standing nearby.

Roland was scowling at his friend. "Did you make certain you weren't followed?"

"I saw, heard, and smelled nothing."

"I didn't see anything either," the other man said. He was about five-eleven with dark blond hair, blue eyes, and a muscular build. Stepping forward, he offered his hand to Roland. "Chris Reordon."

Roland shook it. "I recognized your voice."

Chris offered his hand to Sarah next.

She smiled. "Sarah Bingham."

"Nice to meet you, Sarah."

When Chris gave her a friendly smile, Roland sidled up next to her and draped an arm around her shoulders.

Was he jealous?

The warning scowl he sent the blond certainly seemed to indicate he was as he motioned for them to sit down. "What have you found out?"

Sarah and Roland sat beside each other on the sofa. Marcus took the cushy chair on Sarah's other side while Chris sat in one of the chairs opposite them and dropped a manila file folder on the coffee table between them.

"The vamps seem to have gone deep underground," Marcus said wearily. "Lisette and I have spent every hour of darkness searching for them for the past three nights and haven't found a thing. If they're feeding, they're doing it well outside our territory and are being damned careful to stay under our radar on their way in and out."

"Any idea where Bastien's lair is?"

"None. There's been no sign of him either. It's almost as if they all dropped off the face of the bloody earth."

Sarah watched Roland's scowl deepen and wondered if perhaps he and Marcus had killed them all.

If all of his henchmen and fellow vampires were dead, would Bastien flee or stay and rebuild his numbers?

"What about missing persons?" Roland asked Chris. "Could he be busy recruiting?"

Chris shook his head. "No new missing person reports since he torched your house. And my men at the county morgues said there haven't been any new feeding deaths camouflaged as car crashes, shootings, suicides, or farming accidents. As Marcus said, any vamps in the area are finding their nourishment elsewhere."

So maybe there *were* no more vampires left, she thought hopefully.

Chris seemed to be following the same train of thought, because he leaned forward and braced his elbows on splayed knees. "Is it possible you killed them all and Bastien is on the run?"

"No," Roland immediately responded. "This guy has it in for me. He isn't going to give up after just three skirmishes."

Inwardly Sarah shook her head. Three skirmishes in two days. Three days of training. All together it seemed as though months had passed.

Marcus nodded. "I agree. Whatever this is, it's personal. He isn't going to give up that easily."

"As to that"—Chris flipped the file open—"I've been doing some digging and trying to find out who the hell this guy is. Since you said he looked to be about thirty and is lucid enough to organize and maintain a small army, I figured he had to have been transformed within the past ten years or so. Unfortunately, every Bastien or Sebastien, first or middle name, born in England in the past fifty years has been accounted for. I expanded the search to include Scotland, Ireland, and Wales and came up with the same results, which means it's an assumed name. He's going to be hard to track down."

Vampires were usually fairly easy to trace because, unlike immortals, they tended to keep the names they were given at birth. They might try to change it once or twice to avoid suspicion, but inevitably reverted to the first once the madness kicked in and it became more difficult to arrange and keep up with aliases.

Roland glowered. "So you've got nothing?"

"Not exactly," Chris said, unfazed by Roland's ire and Marcus's growing irritation. "Like you immortals, when vampires use assumed names they usually use family names because they're easier to remember. I put the genealogy geeks on it and they found this."

Rifling through the papers, Chris chose three, turned them upside down, and slid them across the coffee table to Roland.

Sarah, Roland, and Marcus all leaned forward to peruse them.

It looked like something printed off of various Web pages. One said something about the House of Lords. Another was the passenger list of a ship. She couldn't tell what the third sheet said. The writing was too small. However, there was an old sketch, displayed near the top, of a man who resembled Bastien.

"The only Sebastien we could link you with is this man," Chris said, pointing to the sketch, "Sebastien Newcombe, Earl of Marston, born 1783." It couldn't be Bastien then. Roland had said vampires rarely even lived one century. "Now, you and Marston were both in London for much of the first two decades of the nineteenth century. Marston died in 1815 under mysterious circumstances. His body was never recovered. That's a quote and, as you know, a red flag."

"They can't be one and the same. Vampires don't live two hundred years."

"True. But I wonder if you might've killed Marston and all of this is a vendetta handed down father to son to today's Bastien. Thanks to a flood destroying a few pertinent records, information on Marston's bloodline becomes a bit sketchy in the twentieth century, right around the time your man would have been born."

"So Marston was a vampire I hunted?"

"Either that or a human."

Roland's voice turned chilly. "Immortals do not kill innocents when they feed."

"I'm aware of that," Chris said. "But you do kill minions and minions tend to procreate."

Marcus frowned. "You think Marston was a minion and Bastien is his descendant?"

Chris shrugged. "Marston wouldn't be the first member of the nobility to run with the wrong crowd. Nor would your Bastien be the first to be recruited, then later turned by an ancestor. We've seen the virus make its way down through family trees before. Remember that vamp in Virginia who turned both of his grandsons a few years ago?"

Sarah nibbled her lower lip as Roland picked up the paper and studied the sketch more closely.

"I don't know," he pronounced slowly. "I don't recall encountering him in London." He handed the paper to Marcus. "Do you?"

"No, and minions tend to linger longer in my memory because we have to dispose of the bodies."

Uncertain whether they would be irritated by her pointing out the obvious or appreciate her input, Sarah slowly raised her hand.

Roland glanced over at her with a furrowed brow, then smiled. "We aren't in a classroom, Sarah. If you have something you wish to say, you don't have to raise your hand."

The other two men grinned.

Shrugging, she returned their smiles. "Well . . . I was just thinking you might be overlooking something. . . ."

Chris frowned.

"I mean, I could be wrong. It just seems so obvious. . . ." She trailed off.

"What does?" Roland asked, reaching out to touch her hand.

Holding his gaze, she said, "Maybe Bastien isn't a vampire at all. Maybe he's immortal. And the reason Chris couldn't find any information on him is that he isn't a *descendant* of the Earl of Marston. He *is* the Earl of Marston."

Roland and the others stared at her.

"That isn't possible," she heard Marcus say.

Sarah continued to hold Roland's gaze. "You told me yourself not half an hour ago that all immortals share similar physical characteristics. When he landed on the hood of Marcus's car—"

"Is that what happened to it?" Chris said in the background.

"—I got a good look at him, Roland. He has black hair, dark brown eyes, and is over six feet tall. If he stood next to you and Marcus in a crowd, people would think the three of you were brothers."

Chris shook his head. "He can't be immortal, Sarah.

Immortals don't fraternize with vampires, they kill them. And they sure as hell don't try to kill other immortals."

Roland turned to look at Marcus.

Both remained silent.

"Has an immortal ever later turned vampire?" she asked uncertainly.

"No, never," Chris insisted. "Once their bodies mutate the virus, they're safe from the madness forever. And while there might be one or two immortals I would classify as assholes, they're never evil the way vampires are. Immortals are good guys. They don't turn bad no matter what the incentive."

"Oh." Discouraged, she returned her attention to Roland, who still stared at Marcus.

"Could Seth have missed one?" he murmured, his expression grave.

Marcus looked ill. "He never has before."

"Not to our knowledge. Or his."

"Oh shit."

Chris's eyes widened. "You aren't serious, are you?"

Roland met his disbelieving gaze. "It makes the most sense."

"But he tried to kill you! Three times!"

Roland laced his fingers through Sarah's. "If Seth didn't find him after he was transformed and no other immortal happened upon him and took him under their wing, he will have learned everything he knows from vampires."

Marcus dragged a hand down over his face. "He probably doesn't even know he *is* immortal and thinks he's a vampire. No wonder he's so bloody fast and strong."

Sensing how troubled Roland was by the notion, Sarah surreptitiously inched closer to him.

He squeezed her hand. "This changes everything."

Marcus nodded. "We sure as hell can't kill him now."

"Uh, I hate to sound like a broken record," Chris said, "but he—tried—to—kill—you. And if he's been living as a vampire, he's probably killed a lot of humans in the last two centuries and transformed who knows how many others."

Marcus emitted a huff of annoyance. "No shit, Sherlock."

Sarah decided to leap in again before Chris could spout a caustic rebuttal. "You don't know that. If he's immortal, that means he isn't a slave to the bloodlust, right? So maybe he feeds the way immortals did before blood banks came on the scene. Maybe he takes what he needs without killing his victim. He could've killed *me* when they attacked en masse in my front yard, but didn't."

"He told his men to," Marcus reminded her.

"No, he told them I was Roland's weakness."

"Then chased after you when you tried to get away," Roland pointed out.

She chewed her lip. "If he thought you cared about me, he might have thought I would be useful as bait."

Roland swore and dropped his head back.

Marcus frowned. "What?"

"When his minions were dousing the house with gasoline, one of them told another Bastien had said not to light it until they got Sarah out. I assumed he intended to . . . I don't know . . . punish her for helping me or use her to get to me if we managed to escape. But the minions never specifically mentioned taking her back with them."

Chris shook his head. "You aren't actually suggesting he was protecting her, are you?"

Marcus cocked a brow. "If he doesn't kill humans . . ."

Sarah thought Chris looked as if he were about to blow a gasket.

"He commands a pack of vampires! Do you think they're innocent, too?"

"We can't kill him," Roland reiterated. "Not until we know for sure."

"Then what the hell are you going to do—walk up to him, shake hands, and say, 'No hard feelings'?"

"No." Roland shared another look with Marcus. "We'll capture him and turn him over to Seth."

Marcus nodded slowly. "Do you want to tell Seth, or do you want me to?"

Roland's hand tightened around Sarah's. "I will."

Chapter 14

The heels of Seth's boots made sharp percussive sounds on the stone floor as he strode through the castle's many passageways. Up one. Down the next.

There was an urgency to his steps, a tension in his shoulders that held them rigidly squared. The hem of his leather duster flared out behind him as he swung around another corner, confident of his direction despite the stygian shadows unbroken by either torches or electricity.

In his right hand, a cell phone was clutched so tightly, the plastic threatened to crumble. Roland's words still spun through Seth's mind, circling like vultures waiting to pick clean the bones of his reason.

It couldn't be true.

Roland's enemy could not be an immortal. He couldn't have missed one.

Could he?

At last, Seth reached his destination and entered a room large enough to be a ballroom, leaving the door open behind him. Immortals and humans alike were forbidden to cross its threshold or even to open the door and peer within, not that they could. Though there was no visible lock on the large oak door, any who sought to open it in Seth's absence would find the task impossible, even when force and power tools were applied.

Seth took his responsibilities seriously and generously opened his many homes to the immortals he watched over—as well as the humans who served them so honorably and fought by their sides—whether he was currently in residence or not. Anything they needed, he endeavored to provide. But this . . .

This was his alone.

No windows graced the room. No moonlight lit his path.

Were it not for the overhead lights that flickered on at his silent command, he would be standing in a dark void. There was no furniture. No ornamentation whatsoever save the elaborate carving that whorled across the floor and up three of the four pale gray marble walls. Only the wall encasing the door bore no markings.

Seth's hands trembled as he crossed the floor, his steps echoing hollowly in the cavernous room. His heart drummed loudly in his chest. Dread spilled into his stomach, burning like acid.

Hidden amongst the many shadows and crevices the massive engraving created were names, dates, and small notations made in an ancient language that would confound all but the one who had etched them.

Seth found what he sought on the wall opposite the door, tucked away in the northeast corner.

One name. A single notation. And a date.

SEBASTIEN NEWCOMBE, EARL OF MARSTON

EMPATH

1783

The cell phone hit the floor with a clatter.

It was true.

Sebastien, or Bastien, had been a *gifted one.* When he had

been infected with the virus, he had turned immortal, not vampire.

And Seth had not been there to help him.

Staggered by the guilt that inundated him, Seth leaned against the east wall.

How had he missed it?

Though he had never admitted as much to the immortals—to do so would only invite questions he could not or would not answer—there were three phenomena he always felt internally, no matter how far away they took place: the birth of a *gifted one,* the death of either a *gifted one* or an immortal, and the transformation of a *gifted one* into an immortal. The first generated a sort of breathless tingle in his chest, the second a feeling of emptiness, and the third a sick feeling of dread not unlike that he was experiencing now. If he focused on that dread, the individual's fear and pain would come to him and serve as a beacon he could use to track them down much as he had the mystery woman.

He always felt it. Always followed it. Helped the newly initiated immortals through the difficult transition. Schooled them on their new nature. Gave them purpose, guidance, the comfort of a friend. Then either trained them himself or introduced them to another immortal, who would perform the task in his stead and become their mentor.

Who had done that for Sebastien? To whom had he turned in Seth's absence? How many humans had he harmed or killed in his ignorance? His anger? His bitterness?

If he had been taught by a vampire, Sebastien's head would have been filled with lies about the Immortal Guardians who hunted them.

Did he know he was different from his fellow vampires? Did he know he was immortal? Had he ever approached one of the Guardians, hoping for acceptance, and instead been attacked because of his vampiric ways?

Was that what had transpired with Roland, sparking this plot for revenge?

Pressing his back to the wall, Seth slid down and sat on the cold stone floor, boots planted a shoulders' width apart, knees bent.

How had he missed it?

If Bastien had been turned in his thirties, it would have happened between 1813 and 1823. The first two decades of the nineteenth century had been tough ones. Bloody ones. And not just because of Napoleon Bonaparte's perseverance. Another vampire had gotten it into his feeble brain that if he amassed enough vampire servants, he could take over the world.

It happened once every millennium or so. A vampire would start turning humans left and right, instructing them to turn more. But the virus was so corrosive that by the time he had transformed sufficient numbers with which he could plan a campaign, he was too stark raving mad to organize or lead them.

This one had been no different. Lost to the madness, he had quickly forgotten his agenda and just kept turning many of his victims instead of killing them, abandoning them and leaving them to fend for themselves. It had taken Roland, Marcus, and other Immortal Guardians years to track down and destroy him and the many fledgling vampires he had spawned.

And at the end of it all, Seth had found himself with an unusually large number of new immortals requiring aid and training.

The hardest had been Lisette. She had been turned in 1815 and, before Seth could locate her, had unintentionally turned both of her brothers. They had been offering her their blood and helping her hide her condition, none of them understanding that repeated feeding would transform them as well.

Three voices calling out to him at once.

Had there been a fourth, drowned out by their collective cries?

Despair overwhelming him, Seth braced his elbows on his knees and let his head fall forward.

How had he missed it?

Had there been others like Sebastien?

He had been so sure he had found them all, but now . . .

Beneath the self-recriminations and doubt pummeling him, he heard the sounds of bare feet meeting stone and the faint rustle of clothing moving steadily closer.

Through the open door his visitor came. Into the room. *His* room. The forbidden room.

Padding toward him. Slowing. Hesitating.

From the corner of his eye, he saw small pale toes curl against the cold stone, nearly hidden by the frilly hem of a demure white nightgown.

The mystery woman.

Stunned that she would seek him out, he raised his head and glanced up at her.

Caught midmotion, reaching toward him as though to touch his hair, she gasped, yanked her hand back, and took several hasty steps away.

Three days she had been with them and she was still utterly terrified. Though her wounds had been healed that first morning, she was so traumatized by all that had happened to her that she had neither spoken nor slept. He knew the latter because he, David, and Darnell had taken turns watching over her, gently trying to coax her into trusting them.

After a minimum of seventy-two hours without sleep, he didn't know what was keeping her upright. Yet there she was, hands nervously clenched in front of her, red hair charmingly disheveled, brow furrowed with concern as her green eyes met his and clung.

Seth did his best to force a smile, wanting to put her at ease.

She was the one person on the planet who would not be subjected to his wrath for daring to trespass.

“Hello, sweetheart,” he greeted her softly. Since she hadn’t spoken, they didn’t know her name.

Upon returning to Texas after healing Roland and Marcus, Seth had gathered his little crew together and teleported them all to his castle in England, wanting to put as much distance as possible between her and the ones who had tortured her.

She had spent the first day cowering in her room, perhaps expecting them to pick up where her captors had left off. The fact that he and David had healed her many wounds—those that hadn’t already healed themselves—had not lessened her fear of them at all. It only seemed to confuse her.

The second day, she had tentatively ventured out, exploring the sprawling castle and frequently observing him and the others from a distance. Seth had called ahead and dismissed the staff, so it was just the four of them. She watched them alertly when they spoke to her, but didn’t answer. Though her small form was emaciated, she refused to eat or drink anything they didn’t prepare in front of her or taste first themselves. Usually both. And always she kept her distance.

This was the first time she had voluntarily come so close to him or reached out to him.

“Are you all right?” he asked, thinking she looked a bit better, though shadows pooled beneath her expressive eyes. There was more color in her cheeks. She had gained a couple pounds. He suspected she would be a beauty once her body filled out with proper nourishment.

She nodded, indicating she was okay, then cocked her head to one side. Pointing to him, she raised her eyebrows.

“Me?” His own eyebrows rose. “You want to know if *I* am all right?”

She nodded.

He stared at her as understanding dawned. She had felt his distress and had come to see if he was okay. Which meant she was *em*pathic as well as telepathic.

Who *was* she?

Her body possessed incredible regenerative properties.

Both of the fingers and both of the toes that had been crudely amputated had grown back, something even immortals were incapable of achieving (though, with Seth's or David's aid, severed limbs could be reattached). She seemed quite powerful.

Not as powerful as himself, but perhaps as powerful as David, whose bloodline was purer than the other immortals because he was so old. Powerful enough, no doubt, to easily detect Seth's presence if he were to try to peek into her thoughts.

Yet she was neither immortal nor a *gifted one*.

It was a puzzle he had not been able to solve. And he wished now that the minds of the many dozens of armed guards he and David had had to wade through in order to save her had provided an answer. The men in white lab coats who had been torturing her no doubt could have told him but had been slain out of sheer fury, their knowledge dying with them.

She made a motion with her head, urging him to respond to her silent question.

"Am I all right?" he repeated. Looking away, he stared, unblinking, at the wall opposite him. The automated *I'm fine* he usually trotted out in response to the question stuck in his throat. "Not really."

He didn't offer her an explanation. He doubted telling her about the man he had failed so miserably—the man who had needed his help as much as she had—would reassure her and gain her trust.

Sighing, he leaned his head back.

How had he missed it? How had Sebastien's cries gone unheard?

Gathering the loose material of her nightgown around her, the mystery woman lowered herself to the floor beside him . . . beyond arm's reach, of course. Seated with her back to the wall, she covered those tiny feet with the white material, then wrapped her arms around bent knees.

Her movements ceased.

Quiet descended around them.

Seth's thoughts continued to swirl as she offered him silent solace.

Sprawled on the steps that led to the whirlpool tub, Roland watched as Sarah blow-dried her hair. The bathroom, which connected to the bedroom they had claimed for their own, was as sumptuous as the one he had painstakingly installed in his own former home.

He and Sarah had just shared a very passionate interlude in the tub behind him. She was so beautiful and sensual and funny. No other woman had ever made him laugh during sex. But, with Sarah, he would be mindless with lust one moment and roaring with laughter the next when she made some wildly inappropriate or jesting remark between gasps of ecstasy.

And he enjoyed making *her* laugh even more, treasured every chuckle he elicited.

A smile curled his lips.

Yesterday morning, when they had retired, he had tossed her onto the bed on her back, told her to hold on tight to the headboard, then pretended he was so far gone with lust that he couldn't get her pants off. Removing her boots, he had grasped the hem of each pant leg—knowing her belt wouldn't let them slide down her hips—and pulled hard. Sarah had squealed as her body had risen off the bed at least a foot.

The black jeans hadn't budged.

Feigning frustration, Roland had growled and yanked and shook. Her body had swung wildly from side to side and bobbed up and down as though she were on an out-of-control hammock. And all the while she had clung to the headboard, dissolving into giggles that made his heart go soft and warm.

Damn, he loved her.

He loved everything about her.

So much that he couldn't breathe when he contemplated

losing her and returning to his customarily cold, isolated existence.

The scent of ripe strawberries filled the room as she directed hot air through her soft brown tresses. A white towel hugged her slender curves from breasts to midthigh, slipping lower and baring more cleavage as she shifted her weight from one foot to the other.

There were two sinks in front of her, above which hung two oval-shape framed mirrors. They had found everything they needed among David's supplies. His toothbrush, comb, men's deodorant, and straight razor were clustered around the sink on the left. Scattered around the sink on the right were Sarah's toothbrush, ladies' deodorant, comb, styling gel, elastic ties, the toothpaste and shaving cream they shared, and, when she wasn't using them, her brush and the hair dryer.

He liked seeing their things together, mixing and mingling like a married couple's.

He liked watching her perform such mundane tasks as drying or braiding her hair. It was why he hadn't bothered to dry his own, merely running a comb through it and dragging on a pair of jeans before settling in to observe her.

It had rapidly become his favorite pastime. He felt so at peace in these moments. Almost as at peace as he did when he held her as she slept.

The whine of the dryer stopped. Sarah met his gaze in the mirror as she unplugged it and set it aside. "You're smiling," she said softly, the corners of her own lips turning up.

He nodded, still surprised by how naturally smiles and laughter came to him now.

She ran a brush through her hair, then set it on the counter.

He sat up, knees splayed, as she turned away from the mirror and approached him. Her cheeks and the tips of her ears were pink from the blow dryer, her skin warm and deliciously fragrant.

"I like it when you smile," she confessed tenderly, tunneling her fingers through his damp hair.

Sighing in bliss, he leaned forward, wrapped his arms around her, and rested his cheek against her stomach just beneath her breasts.

"You make me smile," he murmured, no longer fighting his feelings for her. He knew it wouldn't last, that he would lose her in the end, but had not the strength to resist the lure of the happiness—however brief it may be—that she brought him.

Tilting his head back, he rested his chin on her flat stomach and stared up at her. "My life was so barren before we met, Sarah. I couldn't feel anything anymore. Didn't *let* myself feel anything." Reaching up, he stroked her lovely face. "Then you came along with your courage and teasing and passion and woke me up."

She cupped his face in one hand, brushing her thumb across his cheek.

"Now I feel so much that, at times, it overwhelms me," he admitted. "I laugh. I want. I need. I *live,* Sarah. Because of you."

Her eyes glimmered with moisture. "I love you, Roland."

He rose and gathered her into a loose embrace. "I love you, too."

A tear spilled over her lashes as she smiled up at him. "I am *so* glad I decided to dig my garden that morning."

He grinned and stole a kiss. "I am, too."

She bit her lip. "Even though I'm going to grow old?"

A sobering fact he tried not to contemplate. "We can't know exactly what the future has in store for us. But I can tell you with absolute certainty that, young or old, I will love you every day we have together and will love you every day thereafter. I don't pretend to understand how this could have happened so swiftly, but it has. I . . ." He broke off, uncertain.

"What?"

"I have little experience with this." He hadn't even *tried* to court a woman in centuries. "So I don't know if it is crass to say this or not."

She gave him a squeeze. "You can tell me anything."

Drawing a deep breath, he shared with her the revelation that had come to him over the preceding days. "This is the first time in my nine and a half centuries of existence that I've truly fallen in love."

The words definitely took her by surprise. "But, I thought . . ."

"I never felt anything close to this with Beatrice. She and I were more like friends with benefits. And with Mary I had even less."

She stared up at him, saying nothing.

Unease crept in as he began to wonder if he had just put his foot in it. "Sarah? You aren't blinking, love. What are you thinking?"

Her stomach growled. "You are *so* getting laid again after I refuel."

Emitting a bark of relieved laughter, he hugged her to him.

The bleating of his cell phone made him swear. "It's probably Chris or Marcus reporting in."

Releasing her, he strode through the doorway into the bedroom and retrieved his cell phone from the bedside table. "Yeah."

"It's Chris. I have something you need to see. *All* of you."

"When and where?"

"An hour. There at David's place. I just didn't want to call the meeting without you okaying it first."

He frowned. "Who are you calling in?"

"Marcus, Lisette, Étienne, and Seth."

"Étienne is in town?" He was one of Lisette's brothers.

Chris made a sound of impatience. "He's lived in Winston-Salem for the past thirty years!"

Roland scowled. Winston-Salem was only fifty or sixty miles away.

Sarah joined him and touched his arm, offering comfort.

"If we meet here, one of you might inadvertently lead Bastien to us and put Sarah in danger."

"Since I assume you won't leave her there alone, that could be said about any meeting place you choose. David's house is the safest bet. It has an excellent security system and several secret escape routes."

"What secret escape routes?"

Sarah's eyebrows flew up.

A long-suffering sigh came across the line and Roland could guess what the man was thinking: If he hadn't shut David out, he would already know.

"I'll tell you when I get there. I have to make these calls."

"Fine," he grumbled, hanging up. "Chris has found some thing and is calling a meeting."

"Here?"

"Yes, they'll be here in an hour."

She went to the armoire and started pulling out clothing. "Who? Him and Marcus?"

"Yes, plus Seth, Lisette, and Étienne."

Even though it had been less than an hour since they had made love, his body hardened as she tossed aside the towel and pulled on a pair of white bikini panties.

"Who is Étienne?" Her bountiful breasts swayed as she reached for a pair of black cargo pants, nipples still rosy from his earlier attentions.

"I can't remember. All the blood in my head just rushed to my groin."

She glanced at the erection straining against his zipper, then dropped the pants. A sly smile tilted her lips as her eyelids lowered slightly. Eyeing him as though she were imagining him naked and plunging inside her, she slowly began to circle the perimeter of the room.

"You want me?" she asked in a low, sultry voice that made his body burn.

He stared, riveted, as she raised a hand, slipped her index finger between her full lips, and sucked, reminding him how it had felt to have those lovely lips close around his cock, her tongue stroking him until he lost all control. "Yes." The word emerged as almost a guttural growl.

"You want to be inside me?"

When she drew that finger down over her chest to stroke her breast, his knees threatened to buckle.

"*Hell, yes.*"

"Then you're going to have to catch me."

By the time the words registered, she was out the door.

Eyes widening, another smile dawning, Roland gave chase. He deliberately refrained from using his preternatural speed, curious to see where she would lead him.

Sarah sprinted down the hall to the training room and darted inside.

Slowing, he entered behind her and paused by the door. Though he wouldn't have thought he could get any harder, he did when he realized where she was heading.

Bypassing the assorted equipment, she crossed a large empty sparring area with a padded floor and turned to face him.

"Here," she said, continuing backward with slow sensual steps as she watched him avidly. "I want you to take me here."

Behind her stretched a wall of floor-to-ceiling mirrors.

Sarah jumped when Roland crossed the distance between them in a single leap. Her heart raced as he prowled toward her with all the grace of a jaguar, eyes glowing, fangs peeking out from between parted lips.

His jeans rode low on his hips, the long, hard ridge of his erection impossible to miss. Barefoot, making no sound on the padded floor, he matched her step for step. The heavy muscles in his chest and rippling abs flexed as he stalked her.

She stopped a few feet from the wall. Roland halted as well, his body so close she could feel his heat, smell his wonderful scent, unclouded by cologne. His head dipped, his warm breath falling upon her neck.

She was already wet and trembling for him.

He inhaled deeply and rubbed his face against her like an affectionate cat as he slipped one arm around her waist. "Turn around," he whispered.

Her pulse leapt.

Swiveling in his arms, she stared at their reflection in the mirror. This is what she had wanted to see. The two of them locked together. So different, but so good together.

She leaned back into him, raising one hand to cup his head as he nuzzled the base of her neck. The arm around her waist, so strong and tan compared to her pale flesh, tightened, drawing her hips into the cradle of his so she could feel his heavy arousal. Heat seared her as his other hand slid around to cup one breast, kneading, teasing, trapping her hardened nipple between thumb and forefinger, then rolling, pinching.

She moaned, letting her head fall back against his shoulder.

"You like that?" he murmured.

She nodded helplessly, sharp darts of pleasure piercing her.

When he pulled back slightly, she moaned a protest and wavered where she stood.

His arms left her. In the mirror she saw him step back and shuck his jeans, tossing them aside.

He wore nothing beneath them.

Then he hooked his thumbs in the narrow waistband of her panties and tugged them down to her ankles, holding her steady while she stepped out of them.

Moving up behind her once more, he clasped her shoulders, trailed his hands down to her fingers, and drew her arms out away from her sides.

"Look at you." His heated gaze, glowing that bright, otherworldly amber, swept her form. "I've never seen anything more beautiful in my life."

"Touch me," she pleaded, every cell on fire.

A wicked grin tilted his lips. "On your knees first."

Heart slamming against her ribs, she sank to her knees.

Kneeling behind her, he leaned forward to take her earlobe between his teeth, ever careful not to prick her with his fangs. "Spread your legs for me."

She did so, watching his hand slide around from behind to recapture her breast.

"Wider."

Breath shortening, she shifted until her knees were widely splayed.

Roland pressed his hard, muscled, very aroused body against her back.

Brushing her hair aside, he pressed heated kisses to the sensitive skin beneath her ear. "Only you, Sarah." He slid his other hand around her waist and down, burying it in the dark thatch of curls at the juncture of her thighs.

Sarah gasped, breath shortening as she watched his long, tapered fingers part the tender folds of her body, warm and slick with welcome, and delve deep inside her. First one finger, then two while his thumb circled and stroked her clit.

"Only you make me burn like this."

She couldn't respond. Couldn't speak as the pleasure spiraled through her, building as she rocked her hips helplessly against him.

Roland groaned. She was so wet for him. So wild for him. Her body clenching around his fingers as he stroked her and inflamed her need, his own building until he couldn't wait any longer. He had to be inside her.

She moaned a protest when he withdrew his fingers, then cried out when he guided his cock to her entrance and plunged into her hard from behind.

The pleasure on her face was almost his undoing.

His whole body trembled as he withdrew, then plunged again. She called his name, raised her arms, and reached back to grip his hair in her fists, drawing his head down.

He slid his hand back into that tempting triangle of curls, stroking her in time to his thrusts. The scent of her was maddening, heightened by her arousal, making him crave more and more of her.

Eyes heavy-lidded, lips parted on gasping breaths, Sarah stared at their reflection in the mirror, watched his hands touch and tease and stroke her.

Pumping his hips, he thrust deeper and faster, the tension rising. She was close. They both were, the pleasure building until it was almost unbearable.

"I love you, Sarah," he whispered hoarsely, his glowing gaze meeting hers in the mirror.

Her body convulsed around him with the most powerful orgasm she had ever experienced. Crying out, she clung to him desperately. On and on the pleasure went as Roland continued to thrust.

Just when she thought it would stop, Roland's body stiffened with his own climax, his fingers danced upon her swollen flesh, and a second orgasm claimed her.

When the last ripples faded, they sank weakly to the floor.

Sarah lay on her side, Roland spooned behind her, and fought to regain her breath.

He tightened his arms around her, holding her close, as though he feared his grasp was the only thing keeping her from slipping away.

Looking over her shoulder, she pressed a kiss to his passion-warmed cheek. "I love you, too."

Chapter 15

The more immortals Sarah met, the more she understood Roland's inability to believe she might be of the *gifted ones*' bloodline.

Marcus arrived first, garbed in the black jeans, long-sleeved black T-shirt, and boots both he and Roland favored. The blades of the many knives and other wicked weapons that adorned him glinted in the overhead light.

Chris arrived next in dark fatigues similar to the ones David kept on hand for his guests. There was a holstered weapon under each arm and a thick file folder clutched in one hand.

The lovely Lisette soon followed. Sarah had hoped female immortals might show a little more diversity in their appearance, but Lisette's long, wavy hair was as black as Roland's, her eyes a lighter shade of brown.

Sarah's heart sank. One would think that the coloring of the *gifted ones* would have been diluted at least a little bit after millennia of breeding with ordinary humans. Nothing drastic. A few hazel eyes mixed in. A brown hair woven through the black here or there. *Something.*

Roland had tried to tell her. No doubt he had wanted to spare her the crushing disappointment that now made her want to weep as Lisette greeted them with a smile.

The only way the Frenchwoman differed from the men was in height and build. She was perhaps five and a half feet tall with a build similar to Sarah's: slender and athletic, yet shapely. Her long legs were encased in tight black jeans that rode low on her hips. A black tank top clung to full breasts and a small waist, over which she wore a long dark coat similar to the mens'.

Marcus smiled as he moved behind her and removed her coat. "Lisette."

The inner lining, Sarah saw, contained a number of throwing knives and other blades she couldn't identify, neatly tucked into loops.

"Marcus." Her voice was low, warm, colored with a faint French accent, and as beautiful as *she* was with her porcelain skin and perfectly proportioned features.

Standing next to Roland, Sarah felt jealousy again stir as the woman left Marcus and approached them.

"Lisette," Roland rumbled.

"Roland, *mon coeur.*" When she offered him her hand, Roland carried it to his lips for a kiss. "I heard you had left your lair, but did not believe it."

"It was either leave it or burn with it."

Even Lisette's laugh was pretty.

Sarah found herself gritting her teeth.

Roland may not have fallen in love with any woman before her, but he sure as hell hadn't been celibate. Had he sated his needs with human women, or immortals like this one?

"Is this the woman who saved you?" the Frenchwoman queried.

Roland rested his large, warm palm low on Sarah's back. "Yes. Sarah, this is Lisette d'Alençon. Lisette, Sarah Bingham."

"An honor to meet you, Sarah," she said with a smile, extending her hand. "We are all in your debt."

Sarah shook it and started to mention she hadn't done anything, but Lisette leaned in.

"He isn't really my heart," she said with a smile, indicating Roland with a nod of her head. "I only tease him because he's shy."

Across the room, Marcus snorted. "He isn't shy. He's antisocial."

Roland cut him a glare.

Lisette turned toward Chris. "Chris, you handsome devil, what have you found for us?"

He grinned. "You know I hate to repeat myself, *chérie*. I'll wait until everyone is here."

Another Immortal Guardian entered. Six-foot-one. Short, raven hair. Deep brown eyes with surprisingly thick lashes.

This must be Lisette's brother.

Black slacks clung to slim hips and powerful thighs as he removed his coat. A dark short-sleeved T-shirt showed off a muscular chest, broad shoulders, and bulging biceps. He, like the others, including Roland, was armed to the teeth with numerous knives and a Glock .45.

"Étienne," Lisette said as he hung up his coat, "come and meet Roland's valiant mortal. I've decided we're going to be the best of friends."

Sarah glanced up at Roland, who winked at her and gave her back a furtive caress.

Étienne came to stand beside his sister, bussing her on both cheeks. Then, smiling at Sarah, he extended his hand.

"You must be Sarah. It's a true pleasure to meet you." His voice was deep and tinged with a French accent as well.

When Sarah placed her hand in his, he carried it to his lips for a kiss as Roland had Lisette's.

"Nice to meet you, too."

"The Internet is all abuzz with tales of your heroics."

"What heroics?" she asked, trying to discern if they were mocking her.

"Saving Roland's life, of course. It's all they're talking about on the Immortal Guardian website."

They had a website?

Étienne released her and extended his hand to Roland with a smile. "Good to see you, Roland."

Roland shook his hand and nodded a greeting.

It was strange, seeing him like this: rather dour and tight-lipped. He was always so warm and open when the two of them were alone.

Étienne turned to Chris and Marcus next. "Chris." He shook Chris's hand. "Marcus."

When Marcus shook his hand, Étienne's face grew solemn. "I was very sorry to hear about Lady Bethany. If there is any way I can be of service to you, my friend, anything I can do, please let me know."

Marcus's lips tightened. "I appreciate that." His eyes acquired the faintest glow and Sarah was dismayed to see they reflected tremendous grief.

Who was Lady Bethany?

Was Marcus one of the immortals Roland had mentioned who had loved a human? Had she died recently?

As Chris motioned for them to adjourn to the spacious dining room, Sarah made a mental note to ask Roland later.

Lisette and Étienne took chairs beside each other at one end of a table long enough to seat twenty.

Roland guided Sarah to two chairs opposite them and sank down beside her. All business, he propped his elbows on the wood surface, splayed his knees, and shifted slightly so his thigh would press against hers.

"Has Lisette filled you in on all that's been happening with Roland and Bastien?" Chris asked Étienne as he seated himself in the chair at the end closest to them and dropped his file folder on the table.

The Frenchman frowned. "She tells me you think he's an immortal, but—"

Sarah gasped and jumped when Seth suddenly appeared beside the table.

Everyone else reached for their weapons, then swore and relaxed.

"Damn it," Marcus muttered, "give us some warning before you do that."

Raising one eyebrow, the towering leader seated himself at the far end of the table and looked to Chris. "You've confirmed that Sebastien is an immortal."

"Yes."

Everyone glanced uneasily at Seth, whose face was like granite.

Even without knowing him, Sarah could tell Seth counted this as a personal failure. Everyone else knew it, too, and seemed to have no idea how to respond. It was a bit like watching children realize for the first time that their parents weren't infallible.

As if they had never before known Seth to make a mistake.

Nietzsche chose that moment to slink into the room and, giving everyone else a wide berth, jump up into Seth's lap.

Chris opened the file folder and thumbed through several pages. "Sarah was right. Roland's enemy is definitely an immortal. He was born Sebastien Newcombe and became the Earl of Marston upon his father's death in 1807. After faking his own death in 1815—he was presumably killed by highwaymen, though, of course, his body was never found—he adopted the name Julien Marston. Julien for his father. Marston for the title. Since he didn't have our resources, he left a sporadic paper trail, moving every twenty or thirty years, sometimes varying his name, though he always used family names. The network's European branches did a phenomenal job locating historic papers that bore his signatures, so we were able to map his movements fairly well."

He passed each of them, Sarah included, a sheaf of papers.

"Whatever made him want Roland's head on a platter happened in London," he continued, looking at Roland, "because he's been dogging your footsteps ever since."

Sarah stared at the papers before her. One half of the page (and all of those that followed) catalogued the many cities in which Roland had lived since his sojourn in London in the early nineteenth century in chronological order. The opposite side did the same for Sebastien, aka Julien Marston, Julien Newcombe, Sebastien Marston, and Marston Newcombe.

Wherever Roland had gone, Sebastien had followed. It had sometimes taken him years to find Roland, but find him he would, usually just in time for Roland to pack up and move again.

"What the hell?" Roland muttered.

"You lucked out when you moved to the States," Chris said, drawing their attention to the last few pages. "He lost you completely and, as you can see, spent the next several decades traveling the globe, I assume in search of you."

Roland slammed the papers down. "I'm telling you, I have never seen this bastard before. Not until the morning he staked me out for the sunrise."

Marcus shook his head. "I don't remember seeing him before either."

Étienne spoke up. "Well, he sure as hell saw Roland." He looked to Roland. "Maybe you killed the one who turned him. He's immortal, not vampire, so he may have been more loyal to the one who infected him."

Roland waved to the pages in disbelief. "To *this* extent?"

Seth cleared his throat. "He had no one else. It's plausible."

An awkward silence fell.

Chris shuffled his papers. "Anyway, Roland's self-imposed isolation worked to his advantage. Once you moved to the States, you forwent servants and refused to have a Second. You very rarely interacted with the other Guardians. So he basically had no way to trace you. When he finally found you roughly twenty years ago, it was probably just dumb luck."

Roland scowled. "So why not try to kill me then? Why wait?"

"This is why." Withdrawing a multifolded piece of paper, Chris spread it open on the table. "I traced him to an old farmhouse outside of Mebane—Julien Marston was the name on the lease—and took some satellite surveillance photos. Here's the first."

It was the size of a road map and showed a large farmhouse and barn surrounded by a sizable clearing, then dense forest.

Sarah's gaze swept over the others. "You have your own satellites?"

Chris shook his head. "Launching satellites into space would draw unwanted scrutiny. I just have friends in interesting places."

"Oh."

"It's why he's the best Cleaner," Marcus commented, then motioned to the map. "So this is his lair?"

"Yes, and this is where the unbelievable factor increases exponentially." Pulling out a second map, Chris unfolded it atop the other.

Sarah, and everyone else, leaned forward with interest.

"I wanted to find out how many, if any, vamp followers he had left, so I had my friend do a broader spectrum sweep with one of their keyhole satellites. The yellow figures are the humans. The violet ones are the vampires sleeping underground."

"Oh shit."

"What the hell?"

Sarah stared at the map.

There were four yellow figures. And dozens of violet ones.

She looked at Roland. "I thought vampires didn't travel in more than twos or threes."

A muscle leaped in his jaw. "They don't."

Lisette's eyes were wide. "There must be at least fifty of them."

"Fifty-seven," Chris corrected.

Étienne stood and spread his hands on the map. "This extends well past the boundaries of the farmhouse."

Chris nodded. "According to the original blueprints, the house had a basement when he bought it, but he's clearly enlarged it."

Marcus frowned. "If it were aboveground, it would fill the whole bloody clearing. Do you have a better layout of it?"

"No, my team checked with every contractor employed in North Carolina and the surrounding states and got nothing. Bastien did the work himself."

Roland tapped the map with his index finger, pointing out a red figure that was distanced from all the rest. Judging by the color, he was too cool to be human and too warm to be vampire. "This is him. He sleeps away from the others."

Marcus grunted. "Probably doesn't trust them. They're fucking vampires."

"Do you think he knows?" Lisette asked. "Do you think he knows he's an immortal?"

Her brother shook his head and retook his seat. "Vampires kill those they feed upon. No immortal could abide living with them, knowing innocent lives were being taken."

"Actually," Chris said, "that's another thing." Out came more papers. "My tech team hacked into his computer via the Internet and found this."

Sarah studied the papers handed to her. It was a list of names and addresses in various cities and towns throughout North Carolina. Some in Virginia and South Carolina.

"We weren't sure what it was until we started looking up the people on the list and tracked Bastien's Internet activity. Or rather his human minions' activity. Most of it took place during the day."

"What is it?" Roland asked, still frowning.

"A list of the vampires' victims."

"He keeps track of them?" Sarah asked.

"No, he *picks* them. Everyone on that list is linked to kiddie porn, either as a buyer, a seller, or a producer, and has either recently gone missing or is dead. Sebastien is telling the vamps whom to feed on and making sure the deaths don't appear to be vampire related."

Étienne shook his head in disbelief. "How the hell is he controlling them?"

Sarah cleared her throat. "Doesn't the medical examiner or whoever examines the victims notice the lack of blood in the bodies?"

"Sure," Marcus said. "But *vampire slaying* isn't something that typically comes to mind when investigating apparent homicides, suicides, or accidents."

Roland nodded. "They usually assume the victims were killed and bled out in an unknown location before the bodies were dumped elsewhere. That sort of thing."

Lisette stared at the map. "It must have taken him the full twenty years to gather so many. They should all be mad by now."

"Unless he's turning them himself," Roland pointed out grimly. "He could have infected them all only recently."

Chris sat down once more. "Or not. All our digging turned up something else I found interesting. I can't be certain, but I'm pretty sure he's making them eat food."

Everyone looked at him as if he were nuts.

Except for Seth.

Seth frowned and continued to stroke Nietzsche, who purred like a Harley-Davidson.

"I sent my ops team out to surveil the place this afternoon—"

Roland scowled. "Then he knows we've found him and could have already relocated."

Chris shook his head. "They were quiet and stayed out of sight. He never knew they were there."

"He's immortal. Have you forgotten our heightened sense of smell?"

"We aren't amateurs, Roland," Chris bit out. "They camouflaged their scent."

"How?"

Sarah was with Roland. Immortals had noses like friggin' polar bears. She found it hard to believe Chris's men could have gone undetected.

"They bathed. No scented soaps, shampoos, or deodorants.

Wore clothes washed in fragrance-free detergent. Then hid whatever scent remained with cover scents and animal urine."

Sarah wrinkled her nose in disgust and saw Lisette do the same.

"Animal urine?" Marcus parroted.

"Sure. Hunters do it all the time. Trust me. No one knew they were there."

Gross.

"What did they see?" Marcus asked.

"A truck delivering a big-ass load of groceries. Mostly fresh vegetables and fruits. My hackers went to work again and found out Julien Marston has a standing order with the supplier. Every two days enough food to feed an army is delivered. According to his payroll, you've cut the number of humans serving Sebastien from thirteen to four but the deliveries keep coming. And even if you hadn't, it would be too much for the humans to consume so quickly. Clearly the food isn't solely for them."

But vampires didn't eat food. Roland had told her the bloodlust struck them so fast and hard, they lost interest in any other form of sustenance.

"He's trying to save them," Lisette declared sadly.

"Will that work?" Sarah asked the table at large. "Will eating food keep them sane?"

All eyes went to Seth.

"No. We tried that. Several times. Those who were already mad only consumed food when forced to through starvation, and it made no difference. Neither did denying them blood straight from the vein and instead feeding it to them in a glass or bag. Once the madness claims them, they're lost."

"And the newbies?" Chris asked.

Seth shook his head. "If we caught them within weeks of being turned, feeding them food didn't prevent the madness from striking. It merely slowed the descent. If they were fortunate, they could have four—possibly five—years, but they were painful ones. The unceasing battle for sanity was exhausting. They had to be watched constantly. And, if they slipped and tried to harm a human, they were tortured by memories of it during their lucid moments. They cannot be saved."

A somber silence fell, ultimately broken by Chris.

"So what's the plan?"

Sarah couldn't see any remotely palatable way to end this.

Roland's hand tightened around hers an instant before he spoke in a cold, determined voice. "We extract Sebastien, then raze the compound."

The faces of Roland's immortal brethren were grim in the aftermath of his proclamation. He didn't look at Sarah, afraid of the condemnation he might see in her beloved face.

What a cold-blooded bastard she must think him.

As the other Immortal Guardians exchanged troubled looks, Roland braced himself for the moment she would withdraw her hand.

Étienne cleared his throat. "Am I the only one suffering qualms about killing vampires who have never harmed an innocent?"

Marcus sighed heavily. "No."

"How do you know they haven't?" Sarah queried, drawing Roland's surprised gaze.

She was still holding his hand.

Chris held up the list of pedophiles. "Trust me, Sarah, no one on this list is innocent."

"Yes, but you're assuming they haven't killed anyone *not* on the list. Is there some rule that prevents vampires from killing more than one person per night? Fifty-seven is a large number to keep track of. Couldn't some of them have strayed without Bastien knowing it?"

Roland had had the same thought. "If they were careful not to get any blood on them so he couldn't discern two different scents . . . yes."

"We don't know for sure that he would even object," Lisette said slowly. "He has lived with vampires for two centuries. I know it is unpleasant, but we must consider the possibility that in some ways he may have come to think like them."

"He certainly shares their hatred of immortals," Marcus said.

A high-pitched ring pierced the air.

Chris pulled a cell phone from his pocket and gave it a glance. "Excuse me. I have to take this." Rising, he held the phone to his ear and strode into the living room. "Yeah?"

"Sebastien's approval or disapproval makes little difference in terms of our goal here," Seth spoke. "I want him taken alive and handed over to me. The others are to be destroyed. If we let them live and do nothing until they lose their tenuous hold on sanity and kill, hundreds of innocents could fall victim before we manage to hunt them all down. That is unacceptable."

Everyone murmured their agreement.

When Chris returned, Roland was debating strategy with the others while he drew soft circles on the back of Sarah's hand with his thumb.

"Well, Sarah was right again," Chris announced, reclaiming his seat. "Andy got his hands on several of the police reports filed for the dead pedophiles and kiddie porn peddlers and Bastien's vamps are unquestionably cheating on their diet." He tapped the list of victims. "Several of these freaks were married and the vamps sent to feed on them killed the wives and children for dessert."

Shit. "How the hell have we not heard about this?"

"None of the victims lived in the Triangle or the Triad."

The Triangle was made up of the neighboring cities of Raleigh, Durham, and Chapel Hill. The Triad consisted of Greensboro, High Point, and Winston-Salem.

"And they were spread out and camouflaged in enough

different ways that no correlations have been drawn between the deaths."

Sarah looked to Roland. "I wish I had been wrong."

Giving her hand a supportive squeeze, he returned his attention to planning their attack.

The hallway outside the mystery woman's bedroom was empty when Seth appeared in it, the sheaf of papers Chris had given him clasped in one hand. A quick look inside showed him the room, too, was devoid of her presence.

No big surprise there. The poor girl still wasn't sleeping.

Worried about her continued insomnia, he had reached out very subtly with his gifts and determined that it was no longer that she was unwilling to sleep. She *couldn't* sleep. Not until she felt safe. It seemed to be some sort of subconscious defense mechanism she was helpless to extinguish.

He, David, and Darnell had all trodden carefully around her and made themselves appear as harmless as possible. He didn't know what else he could do to reassure her.

Of course, she was a tiny thing, barely reaching five feet. It was a little hard to look harmless when one was at least a foot and a half taller than her and outweighed her by a good 100, 120 pounds.

Seth strode down the hallway and began making his way downstairs. The only sounds of life came from the great hall, which—except for the stone walls—now resembled a modern living room. Following them, he saw David standing in the shadows outside the entrance and started to call out a greeting.

David glanced up and placed a finger to his lips.

Seth instantly altered his approach, silencing his footsteps as he joined him and peered into the room.

Darnell was perched on the edge of the sofa, fingers and thumbs working a Playstation controller. On the large-screen television, *Tomb Raider*'s Lara Croft took a running leap from a ledge and grabbed the end of a rope that dangled over a dark, cavernous room.

The mystery woman stood beside the sofa, out of arm's reach as she always did, eyes glued to the screen.

"See," Darnell said with a boyish grin, "I told you she'd make it."

Seth was shocked to see her eyes light up with what would have been a smile if her lips had moved.

"Now I'll make her swing, jump to the next rope, swing again, and land on that ledge over there."

Looking doubtful, she returned her attention to the screen and leaned against the arm of a recliner arranged perpendicularly to the sofa.

The pale blue V-neck T-shirt she wore clung to small breasts and left bare her prominent collarbones and arms that weren't as skeletal now that she was eating regularly. Black and blue pajama bottoms hung on bony hips that had finally gained a bit of flesh on them. Her small feet were bare.

She was still far too thin and looked so fragile it broke Seth's heart. And David's. And Darnell's.

Her face was less gaunt and had more color. It was a pretty face with full lips, a pert nose, and winged brows. Dark shadows still lingered beneath her eyes, however, a testament to her fatigue.

Bearing in mind the fact that this was her eighth day with out sleep, she looked fan-freakin'-tastic.

Seth had once read about a sleep study a university had conducted to see how long a person could go without sleep. The longest any of the participants had lasted was eleven days. By only the fourth, participants' thought processes and motor skills had become sluggish. Problems with short-term memory had arisen. They had had difficulty concentrating, become delusional, and been extremely moody, symptoms that had steadily increased in severity as the days progressed.

Not so their mystery woman. The only evidence of her lack of sleep lay in the bruising under her green eyes.

Beneath Seth's scrutiny, those eyes widened as Lara Croft swung from one rope to another and grabbed it.

"Whew!" Darnell sent her another grin of triumph.

Seth's breath caught when she smiled back.

Darnell went very still for a second but—to his credit—continued as though nothing special had taken place. "Once Lara gets over to the ledge, keep an eye out for medpacks. She's running low and there should be one hidden around there somewhere."

Damned if their guest didn't move to sit on the very edge of the chair's cushion and lean forward to watch Lara Croft's progress more closely.

Seth looked at David and raised his brows. "How long has this been going on?" he asked too softly for human ears to catch.

"The whole time you've been gone," he responded, equally quiet. "Darnell needed to take a break from trying to decrypt those files we snatched."

Music indicating a discovery trilled from the television. "Cool. More flares. *And* a grenade launcher."

Seth winced. "Couldn't he have picked a less violent game?"

David shrugged. "He was already playing it when she came down to watch him."

"Has Lara shot or been attacked by anything yet?"

"Just some bats. And it didn't seem to alarm our girl."

"Good. I'm not sure how much of her rescue she remembers and worry she might not react well to violence, even if it is only in a game. There was a hell of a lot of gunfire that night."

David smiled wryly. "I've never been shot so many times in one night *or* by such high-caliber weapons. Damned things stung." He nodded to the papers in Seth's hand. "Speaking of bloodbaths, what happened at the meeting?"

Seth sighed, feeling infinitely weary. "Sebastien has done the impossible. Excluding the twenty-three Roland and

Marcus have already managed to destroy, Sebastien has fifty-seven vampires living beneath his roof."

David's eyes widened. "What?"

"He's trying to save them," he said, feeling the same sadness Lisette had demonstrated when she had made the declaration earlier. "Making them eat food. Assigning them pedophiles to feed upon instead of innocents. But most are already straying from the path he's chosen for them."

"Did he turn them all himself?"

"I don't know."

The mystery woman suddenly leapt up and hurried over to the television to point at something on the large screen.

"What is it?" Darnell asked, making Lara backtrack a few paces. "Oh, a crevice. I didn't even see that." Lara jumped up, grabbed the edge, and crawled in. "All right! A medpack. Thanks."

Smiling, she returned to her seat.

"How about that," David murmured with a smile of his own. "I should've known if anyone could make her smile it would be Darnell."

Darnell was the least intimidating of the three of them. Exceedingly tall with a lean build and medium-brown skin, he was twenty-six years old and had a naturally cheerful disposition few could resist.

Now if he could only entice her to speak, Seth thought.

David sobered. "So, let's hear it. Tell me what you've learned that everyone else doesn't know."

"Discerning bastard," Seth grumbled.

"No more so than you. Spill it."

Seth hesitated. There *was* something the others hadn't caught. Something he feared would have made them refuse to take Sebastien alive if they had known it. "Sebastien has a grudge against Roland. I don't know the source of it. But he's been trying to catch up with him for two hundred years, tracking and following him to every city he's inhabited."

"Roland doesn't know why?"

"No." Seth held up the papers. "Reordon listed many of the countries, cities, and towns Sebastien has visited, along with dates and . . ." He was loath to say it. "He was in Scotland the year Ewen was killed."

David swore.

The Scottish immortal had been a favorite and had been mourned by them all.

"There were so few vampires in his region and none were banding together," Seth continued. "We always wondered how one could have killed a Guardian of Ewen's strength. It never occurred to us that it could have been another immortal."

"The others can't know."

Seth agreed. "Even if it was in self-defense, they would want his head." And Seth was now burdened with the knowledge that his own failure had caused it all.

David's gaze turned piercing, seeing far more than Seth wanted him to. "You must stop blaming yourself."

"It's my fault."

"No, it isn't," he insisted. "You can't be everywhere at once. You can't be every*thing* to every*one*."

"If I had been there to help him, Sebastien wouldn't have suffered. He wouldn't have begun hating immortals and harboring vampires. And Ewen would still be alive."

"There is no proof he killed Ewen. Only speculation."

"He has tried to kill Roland three times thus far. And probably would have killed Marcus and Sarah if he felt it necessary."

David may not blame Seth for this, but the others did. They had not verbalized it or acknowledged it consciously, but their silence had said it all.

Seth had screwed up. He always aided the new immortals after their transformations and, because he hadn't aided Sebastien . . .

"Did they object to your intention to rehabilitate him?" David asked, abandoning his attempts to ease Seth's guilt.

"No."

"When are you going in?"

"Tomorrow."

"Are you sure you want me to remain here? Five against fifty-seven could get a little hairy."

"I'm sure. I want our guest safe at all times and know that, with you here, she will be."

As one, they turned to look at the mystery woman and were surprised to find her staring back as though she had heard every word.

"Who was Lady Bethany?"

Sarah and Roland lay together in their bedroom as dawn broke, only a dim nightlight warding off complete darkness.

Both were anxious about the coming battle and found sleep elusive.

To take her mind off the danger Roland would soon face, Sarah had decided to ask about the woman Étienne had mentioned.

Lying on his back, staring up at the ceiling, Roland stroked and toyed with her hair as she snuggled closer. "Lady Bethany, Countess of Westcott. Also known as Bethany Bennett."

"Was she Marcus's wife?"

"No, but she was the only woman he has ever loved. And he loved her for a very long time."

Sarah recalled the grief that had flared in Marcus's eyes when Étienne had offered his condolences. "Did she die?"

"It's a little more complicated than that."

Well, that was cryptic.

Shifting, she folded her hands on his chest and propped her chin on them. "Will you tell me?"

Smiling down at her, he drew the backs of his fingers across her cheek. "I don't know that you would believe me if I did. It's a very strange story."

She smiled. "Stranger than vampires and immortals?"

"Believe it or not, yes. It's why every immortal knows about it. Even the minstrels of my time could not have concocted such a sad tale."

"Now you *have* to tell me."

He nodded his ascent but said no more.

"Well?" she prompted, poking him in the side.

He jumped and laughed when she hit a ticklish spot, then promptly grabbed her fingers so she wouldn't do it again. "I am. I'm just trying to decide where to start—the beginning or the end."

"The beginning," she decided for him.

"As you wish." He lifted his head and brushed her lips with a kiss, then relaxed back against the pillow. "Have you ever seen those stories on television in which a dog that has been horribly abused is taken in by someone who treats it well and loves it and, as a result, becomes fiercely loyal to its new owner? So much so that it would die defending or protecting him?"

Sarah studied him curiously. "Yes."

"Well, that's pretty much what happened to Marcus. He was born Brice, heir to the Earl of Dunnenford, in the late twelfth century. His father died when he was a boy and his mother was pressured into remarrying quickly. His stepfather turned out to be a sadistic bastard who beat Marcus and his mother every chance he could get. After he discovered Marcus's gift, he abused him even more. This went on for years and he eventually killed Marcus's mother, claiming she fell down the stairs."

Dismayed, Sarah felt her heart grow heavy as Roland continued.

"He would've killed Marcus, too, if Marcus hadn't fled, sought out Lord Robert, Earl of Fosterly—a man he knew his stepfather feared—and become his squire. Lord Robert was a good man and treated Marcus like a younger brother, giving him the friendship and affection he had been missing. So, naturally, Marcus loved him like a father or the older brother he had never had, respected him above all others, and would have gladly given his life to protect him.

"Then one day, when Marcus was around seventeen—he had been with Robert three or four years I think at that point—Robert brought home a woman unlike any Marcus had ever encountered."

"Lady Bethany?"

"Yes. Robert and three of his men had found her in the forest, covered in blood and searching frantically for her brother, Josh. He told Marcus the two had been attacked by an enemy he was dealing with at the time. But Marcus found out later she was actually from the future."

Sarah stared at him, doubting she had heard him correctly. "I'm sorry—what?"

"Lady Bethany was, in reality, Bethany Bennett, born in Houston, Texas, near the end of the twentieth century. Around the time *you* were, now that I think on it."

"You're kidding, right?"

"No."

Sarah sat up abruptly, the covers falling to her waist. "No way!"

His eyes darkened as they fell to her breasts. "I warned you it was hard to believe."

"How did she go back in time?"

His hands went to her waist. "If I promise to explain it all later, will you let me finish my tale so I can make love to you again?"

Her pulse leapt. Beneath his faintly glowing gaze, her nipples tightened. "Deal."

"Long story short: Bethany and Robert fell madly in love, married, and lived happily ever after."

Her jaw dropped. "What about Marcus?"

"Marcus fell in love with her, adored her as much as Robert did, but never told either one of them. He loved them both too much to threaten the happiness they had found together. And, as I said, he was fiercely loyal to Robert. He would never have betrayed him by pursuing the woman Robert loved."

Sarah stared at him in consternation. "Jeeze. That's . . . that's . . ."

"Fucked up. I know. What's worse is Marcus never stopped loving her. After she died a very old woman, he spent the next eight centuries alternately mourning her and looking forward to seeing her again. When the twentieth century finally rolled around . . ." Roland shook his head. "He was like a child waiting for Santa Claus to arrive. Bethany was born. And Marcus moved to Houston to watch over her while she grew up. He bought the house next door to her when she was sixteen or seventeen, befriended her, Josh, and their father, helped her through her father's death a year later, became one of her and Josh's closest friends, and treasured every moment he spent with her until she went back in time to Robert when she was twenty-two."

Sarah bit her lip. "He never dated her or . . ."

Roland shook his head. "As far as he was concerned, she was Robert's wife. Marcus's relationship with her was always platonic. Even in the future, or present, when it could have been more."

Sarah didn't know what to say. "He never found *anyone* else?"

"No. Some immortals thought he was crazy to pine after her for so many years, then refrain from sleeping with her when he knew her again. But the rest of us are . . . a little awed by it, I suppose. His love for her never diminished in all those years. And when he met her again and could have seduced her, he chose the honorable path and didn't because his loyalty to Robert never diminished either."

"Wow. He could've even tried to keep her from going back in time."

Roland shook his head. "He knew she would be happier with Robert, that they were meant to be together."

"And she's gone now? Is that why Étienne offered condolences?"

"Yes, Bethany went back to the Middle Ages seven years ago. So Marcus will never see her again."

Sarah lay back down. "No wonder he looks so somber whenever he isn't ragging on you."

"He still grieves." Rolling onto his side, Roland slid down until his face was even with hers on the pillow. "I admit that I was one of those who thought him foolish for not pursuing her when they met again." He touched her face, gently drawing his fingers down her temple and over her cheek.

Sarah's heart clenched. He was looking at her as though beholding something precious.

"But I understand now. He loved her enough to place her happiness above his own." He brushed his lips against hers in a tender kiss. "It's how I feel about you, Sarah. I want you to be happy. It's why I've tried not to pressure you into staying with me after we apprehend Bastien."

Sarah bit her lip. She had noticed that he hadn't once asked her to stay with him. "I thought maybe you were feeling ambivalent about it."

"Ambivalent?" He pressed his forehead to hers. "I love you. I would spend eternity with you if I could. But barring that, I would settle for every remaining minute of your mortal life, then pray you'll be reincarnated so that I may find you again."

"I want to have my blood tested." She knew now she would leap at the chance to spend eternity with him and could not yet bring herself to abandon that hope.

He stared at her, his gaze penetrating. "And if it confirms you're human?"

"Your scientists are working on a way to mutate the virus

in vampires and turn them immortal. Maybe they'll find something before I get too old."

"If you were old when you were transformed, the virus would reverse the damage aging had done to your body and you would become young again."

"Cool!"

"But those scientists have been trying to turn vampires into immortals since before the arrival of modern science, Sarah. The outlook is pretty bleak."

He seemed determined to burst her bubble.

"Then I'll spend the rest of my life loving you and laughing with you and will do my damnedest not to let it get to me when you stay hot and I wrinkle like a prune."

Roland wrapped his arms around her and hugged her so tight, Sarah could barely breathe. "I promise I'll try to be less antisocial in the future."

Sarah hugged him back, throat tightening. "And I promise I'll try not to refer to you as my boy toy when I look old enough to be your grandmother."

Chuckling, he rolled her to her back. "Shall I also promise to give you at least one orgasm every day for the rest of your life?"

Sarah smiled as he settled his large, warm body between her thighs, his erection teasing her center. "Only if you start right now."

He dipped his head, lips slanting over hers, tongue dipping inside to send fire burning through her.

She was breathless when he drew back slightly, eyes glowing, and gave her a wicked grin. "It would be my pleasure."

In the next instant, he glided down her body, kissing, licking, and nipping, until he reached her core.

Sarah threw back her head and sank her fingers into his hair. "Oh, yesss."

Chapter 16

Roland fastened the Velcro tabs on his bulletproof vest, then donned a shoulder holster that housed a Sig P226 9mm. The many pockets of his black cargo pants he filled with extra clips and numerous throwing stars. His favored sais were slid into sheaths attached to each thigh.

Pulling a leather strap over his head, he settled it on one shoulder so it draped across his chest like an ammunition belt, then filled the small slits in it with a dozen throwing knives.

His thoughts were chaotic. The cold deliberation that usually overtook him before a fight had completely deserted him.

Bending, he slipped more knives into his boots.

He could feel Sarah watching him and knew without looking up that she was sitting on the foot of the bed, worrying her lower lip as she had been the entire time he had been gearing up.

Once he had packed on as many weapons as he could without hampering his mobility, he straightened and glanced over at her. "Come here, love."

Rising, she moved to stand before him.

Roland picked up the smaller Kevlar vest he had found and began strapping her into it. A shoulder holster with a Glock 9mm followed.

"Have you changed your mind?" she asked hopefully. "Am I coming with you?"

"*Hell,* no." He didn't want her anywhere near that place.

"You've been training me all week, Roland. And I'm an excellent shot."

"We've already discussed this." Several times.

She rolled her eyes, looking vaguely disgruntled. "We didn't discuss it. *I* suggested I may be of some help to you and *you* gave me the finger."

"I did not give you the finger."

"You may as well have. You shot me down so quickly I didn't even have a chance to list all the pros."

He started filling her pockets, back and front, with extra clips and throwing knives. "I don't care if you have a hundred pros. They won't outweigh the con."

"Which is . . . ?"

"You getting killed," he snapped, patience fraying. "Damn it, Sarah, you are not going with us, so would you just drop it?"

He saw her frown as he adjusted her holster and told himself to get a fucking grip. What the hell was wrong with him? Why was he shouting at her? She was just trying to help.

"If I'm not going with you," she broached softly, "then why are you arming me to the teeth?"

"I want to make certain you're as safe as possible while I'm gone." He knew the fight was going to go down at Bastien's lair but still felt riddled with anxiety at the thought of leaving her.

She was so small.

So fragile.

So very mortal.

"Chris's men arrived an hour ago," she pointed out, "and are positioned every two yards around the exterior of the house. A dozen more are patrolling the grounds and there are three stationed at the gate."

He scowled. "I don't know or trust any of those men."

She pursed her lips. "Well, Chris should arrive at any minute and is going to stay inside and guard me himself until you return. You trust Chris, don't you?"

"Not entirely." He examined her black-clad form judiciously. She needed more pockets.

When he reached out to adjust her shoulder holster a third time, she captured his hands in her own and held them still.

"Roland, look at me," she commanded quietly.

He met her hazel gaze.

"What is it?" she asked, studying him carefully. "You aren't usually this antagonistic or abrupt. At least, not with me. So . . . talk to me. Is it Bastien? Are you worried something might go wrong tonight?"

"No, it isn't that." He gripped her hands tightly, memorizing every cherished feature. "It's just . . . different this time. And I'm not handling it very well. I'm sorry."

Her expression lightened a bit. "That's okay. How is it different?"

He forced a smile, though he knew it was a lame attempt. "I've never had anything to lose before. I think it's making me nervous."

Her mouth formed a silent *O*. Then she threw her arms around him and held him tight.

"Careful," he enjoined, gingerly hugging her back. He had a lot of blades with razor-sharp edges lashed to him.

She shook her head and whispered in a choked voice, "I love you."

He rested his cheek on her hair, inhaling her alluring scent. "I love you, too."

"Nothing is going to happen to me."

But so much already had. "I can't help worrying. He always seems to find us."

"Not this time. You're striking during daylight hours. He'll be in Seth's custody and you'll be back here by sunset."

He nodded, though he lacked her confidence. Bastien was

a wily adversary who had proven to be tremendously unpredictable.

"You can't let anything happen to you either, Roland. Come back to me safely."

"I will." Leaning back, he lowered his lips to hers for a gentle kiss. "If Bastien's human minions show up—hell, at *any* sign of trouble—head for the tunnels."

Chris had finally disclosed the locations of the secret escape routes he had mentioned over the phone. Inside the armoire every subterranean bedroom possessed was a false back that concealed the entrance of a tunnel that led deep into the surrounding forest. Each tunnel had its own hidden exit that allowed those who followed it to surface in complete shade (even in winter) a safe enough distance from the house that they would be neither seen nor heard by anyone besieging it.

After examining them all, Roland had decided he would add the same to *his* next home whenever he built or bought it. Had he had such in his last home, he, Marcus, and Sarah could have escaped the fire without venturing into the sun and Sarah would have never been exposed to the minions' gunfire. He had grown too complacent in recent years.

"Thank you for making sure they're free of creepy crawlies," Sarah said, drawing a smile from him.

"Anything for you." He knew her fear of bugs embarrassed her, but he sure as hell didn't think less of her because of it. She was willing to go up against insane vampires and men with guns. Who gave a rat's ass about a little insect phobia?

At that moment, the doorbell pealed. A courtesy, since all the immortals in the area had keys and knew the alarm codes. A second later they heard the front door open.

Sarah sighed. "That must be Chris."

He nodded. "Marcus, Lisette, and Étienne are with him. Time to go."

Linking his fingers through hers, Roland drew her with

him down the hallway, up the stairs, and into the living room. Once there, they both stopped and stared.

Chris was decked out in black fatigues and a Kevlar vest, an automatic weapon under his right arm, a .45 semiautomatic holstered on his right thigh. Fastened to his left thigh was a wicked-looking tactical knife.

Marcus was dressed and armed much as Roland was.

Lisette and Étienne, however, were both clad in what appeared to be dull black rubber pants and long-sleeved shirts that fit them like a second skin. The pants were tucked into heavy boots. The neckline of the shirts rose all the way to their chins. Their hands, concealed by gloves made of the same peculiar material, clutched matching masks and wraparound sunglasses.

Two red shoto swords were strapped to Lisette's back and a pair of Glock 18s equipped with extended thirty-one-round magazines were strapped to the outside of each slender thigh. Étienne had armed himself with a couple of sheathed short swords and numerous throwing knives that hung in a belt across his chest like Roland's.

When Roland and Sarah continued to stare at their odd suits, Étienne spread his arms wide and raised his eyebrows. "They offer us complete protection from the sun."

Interesting. Roland hadn't heard anything about this, even on the Internet message boards. "I wondered how you two would manage to survive the daylight." The younger the immortals, the more sensitive they were to sunlight. And these two were only a couple hundred years old. "Are they comfortable?"

"Not really," Lisette answered. Her long black tresses were slicked back into a neat braid that disappeared into the neckline of her shirt.

Étienne grimaced. "They chafe like a mother when you sweat."

Marcus grinned. "Which is why I'm not wearing them."

Chris motioned to Roland's clothes. "Don't worry.

You're protected, too. All the clothing David provides offers 98 percent protection against UVA and UVB rays. As old as you are, that should be enough. I did bring a couple of extra masks, sunglasses, and gloves, though, in case you were interested."

Roland and Marcus each took a mask, a pair of gloves, and sunglasses. Slipping his hand inside the rubbery ski mask, Roland held it up for Sarah to see.

She reached out and felt it, wrinkling her nose at the automobile-tire texture, then shrugged. "As long as it protects your pretty face, I'm all for it."

Grinning, he turned back to the others.

They were all staring at him with wide eyes.

He scowled. "What?"

They blinked.

"Nothing," Chris mumbled. Pulling an iPhone from one of his pockets, he handed it to Marcus. "Since you're a little more computer and electronics savvy than the others, you get to hang on to this. One of my contacts is going to download another real-time keyhole satellite surveillance photo at precisely five o'clock. It will confirm how many humans and vamps are inside and, since we don't know the layout of that massive basement, will hopefully serve as a guide and help you navigate it and find them all. You'll only get the one photo because he isn't supposed to be doing this shit and is risking his ass to help us."

Seth abruptly appeared behind Chris.

Sarah jumped and emitted a startled squeak, then sighed as she met Roland's amused gaze. "I don't think I'm going to get used to that anytime soon."

He smiled. "It's been nine centuries and I'm still not used to it."

Chris stepped aside so Seth could join the circle. "I've already briefed them."

"Excellent. Let's book."

Roland turned to Sarah as the others filed toward the door.

Her sweet face was pinched with worry as she rose onto her toes and wrapped her arms around him. "Be careful."

He kissed her. "I will." Then he kissed her again. "Remember, at the first sign of trouble—"

"Head for the tunnels. I will."

He kissed her one more time, deeply, drinking in her taste and her scent, then reluctantly set her away from him.

Donning the rubbery mask, gloves, and sunglasses, he followed the others through the front door and out into the late afternoon sunlight.

Sarah's stomach churned as she nervously paced the perimeters of the living room. Low music and voices changed midsentence as Chris channel-surfed from his position on one of the cushy sofas. Every once in a while, she would feel his gaze stray to her, observe her for several seconds, then return to the television.

All the curtains had been pulled back. Golden sunlight poured in through the western windows and spilled across the plush cream-colored carpet. Sparkling dust motes spun and danced as she passed through them.

Curled in an overstuffed chair in one corner, Nietzsche raised his head and peered sleepily at her as she neared him. Sarah paused to rub his fuzzy head and stroke his chin before continuing on.

It was impossible to remain still when worry was twisting her insides into knots.

"How long have they been gone?" she asked for the second time.

Chris checked his watch. "Seven and a half minutes."

She groaned. "That's *all?*" She would've sworn at least half an hour had passed. "How much longer until they get there, do you think?"

"Depending on traffic, about fifteen minutes."

"Why didn't Seth just pop them over there?"

"You mean teleport them?"

She nodded.

"He can only teleport to places he's already been. Unless you're talking to him on the phone. Then he can find you by following the cell signal or zoning in on your brain waves. I can never decide which and keep forgetting to ask."

Sarah almost smiled. "How can you be so . . . relaxed about all of this?" He didn't look at all concerned.

"One: I've been at this long enough to have seen them in action and know that they're extremely good at what they do. And two: I'm not in love with any of them."

Glancing through one of the northern windows as she passed, she saw the back of one of Chris's heavily armed men. "Is it that obvious?"

"As obvious as his love for you is."

Another window. Another guard.

"I'm going to have my blood tested to see if I can be transformed." She wasn't sure why she told him. Perhaps to test his reaction since, according to Roland, no *gifted one* had ever willingly been transformed.

Nietzsche rolled over onto his back and struck a cute pose as she approached again, offering his tummy up for a rub.

Sarah obediently stroked his soft fur, smiling faintly when he rumbled with purrs of satisfaction. Once he had gotten used to her being around, Nietzsche had begun to come to her for treats and caresses almost as often as he did to Roland.

When Chris failed to reply to her announcement, she glanced up and found him turned around on the sofa, watching her over its back, his expression inscrutable.

"You think there's no chance, don't you?" Giving the cat a last stroke, she recommenced circumnavigating the big room. "Roland does, too."

"It isn't im*possible,*" he said slowly, swiveling around as he followed her progress, "just im*probable.*"

And she had thought the day couldn't get any grimmer.

"Roland told me *gifted ones* always have black hair and brown eyes, no matter their race. I have neither."

"Actually, there's a *gifted one* in DC who has brown hair."

Stopping short, Sarah stared at him. "What?"

Chris nodded. "She came to my attention . . . about six years ago when her college roommate was murdered in their dorm room."

"She's a *gifted one?* You're sure?"

"I'm sure. It caused quite a stir when the police ran her DNA. I had to call Seth in to wipe a hell of a lot of memories and to explain things to her."

"And she had brown hair?" Her heart began to thud in her chest.

"Just a bit darker than yours."

"Why doesn't Roland know about this?" He would have told her if he did.

Chris rolled his eyes. "Roland avoids all of us like the plague and this didn't make it onto the Immortal Guardian's website. Not very many people know."

Which would explain why Marcus hadn't said anything either when he had realized Roland was falling for her.

"Does the woman have any special gifts?"

He nodded. "She has minor psychic abilities. Knows someone is going to call before the phone rings or that she's going to receive a package before the postman arrives. That sort of thing. Not enough to enable her to pick the Lotto numbers, but enough for her to notice."

And there came reality, crashing back down again.

She sighed. "My eyes aren't brown and I have no gifts."

His look turned sympathetic. "Hazel is *close* to brown. And maybe you simply have a gift that's mild enough you haven't noticed it yet."

It was nice of him to try. "Thanks, Chris, but—" She broke off, her gaze drawn beyond him to the corner as Nietzsche suddenly flipped onto all fours and looked toward the hallway.

Sarah followed his gaze and saw nothing. The hallway was empty, the doorways leading to the library, bedrooms, and basement all open and equally bereft.

"What is it?" Chris asked, sitting up straighter.

"Nothing, I think."

Nietzsche dropped into a crouch, belly practically touching the cushion, ears laid back, and hissed.

An icy tingle of fear swept down Sarah's spine.

What the hell?

A blur of motion burst from the hallway and rocketed toward the sofa. Blood sprayed from Chris's mouth and nose as his head slammed back. Then he fell sideways, unconscious, onto the cushions.

As the blurry form looming over him stilled, it solidified into a man and turned to face her.

Oh shit. Bastien.

A heavy weight struck her in the stomach as he tossed her over his shoulder.

She hadn't even seen him move!

The room blurred. Her stomach lurched.

Sarah struggled to get her bearings as the light suddenly dimmed and cooler air buffeted her.

Were they down in one of the tunnels?

How had he known about the tunnels?

Heart racing, hands shaking, she reached under her shirt, withdrew the Glock he must not have noticed in his hurry, aimed at the dark blurs she assumed were his legs and fired twice.

The tunnel abruptly swam into focus as his momentum stalled and blood spurted from both of his hamstrings.

Bastien stumbled and went down.

Sarah went down with him. Her back hit the ground first and knocked the breath from her. Her head ricocheting off the hard-packed dirt, she slid several yards, then skidded to a halt. Dust rose up around her, choking her, making her cough. She groaned as her head began to throb.

Rolling to her side, Sarah fought to breathe and ignored the bright sparkles that danced through her vision. Sluggishly, she dragged herself to her feet and glanced around.

The tunnel they were in, like all the others, was dimly lit with low-wattage bulbs activated by motion sensors. She couldn't see the exit, so this must be one of the longer tunnels.

Bastien rose up between her and the entrance, one hand clamped to the back of his right thigh.

Sarah looked around frantically for the Glock she had dropped upon impact. Spotting it a couple of feet in front of her to the right, she dove for it.

Bastien snatched it away before she was even halfway there.

As Sarah jumped back, he turned and hurled it all the way to the entrance. His eyes, when he turned to face her, glowed amber with rage.

"Apparently your immortal friends didn't bother to tell you that shooting vampires doesn't kill us." His lips pulled back from sharp fangs, igniting fear within her. "It only pisses us off!"

She screamed when he raced toward her, expecting him to rip out her throat in retribution.

His shoulder hit her stomach and lifted. The tunnel blurred. Cool wind whipped her as she dangled upside down again. Blood rushed to her head, increasing the pounding in it.

The bullet wounds weren't even slowing him.

Fear made Sarah's pulse drum loudly in her ears. She couldn't let him take her. He'd kill her if he did or—worse—use her to kill Roland.

Her breath coming in panicked gasps, she reached into one of the few pockets still accessible in this position and withdrew a throwing knife. Grasping the wooden handle tightly, she held her breath, drew her arm back, then thrust it down as hard as she could.

Bastien cried out and jerked to a halt.

Sarah kept going, flying forward for a long weightless moment until she slammed into a wall. She heard a loud crack as she hit hard dirt or stone. Pain spiked through her head. Landing in a heap on the floor, she closed her eyes and gritted her teeth.

Dizziness assailed her. Nausea rose.

When she opened her eyes, they refused to focus.

Drawing her knees up under her, she braced a trembling hand against the wall and struggled to rise.

Bastien was an obscure blur a few yards away, though she thought he was standing still.

"*You stabbed me in the ass?*" he roared.

The pain in her head intensified. Tears spilled over her lashes and down her cheeks as she fought to remain upright.

Bastien stared in furious disbelief at the bloody knife he had just yanked out of his right butt cheek.

Was the woman insane? Didn't she understand who and what she was dealing with?

Tossing it the way of the Glock, he sent her a look that, in the past, had been known to make grown men wet their pants.

It didn't seem to faze her in the least, though she *was* crying, he noticed uncomfortably.

Hell, he'd rather have her fight him than cry. He never had been able to abide a woman's tears.

"How many damned weapons are you carrying?" he demanded, hardening his heart. She was a pawn, nothing more. A temporary thorn in his side he would use to bring his enemy down.

Peering around blearily, she abruptly slid down the wall, landing hard on her ass. Her arms settled limply at her sides.

He frowned. "Sarah?"

She didn't respond, just sat there, blinking hard as if something was wrong with her eyes.

When a small stream of crimson liquid emerged from one ear, a cold chill shivered down his spine.

Oh shit.

Bastien swiftly closed the distance between them and knelt before her.

"Sarah? Can you hear me?"

Slipping a hand around to the back of her head, he found it wet with blood.

They had been traveling at a good velocity when she had stabbed him. He hadn't meant to lose his hold on her, but he had had a four-inch blade stuck in his ass.

Had she hit the wall hard enough to fracture her skull?

Damn it! She wasn't supposed to have gotten hurt. She was supposed to have come along docilely, too terrified to fight, and lured Roland into a trap. Then, once the asshole was dead, Bastien would've released her and she would've gone on her merry mortal way.

"Sarah," he repeated softly, trying to get her to focus on him. "Sarah?"

"What?" she whispered.

She was totally out of it. Through his touch, he could feel her pain and confusion. She wanted Roland. Probably wanted him to heal her, since Bastien's research indicated Roland could heal with his hands. Not that he would.

Performing a quick search of her pockets, Bastien relieved her of the rest of her arsenal of weapons. His mind raced as he pulled a mask from his front pocket and jerked it on. Though it wasn't as fancy as those the immortals had been wearing when they had left, it would protect him from the worst of the sun's damage. And what it didn't block, the route through dense forest he had carefully plotted would.

Slipping one arm around Sarah's back and the other beneath her knees, he gently scooped her up into his arms.

"Roland?" she murmured plaintively.

"Easy, princess," he soothed, positioning them beneath the exit. "You'll see him soon."

* * *

Roland peered over Marcus's shoulder as they watched for the satellite image to appear on the small screen.

They had left Chris's van a couple of miles away and, approaching stealthily on foot, had arrived in the forest that overlooked Bastien's farmhouse five minutes ago.

Though the satellite image was due any minute, the wait was excruciating.

Roland continued to feel uneasy about leaving Sarah with only mortals to protect her.

Lisette offered him a sympathetic smile. "I'm sure she's fine, Roland."

Was she reading his thoughts?

Étienne nodded, eyeing him as if he were an exhibit in a damned science fair.

Seth continued to stare through the brush at the vampires' lair.

"Okay, here it comes," Marcus said, drawing their attention.

As Roland and the others gathered around him, an image similar to what Chris had shown them at the meeting appeared on the small screen. Vampires showed up as violet blobs, the humans showed up yellow.

The red blob was notably absent.

Roland scowled. "Where the hell is Bastien?"

Frowning, Marcus touched the screen. "I don't know. Hang on." The image doubled, then tripled in size.

As Roland watched, dread rising inside him, Marcus searched the image quadrant by quadrant and confirmed Bastien's absence.

"He isn't there." Marcus glanced at the others. "Do you think he heard us coming and bolted?"

Seth shook his head. "I would've heard him."

Something like panic struck Roland, tightening around his heart like a fist. "He's gone after Sarah."

"We don't know that," Étienne cautioned just as Seth's head snapped around.

"What is it?" Lisette asked.

Then they all heard it.

A black-clad figure shot from the forest on the far side of the house and entered the back door with preternatural speed. Though the man's face was covered by a mask, Roland knew it was Bastien.

"Anyone get a look at what he was carrying?" Marcus asked.

A scent came to Roland on the breeze.

Fangs burst from his gums and all rational thought fled as rage engulfed him. "It's Sarah."

And she was bleeding.

Moments later, he was tearing the front door off the farmhouse and sprinting inside. Two humans jumping up from the sofa went ignored as he darted past them and flew down the stairs to the basement.

The large main room was empty and offered up four hallways from which he could choose.

Roland didn't hesitate, charging through the only one on the right and plunging into darkness his eyes had no trouble piercing. Almost immediately, the hallway branched off into a number of others, forming an intricate maze that would have slowed Roland substantially if Bastien hadn't been carrying Sarah.

Her scent lit his way like a candle, guiding him unerringly through an endless series of twists and turns.

"*Awaken, vampires!*" Bastien bellowed ahead of him. "*The immortals have found us!*"

Roland's heart slammed against his ribs as he continued forward at top speed. The sounds of battle soon broke out behind him. Gunshots sounded above.

How badly was Sarah hurt? Was she dying? Was she afraid? Did she know he was coming? Would she ever forgive him?

How could he have left her like that? Why had he risked it?

Bastien was *nothing* to him. Sarah was *everything.*

He would kill Bastien for hurting her. For touching her. For even looking at her fucking cross-eyed!

What had he done to her? How badly had he hurt her? Was she suffering?

She couldn't die. Roland wouldn't let her. Couldn't lose her.

Light bloomed ahead.

There. Up and to the left.

Head down, fangs gleaming, Roland charged forward.

Lisette groaned as she watched Roland cover the distance to the farmhouse's front door in a blink, rip it off its hinges, and vanish inside. "So much for stealth."

All but Seth hastily donned their masks.

"*Awaken, vampires!*" a voice bellowed from within. "*The immortals have found us!*"

"How many did you count?" Seth asked grimly.

"Fifty-seven vamps below," Marcus said. "Four humans above."

"If you can prevent Roland from killing Sebastien, do so."

Seth raced for the farmhouse first, followed by Marcus, then Lisette and Étienne.

The French immortals burst inside just as the first two vanished through the door that led to the basement. Two human minions stood gaping in front of a threadbare sofa.

Lisette nodded to her brother. "Go on. I'll see to the humans."

He vanished in a blur.

As she turned to face the minions, they drew handguns and fired. Lisette ducked to the side, slipped behind them, and snapped both their necks. She had been born with the ability to read others' thoughts and theirs had been seriously sadistic.

"I hope Bastien was oblivious to your true natures," she murmured, "because, if he wasn't, he isn't worth saving."

Another of their ilk came running from the kitchen, guns blazing. He died quickly, too.

As the sounds of battle rose from below, she sped down a hallway to the room that had contained the last yellow blob from the satellite image and kicked the door open.

The room was a combination home office and library. The sole occupant was roughly six feet tall, blond, and blue-eyed, with a handsome, youthful face and world-weary eyes.

Lisette guessed he was around thirty-five and, after rapidly scanning his thoughts, definitely worth salvaging.

"Who the hell are you?" he demanded, yanking earbuds blasting metal music out of his ears. When sounds of violence trickled in through the door, he drew a 9mm and pointed it at her. "What the hell is going on?"

Lisette pulled her mask off and drew in a deep breath.

Damned thing made her feel like she was suffocating.

Male appreciation wafted over her. Smiling with a flash of fang, she tucked the mask in her belt. "You might as well put that away," she advised, nodding at the gun.

His eyes widened and his mouth came dangerously close to falling open. "There are female vampires?"

She chuckled. "Of course there are. But, fortunately for you, I am *not* a vampire. Otherwise I would have already ripped out your throat."

He paled. "You're one of *them?*"

"Define 'them,'" she said, strolling toward him across the long, narrow room.

"Immortal Guardians," he sneered.

She shook her head. "I see you are as confused as your employer. As Bastien will soon learn, *we* are the good guys."

"You're murderers."

She shrugged. "We only kill those who prey upon the

innocent. Vampires, on the other hand, kill anyone who strikes their fancy."

"That's not true." He grabbed some papers off the desk with his free hand and held them up. "Bastien's vampires only kill pedophiles."

She tilted her head to the side. "Like the one who murdered your son?"

His Adam's apple bobbed up and down. "How do you know about that?"

"The vampires didn't just kill the men on that list. They killed the men's wives, sons, daughters, grandchildren, and many others who were either oblivious to those men's sickness or had been victimized by it themselves."

"That's . . . That can't be. Bastien wouldn't allow that."

"Bastien doesn't know. That's why we're here. We've seen the police reports and intend to put a stop to it."

A masculine throat cleared in her head. *I hate to interrupt your little chat,* her brother said, *but Roland has gone off to kill Bastien, leaving Seth, Marcus, and me to face the* fifty-seven *vampires spewing forth from the hallways down here. So, if you wouldn't mind wrapping it up, we could really use some help.*

Lisette grinned.

The blond eyed her warily and took a step back. "Why are you smiling?"

"I'm afraid my brother has summoned me. Time's up."

Before he could blink, she leapt over the desk, knocked the gun from his grasp, and yanked the computer's power cord from the wall.

"Relax," she said as she easily restrained him long enough to bind his hands behind his back. "I'm not going to kill you." Shoving him into his chair, she yanked the ethernet cord from both the wall and the computer and bound his ankles as well.

"You can't just leave me like this," he said somewhat desperately as she tied it off. "If you're telling the truth, won't the vampires kill me if they find me like this and Bastien isn't around to stop them?"

"Don't worry." She gave his knee a pat as she rose. "When we're finished here, there won't be any vampires left."

A little faster, please, her brother gritted out.

I'm on my way.

Chapter 17

Roland surged into a square room with cement walls that opened onto a smaller room on the opposite side. Unlike the heart of the basement, which had been furnished like a living room/game room, this chamber boasted only a single tattered armchair. The next room appeared to be empty except for the thick chains and heavy manacles attached to one wall.

Bastien was leaning over Sarah, who was seated in the chair.

Incensed, Roland launched himself at the bastard, knocking him away from her and into the wall beyond.

"Sarah!" he called.

She didn't answer.

Grabbing Bastien by the neck, he hurled him across the room and into the wall with such force that a crater formed in it.

Roland risked a quick glance at her.

She was slumped in the chair, eyes closed, hair falling forward to conceal much of her face.

"*Sarah!*"

He glimpsed none of the blood he smelled and didn't think there was a large quantity of it.

Had Bastien drunk from her? Was that why she wouldn't rouse? Had Bastien attempted to drain her?

Roland couldn't see her neck for her hair but feared that was it.

Roaring his fury, he drew his sais.

Don't kill him, Seth's voice spoke in his head.

He hurt Sarah. All bets are off.

As a stunned Bastien, who clearly hadn't expected Roland to negotiate his maze so swiftly, picked himself up off the ground, Roland leapt the distance between them and swung.

Mere inches from Bastien's neck, the sais rebounded as though they had struck a shield.

I said, don't kill him, Seth spoke, uncompromising.

Damn you, Roland snarled, arms smarting as he watched Bastien stumble backward and draw two short swords.

Beat him. Bruise him. Maim him if you must. But leave him alive, Roland. This is nonnegotiable.

Bastien swung. Metal clashed.

The younger immortal didn't have a hope in hell of emerging the victor. Roland was seven hundred years older. Seven hundred years stronger and swifter. For every gash Bastien inflicted, Roland scored four.

And relished every one.

He was relentless, constantly pressing forward, forcing Bastien onto the defensive, keeping his body between his opponent and Sarah at all times.

Dodging one of Bastien's swings, Roland kicked the sword from his hand, then slashed open Bastien's forehead and cheek, barely missing his eye. Blood gushed, partially blinding the prick as he brought his other sword up into Roland's side.

Roland didn't even flinch, just shoved him back and kept hammering away, cutting and hitting and kicking the crap out of him.

Bastien's other sword went flying.

Dropping one of his sais, Roland grabbed Bastien by the

hair, swung him around, and slammed him face-first into the wall.

Dust and cement slivers erupted outward.

"What did you do to her?" he growled.

When Bastien struggled, Roland drew the immortal's head back and slammed his face into the wall again.

Cement cracked. Bones snapped. Blood spurted from Bastien's nose.

"*What did you do to her?*"

"Fuck you," Bastien bit out, spitting blood.

Yanking him back, Roland hurled him bodily into the next room. Bastien hit the wall, forming a lightning bolt–shaped crevice in it, then fell to the floor.

Roland crossed to him in an instant, jerking him to his feet. Shoving him back against the wall with a hand clamped around his throat, he pressed the tip of his sai to Bastien's chest.

Bastien grabbed the hand holding the sai and strained to keep it at bay.

The blade penetrated skin, pressed forward into muscle.

"Every m-minute you fight me," Bastien choked out, "takes her closer to death."

Panic piercing him, Roland glanced over his shoulder at Sarah. She was still slumped, unmoving, against the cushions.

Careful not to strike the heart or any major arteries, Roland drove the blade home.

Bastien cried out in agony.

It may not kill him, but it would sure as hell slow him down.

Roland withdrew the blade, hurried into the other room, and knelt before Sarah. Dropping the sai, he cupped her face with bloody hands that trembled.

"Sarah?" he called softly. He could see no bite marks on her neck but could tell by her erratic heartbeat that something was seriously wrong.

"Sarah, sweetling, open your eyes and answer me."

Her eyelids fluttered, then rose slowly. Her eyebrows drew together in a pained *V.*

Roland was so relieved to get a response from her that he damned near burst into tears. "That's it, love. Let me see those pretty eyes."

She kept blinking hard and seemed to have difficulty focusing.

"Roland?" she whispered weakly.

"Yes, love, it's me."

As her gaze wandered, he gently drew back first one eyelid, then the other. His heart sank. Her right pupil was dilated. The left one wasn't.

"My head . . ." Pushing his hand away, she closed her eyes.

Roland brushed her bangs back and found no lump. Checked her temples, the left side of her head. When he pulled back the hair on the right side and saw the blood coming from her ear, his insides went cold.

Edward's ears had bled as he'd died.

Tunneling his fingers through the dusty strands, Roland cautiously examined her scalp until he met with more blood in the back.

She moaned when he settled his hands over the wound.

"I'm sorry," he murmured, pressing a kiss to her forehead. "Just sit still. The pain will be gone soon. I promise."

His gift showed him the skull fracture. The hemorrhaging. The pressure it was causing that would kill her if it wasn't relieved soon. The brain damage she had already sustained.

When fury boiled up inside him anew, he vanquished it and forced himself to concentrate. The wounds on his own body ceased healing as Roland directed all of his energy toward healing Sarah.

His hands grew hot.

Light surrounded her head like a halo.

Roland's own head began to ache.

"Just a little longer, love."

* * *

Leaving the human without another glance, Lisette sped down to the basement and stopped short at the foot of the stairs.

It was like nothing she had ever seen.

There were four hallways branching off the main room. One was empty. Étienne, Seth, and Marcus were positioned in front of the others, fighting an endless stream of vampires that flowed forth from each, two and three at a time.

Drawing her Glock 18s, Lisette began to fire.

Blood sprayed the ceiling, walls, floor, and Immortal Guardians as bullets tore through major arteries. Unlike immortals, who could slip into a sort of stasis similar to that of a water bear, vampires died when they bled out.

As many were doing now.

The acrid odors of gunpowder, sweat, and fear permeated the room as she spent sixty-two rounds and the other Guardians' short swords, sais, and katanas flashed.

Kneeling, she ejected the empty clips, dropped one Glock, and pulled replacements from pockets attached to her belt.

A vampire left the others and lunged for her.

Étienne appeared in front of her and cut the vamp down.

"Thanks." She slapped in the clips and rose. "I'm good."

Without a word, Étienne returned to his hallway.

Lisette took out every vamp that sought the stairs or went for Étienne's back, and did the same for Marcus and Seth.

The bodies began to pile up.

The room turned red with blood.

And still the vampires kept coming.

Bastien sank to his knees and probably would have fallen farther if he hadn't grabbed one of the chains bolted to the wall and clung to it.

Every time he drew a breath, it felt as if Roland were plunging that sai into his chest again.

He was in trouble. He had seriously underestimated Roland and didn't see how he was going to make it out of this alive.

Judging by the sounds of things, his men weren't faring any better.

How had Roland become so powerful?

The immortal Bastien had killed in Scotland hadn't been anywhere *near* this fast or strong.

It had happened years ago. Bastien had been feeding upon a woman who sold orphaned children to brothels, fully intending to drain her dry, when the Scottish immortal had pounced. The fight had lasted a lot longer than this one probably would and had left Bastien laid up for three days, but he had won. He had killed the asshole and assumed Roland's skills would be roughly the same.

When he and his men had ambushed Roland in groups, he had realized that Roland was stronger than he had previously believed. But he had imagined him capable of nothing close to this.

Today he was unstoppable. Unbeatable. Carving Bastien up at will and blocking his expert swings and thrusts not only with his wicked sais, but with bursts of telekinetic energy.

His gaze glued to the couple in the next room, Bastien tightened his grip on the chain and pulled himself painfully to his feet.

It wasn't just Roland's astounding power that had caught him off-guard, however. There were other things. Things his gift told him that just didn't add up.

He fought for breath when the lung Roland had punctured collapsed, then struggled to reinflate itself as the virus sapped his energy in an attempt to repair it.

Bastien's gift enabled him to read others' emotions with a touch.

Roland had been a mass of seething rage.

Not surprising. Bastien had stolen his latest toy.

But that rage had been tempered with fear.

Fear that had metamorphosed into panic when Bastien had pointed out that Sarah was dying.

Leaning against the wall, he watched Roland press his lips to Sarah's forehead and cup the back of her head with care.

He was gentle with her. His touch. His speech. And he was healing her.

Sarah wasn't just another victim to him.

Roland loved her. Deeply.

Bastien glanced at the portrait hanging on the wall beside him, out of sight of the next room.

Cold-blooded murderers didn't have those feelings . . . did they?

And Roland hadn't killed him, though he had had ample opportunity to do so. Even when he had punctured Bastien's lung, he had deliberately avoided nicking the heart or any major arteries.

Why? Bastien had felt no intent on Roland's part to torture him at length or save him to kill at a future date.

If he was the heartless murderer Bastien had long believed him to be . . . why hesitate?

He returned his gaze to the next room and frowned.

Roland's hands were glowing brightly. As Bastien watched, astonished, the back of Roland's head began to glisten wetly and blood emerged from one ear.

Bastien looked again at the portrait.

Roland had just fractured his own skull to save Sarah's life.

What the hell was going on?

Aided by the gleaming blade of a katana, the head of Seth's opponent flew from his body and landed in the hands of the vampire behind him. That vampire looked down at his prize, then dropped it with a yelp just as Seth's other katana liberated his head, too.

Behind him (or his collapsing body), three vampires stood,

immobile, in the entrance of the hallway and stared at Seth with terror.

Glad to have a reprieve, Seth checked on his charges to see how they were faring.

Marcus and Étienne were still parked in front of the other hallways, cutting a swath through the vampires the entrances continued to vomit forth.

Lisette blocked the stairs leading out of the basement. She had run out of ammunition several minutes ago and now met any vamp who slipped past the rest of them with the lethal blades of her red shoto swords.

Marcus finished off another vamp and looked over at Seth as the body fell. "How many more of these bastards are there?" he asked as another came at him.

Beyond Marcus, Étienne was battling two vamps of his own.

Seth shrugged. "I don't know. I've lost count."

The bodies were piling up. All four immortals were covered in blood and stood up to their knees in vampire corpses afflicted with various stages of decay.

The stench was overpowering.

Seth returned his attention to the three vampires who lingered uncertainly in the entrance of the hallway he blocked.

One was blond. One was African-American. One was Latino. All appeared to be in their early twenties.

When they seemed disinclined to move, he arched a brow. "Well?"

The blond exchanged a look with the others and swallowed audibly. "You guys are Immortal Guardians?"

"Yes."

The African-American vamp shifted his weight from one foot to the other. "Did you kill Bastien?"

"No, we have no intention of killing him. Bastien is one of us."

His jaw dropped. "Bastien is an immortal?"

"Yes."

"He said he was a vampire like us!"

"Because he thinks he is. Bastien is . . . confused. He was fed false information by the one who transformed him. We're here to help him, not hurt him."

The Latino vampire motioned belligerently to the carnage around them. "Then why are you killing all of us?"

"Bastien's vampire followers have not been confining their feeding to those on the lists they were given. They're killing innocents. I'm afraid we cannot allow such to continue."

"But Bastien said *immortals* kill innocents," the blond spoke up.

"As I said, he was misinformed. Immortal Guardians only kill those who prey upon the innocent, those who threaten to reveal our existence to the mortal world, and those who seek to harm us. We *protect* innocents."

The three huddled together and whispered among themselves.

Seth sheathed one katana, pulled out a throwing knife, and hurled it into the throat of a vampire who had snuck past Étienne and was circling around to attack his back.

According to the conversation he had no difficulty hearing, the blond was Joe, the African-American was Cliff, and the Latino was Vincent.

Joe cleared his throat. "What exactly are our options here?"

Smart vampire. "How long has it been since you were turned?" Seth countered.

"Six months."

"Fourteen for me," Cliff said.

"About two and a half years," Vincent said.

The madness didn't seem to have taken hold of them yet. "How's the bloodlust?"

"Controllable," Joe answered.

Cliff nodded. "Same here."

Vincent hesitated. "It's pretty bad. I . . . I've been having . . . thoughts . . . lately that scare me."

"Have you acted upon them?"

"No."

"He hasn't killed anyone who wasn't on Bastien's list," Cliff said hastily.

Joe nodded. "We made sure. One of us is always with him."

They seemed like good men. It was a damned shame they were destined to become monsters.

"You have two options then, gentlemen. We can either fight to the death today—*your* death, I'm afraid—or, should you prefer it, you can be taken to one of our research facilities. You'll be given individual apartments and anything else you need to be comfortable. You will be supplied with bagged blood and food as well. But you will not be able to leave the building without an immortal escort. We can't risk your killing an innocent."

Joe frowned. "Research facility?"

"Our scientists are attempting to find both a cure for the vampiric virus and a treatment that will alleviate or prevent entirely the madness that inevitably afflicts your kind. Perhaps you would like to be of some assistance."

Vincent snorted. "So you want us to be your guinea pigs? Your lab rats?"

"Look," Cliff said, "if there's a chance they can keep us from going crazy, it's worth it."

"I agree," Joe said somberly.

"But we'd be like their prisoners," Vincent protested.

A tense silence ensued.

Seth threw another knife.

Joe shook his head. "Killing pedophiles is one thing. I don't want to end up killing women and kids and people who aren't violent criminals. If being locked up is the only way to ensure I don't . . ."

Cliff nodded. "Yeah, I don't want to end up like the one who turned me. He didn't just *feed* on people, he *tortured* them."

"The guy who made me tortured people, too," Vincent admitted reluctantly.

"So did mine," Joe added.

Seth lobbed another knife at one of two vamps fighting Lisette. "You won't be treated badly," he assured them. "And, should we not be able to help you, when the madness grows too uncomfortable, you can choose your own end. We won't force you to linger in such a state." To do so would be to truly turn them into lab rats and would endanger the humans at the facility.

The three stared at each other a somber moment.

"Fine," Vincent said finally. "Let's do it."

Seth sheathed his other katana. "I don't have any rope with which to restrain you, so . . . sorry about this." Three carefully placed lightning-quick jabs, backed by Seth's superior preternatural strength, knocked them all unconscious. Grabbing the fronts of their shirts before they could fall, he eased them down to the ground.

A quick look and listen confirmed that the hallway behind them was devoid of further vampires. They must have been the last to rouse.

Drawing his katanas once more, Seth stepped over the mounds of bodies that had dropped around him and headed over to aid Marcus, Étienne, and Lisette.

The vise that was clamped around Sarah's head loosened. Gradually the throbbing that made it feel as if a spike were being driven through her skull eased.

Sighing with relief, she opened her eyes. Vision that was initially hazy cleared and showed her Roland, kneeling in front of her with his eyes closed.

No wonder her headache was going away. He was holding a heating pad to the back of her head.

Smiling gratefully, she reached out to touch his face and froze. Blood was seeping slowly from his ear. More saturated the collar at the back of his neck. Lines of pain bracketed his eyes and mouth as a muscle clenched and unclenched in his jaw.

Oh no. No no no no no!

He was healing her! She must have hit her head or . . .

She didn't know. She couldn't remember.

Reaching up, she tugged at his wrists and looked around wildly.

Where the hell were they? The last thing she recalled was rubbing Nietzsche's tummy. Now they were in a windowless room with blood-splattered, cracked walls and . . .

Terror gripped her.

Bastien was in the next room, staring at them with glowing amber eyes.

Sarah pulled harder on Roland's arms but couldn't break his hold.

"Roland, stop. What are you doing?"

Bastien's face was a bloody mess. A deep laceration creased one side from forehead to jawline. His nose was broken, his chin completely crimson. Too many cuts to count marred the rest of him.

He swayed where he stood. Nevertheless, he scared the crap out of her as he shuffled forward and bent to pick up a sword that lay on the ground.

Sarah tore her gaze away from him and began to struggle violently. "Roland, stop!"

Roland was bleeding from several wounds Bastien must have inflicted. Healing her was diverting much-needed energy away from stopping blood loss that would weaken him. By the looks of it, he was already weak enough that her head wound had opened on him and was leaching more of his strength.

How was he going to be able to defend himself?

Roland's large hands wouldn't budge no matter how strongly Sarah fought.

Her throat thickened. Tears spilled down her cheeks. "Don't do this, Roland. Please, stop healing me. I'm fine now. You have to stop healing me."

His brow creased as his lashes lifted. When his eyes met

hers, she bit back a sob. They should have been glowing amber from his skirmish with Bastien. Instead they were brown and one pupil was much larger than the other.

"You have to stop, baby," she whispered hoarsely, cupping his face in trembling hands. "For me. Please, stop."

He withdrew his hands. The heat faded away.

Sarah cried out when he toppled sideways and hit the floor. Flinging herself from the chair, she knelt over him. "Roland?"

"I'm okay," he murmured. Bracing his hands on the floor, he pushed himself up to sit with his back against the wall. "I just lost my balance for a second." His voice was weak, pained.

"What have you done?"

"What I had to." Reaching up, he stroked her cheek with bloody fingers. "I couldn't lose you."

She covered his hand with hers and held it to her face. "But Bastien is coming." She could hear his dragging footsteps entering the room behind her.

Roland glanced over her shoulder, expression hardening. "Help me up."

"Roland—"

"Help me up, Sarah."

Swearing silently, she wrapped her arms around his waist and, thigh muscles straining, helped heave him to his feet.

Roland leaned against the wall and glared daggers at Bastien.

Sarah looked back and forth between them and thought they both looked as weak as kittens. Yet recent experience had taught her that when it came to vampires and immortals, looks could be deceiving.

"You fractured her skull," Roland growled furiously.

Sarah looked up at him in surprise.

Was that why her head had hurt so badly, why she couldn't recall what had happened?

No wonder healing her had taken so much out of him.

"I didn't mean to drop her," Bastien snapped, surprising

her even more. "I was running with her over my shoulder and she stabbed me in the ass."

Her eyebrows rose.

Roland's lips twitched as he lowered his gaze to meet hers. "You stabbed him in the ass?"

Sarah shrugged. "I don't remember."

She wasn't sure why Bastien felt the need to offer an explanation. He still seemed intent on killing Roland, moving steadily closer with drunken steps.

Sarah bent and retrieved Roland's sai, then positioned herself in front of him, feet braced for an attack.

Bastien shook his head. "Step aside, Sarah. This is between me and Roland."

"What is?" she challenged angrily. "Why are you doing this?"

Bastien turned his head and spat blood, then pointed his blade at Roland. "He killed my sister."

She sucked in a shocked breath.

"What?" Roland asked behind her.

"You killed my sister, you bloody bastard!"

Drawing on what little strength remained, Bastien attacked with a burst of preternatural speed.

Roland grabbed his sai and shoved Sarah aside.

Blades clashed and the battle resumed, slowed nearly to mortal speed by the toll their wounds had taken.

It took only moments for Bastien to perceive he would lose. Roland's swings gained in strength as his own continued to weaken, driving him incessantly backward. Every breath was like a knife in his chest.

"Was she a vampire's minion?" Roland asked through gritted teeth.

"She was an innocent," Bastien denied furiously.

Roland's sai connected with his sword, swung, and propelled it out of his hand.

It landed with a clatter on the far side of the room, where Sarah hurriedly claimed it.

"Then I didn't kill her," Roland insisted evenly.

That he would deny it after savaging Cat the way he had infuriated Bastien.

With no other weapon left him, he drove his fist into Roland's temple.

It must have hurt like hell on top of the skull fracture.

Bastien heard Sarah cry out.

Roland's eyes flashed from brown to glowing amber.

A second later, pain crashed through Bastien's back as Roland hurled him into the wall with the chains in the next room and pinned him there, one of the manacles digging into his shoulder blade, with a hand at his throat.

"It wasn't me, Bastien. The only innocents I have ever killed were my wife and my brother."

"Bullshit!" Sarah blurted from the other room.

Bastien felt Roland's surprise and confusion as Sarah marched toward them.

"That bitch wasn't innocent and neither was your brother. They were the ones who handed you over to the vampire who turned you. Damn it, Roland, I told you to stop feeling guilty about that!"

Love and amusement replaced Roland's confusion but couldn't quite blot out old guilt.

"I stand corrected," he drawled. "They weren't innocent."

When Roland's grip loosened, Bastien drew in several jagged breaths and rested a moment in hopes of rebuilding a final burst of strength. "My sister *was* innocent. She knew nothing of this world, yet you killed her."

"Is that her?" Sarah asked, motioning to the painting.

It was a portrait of Cat and her husband, Blaise.

"Yes."

He waited for Roland's reaction as he looked at it, knowing his gift would tell him the truth regardless of any lies the immortal may spout.

"I don't know her," Roland said simply.

Bastien frowned. Unless his gift was failing him, Roland truly did not recall seeing her. Then . . .

There it was. A spark of recognition.

"You're lying. I can feel it. You recognize her."

Roland's expression darkened as he stared at the painting. "Not her. *Him.* Who was he?"

"Her husband. He was like a brother to me. You turned him after you ripped her throat out and made him watch her die."

Roland looked at him sharply. "Who told you that?"

"He did."

"He lied, Bastien. In all of my nine and a half centuries of living, I have *never* transformed a human."

Bastien stared at him in confusion. He was telling the truth, or seemed to be. He hadn't turned Blaise.

Then the rest of Roland's words hit him. "Nine and a half centuries?"

"Yes."

"That's impossible."

"No, it isn't. There is an immortal fighting your men right now who is millennia older than I. Immortals live far longer than vampires."

"Because you kill them!" he countered, incensed.

"Not all of them," he denied, annoyingly calm. "We aren't everywhere, Bastien. Vampires have always dramatically outnumbered us, finding safe havens wherever they could thrive unchallenged. Even so, the oldest vampire I have ever heard mention of had been a vampire a mere seventy-nine years."

"What of me? I was transformed two centuries ago."

Roland sighed and, releasing his hold, stepped back. "You aren't a vampire. You're an immortal."

Bastien almost laughed. "Now I know you're lying." He wasn't an immortal. He *hated* immortals. Had despised them ever since he had found a hysterical Blaise weeping over Cat's torn and bloody body and learned that an immortal had killed her.

"It's true," Sarah interjected softly.

When Bastien looked at her, he felt a stab of unease.

There was pity in her gaze.

"That's why Roland and the others haven't killed you. You're one of them, Bastien. They just didn't know it until after you attacked him."

A sick feeling slithered through him as he recalled the way Roland had intentionally avoided striking a killing blow. Though he had scored numerous hits during the fight, not one of the wounds Roland had spawned was fatal.

"I'm a vampire," he insisted. The fact that none of them had ever met another two-hundred-year-old vampire didn't mean they didn't exist. It couldn't.

"You were different even as a human," Roland went on, "possessed gifts or abilities you hid from others, gifts your friend Blaise did not."

How did he know that?

"Perhaps you . . . read minds or can discern the emotions of others with a touch?"

Bastien's heart began to pound.

Roland was studying him intently. "All immortals were different as humans. No doubt your sister had special gifts as well."

She had. She had been born with psychometric abilities, receiving glimpses of past events that were related to objects she touched.

"Except immortals were never human," Bastien uttered numbly. "Their . . . your DNA is different from ours."

Roland's gaze sharpened. "That isn't common knowledge amongst vampires. How did you know that?"

"I took a sample of your blood, remember? I had it tested."

Roland exchanged a grim glance with Sarah. "By whom?"

"A biochemist who is helping me search for a cure. He said you were different, that you aren't human and never were."

"If he didn't say the same of you, then he hasn't tested your blood yet."

He hadn't. Always nervous around Bastien, Keegan had said Casey's blood would suffice.

"Have you ever met a vampire who had gifts like yours?"

Not one. But Bastien didn't say so.

"All immortals possess them, though the gifts differ from person to person. They did not acquire them after the transformation. They were born with them, as you were."

Sarah took a step forward, then stopped when Roland motioned for her to stay back. "You even look like them, Bastien. Same hair. Same eyes. Similar features."

It sounded as if she thought he was lucky. What was *that* about?

Mentally, he shook himself. "It doesn't matter whether I'm vampire or immortal." The hell it didn't. "Roland killed my sister and turned her husband. He—"

"I've never seen that woman before!" Roland shouted.

Sarah waved the sword to gain their attention. "Your friend told you Roland turned him?"

"Yes."

"He mentioned Roland specifically by name?"

Roland made a sound of irritation. "He already said he did, Sarah."

"No, he didn't. I know you're grumpy, honey, but be patient and let me finish."

Bastien was shocked when Roland immediately backed down.

"Bastien, did your brother-in-law mention Roland by name when he told you what had happened and that he had been transformed?"

"He didn't know Roland's name then. Only his face." He curled his lip as he eyed Roland distastefully. "He said he'd never forget it as long as he lived."

Sarah spoke before Roland could. "When did he tell you it was Roland?"

"Five years later. We were in London. Blaise had been out feeding and returned white as a sheet. He said he had seen the one who'd turned him and, over the next two weeks, claimed the immortal was hunting him. The night Blaise was killed, I arrived as Roland was leaving and later uncovered his name myself."

"Well, isn't that convenient," Roland said contemptuously. "For years, he couldn't tell you who transformed him, then suddenly decided it was me when he realized I was hunting his sorry ass. Your friend was full of shit. He was slaughtering women in the rookery. When I followed the trail of bodies to him, he got scared and pointed his bloody finger at me, probably hoping you'd kill me."

"Bullshit! He wasn't the one killing women. You were!" And Roland had started by killing sweet Cat.

Roland emitted a mocking laugh. "I suppose he told you that, too?"

Bastien swung at him, wanting to knock the disparaging smile from Roland's face.

Roland dodged his fist, then shoved him up against the wall again. Raising his sai, Roland pressed the tip to Bastien's chest above his uninjured lung. "Did he also tell you I found him crouched over a pregnant woman whose throat was missing? Her blood was all over his face. Her pulse gone. The babe in her belly dead."

He leaned closer, eyes cold as ice. "'Now we can be a family again,' he was telling her. 'We'll be together for eternity, Catherine. You, me, and the baby.' The sick bastard had tried to turn a pregnant woman but, driven by bloodlust, had savaged her throat too badly instead!"

Bastien's heart began to pound.

No hint of deception bled forth from Roland. There was irritation over Bastien's refusal to listen, disgust over Blaise's actions, and anger over the death of the woman and her babe, yet nothing that indicated he wasn't telling the absolute truth.

"And there were others," Roland persisted. "At least six other women murdered just in the two weeks I hunted him."

Mouth suddenly dry, Bastien forced himself to speak. "Were they pregnant?"

"The last three were. Noticeably. If the earlier victims were, you couldn't tell by looking and I didn't check."

Something inside Bastien started to crumble. His disbelief. His faith in his friend. He felt sick.

It couldn't be true. It couldn't. Everything that had driven him for the past two hundred years could not have been a lie.

"What is it?" Sarah asked cautiously.

He met her gaze, wondering if the pain and nausea invading him now was similar to what she must have felt when she had hit her head. "Cat was pregnant when she died."

Sarah bit her lip, her eyes turning sorrowful. "Your sister's name was Cat?"

"Short for Catherine."

Roland sighed heavily and stepped back.

Bastien met the immortal's gaze. "If you didn't kill her . . . who did?"

Roland shook his head regretfully. "You already know the answer to that."

Blaise.

Chapter 18

Sarah watched the emotions flitting across Bastien's battered face. Even though she was angry at him for kidnapping her and trying to kill Roland, she couldn't help but feel sorry for him.

He had been trying to avenge his sister's death and instead had learned that his brother-in-law and best friend was the one who had murdered her, and he had his enemy to thank for bringing him to justice.

What a mess.

"Why?" he asked Roland. "Why would he kill her? He *loved* her. I know he did."

"The bloodlust is very strong in the beginning, even stronger in vampires than it is in us." Roland shook his head. "He may have only intended to take a sip and lost control. It's how I killed *my* wife."

Sarah wished she could find a way to erase that memory for him.

Seth, Marcus, Lisette, and Étienne entered the next room.

Their faces were Jackson Pollocked with scarlet streaks and blotches. Lisette and Étienne's rubber suits glistened wetly and sported numerous neat cuts. Marcus's clothing was torn in several places and boasted large damp patches. Seth's clothes, though stained, were completely intact.

All four, from the knees down, looked as though they had waded through a vat of blood.

As they strolled forward to stand just inside the entrance of the small room Sarah, Roland, and Bastien occupied, Bastien stiffened and straightened his shoulders.

Marcus took in the chains on the wall, as well as Roland's and Bastien's bloody dishevelment, with speculative eyes.

Lisette moved to stand beside Sarah. "Are you all right?"

She nodded. "How about you?"

"I could use a shower."

Bastien stared at Seth. "You're the daywalker."

"Yes." Seth looked past Sarah at the painting, his face grim. "I know this comes inexcusably late"—he met Bastien's combative gaze—"but I would like to offer my sincere condolences on the death of your sister."

Bastien's look turned uncertain.

Seth's words, his expression, his body language broadcasted nothing but genuine regret.

Kindness was surely the last thing Bastien had expected from the leader of the Immortal Guardians.

"Where are my men?" Bastien asked in a low voice.

"*Are* they your men?" Marcus asked. "Did you transform them?"

When Bastien refused to answer, Seth said, "No, he recruited them after others transformed, then abandoned them."

"Where are my men?" he asked again.

Marcus, Lisette, and Étienne looked away.

"They're dead," Seth informed him flatly.

Bastien blanched. "All of them?"

Sarah wondered how close he had been to them, if he had considered them his friends.

"All but one of the humans—"

"You said you didn't kill humans!" Bastien shouted, turning on Roland before Seth could finish.

"I said we didn't kill *innocents,*" Roland corrected.

Lisette nodded. "And those men were not innocent, Bastien. They were depraved. They just hid it well."

Bastien shook his head, his face full of denial. "What about the vampires? Did you kill them, too?"

"All but three," Seth acknowledged.

The next thing Sarah knew, Bastien was beside her, yanking the sword from her hands and swinging it at Seth with phenomenal speed.

Seth vanished before the blade could strike home. The other immortals lunged at Bastien, then stopped short when Seth reappeared behind him. Wrapping one arm around the younger immortal's chest and sword arm and the other around his neck, he deftly restrained him.

"Étienne, you and Lisette take the vampires and the human we spared to the network. They're to be guarded at all times, but treated well. I'll call later with further instructions."

The network.

Sarah's eyes widened. Chris!

She had forgotten all about him. He had been guarding her when Bastien had taken her. Had Bastien . . .

Were Chris and his men dead?

She couldn't remember what had happened.

"Roland," Seth went on, curbing Bastien's struggles as easily as a parent would a child's, "don't kill Chris when you see him."

Relief supplanted worry. Chris was okay, then.

Roland's expression turned mutinous.

"None of us knew Bastien had found the tunnels," Seth said. "Had he been aware, Chris would have been better prepared."

Étienne frowned. "He got in through the tunnels?"

"Yes."

Roland glared at Bastien. "How the hell did you know about them?"

"It's called surveillance, asshole," Bastien snarled.

Sarah sighed. She supposed she could understand his hostility. He had just found out that *Roland's* friends had killed all but four of *his*.

In the next instant, Seth and Bastien vanished.

The tension in the room left with them.

"So," Marcus said, "someone want to clue me in? Unlike Seth and these two"—he motioned to Lisette and Étienne—"I can't read minds. What happened to the sister?"

Roland motioned to the painting. "Shortly after turning vampire, her husband killed her. To cover his ass, he said I killed her, then transformed him. Hence Bastien's thirst for revenge."

Marcus stared at the figures in the portrait. "*She* was Bastien's sister?"

Roland frowned. "You knew her?"

He looked uneasy. "No."

"But you recognize her. How . . ." Trailing off, Roland groaned. "Don't tell me."

Marcus nodded. "She was at your house the afternoon it burned down and she was standing in the corner just now when we came in."

Everyone followed his gaze to the empty corner opposite the portrait.

A chill skittered down Sarah's spine. Roland had told her Marcus could see dead people. Had Catherine's ghost been there, watching, the whole time?

"Is she still there?" Lisette asked uncomfortably.

"No, she vanished when Seth and Bastien did."

Shoulders drooping wearily, Roland dropped his sai, crossed to Sarah, and took her in his arms.

Sarah clung to him, glad it was finally over.

As Roland rested his cheek atop her hair, she buried her face in his chest.

Behind them, Étienne spoke.

"Marcus, I've said it before and I'll say it again. That shit is creepy."

The moment Seth teleported Bastien and himself into the massive entrance hall of his castle in England, he released him.

Stumbling forward several steps, the newly discovered immortal swung around and raised his sword. "What . . . ?" His faintly glowing gaze scoured his surroundings. "What did you do? Where are we?"

"My home," Seth told him. "One of them, anyway."

"Where are the others?"

"Still in your basement, where we left them."

"Why have you brought me here?"

Seth read Sebastien's mind without difficulty, feeling only slightly guilty for the intrusion. His new charge thought Seth was going to kill him and was digging deep to find strength enough to fight him.

"I didn't bring you here to harm you, Sebastien. I brought you here to do what I should have done during the first few weeks after you were transformed: help you understand who and what you are and aid you in making a new life for yourself."

Sebastien barked out a bitter laugh. "Are you kidding me? I *had* a life. I had a purpose, people I cared about, people I was trying to help, and you just slaughtered them all!"

David entered from the kitchen, munching an apple.

Sword held out defensively in front of him, Sebastien angled his body so that he faced both of them.

"You're back," David commented, studying Sebastien curiously and with a complete lack of fear or concern over his weapon. "How did it go?"

"It went," Seth replied. "You may have cared for the men you commanded, Sebastien, but they didn't care for you. They were using you, taking advantage of the safety you provided. They were not your friends."

"And I'm supposed to believe you?" Anger rolled off him in waves.

"Yes."

"I tried to kill one of your own. Two if you count Marcus. Hell, I thought I had amassed an army large enough to kill you all when you came for Sarah. Yet you expect me to just take your word for it that everyone I have associated with for the past two centuries has lied to me?"

"Everyone but the four we spared."

David glanced at Seth. "You found four who were salvageable?"

"Yes."

Darnell entered from the living room/great hall. "What's going on?"

Sebastien started, then shifted so he could keep all three of them in his sights. He was in his enemies' lair, trying hard to deny everything they were telling him, and expected one or more to attack at any moment.

It was about what Seth had expected. Knowing the hard climb he would have ahead of him winning Sebastien's trust, Seth had taken care to touch many of the vampires he had fought before he killed them, leeching from them the memories of the innocent blood they had spilled and how they had hidden it from their leader.

He would offer to show Sebastien the atrocities they had committed now, but thought it best to wait until the younger immortal's head had cleared.

Sebastien began to back away, swinging the sword and his watchful gaze from one to the other.

A faint rustling sounded in the hallway behind him.

Seth's heart nearly stopped when he realized who had made it.

Sebastien swung around, roaring and raising his sword to attack the immortal he thought was sneaking up behind him.

Time seemed to freeze.

Because Seth was the most powerful Immortal Guardian

on the planet, he kept a very tight rein on his temper. So tight very few had ever seen it unleashed.

But when he looked past Sebastien and saw the mystery woman cringe in fear as she stared up at Sebastien with wide, terror-filled eyes and a face devoid of color, the reins slipped.

With only a thought, Seth ripped the sword from Sebastien's grasp and flung it away with such force it embedded itself halfway to the hilt in one of the heavy oak front doors. The stone wall beside them cracked when another thought catapulted Sebastien after it.

Sebastien grunted on impact and fell forward.

With a speed no other Guardian could match, Seth caught him with a hand to the throat before he hit the floor and shoved him back up, feet dangling a foot or more above it.

His fingers tightened, cutting off air, threatening to crush the trachea.

The ground beneath them rippled as though from an earthquake. The castle itself began to rumble and vibrate. Somewhere a lamp crashed to the floor.

Through a red haze of fury, Seth caught and held Sebastien's gaze as that one struggled to breathe. "Listen closely, Sebastien Newcombe," he gritted in low menacing tones. "I will only say this once. I understand the despair coursing through you. I understand the rage that is eating away at your insides like acid. If you want to lash out at me, you are welcome to do so. You can even lash out at David and Darnell. But if you ever give me reason to believe you have been anything less than kind to the woman who resides here, I will strike your head from your body and you will go down in history as the only immortal I have ever killed. Nod your head that you understand me."

Face red from lack of air, Sebastien nodded.

The ground gradually ceased its trembling. The castle quieted.

His fury abating, Seth lowered Sebastien until his feet settled on the floor, then released him.

Sebastien coughed and sucked in great gasping breaths.

"Are you all right?"

He nodded warily.

"Good. Now apologize to the woman in such a way that will make her think you no greater threat than a newborn pup."

Seth stepped aside and turned toward the mystery woman.

She was barefoot again, clad in loose sky-blue pajama bottoms with bright yellow smiley faces on them and a matching yellow tank top. Her narrow shoulders were hunched, her arms wrapped around her middle, as she watched them anxiously.

David and Darnell had moved to stand on either side of her, close but not touching.

Seth felt regret suffuse Sebastien when he saw her. She looked so frail. The younger immortal felt bad for scaring her. A promising sign.

Brow furrowing, Sebastien made a few futile attempts to straighten his clothes and wipe the blood from his face, then cleared his throat. "Forgive me," he beseeched her gently, his voice hoarse from Seth's abuse. "I did not mean to frighten you and have no desire to harm you. You startled me and I overreacted. I apologize. It won't happen again."

When the woman looked to Seth, he gave her what he hoped was a reassuring smile. Returning her gaze to Sebastien, she nodded.

"David, would you take our guest to his room and help him get settled?" Seth requested.

"Sure." Strolling forward, David addressed Sebastien as casually as he would an old friend. "We weren't sure whether you would prefer a room above- or belowground, so we prepared one of each. Both are safe for day sleeping."

"Belowground," Sebastien said uncertainly.

"Belowground it is. Right this way."

Once they were gone, Darnell ambled over and surveyed Seth carefully. "You okay?"

Seth nodded, then proffered his own apology to the woman. "I'm sorry. I thought he posed no threat to you, otherwise I would not have brought him here."

She nodded, her gaze lowering to take in the blood that painted his clothes.

What must she think, seeing him like this, and after all she had just witnessed?

"Did I hear you say you spared four of them?" Darnell asked curiously.

"Yes, one human and three vampires who have not yet succumbed to the madness. Like Sebastien, they were unaware of the others' actions."

"What are you going to do with the vamps?"

He sighed. "Help them any way we can."

"Roland and Sarah and everyone else come through all right?"

"A little banged-up, but they'll be fine."

Darnell looked in the direction David and their unwilling guest had gone. "Sebastien doesn't seem to appreciate your having come to his aid."

"No."

Seth felt a small hand touch his arm and looked down to find the mystery woman at his side, staring up at him.

Her lips parted. "I do," she said softly. "Thank you for saving me."

A tiny thread of joy wound its way through him at the sound of her voice.

He smiled.

Smiling back, she closed her eyes, then sank limply toward the floor.

Darnell leapt forward as Seth caught her and lifted her into his arms. "What is it? Is she sick?"

"I don't know." Frowning, Seth swiftly carried her to her room, Darnell right on his heels.

Darnell hastened to the bed and drew the covers back.

Seth carefully laid her down, then sat beside her on the

mattress. Placing one hand on her forehead and the other on her chest, he sought the source of her unconsciousness.

When he found it, he looked up at Darnell.

"What is it?" Darnell asked apprehensively. "What's wrong with her?"

Seth smiled. "She's sleeping."

Roland and Sarah were curled up on the sofa, watching the news, when his cell phone rang.

Retrieving it from the coffee table, he answered. "What?"

"Are you decent?" Seth's deep voice drawled.

"Have I ever been?" Roland answered wryly.

"Put Sarah on the line."

Frowning, he handed the phone to Sarah. "It's Seth. He wants to talk to you."

Eyebrows raising, she took the phone. "Hello?"

"Hello, Sarah. I know it tends to startle you when I pop in unannounced, so I thought I'd call and warn you this time."

Roland mirrored her smile as she said, "Oh. Okay. Thanks. Pop away."

Seth appeared just inside the front door.

Roland and Sarah both stood as she returned the phone to the coffee table.

"Calling ahead now?" Roland asked.

"Marcus thought it would be wise."

"He told you?" Sarah blurted, face reddening as Seth joined them.

Apparently David had something of an open-door policy. Any immortal who knew the security codes were invited to come and go at will. He always welcomed company and was so powerful he sensed their presence long before they entered, so they needn't even knock.

Out of habit, Marcus had let himself in without knocking the day after they had stormed Bastien's lair and inadvertently walked in on Roland and Sarah making love on the sofa.

Sarah hadn't been able to look Marcus in the eye since without blushing as floridly as she was now.

"Please tell me that didn't make it to the Immortal Guardian message boards," she begged.

Seth smiled. "No, he only mentioned it to me and David so we wouldn't intrude."

She groaned. "Oh, lovely. I'm sure that went over big. *Don't go home without calling first, David. They might be having sex on your couch.*"

Roland laughed and wrapped an arm around her shoulders as she covered her red face.

Seth's dark eyes danced with merriment. "Actually, we weren't given the details. He only said he had accidentally disturbed you when you were not prepared for company."

Lowering her hands, Sarah stared up at Roland with rueful eyes. "Why do you even let me open my mouth?"

Roland dipped his head and stole a kiss. "Because I love that mouth and it says such entertaining things." Sinking onto the sofa, he pulled her down beside him. As Seth settled himself in his favorite chair across from them, Roland draped an arm across the back cushion so he could toy with Sarah's hair.

Two weeks had passed since they had cleaned out the vampire lair. Because Bastien had been unaware of some of his men's activities, Roland had worried that Sarah may not be safe in her home. It had been the site of two confrontations with multiple vampires, and there was no way of knowing if any of Bastien's followers had spoken with vamps who weren't under his guidance. So when she had invited Roland to come and stay with her, he had instead talked her into remaining with him at David's place until they could find a new home of their own to share. (Seth had assured him that Bastien had not disclosed the location of David's home or the tunnels to anyone else.)

"We talked to Chris," Sarah said, her blush lingering. "He seems a little worried about the vampires you guys saved."

Nietzsche meandered into the room, trilled a greeting when he saw Seth, then trotted over and leaped into his lap.

Seth smiled and stroked the small furry body with oversize hands. "Lacking the freedom to come and go at will is a little tougher than they had expected, but I think they're adapting well. They've settled into their new apartments and are already pestering our doctors and scientists, wanting to know how and when they can begin helping them."

Roland wondered how many of the men and women at the research facility had ever actually met a vampire face to face. Those who worked the day shift had probably never even met an immortal. "What do the doctors think of them?"

"They're understandably wary—the whole staff is—but everyone seems to be getting along."

"Have they found the biochemist yet?"

Montrose Keegan had disappeared before the network had had a chance to confront him. Apparently his brother, one of Bastien's vampires, had managed to call and warn him before he was killed in the attack at the farmhouse.

"No. Reordon has tagged his cell phone, social security number, bank account, and credit cards, but there's been no activity. He's living off the grid."

Great. "I understand Tanner fit in instantly and is well-liked."

Sarah glanced up at him. "Which one is Tanner?"

"The human Chris inducted into the network."

"Oh, right."

Seth nodded. "Once Sebastien and Tanner have both been trained, I intend to assign Tanner to be Sebastien's Second."

It made sense. The two were already friends and worked well together.

"How *is* Bastien?" Sarah broached hesitantly.

Roland was still fuming over Bastien hurting her, so she tended to avoid mentioning his name lest she set off another rant.

"Not good." Seth paused while Nietzsche sprawled on his

side, then twisted his upper body so that his head was upside down and his chest, front paws, and chin all faced the ceiling. "He doesn't eat. He doesn't feed. He is consumed with anger."

Sarah frowned. "Anger at whom?"

"Everyone, I think."

Roland brushed his fingers across her black T-shirt–clad shoulder. "Did you show him the memories you took from his vampires?"

Seth nodded. "It only infuriated him more, knowing they had found a way around his gift and lied to him, perpetrating such atrocities while he was trying to save them."

Roland glanced down when Sarah rested a hand on his thigh and looked up at him.

"Maybe you should go see him," she suggested.

He gazed at her in disbelief. "What?"

Reaching up with her free hand, she laced her fingers through his at her shoulder. "Who better for him to talk to? He's going through the same thing you did, only on a larger scale. Maybe you could help him."

"You're delirious, aren't you?"

She smiled, hazel eyes sparkling. "Come on, Roland, think about it. You were betrayed by your wife and brother. He was betrayed by his brother-in-law and best friend."

Seth held up a finger. "Who *was* the one who turned him, by the way. He told Sebastien it was an accident, that he hadn't known feeding from him repeatedly would transform him, but—considering his other lies—I have my doubts."

"You see?" Sarah said as if that proved her point. "Then you were betrayed again by Mary. Bastien was betrayed by—what—seventy of his closest friends?"

"What's your point?" Roland asked, hardening his heart against the sympathy that threatened. It must be Sarah's influence. Normally he wouldn't have felt anything for Bastien but contempt.

She rolled her eyes. "That you had Seth and Marcus to help

you through it, unappreciative though you may have been, and Bastien probably feels like he has no one."

Roland glanced at Seth, who was watching him with a neutral expression. "I appreciated it," he admitted.

Seth shifted his gaze to Sarah. "You're good for him."

She squeezed Roland's thigh and tossed him a teasing glance. "I know."

"Actually, Roland, I agree. That's one of the reasons I dropped by. I think it would help if you spoke with Sebastien."

"No. He hurt Sarah."

"It was unintentional and he regrets it. He expected her to come along docilely, not shoot him in the hamstrings and stab him in the ass." He smiled at Sarah. "*That* made it to the message boards."

Roland was guilty of that one himself. When speculation had arisen on the boards regarding Sarah and the role she had played in the battle, he had posted a message for the first time ever, boasting of her quick thinking and bravery.

"Please, Roland," Sarah entreated, unfairly irresistible.

"I'll think about it," he grumbled, knowing he'd cave in the end. He could deny her nothing. "You said that was *one* of the reasons you came by," he told Seth before she could elicit a solid "yes" from him. "What was the other?"

The older immortal was quiet for a moment. "Chris told me you took Sarah to the lab to have her blood tested."

Roland stiffened. Every immortal he had ever heard of had either been transformed forcibly against his or her will or accidentally, as Étienne and his brother, Richart, had been. If Sarah, against all the odds, turned out to be a *gifted one,* she would be the first to actually *ask* to be infected.

Did Seth intend to forbid it?

Roland's heart thudded loudly in his ears. "And?"

Seth focused on Sarah. "You wish to be transformed?"

"Yes," she answered somewhat nervously.

"Why?"

Her grip on Roland's fingers tightened. "I want to be with Roland. Always."

"You love him that much?"

"Yes."

"Has he explained the negative aspects of his existence?"

"Yes."

Seth studied her intently.

Too intently.

"Stop reading her mind," Roland snapped, wrapping his other arm around her protectively, as though that could stop it.

Her eyes widened.

Seth shrugged. "I had to be sure she understood, that she was certain."

"And?" he demanded shortly when Seth said no more.

"She does and she is." Scooping Nietzsche up, he rose, then lowered the sleepy feline to the cushion he had just vacated.

Roland and Sarah rose as well.

It was like waiting for a judge to hand down a sentence.

Sarah's arm crept around his waist. His tightened around her shoulders.

One corner of Seth's lips tilted up. "You need not wait for the lab results. She's a *gifted one*."

For a moment, Roland couldn't breathe. "What?"

Seth smiled fully. "She's a *gifted one*. I don't need the blood test to be sure."

Sarah squealed and hugged Roland, jumping up and down until he laughed, though he was still afraid to believe it.

"But she doesn't have any gifts."

"Of course she does. Her dreams foretell the future."

Sarah stopped jumping and stared at Seth. "They do?" she asked incredulously, continuing to cling to Roland.

"Yes, you simply haven't learned to decipher them.

Contrary to popular belief, prophetic dreams are only literal in the most powerful of the *gifted ones* and immortals. For the rest, there are symbols that must be learned and deciphered and the meaning of the dreams can be vague. For example, a week or so before you met Roland, you dreamed there was a large cockroach in your living room that you had difficulty killing. The living room represented daily activities, such as work. The cockroach, due to its size, represented a substantial irritation. The next day, your student went to the head of the department and lodged a complaint against you."

Which *had* been a major irritation, she thought.

"A few days later you dreamed of tornadoes."

"I did," she said, amazed. "It was like in that movie *The Day After Tomorrow,* when all the tornadoes spiraled down and hit Los Angeles. They were all around me. And one even seemed to be chasing me. It was terrifying."

"Tornadoes represent great emotional turmoil, danger, and, at times, death . . . all the things that accompanied Roland when he entered your life shortly thereafter."

Wow. She had never paid much attention to her dreams beyond wondering why so many people believed dreams only came in black and white when hers were always in vivid color.

"I can aid you in learning how to interpret your dreams, if you wish."

Realizing her mouth was hanging open, Sarah hastily closed it. "That would be great. Thanks." She looked up at Roland, who was frowning. "My dreams foretell the future."

"So I heard." He grimaced. "Sorry about the turmoil, danger, and death thing."

She smiled. "It was worth it."

Roland looked to Seth. "What about the physical characteristics?"

"They've begun to weaken a bit in the last century or so. Nothing dramatic. Dark brown hair instead of black.

Hazel eyes instead of brown. Even those changes are still extremely rare."

"So I can be safely transformed?" Sarah pressed, just to be certain.

"Yes."

Roland's hold tightened. "You don't object?"

"This is Sarah's decision to make, not mine. If she wishes you to transform her, you may do so whenever you choose."

Now that she knew it would happen, Sarah felt both excited and nervous.

Seth's features softened. "It won't be too bad. Roland will drain you until you are near death, then infuse you with his own blood. You'll feel like you have a bad case of the flu for a few days. Then all will be well."

He shifted his gaze to Roland. "You look as nervous as she does."

Sarah glanced up and had to agree.

Roland's lips tightened. "What if something goes wrong?"

"It won't. She'll be fine. And I'm only a phone call away if you have any questions or concerns. I'll leave her training up to you, if that's all right."

They both nodded.

"I should be going now. I need to stop by Seattle on my way home."

"Thank you, Seth," Sarah said, "for everything."

He smiled. "You're welcome."

An instant later, he was gone.

Sarah smiled up at Roland. "I'm a *gifted one.*"

"I know. I can't believe it. But, Sarah . . ." He lightly clasped her upper arms and stared down at her, his expression earnest. "This doesn't have to change anything. The fact that you *can* be transformed doesn't mean you *have* to be. I don't want you to feel you—"

"I want you to transform me," she interrupted.

Extreme relief blanketing his features, he slid his arms

around her, lifted her feet off the floor, and twirled her around. "Thank you, thank you, thank you."

She laughed and, wrapping her arms around his neck, hugged him back. "So you're happy?"

He nodded, his face buried in her hair. "I wouldn't love you less if you said no. But, given the choice of spending either decades with you or centuries, I'd much rather have centuries."

"Me, too."

Setting her down, he drew back slightly and touched his lips to hers, first buoyantly, then tenderly.

Her heart did a funny little skip when she met his faintly luminous eyes.

"I love you, Sarah."

"I love you, too." So much more than she had dreamed was possible.

He kissed her again, held her close. "I'll leave it up to you to decide when you're ready."

"There's no time like the present."

His face lit with surprise. "Now?"

"Yes."

"Are you sure?"

She didn't blame him. She had expressed, more than once, uneasiness over how quickly all this had happened. But she felt no such uneasiness now.

"I'm sure. I'm not going to change my mind. And the longer we put it off, the more nervous we'll both become."

His lips twisted ruefully. "You weren't supposed to see that."

"What? That you're nervous?"

"Yes."

She shrugged. "I would've known even if you'd hidden it. You've never transformed anyone before and you're a tad obsessive when it comes to preventing me from experiencing any discomfort." When his arms tightened and his face filled with dread, she patted his back comfortingly. "That look right there is why we need to go ahead and get it done. I know Seth said it's like having the flu, but the longer we put it off, the more we're both going to imagine it being worse."

He drew in a deep breath and let it out slowly. "You're right. Now it is, then."

Thump.

Roland's head snapped around at the odd noise that came from the kitchen. Eyes flaring, fangs descending, he was gone before Sarah even finished tensing.

"It's all right," he called a second later. "Come and see."

Curious, she strode to the kitchen and paused just inside the entrance.

The largest gift basket she had ever seen sat in the middle of the floor. Decked with ribbons and bows, it was so large that if the contents were removed, she could curl up in it like a cat and take a nap.

"It's for us," Roland pronounced, opening a white envelope.

"Who's it from?"

As he pulled out a folded sheet of paper, she moved closer and began to pick through the basket's contents.

"It's from David."

There were several enormous bags of organic oranges so fragrant they made her mouth water, bottles of club soda, all-natural crackers sprinkled with sea salt, icy gel packs. . . .

"Seth must have told him I'm going to transform you. David says you'll have difficulty keeping food down for a couple of days, but fresh-squeezed orange juice and club soda will help."

"And crackers?"

"Crackers and pita chips."

Sure enough, there were several bags of super-crunchy baked pita chips with sea salt included.

Had David known it was her favorite brand or had it simply been a lucky guess?

She looked at Roland.

His eyes had lost their glow and were once more brown, his expression just this side of stunned.

"This is really nice," Sarah said, a little stunned herself. David didn't even know her and had only encountered Roland a few times, yet he'd opened up his home to them, told them they could stay as long as they wanted to, and now this?

Roland nodded slowly. "It is."

She smiled. It was going to take him awhile to get used to having friends rather than acquaintances. "Let's put the soda and the oranges in the fridge and get the gel packs in the freezer."

There was so much it took them several minutes to finish.

"So," she broached when they were done, "how are we going to do this?"

She was nervous. She didn't want to be but couldn't help it.

He swooped down and picked her up, one arm supporting her back, the other under her knees. "First, I will carry you to our bedroom."

"Ooh," she crooned, wrapping her arms around his neck as he left the kitchen and put action to words. "I like it so far."

"Then . . . I'm going to place you on our bed."

She nuzzled his neck and felt a shiver ripple through him. "Go on."

"Peel your clothing off with my teeth."

Her body melted at his words as he descended into the basement and made his way to their bedroom. "What next?"

"Make a slow exploration of your body with my tongue."

His tongue, she thought as he crossed to the bed. His wicked, wicked tongue. "And then?"

"And then," he said, placing her gently atop the covers, "as your body clenches in one of the many orgasms I intend to give you"—he knelt on the mattress beside her, leaned over her, kissed the base of her neck where her pulse hammered just beneath the surface—"I will bite you right here and make you mine forever."

She arched against him when he drew his tongue across her skin. “Mmm. Don’t forget the stripping me with your teeth part.”

He chuckled, a warm, growly sound that sent excitement skittering through her. “I wouldn’t dare.”

Roland was true to his word. With teeth, tongue, and hands, he aroused Sarah to a fevered pitch, distancing himself from his own desire and gently rebuffing her attempts to pleasure him, too. It was imperative that he keep a clear head, which meant ignoring his own needs and focusing solely on hers.

And, as her body writhed in orgasm for the third time, he gently sank his teeth into her throat and, exalting in the life that flowed into his body, devoured her like the monster he had so often been named.

Chapter 19

Okay, clearly Seth had never had the flu.

The first day of the transformation was about what Sarah had expected. Once she had regained consciousness (she had passed out while Roland was drinking from her and had no memory of him biting her), she had gradually begun to feel unwell. Mild fever. Chills. Nausea that was sometimes assuaged by the orange juice and club soda and other times brought it right back up again.

She had tried to keep Roland from following her into the bathroom (there were just some things she'd rather he not see her do, and vomiting was one of them), but he insisted and she rapidly grew too weak to prevent it. So he held her hair for her, physically supported her when she needed it, loaded up her toothbrush with toothpaste once her stomach had emptied itself, and when her mouth was minty fresh again, carried her back to bed.

He brought a television and a DVD player down to their room, played cards with her, read to her, regaled her with tales of his amazing past. He squeezed dozens of oranges, made sure she had plenty of fluids, soothed her aching head with gel pack after gel pack.

He was wonderful. Patient. Had an excellent bedside manner.

It made her love him all the more.

Then everything sort of . . . deteriorated on the second day. Her fever rose. And rose. Things got pretty hazy after that. Sarah later recalled very little of it. Just flashes here and there of Roland's worried face peering down at her as he urged her to drink more juice. Hearing him shout *flu my ass!* and *if you aren't here in five fucking seconds . . . !* Being submerged in an ice bath with Roland's big body behind her, his arms locked around her, both supporting her and restraining her as she thrashed about, his choked voice in her ear, murmuring over and over again that he loved her. A man with the darkest skin she had ever seen, dreadlocks down to his hips and the face of a pharaoh leaning over them.

There followed a large block of nothingness, during which her fever evidently broke. Midway through day three, she awoke lucid, her stomach settled, with a massive toothache.

Roland, who was slumped in a chair by the bed with one of her hands clutched in his, looked more haggard than she had ever seen him. His cheeks and chin were coated with dark stubble. New creases lined his forehead and bracketed his mouth.

His relief when she squeezed his hand and gave him a weak smile was heartbreaking. Climbing into bed, he spooned up behind her, buried his face in her hair, and hugged the stuffing out of her for at least half an hour.

"You scared the hell out of me," he whispered brokenly.

"I'm sorry. I didn't mean to."

His lips brushed the back of her neck. "I love you, Sarah." He pressed closer, as though he would burrow beneath her skin if he could. "I love you so much."

Smiling, she closed her eyes as drowsiness slunk through her. "I love you, too."

* * *

Seth and David were in the kitchen, preparing dinner, when they sensed Darnell's approach. David paused in the midst of basting the organic Cornish hens. The knife Seth was applying to several carrots for a salad stopped slicing.

Both felt their human friend's emotions fluctuating wildly and exchanged a concerned glance before turning toward the entrance.

When Darnell filled the doorway, he was carrying a sheaf of printed papers and looked shell-shocked.

"What is it?" David asked, setting aside his spoon and wiping his hands on a nearby towel.

Darnell's throat worked as he swallowed audibly. "I finally managed to decrypt the files on one of the laptops you stole when you rescued Amiriska."

The mystery woman had finally disclosed her name when she had awakened after sleeping for nearly two days.

Seth abandoned the knife and carrots as Darnell approached them. "And?"

"They're all about Ami," he said, pronouncing the nickname he had given her as one would *Amy*. "How long they held her. The tests and experiments they performed on her. Horrible, torturous experiments. And there were so many of them."

Seth cocked his head to one side. "Do they say who she is? Where they found her?" She was powerful enough that Seth couldn't read her mind and glean the information himself without her knowing. And he didn't want to frighten her.

Slowly Darnell nodded. "You aren't going to believe it. Hell, I've read it five times and *I* don't believe it."

Seth took the papers he proffered and held them so David could read them, too.

When Seth reached the first significant passage, shock filtered through him.

"Are you serious?" David breathed beside him.

Movement drew their gazes to the entrance.

Amiriska stood there, watching them, eyes wide, her pretty

face filling with trepidation as she realized they now knew her secret.

Sarah smiled as Roland took her hand and twined his fingers through hers. Though there was only the barest sliver of a moon, she had no difficulty seeing and gazed with wonder at the night scene around her.

It was all so clear. As clear as it would be on a cloudy afternoon.

Tall majestic trees that thickened into a forest. Fireflies sparkling in their midst. A rolling meadow liberally sprinkled with low-growing wildflowers, many of which had closed their petals for the night.

In the center of it all rested their new home: a spacious one-story with an equally spacious basement and three escape tunnels similar to David's. All had been completed in only a few weeks' time, thanks to Chris and the network, while Sarah had adjusted to the changes taking place in her body.

As they strolled up the pretty cobblestone path that led from the driveway to the front porch, Sarah again marveled at the proliferation of scents that danced on the summer breeze. The most compelling, of course, was Roland's. No cologne. Just soap and water and him. *Yum.*

And the sounds . . .

Before there had just been the *ch-ch-ch* of those weird bugs and the croaking of frogs. Now she heard the wind brushing her clothing, field mice scuttling through distant grasses, an opossum lumbering through the forest a mile away, and the soft clop of deer hooves and the grinding of their teeth as they grazed near a stream beyond that. An owl's feathers beat the air overhead as it scouted for prey. Bat wings flapped as the night creatures gorged themselves on insects.

Roland's heartbeat, strong and steady, picked up a bit when she smiled at him.

Her senses were so much sharper now. All of them. Even touch. And her strength . . . !

She was even stronger and faster than Étienne and Lisette, a fact that astonished them all and titillated the hell out of the scientists at the network. No one had expected that. Not even Seth. Younger immortals were always weaker than older immortals.

Had being turned by an immortal instead of a vampire made the difference?

Was there something unique in Roland's blood?

Was it because he was so much older, his bloodline purer?

No one knew.

The network had been hounding Roland to bring Sarah to the lab ever since word had gotten out, but he had flatly refused. He was protecting her, she knew, and had no interest in submitting to their tests himself. It was important, though, so Sarah decided she'd work on him later and see if she couldn't coax him into changing his mind.

He may be a grumpy Gus with others, but with her he was a real softie.

"You really like it?" he asked.

"I love it," she vowed as they climbed the steps to the covered front porch.

He paused and drew her into the circle of his embrace. "And I love *you.*" He dipped his head, capturing her lips in a slow sensual kiss. "Wife."

"I love you, too," she whispered against his lips, "husband."

A soft growl rumbled forth as he deepened the kiss, sliding his hands down to cup her bottom and clutch her to him.

When she drew back, she knew her eyes were glowing green, could feel her fangs descending as they did whenever she was in the grip of strong emotion. Seeing herself like that for the first time had been quite a shock. She and Roland had just made love in the shower and she had caught her reflection in the mirror as they emerged.

Stunned speechless, she had gaped at her reflection so long the fangs had receded and her eyes had faded back to normal. Roland, seeing her disappointment and always happy to be of service, had stepped up behind her and palmed her breasts, teasing her nipples to hardness and making her breath catch. Her eyes had almost instantly begun to glow again. Her fangs had descended. Astonishing. That was going to be even harder to get used to than drinking blood, which really wasn't that bad since she didn't actually *drink* it. She just bit down into the bag and her fangs siphoned the liquid into her veins.

"Your eyes are glowing," he murmured, rubbing noses with her.

"So are yours."

He smiled. "They'll always glow when I want you."

Releasing her, he unlocked the door and punched in the security code. Then, turning, he lifted her into his arms, carried her across the threshold . . . and stopped short.

Sarah followed his gaze and stared at their living room in disbelief. "Wow."

There were brightly wrapped gifts everywhere. On every surface. Every piece of furniture. Stacked nearly as high as the ceiling.

Roland lowered her feet to the floor and closed the door. "Seth warned me there would be wedding presents, but I didn't expect there to be so many."

The two of them had been married earlier that evening in David's backyard in a private ceremony attended by Seth, David, Marcus, Chris, Lisette, and Étienne that was presided over by a minister friend of Chris's.

Well, private wasn't entirely accurate. The wedding had been broadcast live over the Internet on a heavily encrypted website only other Immortal Guardians and their Seconds could access. So many around the world had been awed and enchanted by their story that they had wanted to witness the historic event themselves.

Sarah and Roland had consented.

"Are these all from Seth and David?" she asked.

Roland glanced at the cards on the packages closest to them. "They're from . . . everyone. Every immortal on the planet sent something, by the looks of it."

"But they don't even know me."

"Most don't know me either. And few that do like me. I'm as stunned as you are."

They stood there for a long moment before he took her hand. "Why don't we put off opening these until later. There's something I want to show you."

"Okay."

Wending his way through the mountains of boxes, Roland led her to the back door. Sarah followed him out into the shadows that darkened the large deck.

A pretty meadow spread out before them and off to the side was . . .

She gasped. "A veggie garden!"

"I regretted that you never got to plant yours."

Throwing her arms around his neck, she hugged him tightly. "Thank you, Roland. It's perfect."

He grinned, locking his arms behind her back. "*You're* perfect." Bending, he kissed her forehead, her cheeks, then her lips. "Thank you for saving my life, Sarah, in so many ways."

She kissed him back. "Thank you for transforming mine."